"Hope."

One look and her body froze. Even under the beating sun, she couldn't even feel her heartbeat.

Joel Kidd, the boyfriend who'd walked out on her eighteen months ago, stood next to the helicopter.

Black T-shirt, olive cargo pants and sunglasses to hide those dark eyes. From this distance she could see the ever-present dark scruff around his chin. His black hair was longer, grown out from the short military style she remembered.

She could see the gun strapped to his hip and knew Joel knew how to use it. That used to scare her a little. Now it comforted her frazzled nerves.

"What are you doing here?" The whip of her voice mirrored her frustration.

He hesitated, as if weighing what to say and whether to let his question go. Whatever he saw in her expression had him closing the distance between them. "I came to find you."

LAWLESS

BY
HELENKAY DIMON

MILLS & BOON®

Published in Great Britain 2014
by Mills & Boon, an imprint of Harlequin (UK) Limited,
Eton House, 18-24 Paradise Road, Richmond, Surrey, TW9 1SR

© 2014 HelenKay Dimon

ISBN: 978 0 263 91359 0

46-0514

Award-winning author **HelenKay Dimon** spent twelve years in the most unromantic career ever—divorce lawyer. After dedicating all that effort to helping people terminate relationships, she is thrilled to deal in happy endings and write romance novels for a living. Now her days are filled with gardening, writing, reading and spending time with her family in and around San Diego. HelenKay loves hearing from readers, so stop by her website, www.helenkaydimon.com, and say hello.

To my husband for agreeing to watch all those
big budget Hollywood action movies with me and
pretending I was telling the truth when
I called them writing research

Chapter One

Hope Algier preferred sunshine and fresh air to a stuffy office. Except today.

She spent most of her life outdoors. Her father had tried for years to entice his baby girl into the boardroom of the family business with promises of expensive cars and impressive bonus packages. She turned them all down without a second thought, but right now a leather chair behind a big desk sounded good.

Trees towered over her and surrounded her on every side. This section of land adjacent to West Virginia's Cranberry Wilderness was called the Cranberry Backcountry for a reason. It consisted of more than eleven thousand acres of hills and woods and little else.

Animals skittered around her. Leaves rustled as the summer wind blew warm air under her ponytail and across the back of her neck. Thick branches blocked most of the sunlight, giving her an eerie sense of isolation.

No people, no houses and no easy way out.

Turned out, this patch of forest messed with her satellite phone. She needed open sky for a signal, and she could only see peeks of blue through the canopy of summer green leaves above her. Right about now she'd give anything for a second of heat on her face.

She slipped behind a large trunk and leaned against it.

Her heartbeat hammered in her ears as she slipped the sat phone out of the pocket of her cargo shorts. It measured a bit longer than a cell phone and fit in her palm. The map she'd memorized earlier and carried in her back pocket pointed to a clearing up ahead. She hoped she was close enough to catch a signal.

Please let it work this time.

She pushed buttons. When that didn't do anything, she smacked the side, hoping to jolt it into action. She even thought about smashing it against the cushion of dirt and leaves under her hiking boots.

She was about to repeat the hitting cycle when something crunched off to her right…again. The same subtle crackling she'd been hearing on and off since she'd dove deep into the trees. A squirrel, probably. She repeated the comment in her head over and over, hoping to reassure her brain and stop the sudden subtle shake moving through her hands. She refused to think bear or, worse, predator of the two-legged kind.

As she shifted, the stray branches scratched her bare legs and caught on the short sleeve of her cotton tee. She balanced her head against the hard bark again and counted to five. It took all of her control not to call out for Mark Callah, the vice president of finance for Baxter Industries.

He'd been all gung ho about "roughing it" on this corporate retreat. So much so he had brought a gun along without telling her. She saw it when he had waved it around last night at dinner. As the person leading the retreat, she had confiscated it. That didn't go over well. Now he was missing.

Crack.

There it was again. That made the fourth time she picked up the sound she wanted to write off as nothing.

Something furry and four-legged and small…she hoped. But the gentle thuds sped up.

She peeked around the tree she was using as a shield and spied what looked like a flash of blue in the distance. The same flash she'd seen twice so far on this journey to find Mark and grab a clear shot to the satellite to jump-start the phone.

She'd left the rest of the executives back at camp with orders to make breakfast and clean up. Except for Mark, they weren't exactly the venture-out-alone types. She strained to remember any of them wearing navy this morning at roll call, but her brain refused to focus.

Crunching and snapping echoed all around her until she couldn't tell from which direction the noises originated. The tunnel effect had her doubting her hearing and her vision. If she spun around one more time or ventured too far in any direction, she'd need the GPS to guide her back to camp.

What she really wanted was a view of open sky. If she could get to the edge of the field and send out a call for help, then she could duck back into the woods again.

Maybe she could lure out her visitor. Not that the option sounded too reassuring to her right now.

Without thinking, she reached for the leather sheath hooked to her belt. Her fingers skimmed over the hilt of her knife. She wanted to slide it out for protection, but running on uneven ground with a blade struck her as a distinctly stupid thing to do.

Still, having the makeshift weapon lessened the anxiety pounding through her. A little.

With one last glance into the thick columns of trees behind her, she took off. Her hands swatted at the branches blocking her forged path as her feet slipped over rocks and roots and her pace picked up to a jog. The wind whistled by her and the slap of leaves hit her face. She made enough noise to put a target on her back, but she didn't care. She needed that open field.

Footsteps fell hard off to her left this time. The thump of shoes against the ground kicked up and the person drew almost parallel to her position. She tried to zigzag even though she knew her white shirt would give her position away...wherever she was.

But she needed space and enough distance to make the call and pull her knife. Regardless of whatever or whoever else was out there, she would not go down without a fight.

The trail in front of her brightened and sunlight puddled on the forest floor. Even without the thinning of branches she knew she was close from the beep of her GPS as she zoned in on the preset location. The sat phone smacked against her leg with each step. She fumbled to pull it out of her pocket and hold it as she ran.

The log came out of nowhere. A fallen tree too thick to jump over right in her path. She tried to pivot and her ankle turned. One second she was on her feet and the next her knee cracked against the hard ground and something sharp dug into her palm.

She was down for only a few seconds but long enough for heavy breathing to pound in her lungs and float through the trees. The labored sound drowned out everything. The running near her seemed to stop. She feared that meant someone or something circled nearby ready to grab her.

Ignoring the pain thumping from her foot to her hip, she pushed up. With her hands on the log, she skirted the end and ran. Each punch of her right foot against the hard ground made her teeth rattle with the need to cry out.

But the bright light was right there. A few more feet

and she'd be free. She dodged a massive tree trunk as the crashing of footsteps beside her picked up again. A blue blur raced close enough for her to make out a figure, but the heavy hoodie pulled down low made it impossible to identify who it was.

But the *who* didn't matter right now.

She broke into the clearing and reached into her pocket for the phone. Nothing. She patted her shorts and spun around in a circle as desperation swamped her. Fear rumbled through her until her knees buckled.

The log. The fall. The memory came rushing back. She must have dropped the stupid thing on the ground when she went down.

With her back against a tree, she scanned the forty feet of open field in front of her and the miles of woods beyond that. She tried to calm her breathing and slow her heart enough for her to concentrate.

The adrenaline kept pumping. She knew she should welcome it because it kept the pain at bay and her mind off the blood around her knee and throbbing in her hand, but she needed to focus.

The figure, whoever it was, stood still, right behind a tree about fifty feet away. She slipped her knife out again and tightened her grip over the handle, ignoring the fresh burst of throbbing from her injury. She opened her mouth to call out, to make the idiot face her instead of trying to terrify her in silence.

A strange thwapping drowned out her yell. She shielded her eyes with a hand and squinted up into the sun. Blue skies greeted her. She didn't see anything, but the noise grew louder.

Whop, whop, whop.

A helicopter broke into sight as it came in for a landing. She blinked twice, not trusting what she was seeing. Out here, in the middle of nowhere, it didn't make sense.

Her breath hiccupped as a new panic crashed over her. She could have walked into anything. Drug runners or criminals of any type. And if the pilot was a partner to her tracker, there was no way a knife would save her.

The helicopter hovered over the ground. The blades kicked up grass and leaves. When it finally touched down, she could make out two men, but the glass, and probably the waves of fear, distorted her view.

She was about to slip back into the blanket of the woods where she at least stood a chance when the rustling off to her left had her attention dragging back to the tree and the person hiding there. The hoodie was gone. Fearing the attacker could sneak up on her, she backed to the edge of the open field and held her knife in front of her as she faced the woods.

"Hope."

She thought she heard her name over the chopping of the helicopter blades, but she knew that wasn't possible. No way had one of her executives ventured away from the camp and somehow made it this far.

Her mind had gone into shutdown mode. That was the only explanation. She was hearing things and jumping at every sound.

The helicopter's engine wound down and the propeller slowed to a lazy turn. The change had her spinning around to face the new threat. One look and her body froze. Right there in the beating sun, every organ inside her whirred to a stop. She couldn't even feel her heartbeat.

"Hope, what are you doing?" Joel Kidd, the boyfriend who had walked out on her eighteen months ago rather than fight for a life with her, stood next to the helicopter.

Black tee, olive cargo pants, and sunglasses to hide those near-black eyes. From this distance she could see the ever-present dark scruff around his chin. His black hair was longer, grown out from the short military style she remembered. He might even have been thinner. And none of that explained what he was doing in West Virginia.

With one last look into the menacing woods behind her, she stepped forward. She could see the gun strapped to his hip and knew Joel was well trained in how to use it. That used to scare her a little. Now it comforted her frazzled nerves.

"You cut your leg." He ripped his sunglasses off, and concerned eyes traveled over her. "What's going on?"

Seeing him hit her like a kick to the stomach. She almost doubled over from the force of it. She'd loved him and mourned his leaving, then had spent some time pretending she hated him. As she looked at him now, old feelings of longing came rushing back. So did the urge to punch him.

"What are you doing here?" The whip of her voice mirrored her frustration.

He hesitated as if weighing what to say and whether to let the question go. Whatever he saw on her face or in her expression had him closing the distance between them. "I came to find you."

"Why?" Truth was, he devoted his life to gathering intelligence and protecting others. Right now she could use a bit of both.

The sound of the helicopter seemed to have scared off her tracker, and for that reason alone she was willing to hear Joel out. For a few seconds.

"You haven't been picking up your phone." His gaze

did another bounce up and down her body, hesitating over her torn-up knee. "Where is it?"

Good question. "Lost."

His near-black eyes narrowed. "Really?"

"Long story."

"Any chance of hearing it right now?"

"First, you answer a question of mine." She glanced past Joel to the pilot. He jumped down and headed for them.

"Shoot," Joel said.

"There is no way you just happened to be out here, tooling around West Virginia, when you live in Annapolis. So, what's going on?"

The corner of his mouth lifted in a smile. "You know where I live now?"

No way was she walking into that discussion. "Let's stick to my question."

"Fine, it's not a coincidence." Joel's expression went blank. "Your father sent me."

Figured. "It's still your turn to explain, so keep talking."

She loved her dad, but his protective streak stayed locked in hyperdrive. He ran a private security company, one Joel used to work for. All that danger made her dad a bit paranoid. Though, admittedly, in this instance that was a good thing.

"Your dad and Baxter Industries." Joel shifted his weight, putting his feet hip-distance apart. "Seems your dad wanted you to have backup out here. Combine that with the twitchiness of the Baxter Board about having a twenty-six-year-old woman, alone, guiding the male executives, and you get me."

"How very sexist of them."

"They clearly don't appreciate how competent you are outdoors."

She had no idea if that was a shot or a compliment, so she ignored it. "If the phone isn't working, how did you... oh, right. The GPS locator still functions."

"Yes."

"So, Dad tracked me down and sent you by helicopter."

Instead of answering, Joel motioned to the pilot. "This is Cameron Roth."

She wasn't in the mood for meeting people just now, but there was no reason to be rude. "Okay."

"We work together," Joel explained.

"At where exactly?" She'd tried to find out where Joel went when he left her dad's company. One night, bored and feeling lonely, she conducted a search, hoping to locate him, and uncovered nothing.

Her father finally let slip Joel lived in Annapolis, less than an hour away from her place in Virginia, the same place he used to live with her but never bothered to visit now. Being ignored made her stop checking in on the guy. If Joel didn't care enough to make contact, she wouldn't either.

"Ma'am." The other man butted in with a nod of welcome. "You can call me Roth or Cam."

The guy looked about the same age as Joel, a few years older than her, and shared Joel's used-to-be-in-the-military look. Broad shoulders with muscles peeking out from under the edge of his T-shirt. They both carried their bodies in a permanent battle stance, as if they could shoot or tackle at any moment, if needed.

Joel had the Tall, Dark and Whoa-He's-Hot thing down. That hadn't changed in their months apart. Cam's lighter hair and blue eyes made him seem less intense, but knowing the male type standing in front of her, she doubted that was actually the case.

Joel clapped. "There. That's settled."

Looked like the menfolk thought explanation time was over. She disagreed. "Let's go back to my question. Why are you really here? And skip the sat phone talk this time."

"Your father sent me to look for you." That smile widened. "Now it's my turn to ask a question."

"Did you really answer mine?"

Cam laughed. "She has you there, man."

Joel nodded in the direction of her hand. "Is there a reason you're carrying a knife, or is the plan to stab the helicopter?"

She glanced down, then back at Joel. "Are you worried it's meant for you?"

"I take it you two know each other pretty well," Cam said.

The conversation kept jumping around. She'd only remembered the knife when Joel mentioned it. The burning from where it pressed into her palm suddenly hit her.

Then Cam's comment grabbed her attention.

"Joel didn't tell you who I was to him?" She wanted not to care, but the hurt swallowed up her indifference.

Cam looked from her to Joel and back again. "Let's just say I'm thinking he left out some important pieces about your joint past."

"Hope." Joel snapped his fingers and brought the focus back to him. "The knife?"

She stared at it in her hands. "What about it?"

"Why are you holding it as if you're ready to attack?"

She couldn't come up with a reason to stall and certainly had no reason to lie. Not about this. Not to him. "Someone was following me."

Both men leaned in closer, all amusement gone from their faces. Cam's mouth opened, but Joel was the one who barked out a question. "What?"

Now that she had their attention, she decided to spill it all. "And I think one of my executives might be dead."

Chapter Two

Joel called up every ounce of his practiced control to stay calm. Before he'd joined the Corcoran Team, a private security organization out of Annapolis, Maryland, that specialized in risk assessments for companies and governments, this sort of thing would have had him spinning and drilling her with questions.

Connor Bowen and the rest of the Corcoran Team had taught him the importance of patience and holding still for the right opening. Without those skills, the high-priority, under-the-radar kidnap and rescue missions they conducted would fail. Because when you worked outside the legal parameters and without a safety net, mistakes couldn't happen.

After a lifetime of kicking around in the intelligence field, Joel knew he'd finally landed in a place that felt right. He'd buckled down, used his tech skills to fill in after the last tech guy left and tried to forget about her. Hope, his greatest weakness.

Now he seriously considered telling Cam to get lost for a few minutes, though he doubted the guy would budge. Not when he was staring as if he'd never seen a woman before and was hanging on every word of the discussion.

Joel couldn't really blame Cam on the gawking part. Hope looked as good as Joel remembered. Better, even.

The long dark brown hair and near black eyes hadn't changed. From the dimple and girl-next-door hotness to the tanned legs and smokin' petite frame, he found her almost impossible to resist.

Add in her smarts, competency with weapons and near fearless determination when she wanted something and he'd had no choice but to dump his job and move to the next state to keep from falling deeper into her. Or that's what he'd rationalized at the time.

But right now he worried more about the danger that appeared to be haunting her. "Say that again."

She cleared her throat. "I have a missing executive."

Joel had no idea what that meant. "You said dead a second ago."

She shrugged. "I'm hoping that was an exaggeration."

Well, that cleared up…nothing. He glanced over at Cam.

He shook his head. "Got me. I have no clue."

"Hope." Joel reached out to touch the hand with the weapon in it and felt the subtle tremor running through her. Yeah, forget how comfortable she looked hanging around outside, something bad had happened and she was throwing off the desperation vibe.

His protective instincts kicked into high gear. He folded his hand over hers and slid the knife out of her palm. Not an easy task since she had a death grip on it.

Moving nice and slow, he eased the blade back into its case at her waist as he rubbed his thumb over the deep creases on her palm. "Where is this executive?"

"His name is Mark Callah."

"Okay." Joel didn't dig too deep for details. Not yet. "Where is Mark?"

"I have no idea since I lost him."

Cam grunted. "She's giving you a pretty logical answer, actually."

"I got up this morning and he was gone from camp." She tugged free of Joel's hold and rubbed her hands together. "I headed for this clearing to use the sat phone and realized some guy was following me. Then your helicopter—"

"Hold up." For the second time, she jumped right past the most interesting part. "Go back a second."

"To where?"

Stray branches crunched under Cam's feet as he shifted his weight. "I'm guessing to the 'following me' part."

She spent a second frowning at both of them. "Blue hoodie. The guy stalked me, then started moving faster and came up the side until we were parallel. He didn't look up and stayed close. Your helicopter scared him off."

"Stalked?" Joel didn't hear much after that word.

"Yes, Joel." She didn't roll her eyes, but she looked like she was right on the edge of doing so.

She could sigh at him all she wanted because he was not letting this conversation drop. Not until he assessed the level of danger. "Could this person be one of the executives you have out here on the team-building retreat?"

This time her face went blank. "Wow, my dad really did fill you in on this job."

"Let's stick to your story for now." One more diversion and Joel worried he'd never be able to pull the tale out of her. And he knew from experience any talk about her dad and his protective nature would not make this exercise go faster.

"Except for Mark, most of the Baxter Industries management talk tough but are terrified of being out here. One guy jumped around demanding to go home because he found a tick on his upper arm." She snorted. "I mean, come on."

Joel bit back a laugh. "Very manly."

"Right. So, you understand why I can't imagine any of them chasing me through the woods, being covert and ducking out of sight for no good reason."

"You're throwing out some scary words there."

"So?"

She could shoot and run and build a camp from twigs, but that didn't make her invincible. He wondered if she understood that. "My point is this story gets worse the more details you add."

She glanced over her shoulder and deep into the woods behind her. "Anyway, I'd like to think if it was one of my guys, he would have helped or at least called out when I fell."

The bad news just kept coming. Joel glanced at Cam. "And now we have a fall."

She faced them again. "What?"

"You skipped that part before," Cam said.

Joel guessed that was intentional. "Let's just say your linear storytelling needs work."

"I'll run through all of it if you need me to—"

"I do." Joel wanted her comment to stop right there.

She talked right over his interruption. "But since you're here, you can come with me while I get my sat phone and then we can spread out and hunt for Mark."

Joel caught her in the second before she took off. Never mind her tale about a stalker and the terror in her eyes only a few minutes ago. Now she was ready to head out. "I thought you lost the phone."

"Yeah, but I know where."

"Your definition of lost is no better than your story-telling ability."

"We don't have time for chitchat." Her gaze dipped to where his fingers wrapped around her elbow, then bounced back up again. "I'm assuming you guys need to get out of here and head off to some other covert action-movie adventure, so let's move."

Nice try. "You're my job this week, remember?"

"Yeah, we're going to talk about that later."

"Talk all you want. I'm staying." That had been the plan before the knife and the story about the fall and every other bizarre fact she threw out, and he wasn't changing it now.

But there was some good news here. Her feistiness clicked back into place with full force. While the verbal jabs about his job used to drive him nuts, he missed this side of her, too.

She didn't back down. She didn't care about his size or ability with a weapon. She understood he'd never hurt her and held her ground. Probably had something to do with having a former special ops father who made sure his precious daughter and only child could protect herself no matter what.

The attitude had gotten her in trouble more than once. Not with him, but some of the men in her father's business, Algier Security, didn't appreciate her refusal to be a good little girl and sit down.

Sexist idiots.

Still, she could be rough on the male ego. He glanced over at Cam to fill him in with a simple explanation. "She doesn't approve of what we do."

"Understood," Cam said with a nod.

Hope wasn't having any of it. She shot them both one of her men-can-be-clueless frowns. "That's not true."

Cam kept nodding, as if he'd figured out some great big secret. "Is that why you left him?"

Damn. "Let's not go there." This was just about the last topic Joel wanted to discuss.

Strike that. It was *the* last. Dead last.

"I figured it out." Cam smiled. "She's the ex."

Suddenly Joel regretted that one night a month or so ago with too much beer and too much talking. Cam had wanted to know why Joel never dated and he mentioned a tough break-up. Cam clearly put it all together.

"Didn't he tell you the story?" Hope's eyebrow lifted. "Interesting."

"How so?" Cam asked.

"Joel left me."

Cam's eyes bugged as his jaw dropped. "No way."

"I know, right?" She shook her head. "Whatever."

Cam whistled. "I didn't see that news coming."

That was enough of that. Joel cleared his throat to get everyone's attention. "Can we get back to the missing guy and the stalking?"

"Camp is back here." She didn't wait for a discussion or arguments. She headed off through the thick branches, with twigs and other debris crunching under her boots. She slowed down only long enough to glance over her shoulder and gesture for them to follow.

"Hope…and she's gone." Joel took a step in the same direction.

Cam slid in and blocked his path. "You dumped her?"

"Let it go."

Cam laughed. "I think we both know that's not going to happen."

It was a long story and Joel knew he didn't exactly come off well. With his messed-up upbringing, a quiet life in the suburbs wasn't on the table. But she had tempted him, made him think even for a little while that he could do normal. Then he got offered a dream job with the Defense Intelligence Agency and, like an idiot, picked it over her.

Funny how karma nailed him on that one.

Cam leaned in with a hand behind his ear. "Not talking?"

"Nope."

"You will." He winked, then called out to Hope. "Hey, where was this stalker walking?"

She stopped and gestured to the line of trees directly across from her. "About fifty feet that way, running parallel with me."

Joel tracked her white shirt as she pushed long branches out of her way and kept walking. "Notice how she acts like whatever happened wasn't a big deal."

"Was she ever an operative?"

"Mountain climber, archery expert, like Olympic skill level, outdoors type and can shoot better than some members of the Corcoran Team."

"You're talking about Ben, right?" Cam asked.

Ben Tanner was the newest member of the Corcoran Team and a former special agent for NCIS. The guy could shoot but he lacked the sniper skills of many on the team. And they never let him forget it. "Obviously."

Cam stopped staring at Hope, and it looked like that took some control on his part. "Explain to me why you left her again? Because, gotta be honest, man, between the way she looks, the way she moves and that list of skills you just read off, I think I'm in love."

"Get over it."

Cam nodded, which he often did. "Ah, okay. Interesting."

Hope's white shirt got farther away. That meant one thing—the time for talk had ended. "Stop with that crap."

Just as Joel lost sight of her, she peeked out from behind a massive tree trunk. "You guys coming?"

This time Cam laughed. "Your ex wants your attention."

"Don't call her that." Correct or not, the term grated on Joel's nerves. It meant she was free to find someone else, and even though he knew that was fair and the right thing, he despised the idea.

He'd spent the months away from her pretending he didn't care when her father had called to alert him that she'd gone out on a date with this guy or that one. The old man was on a warped matchmaking mission. One that slowly broke Joel until he thought he'd go insane imagining her in bed with someone else.

"I am so happy I was available to fly you in for this op. Wouldn't have missed this for anything." Cam clapped Joel on the back. "Not sure who will enjoy this more—the guys back at the Annapolis office or the guys on my traveling team. Tough call."

Both options sucked for Joel. "I could hide your body out here."

"You're welcome to try."

Because Cam came to Corcoran with the nickname "Lethal" and rumor was he'd flown Navy missions so secret just mentioning the operation names would bring the FBI running with guns firing, Joel decided to switch the subject. "And this is a favor for an old friend, not an op."

"If a businessman is missing and someone is chasing your woman, it's an op." Cam didn't wait around for an argument. He headed in the direction Hope indicated as the stalker's path. "I'll be over there, straining to hear every word."

Joel took off after Hope. She'd stopped, and with his

long stride, he caught up fast. When he drew close he saw her standing near a fallen tree, staring at the dirt.

"What's going on?" he asked.

She looked up, the anger obvious in her tight jaw and the flush of red on her cheeks. "My phone is gone."

"I thought we already knew that."

"No, I mean I had it in my hand while I was running—"

"You ran through this?"

"—and stumbled here. I dropped the phone and now it's gone."

There was no trail and no obvious signs of a path. Roots poked out of the ground, and the trees had grown to the point where they blanketed the area. Any sane person would watch her step. But she had run. Figured.

He thought about lecturing her but abandoned the idea when she bent down and started patting the rough terrain with her palm. Hope knew the outdoors, loved and cherished the openness. It was one of the things they had in common.

Still, a phone could only bounce so far. "Any chance you lost it somewhere else?"

"No." She tried to reach her arm under the log. "I'm not exactly easy to spook. I know what I'm talking about."

"But you are."

She tugged on her arm but didn't remove it or sit back up again. Twisting around, she looked up at him. "What?"

"Spooked." And stuck. He wondered how long it would be before she admitted that. "Your pulse is racing and you're jumpy. Not that long ago you were shaking and holding that knife like you were ready to slash anyone in your path."

"Someone was chasing me." She kept shifting and squirming. The heels of her boots dug into the dirt as she wrenched her shoulder.

Much more of this and she'd really injure herself. Any second now she'd ask for help. Well, most people would. With Hope, who knew?

He was ready to jump in. She just had to say the word, but he'd bet all the cash on him she wouldn't.

"I get the chasing part," he said.

She stopped moving around and shot him a big-eyed stare. "You don't believe me."

With Hope, he figured that was as close as he was going to get to a plea for help. He crouched and did the quick math on the best angle to pull her out without dislocating her shoulder. "I didn't say that."

"I am not a little girl who needs protecting. Your days of holding that job are over and, in case you missed it, I was never a little girl on your watch."

"Oh, I noticed." He jammed his fingers into the hard ground as dirt and peat moss slid under his nails. Ignoring the closeness and the way her arm brushed across his chest, he wedged his hand under hers and dug a shallow tunnel with his knuckles. "For the record, I noticed everything about you. Still do."

Before he could add to the comment, footsteps echoed around him and boots appeared in front of his face. He strained to look up and got as far as the familiar utility pants.

"Our company is back," Joel said into the relative quiet of the forest.

She tried to spin around and hissed when her trapped arm stopped her movements. It took another beat for her to get a word out. "Where?"

"He means me." Cam dropped down to the balls of his feet with his body between Joel and Hope. "What are you two doing?"

With his hand caked with dirt, Joel wrapped his fingers around her bare arm and gave a quick pull. "Rescuing her."

"I don't need rescuing." She popped free and fell back on her butt. Next she rubbed her shoulder joint. "Ouch."

Joel refused to feel guilty for getting her unstuck when she'd been too stubborn to ask for his assistance. "Good thing you weren't caught then."

"Glad we cleared that up." Cam stood. "She's right about being followed. There are footprints over there."

"Any clue about who or why?" Joel got to his feet and put a hand down, surprised when she took it to jump up next to him.

"Some interesting information." Cam turned his camera around and flashed an image most people would think showed nothing but leaves but really showed an outline of a shoe. "Men's size eleven. Probably a hundred-seventy pounds."

She leaned in closer to the screen, her eyes narrowing. "You can tell that from a grainy picture?"

Cam nodded. "And your stalker is an overpronator."

Joel had to smile at that. "Now you're just showing off."

Cam shrugged. "I'm good at my job."

"Which is what again?" she asked.

No way was Joel entertaining an impromptu debriefing in the middle of an isolated forest. Protocol was very clear. The Corcoran Team operated on a need-to-know basis.

To the world they provided risk assessments and moved in to help if things went wrong. Important but not the complete story. The definition missed the reality of the constant danger and huge amount of shooting.

Fact was, telling the woman he once dated about his

current occupation had to violate some rule. "Not up for discussion."

She sighed. "I've been hearing that my whole life."

A stark silence followed her words. Joel didn't bother to explain the real-world need for not filling her in. She knew how this game was played. She'd lived with a man known for having secrets. Joel got that she hated the game, but that didn't change it one bit.

Cam finally broke the quiet with a clap that thundered through the trees. "So, we have someone skulking around the woods."

"And a missing phone." She turned on Joel with a finger in his face. "Do not ask me if I'm sure this is where I dropped it."

Those words died in his throat because saying them could get him punched. "No, ma'am."

She treated him to a smile then. "That's new."

He tried not to notice how it lit up her face. "I'm not always difficult."

"Yes, you are," she said.

Cam nodded at the same time. "Not always, but mostly."

"We should head back and make sure none of these weekend warriors cut off a toe." Falling back into command mode kept Joel from telling both of them off. "We also need to check out Hope's knee."

She glanced down.

Cam nodded. "Maybe this Mark guy wandered into camp and there's some reasonable explanation for all of this."

The men started to walk but she stayed still. "What about your helicopter and wherever you were planning to go after stopping in here?"

Sounded like she still wasn't understanding his assignment here. Joel tried again. "This is my final destination. With you."

Cam slid his foot over the piles of leaves stacked around them. "And I'm good to hang out for a few hours."

Her hands went to her hips, and her legs still didn't move. "You both think something is seriously wrong."

Joel decided not to sugarcoat this. Sure, the past half hour could mean nothing. Or it could mean Baxter Industries and her dad were right to send in reinforcements. They wouldn't know until they got back to camp. "Stolen phone and a stalker? Yeah, Hope. Something is not right."

Her smile came roaring back. "Good."

He wondered if he would ever understand her mood swings. "How is that good?"

"Because you believe me. You're not writing this off as some hysterical woman thing."

Of all the things she could have said, that one came out of nowhere. "I've never known you to be hysterical."

She eyed him up. "You know, you seem slightly smarter about women now. Maybe some things have changed about you since we last went out."

And he worried the most obvious—how much he wanted her—hadn't.

Chapter Three

Hope tried to ignore Joel for the entire walk back to camp. His constant stream of questions didn't make that easy. He wanted to know about the campers and what her plan had been to get the men in and out of camp. She gave the details, even though she really wanted to stop and demand an explanation for why it was so easy for him to walk out of her life.

Then again, maybe she didn't want to know. Her ego could only take so much, and he had the power to break her. Had from the minute she'd met him.

The forest floor crunched and crackled under their feet. Their steps echoed around her, and Cam whistled as he walked a half step behind her. It all seemed so normal...except for the missing businessman and lost phone. And who could forget the scary stalker?

Amazing how a nice morning could make a left turn into awful so quickly.

She had taken this job to emotionally recuperate. The double whammy of losing Joel and the disaster on her last climbing expedition had sent her world into a tailspin. A new career conducting business retreats and leading simple hiking and camping outings was supposed to be soothing. The way her nerves jumped around was anything but.

"Looks like we're here."

The sound of Cam's voice over her shoulder made her jump and knock into Joel next to her. When her hands brushed against his, a new sensation spun through her. Something like excitement, and that didn't make her happy at all. She wanted to be totally over him, or at the very least not feel anything. She'd do anything for a bit of indifference at the moment.

She settled for doubling her pace and broke through the trees and into the camp clearing a step before her self-appointed bodyguards. The businessmen sat on logs turned into benches around the fire pit area. They looked up as she approached.

They all started talking a second later. Shouting over each other in an attempt to hold the metaphorical floor.

Yeah, she hadn't missed this part of their company dynamic during the past hour.

"Where have you been?" Jeff Acheson, the Baxter director of marketing, dumped his plate on the ground and stood up. His distaste for her was on full display, from his puffing red cheeks to the scowl marring what she guessed most women found to be his perfectly chiseled model face.

She took a long look at him in the bright sunshine and decided he was a bit too buffed and polished for her taste. He had a phony air about him. Probably because he listed his age as thirty-four on the questionnaire she had handed out last night to assess their skill levels, when she knew from the files Baxter gave her the number was more like forty.

That sort of thing struck her as ridiculous. She'd bet he took twice as long to get ready for a big date than she did.

She could still remember the up-and-down sweep he gave her when they'd first met in the Baxter offices. He'd turned on the charming smile back when he thought she was some sort of assistant to the *real* leader on the trip. That disappeared when she'd made it clear she was in charge.

But he picked the wrong time to get all uppity with her. She wasn't in the mood. "Is Mark here?"

"What?" Lance Ringer, the Baxter personnel manager, asked.

Lance was the one guy Hope had liked immediately. He was the youngest on the retreat but didn't try to impress her. He owned up to the fact he hadn't been camping since he was a kid, more than twenty years ago, and would rather be home with his newborn and wife than out roughing it with the guys. Hope found his honesty refreshing.

"Mark was missing this morning and I went to look for him," she said, waiting for Joel and Cam to pipe up and feeling a bit dazed when neither rushed to take the lead. "Did he ever come back?"

Jeff took a threatening step in her direction. "Why didn't you tell us there was a problem before now?"

"Probably because of this type of overblown reaction." Joel morphed from calm to a shield of muscles in two seconds. He reached around Hope, blocking some of her view of Jeff, and put a hand on his chest. "Back up."

Jeff tried to push Joel's hand away. "Who are you?"

"Not relevant at the moment."

Joel didn't move and Cam just smiled. Hope was smart enough to know those reactions meant brewing trouble. Joel's protective nature made it tough for him to back down, and when he was faced with a pontificating blowhard like Jeff, there was no telling what could happen.

"You have a gun," Jeff said.

Joel motioned toward Cam. "We both do."

With the tension building and washing over all of them, she decided this might be a good time to make one point clear. "Joel is my assistant."

She put her hand over his and it dropped away from Jeff. But the battle stance stayed, as did Joel's unwavering gaze on Jeff.

Cam covered his smile with his hand as he mumbled, "This should be good."

"What are you talking about?" Jeff asked as he turned his attention back to her. "I thought you were the supposed leader of this outing."

She said the word *assistant* and Jeff assumed she was no longer in charge. The man heard what he wanted to hear.

Before anyone said anything else that made her grumbly, Hope made the necessary introductions to keep the chain of command clear. "This is Joel Kidd, my helper, and Cameron Roth."

Joel cleared his throat. "Helper?"

With a raise of the chin she held her ground. "Yes."

The silence lasted for only a second before he nodded. "Alrighty then."

Relief poured through her when he didn't push it. She turned back to Lance. "Where's Perry?"

"Who's that?" Cam asked.

Lance got up and brushed off his pants. He stopped to shake hands with everyone. "Perry Kramer is our sales manager."

"What does he sell?" Joel stared at Hope when she shoved an elbow into his stomach. "What? It's a fair question."

Lance shrugged. "But it's probably not important information right now."

Hope heard the rustle of branches and glanced over in

time to see Charlie Bardon, the camp owner and cook, break through the trees on the far side of the last cabin. He was out of breath and running his hands over his grimy chef's apron as he walked.

"What's going on out here?" he asked.

Joel looked to the newcomer. "That was going to be my question."

Charlie didn't look any more willing to back down than Joel. They stood face to face and shared the same former military in-command presence. Pushing fifty, Charlie had been out for decades, but Joel seemed just as determined and set in his ways at thirty-three.

Before this could blow into a full-blown argument, Hope tried to step in. "Mark is missing."

"I was hoping he was with you." Charlie turned his attention to Joel. "Where did you come from?"

Joel shrugged. "Annapolis…or are you looking for an explanation about how birthing works?"

The older man's eyes narrowed. "Are you trying to be funny?"

"Not really."

"Okay, enough." She wasn't sure who deserved the bigger kick to the shin—Joel for acting disinterested and maintaining his monotone voice through the snide comments or Cam, who couldn't stop smiling. "Cam and Joel came in by helicopter to help me."

If possible, Charlie's scowl deepened. "With what?"

She had no idea how to answer the question, so she skipped it and talked to the campers, trying to ignore the fact another one appeared to be missing. "When is the last time anyone saw Mark?"

Taking a long time and making the movement last longer than necessary, Jeff folded his arms in front of him. "When you two fought last night."

Joel turned to face her. "Really?"

"He stormed out, saying he was going to the cabin," Lance said. "But he wasn't in there when I went to bed."

"What time was that?" Cam asked.

"Around midnight."

Charlie blew out a long breath as he talked. "You didn't think that was odd?"

"He was ticked off that Hope took his gun. I thought I heard him coming in later, but he wasn't there this morning." Lance looked at Joel as if he expected backup.

Joel leaned in closer instead. "His what?"

She knew there was no way that comment would slide by. "Gun, and I'll explain later."

"Yeah, you will," Joel said.

But not now. Not when all those eyes focused solely on her. "Go on, Lance."

"That's it. I figured he was walking it off or getting something to eat. Honestly, I didn't think it was a big deal. He got scolded. Get over it."

Hope didn't know what to do with any of that information. Mark had gotten angry and stormed off. She knew that before she took off on her search. But maybe she could get an answer to one question. "Were either of you out in the woods this morning?"

She got a lot of head shaking and mumbling but no answers. She scanned the crowd. Only Lance didn't possess the right body type. He'd joked about gaining more weight than his wife during the pregnancy. Hope doubted that was true, but he was carrying around a few extra pounds that would have made it a bit tough to dodge in and out of the trees.

Still, that didn't mean none of them had done it. Someone had and the nerves jumping around inside her wouldn't quiet down until she had answers, the right number of campers and her phone.

"And where were you this morning?" Joel asked the man in front of him.

Charlie didn't move. "Checking on the food situation."

From the question Hope guessed Joel wasn't as willing to believe as easily as she was. Then again, he'd just met the group, and they were down two members.

"Let's try it this way." Joel shifted his weight. Not a big move. Barely perceptible but something about it made him appear taller and less willing to play games. "When did you last see Mark?"

Charlie's gaze bounced from Joel to Cam and back again. "What's with the weapons? Are you police?"

The look on Joel's face, the way the corner of his mouth inched up, came close to a smile. "Pretend I am."

Charlie didn't share his amusement. "I don't think I will."

Much more of this and they'd never get to an answer. As it was, Lance and Jeff stared, watching the verbal volleys with their mouths hanging more open with each sentence.

Hope decided to act like what she was—in charge. "Charlie, help me out here. Mark wandered off and now I don't know where Perry is."

"I'm pretty sure Perry is in taking a second run at the chow line."

This time the relief walloped the air right out of her lungs. "So, you've seen him this morning?"

Charlie nodded. "About fifteen minutes ago."

"That's a relief," Lance said.

She saw Joel opening his mouth to say something and jumped in first. "But it doesn't explain the Mark issue."

Charlie waved her off. Even threw in a "bah" right before he started talking. "He's just blowing off steam."

The men kept saying it, but the explanation wasn't good enough. "I can't find him and I need him to check in before we do one more thing."

Jeff swiped his thermos off the ground. "We need to go out looking for him."

"How exactly?" Joel asked.

The question caused Jeff to go still. "What?"

Hope knew where this was going. She felt the conversation rolling downhill and couldn't grab a two-second break to throw her body in front of it.

She couldn't speak for Cam's expertise, but she guessed it was off the charts. But Joel knew everything about surviving outdoors. He was the one person in the group better at outdoor activities than she was, and that was saying something.

He thrived in this environment. His father had groomed his kids to fight and shoot, readying them for the domestic civil war he insisted was coming.

Lost in paranoia and reeling from the unexpected loss of his wife, Joel's dad believed the government had lost its way and only small pockets of freedom-loving people would save the world. He went about it by toughening up his kids, making them sleep outside and denying them an education until the state stepped in.

The upbringing was sick and wrong and it shaped Joel in ways she still hadn't explored. He liked to joke and act as if certain things didn't bother him, but she knew. But there were times when his gaze would wander and those dark eyes would glaze. He'd go to whatever place he built in his mind to find normalcy. And he wouldn't let her in.

"Do you know anything about wilderness survival?"

His voice stayed deceptively soft as he aimed the question at Jeff.

The other man held eye contact for a few seconds, then broke it. "We studied up before we came out here."

"Oh, good." Joel stared at Cam. "They studied."

She got the point, but the conversation promised to run them right into a brick wall. "Joel, that's enough."

Not that he heard her. He continued to stare at Jeff.

She knew the hard truth. None of the testosterone-jousting did anything to help them locate Mark.

"Which cabin belongs to this guy?" Cam asked.

"That one." She pointed to the building directly next to where hers sat in the middle of the makeshift line. Because she appreciated the assist, she followed Cam's lead. "Charlie, can you take the guys and put together some provisions? If we're going to spread out and search for Mark—"

Joel frowned. "Are we?"

"—they need to be ready."

Charlie started shaking his head before she finished the sentence. "I'm not convinced this is necessary. He's probably sulking. Struck me as the type."

"He's the vice president of finance," Jeff said, as if that explained everything.

When Joel finally performed that eye roll it looked like he'd been dying to do since Jeff stood up, it was obvious he wasn't convinced. "So?"

But she had a plan and it depended on everyone agreeing and moving on. "Charlie, if you could, maybe, keep everyone together, that would be a great help."

He stared at her, not saying a thing. A gust of wind shook the leaves and the sun beat down on the campground, but the silence stretched out. Finally, Charlie began a slow nod. It picked up in speed as it went and seemed to last for a long time. "Ah, got it."

She blew out the breath she'd been holding. It scratched her throat as it rushed out. "Thanks."

"Gentlemen?" Charlie motioned for the managers to follow him. "Let's go find Perry and get packed."

Joel didn't speak until the place cleared out and the voices faded as everyone slipped through the path between the cabins and headed for the kitchen cabin and open seating area about thirty feet away before he faced her. "What's with the search party talk?"

"Some of this crew think they are mountain men. I was worried they'd run off with butter knives and try to slay bears or something equally stupid." She'd dealt with the type for a long time and developed some skills, the top one being not to let them rally and slide into attack mode.

Cam nodded. "You wanted Charlie to keep them occupied while we searched."

She looked at Joel, waited for him to say something. She expected a lecture on knowing the parameters of her job and leaving the investigation to him, the professional.

Instead a smile broke across his lips. "Your dad would be proud of your covert abilities."

The compliment rushed right to her head, making her as dizzy as drinking the finest wine. "You don't grow up with a former special ops guy and not learn a few things."

That smile only widened. "Apparently."

"Besides, Charlie gets it. He knows the kind of people who come out here," she said, hoping to focus on all she had to do and drag her mind away from Joel. "He can help."

Cam chuckled. "If Joel doesn't tick him off."

Very true. "Well, there's that."

They walked to Mark's cabin. The men's footsteps matched and she had to push her gait to keep up. They had long legs and moved quickly and quietly. She had a case of nerves that shook her hard enough to knock her over. She wanted to believe there was a reasonable explanation, but as the minutes passed her faith waned.

She used her master key to open the lock. All three of them stepped inside and stopped. Their shoulders touched and they still took up most of the open space.

They kept silent as their gazes scanned from wall to wall. The room consisted of two double beds and a small sitting area. With only a few suitcases, a coffeepot on a hot plate and rows of clothes on hangers inside the open closet, the visual inventory didn't take long. There was one door, which went to a bathroom only slightly larger than a closet because the shower was outside the cabin in every building but hers.

Joel's shoes scraped against the wood floor as he stepped farther inside. "There's not much here."

She had to take the blame for that one. "I found I have to really limit what they can bring along or some folks come out here with laptops and three suitcases and think someone else will drag it along."

"Very practical." Joel rummaged through a duffel bag on the floor and peeked under the cushions on the loveseat.

Metal screeched as she slid the hangers on the old rod. She spotted a few shirts and extra sneakers on the floor. There wasn't as much as a chest of drawers in the place.

"Blood." Cam didn't add anything else. One word and so deathly serious.

She spun around to find Cam standing by the bed closest to the door. "What?"

Joel got there first, but she was right behind. They all crowded around the bed, staring and unmoving. No one touched anything.

She tried not to state the obvious, but she didn't see anything except crumpled white sheets and a stack of pillows with a clear head indent in them. "What am I looking at?"

Cam nodded in the direction of the bottom of the bed. "The underside of the cover."

Before she could reach over, Joel put out an arm and held her back. Two steps put him at the small table on the other side of the room. He was back in a flash with a pen in his hand.

With the tip, he lifted off the cover and flipped it back. Dark streaks ran about a foot along the underside. Splotches stained the navy blue blanket underneath. The dark shade hid the color. But she knew.

The dizziness hit her full force and the room spun. She would have grabbed for Joel but he'd crouched down to study the bed close up.

"It's not a lot," she said, looking for any positive spin on this horrible find.

"Well, it's more than a few drops," Joel said. "Almost like the spill of a glass of something."

"Are you sure it's blood?" She wanted them to say no, but she knew they wouldn't.

Joel stood back up. "Not without tests, but I think we should assume it is until we see Mark walking around here."

"Maybe he cut himself and didn't tell me?" She was willing to believe anything at this point, so long as the man was healthy and fine.

"What about this gun?" Joel asked.

The question shot out of nowhere and slammed into her with the force of a body blow. They could add the weapon to the list of things suddenly gone missing.

Dread washed over her and she would have sat down hard on the floor, but Joel reached over and settled a hand on her elbow. Technically, he wasn't holding her up, but inside she felt as if he were holding her together.

She tried to explain over the knot of anxiety wedged in her throat. "Unbeknownst to me, he brought it along. He waved it around at dinner, acting like a big shot."

"Guy sounds like a jerk," Cam said.

She felt obligated to defend him on some level. "He was showing off, but my rules are clear. No weapons."

Joel shrugged. "I'm armed."

"So am I," Cam agreed.

They acted as if they were the only ones concerned with safety. "Yeah, well, that makes three of us."

Cam smiled. "Really?"

"We all know the most dangerous person in a situation like this is the nervous novice with the gun." Joel nodded and she took that as approval and kept going. "I can't have people out here with weapons, or sooner or later one of them will shoot off a hand by accident."

He looked around the room. Even opened the bathroom door. "So where is it?"

"What?"

"The gun."

"I have it." She remembered the fight and what she did. "It's in a small lockbox in my cabin." But somehow deep down, she knew it was gone.

Joel stopped in the middle of the room and fixed her with a serious glare. "A hundred bucks says it's missing."

Just went to show how alike they were. She knew, he knew. Heck, maybe even Cam knew.

Still, she had to ask. "Why would you say that?"

Joel didn't hesitate. "Experience."

Chapter Four

Ten minutes later Hope had her leg wound bandaged and cleaned by Joel and carefully kneeled on the floor of her cabin, putting as little weight on the injury as possible. After a quick check under the bed she sat back on her heels and stared up at Joel. "Can I panic now?"

As far as he was concerned, they'd passed that point one missing businessman ago. "Soon."

Joel had come out here as a favor. He'd dragged Cam because he needed a ride. Now they had a full-fledged mess on their hands.

Time was the issue. Mark had been missing for potentially twelve hours or more. That amounted to an emergency. The weather had stayed warm, but the breeze had kicked up and the air carried the scent of rain.

From all accounts Mark wasn't a seasoned hiker. Animals, accidents, falls—the list of dangers went on and on. He could be hurt or worse.

Joel needed to get word to the rest of his team in Annapolis of the potential issue in West Virginia. They might need search and rescue, or air support, and he sure as hell wanted an answer to who was stalking Hope.

Then there was the bigger problem. The lingering sense of something being off. This should have been a routine assignment for Hope. He understood her dad's worries, and Joel shared them when it came to her safety around a bunch of idiot men in the middle of nowhere, but this felt bigger. Targeted.

Joel didn't like it, and the frown on Cam's face and way he walked around, staring at the floor, suggested he wasn't a fan either. Joel wanted to chalk it up to the mix of guilt and want that pummeled him every time he looked at Hope. She was the one woman who tempted him to give it all up and hunt for a normal ending to his story.

Leaving her was the one time when he'd acted like a complete jerk with a woman and deserved a swift kick. He was lucky she hadn't treated him to one.

But the tic in the back of his neck wasn't about his feelings for her. He loved her until he couldn't see straight. Probably always would. No, this was something else.

He'd been attuned to danger—real danger, not the kind his father manufactured in his sick head—since he joined the military to escape his childhood. He learned to recognize it during his short tenure at Algier Security and honed it at the Defense Intelligence Agency. With Connor's help and the support of the Corcoran Team, he understood not to ignore it and instead figured out how best to handle it.

And he was into it up to his eyeballs now.

"Let's do a weapons check." Joel touched a hand against the gun strapped to his side, then performed a mental rundown of the rest. One at his ankle and the two knives hidden under his clothing, plus the others in the lockbox on the helicopter.

He glanced at Hope. "What do you have?"

"Charlie has a gun." She stood up next to Joel at the side of the bed. "I have a knife and a bow."

"Bow?" Cam broke off from his staring to watch her from across the mattress. "Is that really practical?"

That was the kind of talk that usually led to a demonstration. People underestimated Hope. They saw the pretty face and tight body and decided she must be the type to sit on daddy's piles of money and do nothing.

Joel had made that miscalculation for exactly three minutes before he saw her do a verbal takedown of a guy in her father's office who called her sweetie. Joel had been about to give the guy a lesson in respect, but she'd handled it.

And he'd been hooked ever since. He found other women attractive, but none of them were her. None came close.

He decided to fill Cam in on the nonprivate part. "She was basically a Junior Olympics champion."

"Not just basically." Bending over, she pulled the case out from under the bed and opened it. "Want to see my medals? I have several bows—recurve, long bow and a few compound. You'll have to trust me that I know how to use all of them."

Cam stretched and looked over the bed from his side. "Why did you bring one here? That one's recurve, right?"

She flashed him a smile. "The man knows his hardware."

"Definitely."

"Well, I figured I could show the men how to use it. People generally assume it's easy and have no idea how much strength it takes. And…" Her smile grew to high wattage as she closed the case. "Having a bow and arrows in the room tends to cut down on drunken male idiocy."

That time Cam laughed. "Impressive."

"What do you guys have?" she asked as she sat on the bed.

The laughter in her voice caught Joel in a spell. Seeing

her lighthearted and happy, if only for a few seconds, touched off something inside him.

Near the end they had fought a lot. Then he'd made her cry. He could have gone a lifetime without seeing that, without having her despair rip through him, shredding him from the inside out.

He forced his attention back to the present before the old feelings of guilt swamped him. "Guns, knives." Joel thought about a man tracking her through the woods. "My bare hands."

Her head fell to the side and her hair cascaded over her shoulder. "Strangely, I find that comforting."

A stark silence zipped through the room. It was charged and uncomfortable enough to have him thinking about the big bed right in front of him and Cam squirming as if he wanted to bolt.

He inched toward the door, looking like he was about to do just that. "I should head back to the helicopter and lock it up. Also need to check in with Connor."

Joel nodded. "Fine."

"Who is that?" she asked, seemingly unaware of the firestorm she'd set off in the man she'd once dated.

Joel swallowed a few times and thought about every unsexy thing he could to overwhelm the other thoughts in his head. After a few seconds, his control zapped back to life. "Our boss, Connor Bowen. He runs the Corcoran Team."

"Yeah, like I said, I should contact him." With his hand against the door, Cam appeared to want to do it right then.

Joel didn't disagree. He'd been toying with yelling for the cavalry, but he didn't want to rush everyone in before they conducted a few more easy steps. "Let's see if we can figure this out first. It's still possible we have an annoying businessman acting like a spoiled child."

"How do you explain the gun?" Cam asked.

Joel couldn't. Not without hitting on options that had his temper spiking. That was the problem. "I'm thinking Mark snuck in here and took the box."

"What?" Hope jumped off the bed and wrapped her arms around her body.

"I know that sounds bad, but—"

"While I was sleeping? No way." She rubbed her hands up and down her arms. "Don't you think I'd hear him?"

Cam winced. "Maybe not."

She visibly shivered. "That's just creepy."

"And one of the reasons your dad wanted me here." Joel slid that in there in the hope it would cut off any argument he'd get on the helicopter when they flew out of there the second after they located Mark. Thanks to all she'd described about this retreat so far, he'd leave when she did and not a minute earlier.

She held up a hand. "Don't start."

Looked like her fear or disgust or whatever it was about the lockbox had disappeared. "Your dad is being practical." Joel suspected her father was also engaging in a bit of matchmaking, but Joel decided not to share that thought.

"The word you're looking for is overprotective."

"Hope, I think—"

She turned to Cam. "So, now what?"

He bit his bottom lip in what looked like a poor attempt to block a smile. "We check the helicopter and do a quick search around the campground."

Those priorities worked for Joel. "Cam will question the men here at the campground and maybe see if Charlie knows anything or can give us some direction."

"He knows these woods better than anyone and probably can tell us where someone might hide." She sighed as she shook her head. "I swear if Mark is just being a big baby and staying away because a woman yelled at him, I'm going to hit him."

"Absolutely fine, since nailing him with an arrow is out. Unfortunately," Joel said.

Cam nodded. "Sounds like a reasonable plan."

She let her hand drop to her side again. "But Mark being a jerk still doesn't explain the missing satphone and the stalker."

"You're sure Mark wasn't the one following you?" Man, Joel wanted that to be the answer. It was simple and clean, but he knew life rarely worked that way. Not for him.

"The build was all wrong. Mark is stocky and a bit out of shape. This guy was lean and moved fast."

"I don't like that at all." Cam shook his head as he peeked out the small window next to the cabin's front door. "Heads up—the troops are gathering by the fire pit again. Looks like Charlie is giving them orders."

"I bet Jeff pays attention to Charlie," Hope grumbled.

Cam snorted. "Annoying but at least they're listening. Good to know they can."

Sounded like time had run out. Joel didn't want to spend one more second in planning mode. "Okay, we meet back here in two hours. If we haven't found anything, we start looking in the other cabins."

Hope reached down. "I'll bring—"

No way was Joel dealing with that. "The bow stays here."

"Fine." She got up and joined the men at the door. She glanced at Cam. "I thought you had to be somewhere else today."

He nodded, like he always did. "I'm fine for now."

"Maybe we should all be in on the questioning. I mean, I already checked the woods."

Joel knew that would eat up too much time. "This go-round we'll look for tracks."

"Want me to do that? It's more of my specialty than yours," Cam said.

"We'll be fine."

Cam reached for the doorknob. "I bet."

"Can I have a gun?"

Her question stopped both men. Cam froze and Joel did a quick count to ten. She could handle it, but she was still spooked and he had to be sure she was back in full control before he handed her a loaded gun. Still… "No."

"Can you shoot?" Cam asked.

"Been practicing since I was ten."

Joel wasn't having this conversation right now. He reached around and shoved the door open, bringing the warm breeze inside. "Shooting a person is different."

Her head snapped back. "Are we doing that?"

He hoped not. "Maybe."

"And you would know how hard that is."

He glanced at her over his shoulder. "Yes, I would."

THEY'D CROSSED OUT of sight of the campground before Hope broached the difficult subject. Actually, about a hundred feet away she opened her mouth and then closed it again, focusing on the sway of branches against the increasing wind and the clomp of their feet against the ground.

Later they hit the point where she could see sunlight up ahead and knew the helicopter sat a short distance away. She didn't hold back. "Are we going to talk about it?"

He stopped scanning the trees and large expanse of forest around them to spare her a glance. "About what?"

Men were clueless. "Us."

He exhaled. "Hope—"

"I know. You don't have to list off the reasons why we should pretend we've never slept together."

"I never said that."

"You act like it."

"And, for the record, it was more than sex."

"Was it?" She asked even though she couldn't stand to hear him dismiss their relationship as unimportant—again.

True, they hadn't been together in what felt like forever. She'd convinced herself she didn't care and could move on, but seeing him made her realize how untrue that was.

He picked a leaf off a branch that nearly whacked him in the face. "We can't do this now."

The world around her barely registered. Not when this topic came up.

She'd heard all of the excuses. They ran through her mind on constant play. They spilled out of her now before she could call them back. "This is the wrong time. I'm the wrong guy. You deserve better. My background is a mess. My job is dangerous."

He stopped. "Excuse me?"

"Have you invented more reasons? I've heard all of those, and none of them sent *me* running."

"Wow."

She debated storming ahead, leaving him floundering, but refrained. Childish wasn't the answer when what she really wanted was for him to treat her the way a woman deserved to be treated. "Imagine how I felt as you ticked off that list, or some version of it, day after day. You always had a new reason to push away and leave, but you never found one to stay."

"That's not true."

She knew it was because she had lived it. "All those months ago I asked you to move in with me since you were basically staying there every night anyway, and you flew out of town on a business trip the next morning instead of giving me an answer."

"That was legitimate."

"Joel, come on."

The leaf disappeared as Joel crushed it inside his clenched fist. "Your father said you were dating again."

Her gaze slipped back up to his. "What?"

"No?"

The conversation had her mind spinning. Her dad still talked with Joel? And since when was her dating life up for discussion? Not that she really had one. She struggled through a few setups from friends and had a perfectly nice time with a guy from her climbing club.

Handsome men, fun places and she didn't experience so much as a spark. Not even a tiny nibble of interest.

But that's not where her mind went when Joel asked the question. It zoomed right to her nightmare scenario. The one where he walked away and found someone else. Where the truth turned out to be not that he wasn't ready to make a commitment but that he didn't want to make one to *her*.

"Are *you*?" Two simple words, but it actually hurt her to say them.

"I didn't leave you so I could date other women. My decision wasn't about being a playboy." His voice rose and anger slipped in as he spoke.

As if he had a right to be upset about the fallout. "Well, I guess that's good to know."

Instead of standing around arguing, she headed in the direction of the helicopter. This was a waste of time and they had more important things to worry about than her broken heart.

Joel grabbed her arm before she got more than three feet. "Hey, wait up."

She didn't shake out of his grip, though she could have because his hold was more gentle than confining. Seeing the pain in his dark eyes killed off any thought of pulling back anyway.

He closed in, bringing his body within a few breaths of hers. "You know I'm telling the truth, right?"

"I know you had a lot of excuses. Still do." And she couldn't hear them again. Not and still function.

"Hope, look...I want..."

"What?" She heard the pleading in her voice.

His eyes closed and when they opened again the wary expression hadn't faded. "Maybe we should stick to finding Mark."

Just like that, the mood changed. Something snapped and the tension that had been building blew away.

Because he seemed to want an out, she gave him one. Maybe a change of topic made sense. There had been so much pain and disappointment, so many tears. She needed her head in the game and her mind on Mark. "Fine. Why are we headed back to the helicopter instead of following tracks?"

"I want to check in at work."

"And?" Joel's face went blank and she wasn't falling for it. "Oh, please. Maybe I didn't see you walking out on me, but I do know you. Part of you, and you are fixated and worried."

"I didn't leave you—"

"Joel."

His hand dropped. "Okay, yes. I'm concerned."

"You're admitting it?"

"You deserve that much." He motioned with his head for them to start walking again. "This is your job, and I think something is very wrong here."

The honesty flooded her with relief. "Good."

"Why good?"

"Sharing even that much is a big step for you."

"I thought you'd be happy I left." His voice dropped to a near whisper. "Back then, I mean."

The words stunned her and she stumbled. She stared at him, thinking he had to be playing a sick joke, even though that wasn't his style. But he looked ahead, not even blinking.

"You've got to be kidding." She was about to pull him to a stop when a crack echoed through the trees. Dirt kicked up a few feet away from her, and birds swooped out of the trees in a rush.

"Get down!" His full body smacked into her before he finished talking.

The ground rushed up and she put out a hand to stop the free fall. Her legs twisted with his and the second before she slammed into the ground he turned them.

Landing on his side with a grunt, he absorbed the majority of their combined body weight on his shoulder. His body bounced and she tried to move away and let him brace for impact, but he curled her body into his. Still, the jolt rattled her teeth and she heard him swear under his breath.

She could taste dirt and feel sharp sticks jabbing into her bare legs and ripping off her bandage. Her mind finally focused and the sounds of the forest came rushing back. "Joel—"

"Don't move."

It had sounded like… But it couldn't be. "What was that?" She whispered the question as she frantically looked around.

Before she could scramble to her feet, he shoved her against the ground and covered her body with his. His fingers slipped into her hair as he held her down. She heard a steady stream of reassuring words, but they barely registered over the fear and panic pounding through her.

She expected shouts and more pops. When nothing came, she glanced up. His gaze scanned the area, and his gun was up and ready. She swallowed hard at the vulnerability of their position. Right there on her makeshift path with nothing covering them or blocking their view in any direction.

"A gunshot." He was so close the words vibrated against the side of her head.

Adrenaline pumped through her, and her heartbeat hammered in her ears so loudly she thought for sure she'd give away their position. "Where did it come from?"

"I'm more worried about who and how many." He shifted his weight until most of it fell away to her side. "Stay under me."

"Are you wearing a bulletproof vest?"

"Didn't think I'd need one."

She waited for the attacker to rush them. Listened for another shot. "I can't hear or see anything."

"I need to get to the helicopter."

A vision of him running and getting shot hit her with the force of a crashing train. The horror of it stole her breath and had her fingernails digging into the dirt. "No."

"I have a vest and binoculars in there." He slipped farther off her. "Other weapons."

"You can't risk going into the open."

With barely a touch he moved them to the left. She felt his deep inhale before he rolled them over and stopped close to a large tree trunk. He tapped the back of her legs. "Curl up."

When the world finally stopped spinning she looked up and saw rough bark right in front of her face and threw a hand out to touch the surface. "What are we doing?"

"You are going to make yourself as small as possible." He gave the orders without looking at her. His head kept moving as he glanced around them. "Then you're not to move."

"You can't—"

"I'm serious. You move and I will come back, which is more of a threat to me than racing over there." With a hand between her shoulder blades, he lowered her closer to the ground. "Stay down."

Before she could grab on or call him back, he was gone. In a crouch, zigzagging he broke through the last line of trees. He hugged close to the helicopter as he lifted a hand. The door must have stuck or his angle was off because she saw him pulling and tugging.

With all her concentration, she focused on him. Her teeth clicked together as terror spun through her. She waited for footsteps to fall and a hand to pull her up. The only thing that kept her from screaming was watching Joel. Even as her vision blurred around the edges, she stared.

After some fiddling and a yank, he got the door open and bonelessly slipped inside. One minute his dark hair provided a beacon and the next he was gone.

Her breath hiccupped in her chest as she fought the urge to run after him. She'd just decided to do that when she saw his head again. He held binoculars and swept his gaze over the forest. The door inched open and he was off again, this time running toward her.

He slid in beside her, kicking up twigs and leaves around her. He held up a vest. "Put this on."

"You need it."

"I think the person is gone, but I don't want to risk you getting shot."

When he continued to hold the vest, she took it and slid it on. The way he stared at her with that I-can-wait-all-day expression had her adjusting the straps and securing it tighter to her body. "Happy?"

"Not really."

That made two of them. She looked at the binoculars. They weren't the standard bird watching kind.

"Do they do something special?" She half hoped they functioned as a grenade launcher. She'd be satisfied with any weapon that could protect them all and get them out of there fast.

"Increased magnification and brightness. Plus the universal mil reticle." He spit all that out without lowering the glasses.

"Um, okay."

"The last is a special feature snipers use." This time he looked at her. "It allows for better targeting and range estimates."

The techno-jargon filled her with a strange sense of relief. It was as if they had walked right into his wheelhouse. She was fine to stay there with him.

Despite all their personal troubles, she never doubted his competency on the job. He was the man any sane person would want on her team when things fell apart. Now qualified.

Still, the sniper talk had her attention. "I don't know most of the words you just used."

"It means—"

She put a hand on his arm. "Don't explain. I'm just happy you know what you're talking about."

He nodded. "We need to get back."

The comment started a new round of thundering in her chest. "How do we know it's safe?"

"I'll feel better when we're in the cabins."

She'd feel better in her town house. "Any chance your team is on the way?"

"I called them. Yes."

"That's good news." But she noticed he wasn't smiling and didn't look one ounce more relieved than he was before he crawled into the helicopter for reinforcements. "Right?"

"I'll explain later."

Something inside her shriveled. "I was afraid you'd say that."

Chapter Five

Tony Prather had no idea who or what Connor Bowen was, but the man was on his way up to the executive floor of Baxter Industries. Tony glanced out of his conference room window to the Washington, D.C., skyline in the distance. His Rosslyn office had a view across the Potomac River to Georgetown.

He'd worked hard for his position with the big office, complete with private executive bathroom and two administrative assistants. He wasn't accustomed to jumping when others issued orders. If anyone other than Rafe Algier had phoned in from a trip abroad and asked, Tony would have had someone on his staff offer an excuse and insist he couldn't be disturbed.

But Algier Security had sent work Baxter's way, and back when business was floundering Rafe had provided some much-needed contracts and personnel to help keep Baxter's doors open. Tony had a strong loyalty to the man. It was why he had agreed to hire his daughter for the executive retreat.

Well, part of the reason. Tony didn't get where he was by being soft. His obligation didn't pass from Rafe to his daughter.

Tony had taken over the reins of Baxter after a coup by the old board of directors. When the bottom fell out of the financial markets and business dried up, the old president and chief executive officer lost the confidence of everyone from shareholders to the management staff. Tony stepped in and got the place running again. He expanded the company's services.

They no longer just provided tech and personnel to government agencies. Now his people staffed Fortune 500 companies and smaller businesses. Anyone who didn't want to pay employee benefits and could afford Baxter's bills was welcome.

But that didn't mean he had time to babysit some guy with an agenda. And Rafe hadn't taken the time to explain anything, which ticked Tony off. He had other worries. All his plans, those tenuous pieces he needed to come together and fit just so, were breaking down. He had a partner he didn't trust and a problem he needed to fix.

He'd rebuilt it all and couldn't afford to have it crumble now. Not when he was so close to the end.

The phone on the credenza buzzed and he gave the okay for one of his assistants to usher in their unwanted guest. Better to get it over with and move on.

The man who stepped through the glass doors and stopped was not what Tony expected. Tall with dark hair, he wore a business suit minus the jacket. But that's not what stuck out. It was the lethal look. The man appeared ready for battle. So did the muscled man behind him.

Earlier, Rafe had talked about needing to get in touch with his daughter. Tony had barely listened because the mere mention of Hope Algier's name at this point in the process had Tony speed dialing his partner. Not that he could get through.

"I'm Connor Bowen." The man motioned to the guy with him. "This is Davis Weeks."

"Gentlemen." Tony nodded because that's what protocol demanded.

Inside, his rage boiled. He'd prepared for one of them. Bowen was president and owner of something called the Corcoran Team. The Internet and paperwork trail pointed to a threat assessment group. The kind of team that taught businessmen how not to get kidnapped while playing in Mexico and made plans for getting them out when they did.

All aboveboard and clean, but Tony recognized an off-the-books undercover operation when he saw one. And that had his interest. So did this Weeks character. The guy hadn't blinked and if the bulge under his jacket was an indication, he'd somehow snuck a gun through security.

"I'm Tony Prather." He motioned toward the seats across the conference table from him. "I was told only one of you would be coming."

"Davis is my second in command. He understands the situation."

Because Tony needed to know what that was, he played along. Still, this was his turf, so he took the lead. "What can I help you with?"

Connor leaned forward with his elbows folded on the table in front of him. "There's a problem at your management retreat."

A stark silence followed the statement. Tony guessed that was the point. Drop the bombshell and then assess his reaction.

He had no intention of giving them anything. "Meaning?"

This time Davis spoke up. "One of your executives is missing and there's been some other trouble."

"This is a get-away-from-it-all retreat. How would you

know what's happening there?" Tony had been trying to check in, and the messages he'd received made no sense.

Connor's hand dropped to the table, and his fingers drummed on the top. "Some of my people are there."

The information would have been good to know before now. Funny how Rafe had left that out. "Some?"

"More than one."

The steady thumping touched off a headache. Tony had enough of that right now. "Care to tell me why?"

Connor shrugged. "As a favor to Rafe."

Looked like he wasn't the only one indebted to Rafe Algier in some way. Tony wasn't sure how he felt about that. The idea of the old man moving the chess pieces around, using them all, had Tony balling his hands into fists on his lap.

"Does he know his daughter is tangled up in this?" Tony had put her there for a reason and now it could all unravel thanks to this Corcoran Team and Rafe's meddling.

"Not all the details," Connor said. "Rafe is breaking away from his meetings in Vietnam and should be taking off soon to head back."

"This is that serious?" Tony noticed only the one in charge talked. Tony appreciated the chain of command as much as the next guy, but the silence from Davis proved unnerving. The guy sat and stared.

A lesser man would get twitchy and start talking. If that was the plan, these two sorely underestimated him. Tony Prather could not be intimidated. Others had tried and failed at using that tactic.

He hadn't won his current position by shaking hands and saying yes all the time. He'd pushed his predecessor out and never looked back. He'd won the office and the hot young wife. That's what he did—he won.

Davis finally shifted in his chair. The movement was slight, but it had the focus switching to him. "You didn't ask which executive is missing."

Tony knew all about Mark's situation. Knew and was watching, but these two didn't need that information. "I'm assuming whoever it was got lost on a hike and this isn't really a big deal."

Davis and Connor exchanged glances. Connor started talking again after Davis nodded. "Right before I spoke with one of my team members earlier today, he came under fire."

Tony was more interested in which man was in charge than about this conversation. Still, he had a role to play. "You mean—"

"Gunshots." Connor exhaled as if explaining bored him. "At the camp."

Time for concern. Hitting the appropriate level would be the trick. Tony went with pushing his chair back and reaching for the phone. "I need to get them all out."

"My people are working on that." Connor glanced at the phone and continued when Tony returned it to the cradle. "Once the weather breaks we'll move in."

Not the response Tony had expected. He figured they'd rush in and rescue, or whatever they normally did. The change in expectations and protocol sent a new push of adrenaline rushing through him. "Send in the park rangers. Do something."

Davis's eyes narrowed. "If we didn't have a 'shots fired' situation, maybe, but we can't risk putting anyone else in danger."

All reasonable answers. But Tony couldn't shake the feeling he was being sized up and checked out. That was probably fair because he was playing the same game at the moment.

Right now he needed to know their real plan. He guessed they wouldn't share most of it, but maybe he could drag out something. "So, what's next?"

Connor thumped his fingertips even louder. "My guys will secure the scene until I can get emergency personnel in there."

Tony glanced down but Connor didn't stop. "And in the meantime what happens to my executive?"

"We try to find him," Davis said.

Definitive and solid. Tony looked for a chink in their show and didn't see one. The routine came off as practiced but appropriate. He had to admit a part of him was a little impressed. These two could give lessons in remaining cool and detached.

"Should I contact his family or at least notify the board?" he asked.

"Let's see where we are tomorrow." Connor stood up. "We need to get back, but I'll keep you updated."

"Absolutely." Tony reached across the table and shook their hands. "Thanks for coming in."

Connor nodded. "I'm sorry I don't have more definitive news."

"I'm going to continue to believe this is a case of wandering away from camp and not a disaster."

"Except for the gunshots." Davis delivered the line in a flat voice. He didn't say much, but what he did force out came with a punch.

Tony admired the skill. "That could be hunters, anything."

"I have a conference call scheduled with search and rescue. You're welcome to listen in." Connor slipped a business card out of the pocket of his dress shirt and set it on the table.

Tony left it there. "I appreciate that. My assistant

can give you all my contact information, including the home numbers."

"Good." Connor headed to the door with Davis right behind him.

At the last minute, Davis turned around again. "Mark."

That fast the air sucked out of the room. "Excuse me?"

"Your missing executive. His name is Mark Callah." For the first time, Davis smiled.

Tony found it more intimidating than the staring. "Connor already told me that."

"Did I?" he asked.

Tony stuck with the story because he refused to believe he'd messed up and not asked what would be the obvious question. This was a trap and he would not fall into it. "Yes."

"I'll call in a few hours." After one last up and down, Connor left, taking Davis with him.

JOEL TRIED TO think of a way the past hour could have gone worse. Hope wanted to have "the talk" in the middle of a potential missing persons case. Add in bad weather, gunshots and no answers, and Joel wanted to yank all of them out of there and go home.

He might have done so if the flight wasn't dangerous and he didn't have a missing camper lost out in the unforgiving woods somewhere. Still, the idea of shoving Hope on the helicopter and telling Cam to fly her to safety was compelling. The fact that she would refuse wasn't Joel's biggest concern. He could—would—make her if that's what he had to do to keep her safe.

He had left her to give her a normal life. Forfeiting that now was not okay with him. Not after all he'd lost.

They stepped into camp. When Joel saw the flat expression on Cam's face, he knew something was wrong.

"What's going on?" Joel called out.

Cam joined them at the line where the trees met the open space. "Perry's officially missing."

Hope let out a stifled gasp. "You've got to be kidding. We're missing two now?"

"Charlie last saw him in the kitchen area around breakfast, but there's no sign of him at all." Cam kicked the dirt under his feet.

Joel tried to ignore the uncharacteristic shifting, but it made him nervous. "His bed?"

"Slept in and all of his stuff is in his cabin." Cam looked up. "Good news is we don't have blood this time."

"I can't believe that now qualifies as good news." She leaned against Joel.

Cam shrugged. "Well, it's not as bad as it could be."

Without thinking, Joel put a hand against her lower back and brought her in closer to his side. Despite the warm weather, her skin felt cold and the chill seeped through his clothes to his skin. The wind had cooled, but not enough to explain the shivers running through her.

Cam's gaze shot to the lack of space between Joel and Hope, then back up again. "Jeff and Lance are pretty jumpy. Charlie is on the side of that last cabin, walking them through some camping tips."

As far as Joel was concerned, that was the sort of thing that should have happened before the retreat started. "Now?"

"I did that before," she said.

Cam waved off the concern. "I think he's trying to keep them calm."

"Well." Hope rubbed her hands up and down her arms. "Maybe I should listen in then."

Joel knew she was suffering from a case of nerves. She didn't need a class on wilderness survival. In their months apart she'd taken more and more risks, climbing higher mountains and guiding tours thousands of feet into the air. He hated the idea of her up there, but he knew she loved it. And they were no longer together, so he limited his complaints to her dad. Not that they worked.

The corner of Cam's mouth lifted as his gaze wandered over Hope and Joel. "What happened to you two?"

"Get ready for more bad news," she said.

Joel didn't feel like playing games, so he skipped right to it. "Someone shot at us."

Cam's mouth fell into a flat line again. "What?"

She blew out a long, labored breath. "One shot but it had us ducking."

Cam nodded. "I'd think so."

"Well then." She stepped out of Joel's hold. "I should go do some work."

Joel admired her courage to not sit in a corner and rock. Most people would, but not her. But he still worried about her shell-shocked expression and wavering voice. "You okay?"

Cam cut off any chance of getting her to stay. "I need to talk with you."

Even though he wanted to follow her, Joel let Hope go but not before one more reminder. "You need to check your knee and put on another bandage."

She nodded but didn't say anything. That didn't stop him from staring. He watched her walk across the campground, ignoring the gentle swish of her hips and not breaking focus until he saw her stop next to Charlie in the distance.

Cam took a few steps and came to stand beside Joel. "The others were with me the whole time. None of these three could have taken the shot at you."

Joel had already come to that conclusion. Ruling some

people out narrowed their choices. He didn't like any of the remaining ones. "Then we need to deal with the very real possibility either Mark or Perry, or both, are at the bottom or this."

"There's another possibility." Cam matched Joel's stance and stared at the others as well. "We could have an unknown out here stalking people."

There it was. The worst possible answer. An unknown meant they were dealing with a surprise. The person could be on drugs or unstable or just enjoy killing.

Joel didn't want Hope near any of those types. "I've been trying not to think about that option."

"It would explain the gunshots." Cam stared at him then. "I'm guessing you didn't see anyone."

"Nothing. The guy totally got the drop on me."

Cam made a face. "Weird."

"I know." Joel understood the surprise. He wasn't the type to miss someone sneaking up on him.

He'd been training for surveillance his entire life. He had tracked and practiced from the day after he turned seven and his dad insisted the family go totally off the grid. Maybe those early lessons grew out of his father's sick paranoia, but he instilled a sense of caution and taught certain skills. The same skills that served Joel well as he passed from one position to another in the intelligence community.

That likely meant the attacker was equally well trained. Joel hated that prospect.

Cam let out an impressive line of profanity. "What did Connor say?"

"He's on the way and will bring everyone from the forest rangers to the local police with him."

Connor was solid that way. No questions or explanations needed. Joel was on a few days of leave, but he knew if he sent up the red flag, the team would come running.

He'd missed that in his other employment positions and throughout most of his life. He didn't know the sensation of someone putting it all out there for him. His mom had died before he could really know her, and his father's idea of love was handing over a rifle and teaching him to shoot.

Now Joel needed to fill Cam in on the bad part. Joel owed him that since Cam was only out here as a favor. "One problem."

"I'm not sure we need another."

"A storm is moving in."

"Of course it is." Cam groaned. "There's always a storm right when you don't need one."

"Connor can't get in until morning, and even then that's not a guarantee." Joel doubted the timetable anyway. He could smell the rain in the air and feel the dampness on his skin, even though not a single drop had fallen. But Connor talked about violent thunderstorms rolling in and Joel guessed they were headed this way. At the very least, the weather grounded planes. "So, we hunker down."

"I was afraid you were going to say that."

And it was about to get worse, so Joel braced. "I say we do a quick meal, stick together until dark or rain or whatever comes first. Then those of us with weapons split up and bunk with the others."

Cam's mouth broke out into a full grin. "Let me guess which cabin you'll be in."

Knowing the ribbing could go on for hours, Joel ignored the first shot. "You with Lance and we'll let Charlie handle Jeff."

"And you with Hope."

Joel rolled his eyes. "Yes."

"You ready to tell me what happened with her before you came to Corcoran?"

He still battled with the details. He couldn't lay it out there. Not after he was barely holding together from Hope's insistence they pick at it. "No."

Cam nodded and Joel thought he might be in the clear. They needed to concentrate and—

"I'm thinking you'll need practice," Cam said, breaking into Joel's thoughts.

He bit back a groan. "Meaning?"

"I don't know much about women—"

"True."

"—but even I know there's no way you're going to spend the night together without the topic of your relationship implosion coming up." Cam ended the comment with a knowing look.

Joel ignored the description of his upcoming evening, even though he wanted to deny it. "We're grown-ups."

The nodding came back. Cam did love to nod. "I'm guessing that's what she'll say before she demands an explanation."

"What makes you think we didn't work this out already?"

Joel wished. He wanted to fix the damage and move on. Because forgetting her appeared to be out of the question, he'd settle for a healthy parting. One that took away the sadness that moved into her eyes when she talked about them.

"What was the word you used earlier on her?" Cam looked up and closed one eye, as if he were pretending to mull it over. "Oh, right. Experience."

"We're the same age and I doubt you're any better at

this women stuff than I am." Joel hoped for Cam's sake that wasn't true.

"But I wouldn't be dumb enough to let that woman go."

This time Joel nodded. There was that.

Chapter Six

Hope tried busywork to calm the nerves somersaulting in her stomach. With her knee bandaged and everyone tucked away, she tried to settle in. She drew down the bed covers, then drew them up again and tucked them around the pillows.

Next came sitting. She dropped onto the mattress and looked around the cabin. It was a utilitarian space with dark furniture and windows that rattled when a strong gust of air blew in, like right now. Her space measured about twenty square feet more than the others and included an inside shower.

That was pretty much a prerequisite for her on a retreat like this. She'd rather go without than risk flashing half the camp. Here she didn't have to make the choice.

But she had bigger problems ahead. Well, one. Joel.

He stood with his broad back to her and stared out the small window next to the door. He wore the same pants he was wearing when he'd landed. Charlie had lent him a clean T-shirt. The rest of Joel's clothes sat in his bag on the helicopter. He insisted another run was too risky in light of the guy practicing his sniper skills out here.

Rain pelted the windows and had kept them all trapped inside for the past few hours. Now the sun had gone down and the ceiling light in the center of the room highlighted everything, including all six-feet-whatever of him.

The ruffled dark hair and scruff around his chin had always been her favorite look for him. Made him look rugged and reminded her of his sexy ability to handle almost any situation.

"We've slept in the same room before." He made the comment without looking at her.

She had to smile. "Many times, but we were dating back then."

Sometimes she thought the phrase "eyes in the back of his head" was invented to describe him. He always seemed to have a clue about what was happening around him, even if he acted like he didn't care or his eyes were closed.

"True." He turned but didn't move one inch closer. "And no one was shooting at us."

"Now look at us." She sat on her hands to keep from fidgeting or waving them around.

His gaze bounced to her lap, then back to her face. "I'll sleep on the floor."

Interesting how he had his lines and she had hers. Having him nod off during the next shoot-out was not her idea of a good time. "You'll sleep in the bed with me."

"That's not a great idea."

Oh, she knew that. His scent, his arms. The way he wrapped his body around hers and pulled her in tight. All dangerous for her self-control. "Agreed."

He held out a hand. "Then throw me a pillow and—"

"But it's still happening."

With that his arm dropped to his side again. "You go to my head."

And he didn't look particularly happy about the idea.

His face stayed blank and his eyes flat. He froze in place and looked as likely to bolt as he was to take a step closer.

The words both freeing and empty went to her head and stuck there. "What does that mean?"

"I've never been attracted to a woman the way I'm attracted to you." He pushed away from the door and walked across the room.

With each step, his hiking boots fell quietly against the hard floor. The cabin walls creaked and thunder drummed in the distance. The harder the winds and heavier the sheets of rain, the more she waited for the outside to storm in. The sturdy structures held, but a dribble leaked in at the back left corner near the open closet.

All she could focus on was the soft tap of his steps until he stopped in front of her. With only a foot separating them, she could smell him. Feel the weight of his gaze upon her.

As she stood, her gaze traveled over his flat stomach and the smooth muscles under his damp tee. "So, naturally, you left me."

"Normal doesn't work for me."

How many times had she heard that excuse? It appeared to be his favorite, which made it her least. "You say that often enough for it to be your motto."

"The way I was raised…" He broke off and shook his head. "Look, things can work for a little while but that's it."

There it was. The blanket statement that ended it all. The sentiment would have been sweetly misguided if it hadn't driven them apart. He believed. It amounted to nonsense talk, but in his head he viewed it as truth.

Shame that on this one issue he ignored the reality that life could be better than what he was handed. "How do you know?"

His eyes narrowed. "What?"

"How many long-term relationships have you had?" She steeled her body for the verbal blow. She had a theory and put it out there, hoping she'd turn out to be right.

"We should talk about something else." He started to pivot.

"I'll narrow it down for you." She spoke louder and put a hand on his arm to hold him there. "Did you ever live with a woman?"

He blinked a few times. "Just you, and that was informal."

The relief crashing over her nearly knocked her down. "Ever date one woman for more than three months in a row?"

He didn't hesitate. "You."

The last of the tension whooshed out of her. Even though she seemed to be the only one fighting for them, at least he refrained from using her weakness for him against her. "Then you have no idea what you could or couldn't do long term."

"I didn't go to school until I was eleven." He folded his hand over hers where it lay against her arm.

"Do you think that's a test for something?" The rain cast dampness over everything and had her shivering, but his touch sent warmth spiraling through her.

"Yes, for everything."

His palm brought the heat back to her limbs. "All it says to me is your father was a sick man, which I already knew. He grew paranoid and scary and died from a brain tumor. You didn't hide that from me."

His hand squeezed hers. "That wasn't really an option since your father had my information and knew."

Not a surprise. Her father specialized in collecting information. The more confidential and harder to find, the more he liked hunting it down. He was a specific type of person. The same type as Joel.

"Believe it or not, he didn't hand me your personnel file," she said.

This time Joel smiled and life sparked behind those serious eyes. "I bet he tried."

"Yes." He'd lectured, done everything but make a pros and cons list about Joel.

Not that her dad would put anything on the con list. He loved Joel like a son and wanted him to be *the* one for her. Dad had never been subtle on that point.

"Why didn't you take it?" Joel asked.

That was easy. "I wanted to learn everything about you in the *normal* way. Date like normal people. Eat together like normal people. Find out about each other like normal people."

"I remember our first date." His free hand went to her hair. He slid it forward and weaved his fingers through.

"Italian food. We ate for three hours."

He wrapped a lock around his forefinger. "I was done in ten minutes, but I moved a few stray pieces around on my plate because I wanted to be with you as long as possible."

Her heart did a perfect backflip. "When did that stop?"

The sadness moved back into his eyes as his thumb traced her lower lip. "Never."

"So, you left me for a job." The words stuck in her chest, but she shoved them out, letting them rip and tear as they went.

"Yes."

The word hit her like a punch. "And then you left that job for the one you have now."

She didn't understand that choice. He had confessed how much he wanted the position at the Defense Intelligence Agency, how he needed to be available to come and go. That the work would be dangerous and the hours impossible. He'd pick up and leave and couldn't tell her… so they should move on from each other.

The memory of how easy it had been for him to deliver the horrible news still haunted her. She'd begged and he'd walked away. Never looked back.

But now she saw a different man. This Joel didn't celebrate leaving her. When he looked at her he acted as if the need crushed him. She just wished he could see it. She wished he was willing to do something to fix them.

His chest rose and fell on heavy breaths as his fingertips brushed against her cheek. "The DIA job was a mistake."

Not the answer she expected. Not really the question in her mind either. "Was leaving me a mistake?"

He closed his eyes for the briefest of seconds "Hope, don't—"

She stopped his words by putting her palms on either side of his face. "Kiss me."

"No." There was no heat behind the word.

"Why?"

"I won't stop."

She leaned in closer, letting her breath mingle with his. "You will. We'll kiss and then we'll get in that bed and sleep."

"You have more faith in my control than I do."

He acted like this was easy for her. Like she wasn't waging a battle to win *them* back. "You would never touch me without my permission."

"Of course not." His hands went to her waist and with a tug her chest pressed against his.

"You don't have it." She dropped a small kiss on his chin. "You would have to earn it."

"You're killing me." His face went into her hair, and his mouth nuzzled her ear.

The brush of air across her skin sent a tremor racing down her spine. The shiver brought with it an ache. A need to be near him. "That pretty face of yours isn't enough for me to drop my common sense."

He chuckled. "Good to know."

"But you could—"

"Kiss you."

He didn't ask for permission a second time or for an order from her. He dipped his head and his lips touched hers. The kiss slipped from sweet to hot before one second could pass to the next.

Fire rolled over her as her nerve endings sparked to life. Her hands tingled. She wanted to crawl in closer and never let him go.

His mouth passed over hers and a grumble built in the back of his throat. He kissed her hard and deep and kicked life into every fantasy she'd ever had of him, every memory she held as sacred.

When he lifted his head the room continued to spin. Her fingers gripped his back, and her pulse thumped in her ears.

With a groan, he leaned his forehead against hers. "You think we can stop cold after a few more of those?"

She could barely catch her breath. It rushed out of her in huge shuddering gasps. "We're going to stop because we need our rest, although I bet you're going to stay up most of the night keeping watch."

"You do know me." He lifted his head and kissed her again, this one short yet determined.

She pulled her head back before either one of them was tempted to deepen it. "Parts."

He sighed, exhaled, treated her to the whole "you win" vibe males had. "There hasn't been anyone else."

Deep down she knew that. He couldn't look at her the way he did and then run home to someone else. He wasn't that guy. It wasn't his style.

Knowing that and knowing the reality of how people worked were two different things. People moved on. They had sex and fell in love. He was worth it and believed to her soul he eventually would believe it, too. He was a catch, whether or not he realized that.

"But there will be. Someone else, I mean." She whispered the phrase because it hurt to say it louder.

"No."

The quickness of his comeback had the hope inside her surging again. "I'm wondering if you'll ever trust me enough to stay."

He cupped her cheek. "It's not about trust."

That's the part he never got. If he really loved her and trusted her to accept him for who and what he was, he wouldn't run. He'd stay and fight.

But he didn't and she could feel him slipping away again.

She covered his hand with hers and stepped back, breaking the connection between them. "Yeah, it is."

THE CHAIR WITH its thin cushion turned out to be pretty uncomfortable. The longer Joel sat there, the more his lower back ached. But he didn't plan to move. Not when the seat gave him the best view of her on the other side of the cabin.

He'd found a small lamp stuck in the corner. With it plugged in across the room from the bed and the shade turned toward the ceiling, it bathed the cabin in a soft light. Most of the small space stayed hidden in shadows, but he could see her face.

Lying there with his arms wrapped around her and that body pressed against his for hours had amounted to slow torture. Hours with her curled up so close. The position, the smell of her hair, it all brought the memories back.

Eighteen months ago she'd handed him the key to her apartment and temptation pulled at him to stay. He'd wanted to grab it and try to make it work. He'd toyed with the idea even though he always promised himself years ago he would never drag another person into his messed up life.

He'd switched jobs and got antsy. He craved the outdoors and didn't have time for the bar scene. Even now he lived in the third-floor crash pad of the Corcoran Team headquarters instead of taking the time to find his own place.

Committing came hard for him—to a job, to a plan, to a path that got him somewhere other than slinging a gun while hiding in the woods. He didn't want to settle in and act the way other people did.

His time in the DIA ended when his boss accused him of selling the team out for cash. The man pivoted right off the charge, almost immediately, and Joel didn't do anything wrong, but the damage was done in Joel's mind.

He'd spent a lifetime bouncing around from obligation to obligation and hadn't stayed anywhere for long. His upbringing had taught him to keep ties to a minimum and possessions to almost nothing. He'd tried to break the cycle, but since he didn't even have a closet to his name, he'd clearly failed.

Still, the Corcoran Team had changed him, given him focus and a place. Connor set down enough rules to pro-

mote excellence and consistency but didn't microman-
age. That balance let Joel breathe.

In exchange, he filled any role the team needed. He
honed his tech skills to make his work indispensable and
spent hours at the shooting range perfecting his game.
He refused to disappoint the members who had become
closer than family to him.

Then there was Hope. She was everything he wanted.
Smart, athletic, driven and fun. She didn't get caught up
in her father's wealth and wasn't impressed with fancy
cars or the usual trappings. Her one weakness was for
big comfy beds stacked with pillows. He smiled at the
memory of the bedroom in her town house. A man could
fall into it and get lost in the mass of blankets.

Of course, most things about her made him smile. She
didn't pester. She understood the concept of work secrets
and didn't push. Her easy acceptance had almost made it
harder on him. He'd kept waiting for the bottom to drop,
and the tension built with each day it didn't. Another sick
cycle he couldn't figure out how to break.

"I can feel you staring at me." Her sleepy voice floated
through the room.

Even in the limited light he could see her eyes remained shut and her body buried in the covers. She
claimed the whistle of the wind helped her sleep. Could
be, but the humidity hadn't faded and until it did he'd
prefer to sleep without clothing, and that could not happen with her if he hoped to keep his "hands off" promise.

He watched her mouth curve into a smile and tried
to cut off whatever was happening in her head to put it
there. "You should be asleep."

She shifted and made a sexy little grumbling sound.
"With you."

"Being even this close to you is killing me."

Her eyes popped open. "Good."

Funny how she liked that word, especially when she used it for instances he found to be the exact opposite of good. "Why?"

She lifted herself up on her elbow. "You should suffer."

The words stung. They didn't slice through him as they once would have, likely because of her softer delivery this time, but they bit. "Because I hurt you."

She shook her head, and her hair fell over her shoulder. "Because you still are."

Debating how far to go, he decided to give her the truth. Man up and take the deep plunge.

He leaned over and balanced his elbows on his knees. "You know I love you, right?"

"Yes."

Her expression didn't change, but he thought he saw a hint of satisfaction mirrored in her eyes. This woman… "That was easy."

After a sigh, she rolled her eyes. Ran through the entire "men are clueless" list of gestures he'd seen before. "Joel Kidd, nothing about you is easy."

Not really a point he could argue with, so he stuck with rubbing his hands together where they hung between his knees. "Fair enough."

"Come to bed." Her gaze roamed over his tee and down his bare legs.

He wore his boxer briefs and was ten seconds away from stripping them off. Which made his answer very easy. "I should ride out the night over here."

Instead of taking the hint and gathering up the blanket around her again, she threw back the sheet and patted the mattress. "Do it here."

He should have said no. Insisted they'd pushed their

control far enough. He repeated that refrain as he walked across the room and slid in next to her.

The mattress dipped. Before he could think it through, he rolled her to her side and wrapped a hand around her waist. Her back pressed against his chest, and his nose went into her hair. "You feel so good."

She brushed her hand across the arm banding her waist. "Go to sleep."

"I have to go out looking for Perry and Mark tomorrow."

She shifted until her hair hit the pillow and his body hovered over hers. "That's too dangerous."

"It's what I do."

She lifted a hand and skimmed her fingers over his cheek. "You could wait for the rest of your team to arrive."

"Mark and Perry might need help and, if so, the clock would be ticking."

"But you think they're dead."

He hesitated, but her clear eyes had him telling the truth. "That's the worry, yes."

Thundered cracked in the distance and rain pounded the window. Being out in this would be rough on an experienced camper. He doubted two soft businessmen with little experience were faring all that well. Which left Joel with no choice—he had to get out there at sunup.

"I'm going with you."

"Not going to happen," he said in a scratchy voice.

The soft touch of her fingertips against his skin set off a fire inside him. He wanted her, would have been all over her, but he had promised. She'd set down the rules, and he intended to follow them. Even if it killed him, and he was starting to suspect it would.

She lifted her head and treated him to a lingering kiss

before dropping back down again. "Then you really better sleep because tomorrow you'll have a fight on your hands."

The playful side of her...he loved this part. "Is that a threat?"

She winked and flipped over again, facing away from him. "You'll find out in a few hours."

Chapter Seven

The monster thunderstorm moved out, but the rain continued to fall in an annoying drizzle the next morning. The sky turned a hazy gray as the temperature held steady and the humidity rose. Dampness hung on the air and highlighted the smells of the forest. Fresh evergreen and the earthy scent of dirt and grass.

The scene felt familiar and, except for feeling sticky in her clothing, comfortable to Hope. She thrived in this environment. She also had packed the right gear. Sitting on the log turned into a makeshift seat, she wore a rain jacket and kept the hood up, ignoring the pings of raindrops against her face.

She would have stayed inside, where it was safer and certainly drier, and waited for the official breakfast hour to begin, but she had to deal with Joel. More like it, she had to deal with him being gone.

"There he is. Finally." Cam stood over her, staring into the mass of greenery off to the right of the cabins. "He's headed back in."

She could hear the relief in Cam's voice. The same feeling flooded through her. Joel had taken off, without a word to either of them, and headed out to sniper territory. In the world of dumb ideas, that one ranked pretty high up there.

"I should have known he'd skulk off." She blew out a long breath as the anxiety pinging around in her belly slowed. She stretched her legs out in front of her. "He's good at that."

"Not that I know anything about what happened between you two, because I don't." Cam sat down next to her and mimicked her position. "But he's not out in Annapolis partying with other women. I've never even see him checking out the ladies or making moves, and he's had opportunities."

That grumbly sensation came rushing back. "I bet."

"I'm just saying he attracts attention now and then, not that I'd ever admit that in front of him because I'm pretty invested in telling him how he lacks game."

She tried not to smile at that, at all of it. "Sure."

"At least now I know why he keeps the monk's existence."

That part made her beat back a dose of skepticism. Even when they were together she'd see women check him out and look for the chance to make a move. The fit body and hot smile combined with those dark looks and that bit of naughtiness in his eyes. Many women took a second look. He never noticed, that she could tell, but she'd assumed once he was free of their relationship he would. Just one more example of Joel reacting the opposite of how she thought he would.

"In some ways he's really complex—this mass of contradictions and frustrations—and in another he's transparent." Like the part where he ran scared from emotional entanglements. She was far too familiar with that side of him.

"His dad messed him up." Cam shook his head. "I never really saw how much before."

Her gaze snapped away from the man walking toward her and back to Cam. "He told you about his upbringing?"

"The end-of-the-world fears imposed on him. The foster homes. Being separated from his sisters and never truly reconnecting with them again." Cam whistled. "Sometimes I'm amazed he can function, that he's as normal as he is. Don't tell him I admitted that either."

Joel's openness with Cam stunned her. Joel never hid his background or shied away from using his survival skills, but the idea of him talking it out with Cam was a surprise. She liked that Joel had someone close enough, and now she knew Cam wasn't just some random work friend.

But he'd used the magic word. The same one Joel loved to throw around. "That's the problem."

Cam frowned. "You lost me."

Through the dripping of the rain and soaking of the ground, Joel broke through the tree line. His footsteps hesitated for a second, and then he made a beeline for them.

She lowered her voice. "He thinks he can never be normal."

"Then he needs a good kick in the—"

"What are you two doing out here? You shouldn't be in the open." Joel stopped right by her feet. The scowl stayed as he scanned the area around them.

"We were waiting for you to wander back in," Cam said.

"I walked out a few hundred feet and did a perimeter check." Joel turned in a semicircle as his hand traced the trail through the air.

He acted like leaving was no big deal if he was the one doing it. He wasn't wearing a jacket and his shirt was soaked clear through. Never mind the fact there was some guy sitting out there waiting to shoot at them again. "Good thing a bullet can't reach that far."

"I was fine."

She rolled her eyes as she wondered how he would react if the roles were reversed. "This time."

Shuffling started behind her, then she heard footsteps and the low mumble of male voices. Following Joel's gaze, she watched Lance and Jeff walk out to the fire pit area. Apparently no one wanted to stay inside where it was safer.

It wasn't exactly easy to take the two businessmen seriously with the drawstrings pulled tight on their hoods so only a fraction of their faces stood out. They acted as if acid fell from the sky.

She bit back a joke as she stood up, doubting Jeff would appreciate the humor. He'd dragged designer gear with him, most of which was more suitable for Himalayan climbing than camping in cabins.

Amateurs.

Joel nodded to the new members of the group. "Good morning."

"Where's Charlie?" she asked.

He popped up in the distance over Jeff's shoulder a second later carrying a steaming mug of something. "Breakfast is almost ready."

"Forget that." Jeff frowned at all of them. "What's the plan?"

Joel didn't move. "Survival."

One second he stood there alone. The next, Cam got up and took the place beside Joel. Together they formed a wall of lethal males.

Not that everyone got the message or understood the peril. Jeff sent Joel a withering look, one that probably worked when he tried intimidating his assistants. "I'm serious."

"So am I," Joel shot back.

Jeff dragged a foot through the mud before balancing it on the edge of the log. Never mind that people sat there. "Your timing is interesting."

Hope felt the conversation sliding sideways. Whatever point Jeff was trying to make had tension pounding harder than last night's thunder. He kept poking the bear and sooner or later, Joel would unleash. He had the skills to make Jeff look like an idiot, and she feared that showdown inched ever closer.

"What are you talking about?" Joel asked as he spread his stance and folded his arms behind him.

"You two show up and Mark disappears. Now you claim to have heard gunfire."

Joel's eyebrow lifted. "Claim?"

Enough testosterone-fueled nonsense. She stepped in. "It happened. I was there."

Jeff didn't even spare her a glance. "I'm just saying there are easier ways to get a woman into bed."

Joel took a threatening step forward. "That's enough." Only Cam's arm held him back.

"You're out of line, Jeff. Apologize," Charlie said at the same time.

But Jeff wasn't done. Clearly warming up to his theory, he stood taller and crossed his arms in front of him. "Maybe Mark snuck up on you? Maybe he was in the way? After all, the fight between Mark and Hope was explosive. Made me wonder if there was something behind all that anger."

She was two seconds from kicking the guy in the shin. "You should stop talking."

Joel nodded. "Listen to the lady."

Jeff threw his arms wide. "You going to make me?"

"Damn, you're stupid." Cam shook his head as he mumbled.

"Oh, really?"

Before Jeff could move, Charlie clamped a hand on his shoulder. "Sit."

Jeff shirked it off. "Why should I listen to you?"

"Because it's obvious Joel could take you out in a second, and I know the truth." Charlie took a long sip, drawing out the moment. "You and Mark had quite the argument after the gun incident."

Now, there was news that would have been helpful yesterday. Could have lessened some of her guilt, too. Confiscating the weapon had been the right answer, but doubts had bombarded her ever since. Maybe she could have been less firm about it or taken him aside. She'd always found that a show of strength cut down on some idiocy, but maybe she'd miscalculated this time.

"About what?" she asked, not trying to keep the seething anger out of her voice.

"Nothing you need to worry about." Jeff stepped back, separating himself from the group as he glanced around like a cornered animal. "This is insane. Charlie is just protecting her."

"My name is Hope." The guy was just not getting it. His coworkers were missing. This was not some game. "And what fight?"

Charlie shrugged. "I couldn't hear, but there was a lot of pushing and shouting."

Lance had stayed quiet, just watching and frowning. Now he moved, shoving a hand against Jeff's chest. "About what?"

"Don't touch me."

The more the minutes passed, the less Hope liked Jeff.

He acted entitled and childish, and because neither Cam nor Joel looked ready to step in.

She did. "Boys, knock it off."

The shots rang out as she said the last word. Through the misty air and steady wind, the pings echoed.

"Everybody get down!" Joel yelled the order as he made a dive for Hope.

Lance beat him to it. He knocked into her stomach and they both went flying. She hit the ground hard, making a breath hiccup in her lungs. Knowing she had to move, she scrambled up and crawled on her knees and elbows to the log and tried to lie flat behind it.

Lance half covered her as he reached up and tugged on Jeff's sleeve, breaking the spell that had frozen him in place and dragging him down in the mud beside them. Gunfire rang out. Glass shattered somewhere behind her and pieces of wood kicked up when a bullet slammed into the log right by her head.

She heard shouting and scuffling. The sharp smell of gunfire hit her, and a smoky haze filled the air.

Then Joel was there beside her. After a quick look up and down her torso, he and Cam crouched like a protective shield around the group. All but Charlie, who took off for the cabins behind them.

Noises blurred together and crescendoed to a rolling thunder. Everything seemed to rattle as her stomach rolled.

To steady her body, she reached forward and put her palm against the back of Joel's shirt. She wanted to pull him down and out of target range but settled for the touch. Anything to keep the contact.

In a blink it all stopped. No more loud banging and constant movements. Silence fell over them.

The wind blew and branches shifted. But the roar of

noise that filled her ears ceased. Her hand clenched in Joel's shirt as the world came rushing back to her. She could make out Lance's heavy breathing as his weight fell against her. Jeff's whimpering sounded in the background. At least he'd stopped screaming his wife's name.

She heard the crunch of metal and looked behind her. Charlie stood on the cabin porch, half behind a post, with a shotgun in his hands. She had no idea where that had come from.

"Okay, let's double-time this before our friend comes back." Joel shifted around in his position, his gaze taking in the huddle of people behind him. "We need to get everyone inside."

Cam nodded as he came around the far end of the log and pulled Jeff to his feet. "Go right into Hope's cabin. Do not stop or hesitate."

An eerie quiet whispered through the trees. It made her want to bolt for the indoors. Sitting up proved impossible with Lance pinning her leg to the ground.

"We need to go." She pushed against his shoulder, trying to get him to pull out of his ducking position, but he didn't move. "It's okay now. You can move."

Joel stood watch. "Cam, get them inside now."

A new sensation stabbed at her. One of pure panic. The type that had something twisting in her gut. "Lance?"

The tone must have caught Joel's attention because his sweeping gaze landed on her. "What's wrong?"

She put a hand on Lance's shoulder and shook. Still nothing. Pulling it back, she saw the red.

The color drained right out of her as she looked up at Joel. "Blood."

TONY HADN'T ENJOYED his first conversation with Connor Bowen and didn't relish a second one. From the time the man left the office yesterday until this morning, Tony had conducted an impromptu investigation.

It paid to know the man on the other side of the conference room table and be ready for anything. Tony always was, but he hadn't counted on this guy. He expected Hope to be connected, thanks to her father, but word was her life focused on climbing and, now that she'd messed up that career, she was floundering.

That had proved to be only part of the story. Looked like she knew powerful men in dangerous places. Men who didn't know when to back off.

Connor and his team worked in the intelligence field, and his record possessed the shiny, perfect look that came with false IDs. Tony would bet they dealt in hush-hush projects. That made Connor and anyone who worked for him a huge liability.

Tony stared at his closed office door and reasoned out his next steps. He'd worked too long and too hard to get to this uncertain place.

He'd earned his reputation for being ruthless the honest way. He'd move into a company and cut staff and streamline costs and personnel, rarely getting the credit he deserved. The career had him relocating and trading positions while trying to make a series of corporate boards happy.

But this position was his ticket. Show the right numbers and growth, and the big desk would stay his. He would be in charge and the impressive paycheck and windfall bonuses would come his way.

With one sharp knock, his office door opened. So much for his crack staff and the security measures he'd put in place to keep anyone from getting into his office without permission. Connor somehow broke through the protocol after one visit to the place.

That meant one thing: Tony had to get the pseudo-detective out of his business and off his trail. Fast.

He didn't give Connor the satisfaction of mentioning the unapproved entrance. "You're back."

Connor didn't bother with small talk. He walked right across the large office to stand in front of Tony's desk. "I have a few questions."

Not that Tony had any intention of answering them. "Where's your assistant?"

"Second in command."

He leaned back in his chair and slid his palms over the smooth leather of the armrests. "Is there a difference?"

Connor took a quick look around the office. His gaze roamed but he didn't move. "Davis is back at the office, working on this case."

"Case?"

"Yes."

"Exactly how long are you in town?" The man needed to head back to Annapolis and stay there. Tony was half ready to throw him in a cab to make it happen.

"For as long as it takes."

"Interesting response."

Connor's stance relaxed from attack mode to soon-to-attack. The dark suit didn't fool Tony. He knew a fellow fighter when he saw one. This man could ruin everything. He would dig and push, and those were the two things Tony could not afford to have happen.

Without being asked, Connor launched into whatever he came to say. "I thought you could give me some intel on your officers."

The man had guts. Tony had to give him that, but the request, if that's what it was, would never happen. "Intel?"

"Who, what, backgrounds. Personality types." Other

than blinking, Connor still didn't move. "Likelihood for trouble."

Tony tapped his fingers against the end of the armrest. He aimed for mild disinterest. Inside his mind was spinning with ways to end the conversation. "This is starting to sound a bit like an interrogation."

"If it helps you to think of it that way, I'm good with that." The flat tone only added to the feeling of menace.

"It's also a clear case of overreaching."

"Your executive *is* missing."

And what a mess that had turned out to be. "I let you get me upset last time, but this is nothing. Mark wandered away from camp. That's hardly a reason to dig around in people's personal lives."

Connor's eyes narrowed a fraction. "Why do you say that?"

"Because it's not your business where they—"

"I meant the part about Mark. Why do you think he walked off?"

"It's the most logical explanation." That was the story. That was the plan. Simple and straightforward. Except for the part where it all blew apart and now Tony had to deal with bad weather, Rafe screaming on the phone from thousands of miles away about his baby girl's safety and the man across the desk who wanted to rush in and save everyone.

"I told you there were gunshots."

"I doubt it," Tony said. "If that were true, if there were really trouble, the police, park rangers and everyone else would be out there. I'd be getting calls and this would be on the news. You see, Mr. Bowen—"

"Connor is fine."

"Conner then." Though Tony would prefer not to get

so personal. "I turned this company around by being patient. I don't run off or act in panic mode."

"You think I do?"

"Technically, isn't other people's panic your business?" Tony continued to drum his fingers. With each tap he inhaled, trying to slow down his pounding heart and keep his breathing under control. There was no need to show weakness. "Look, Mark likes to show off. He wasn't thrilled with the idea of a young woman running the retreat."

"How evolved of him."

Little did Connor know the woman, Hope, had been a vital part of the plan. Talk about a miscalculation. "My guess is his male ego got wounded and now he's stuck trying to find a reasonable way to save face and come back to camp."

"Is that it?"

"Excuse me?"

"Are you done?" This time Connor moved. He leaned forward with his fists on the far edge of Tony's desk and kept the eye contact locked on him. "If so, let me tell you about my men. They don't panic. They also know what gunfire sounds like because they're experts at rescuing. When they issue a warning it's because something is seriously wrong."

"So you're impressed with your men." By the time he finished, the words rang out in the room. It took all of Tony's control to keep his expression blank and not shift in his chair. "Your point is?"

Connor pushed up and stood straight again. "I take off as soon as the weather clears."

"This is a waste of time and money."

"Possibly, but it's my time and my money to waste."

"Not really since it's my men out there on the retreat." Tony needed to bring them in clean and without them being subjected to questioning. Not unless he could control it, and he knew Connor wouldn't let that happen "My suggestion would be to let this play out. I paid for a certain number of days and want those men out there, including Mark, who will show up soon, in the woods, building rapport as promised."

"While getting shot at."

"I think we've discussed that issue enough." Until Tony knew more about the who and why of the gunshots, he pivoted around the topic.

"I agree."

Forget relief. Anxiety smacked into him. "You're still going."

"I'm getting my people out."

That superman complex was going to ruin everything. Tony sensed it. "I guess that's your choice."

Connor nodded. "I'll let you know what Mark says."

"Meaning?"

"When I find him, I'll get him to talk. Because, *Tony,* I will find him. That's what I do."

Chapter Eight

Hope stood behind Cam and looked out the small window next to her cabin door. The rainy gray sky beyond didn't provide much light, so they had to rely on a few dull bulbs.

The small space was lined wall to wall with mud-soaked men. The mixed scent of wet clothes and stale air in the confined room gave it the feel of a locker room, though he'd smelled worse, but for her this couldn't be good.

After the frantic racing around outside and piling inside the cabin, Joel could finally breathe. Hearing the familiar crack and watching Hope fall had taken a good twenty years off his life. When she'd moved and Lance had covered her, Joel forced his mind on the attacker, but the twisting-gut fear about her getting hurt had kept him off his game.

Somehow they'd made it with minimal injuries. Hers being the biggest cabin and having the only indoor shower, it won as the staging area—a good place to regroup and plan. And in Lance's case, receive medical treatment.

Charlie was in the other room now while Jeff paced outside the door. Joel had ordered they all rotate in the bathroom and then put on dry clothes. He had enough to worry about without having someone get deathly ill, and he was willing to do anything to keep Jeff occupied. The man was walking around in circles mumbling about finding a new job.

Now Joel hovered over Lance where he sat on the arm of the couch. The stitching would have been done five minutes ago if the guy would stop jerking and hissing. You'd think he'd never been injured before.

Sure, the shot was a bit more than a flesh wound, but not much more. They all had scrapes and bruises, but Lance delivered most of the flinching. How he'd ever made it through his wife giving birth was a mystery.

With one last stitch, Joel dropped a bloody bandage in the small trash can by his feet. He kept up a running dialogue with Lance, thinking it might calm the man down. "You got lucky."

Lance winced as Joel wrapped a clean bandage around his upper arm. "We might have different definitions of that word."

"I'm not even going to mention that you passed out from a puny shot in the arm." Okay, maybe he'd mention it that one time, but now he'd stop.

"I thought I was dead."

Joel had worried a bullet hit Hope, and the punch of pain had nearly knocked him over. Although he didn't want anyone hurt, he wasn't upset Lance had caught it instead.

He was about to thank him for trying to protect Hope, but she broke in. "There isn't a special prize for the least amount of tears when shot."

"I didn't cry." Lance's voice rose as if swearing under his breath didn't telegraph his disgust for the suggestion.

"Because you were unconscious," Cam said without ending his surveillance on the world outside the cabin.

Joel chuckled. He could go a lifetime without seeing whiny Jeff again, but Joel liked Lance. Charlie, now, he was an enigma. Joel had no idea what to think about that guy.

When Lance glanced down at the white bandage and the line of red seeping through, the color left his face. Joel rushed to reassure him. It was either that or risk having the guy pass out again. "The bullet went through and didn't knick anything important."

"It hurts like a—"

"I have some painkillers," Hope broke in as she left her position by the window and squatted down to drag a bag out from under the bed.

"That would be good." Joel pointed at Jeff. "You're next."

The guy stopped mid-pace. "I wasn't hit."

"I meant answers."

Hope frowned at Joel. Took a second and shot most of the men in the room a frown, even Cam, and he wasn't looking at her. "Now might not be the time for a chat."

This topic was not up for debate. Joel's patience had expired. So had his willingness to sit around and wait to become a target. "Someone is shooting at us and we have two unskilled men missing in this miserable weather. So if Jeff here knows something, it's time to speak up."

"I don't."

Hope got to her feet and grabbed a water bottle on her way over to Lance. Her gaze never left Jeff. "Why did you fight with Mark?"

"It has nothing to do with…" Jeff exhaled as he ran a hand through his wet hair. "Look, it was a work issue."

That got Lance's attention. "What was it?"

Whatever Jeff heard in Lance's voice or saw on his

face had his shoulders slumping. "He had these private meetings with Tony—"

"Who?" Cam asked.

"Tony Prather, Baxter's CEO." Jeff kept up the steady stream of sighing. "It felt like Mark was making a play. Going around my back."

"Doesn't Mark rank above you in the corporate scheme?" Hope asked. "He's the vice president, not you."

Leave it to her to point that out. Joel wished he had. "Exactly my question. Jeff?"

"I had some ideas about positioning the company moving forward. One of the divisions had a down quarter but seemed to be bouncing back, and I wanted to capitalize on the upswing." Jeff leaned against the wall and let his head fall back. "I give Mark some notes, he studies them and all of a sudden he's having private meetings with our boss."

Joel could see it all playing out. Jeff, with his oversized ego, wouldn't accept being pushed out. He'd want every ounce of credit he could squeeze out of an idea. "That ticked you off."

Jeff looked around the room. "Wouldn't it do the same to you?"

"Don't know since I've never worked in an office," Cam said.

Joel reached into the specialized first aid kit for another bandage roll as he turned over Jeff's comments in his mind. The man had just handed them a motive. Not a compelling reason to kill in Joel's view, but for Jeff's type it could be. Always looking for an angle, expecting to rise in the ranks at record speed, wanting the perks and big title. Watching someone grab that away could be a brutal ego blow for someone like Jeff.

Reading people was not his strength. Joel glanced at

Hope, looking for her take on the situation. She had good instincts. But because she stood right at Cam's shoulder, looking out the window instead of at Jeff, Joel couldn't tell what she was thinking.

Now Joel wanted to know what had caught her attention and held it so long. "Cam, can you take over for a second?"

"Sure."

The men passed each other in the middle of the room, exchanging gun for bandage. By the time Joel got to the window, Hope stood right in front of it. Talk about becoming a target. With her damp, freshly showered hair pulled in a ponytail and clean white shirt, she stuck out among the group.

Without making a big deal of it, he shifted her out of the direct firing line through the window and lowered his voice. "You okay?"

"You're very handy with a first aid kit."

He noticed she skipped his question, but he decided to let it slide. "One of the many skills demanded by my father."

"He brought about so much bad, but every now and then there's something positive."

"I think you're reaching for a silver lining."

Joel remembered every minute of the last day as a family—protective services ripping his sisters away, the standoff with the police, the shot his dad fired that finally landed him in jail—so he knew the truth. Nothing good happened. Joel couldn't point to one decent thing about the way he grew up either before or after the final takedown of the Kidd family.

She bit her lower lip. "I keep hoping to find something positive about your upbringing."

"That's not an easy task."

She clearly tried to get it. She listened and shook her head at all the right places.

The pain in her eyes as he relayed the facts, some of them anyway, was genuine. It bordered on pity, and Joel hated that. Knew it was human nature but still despised it. Connor and Cam and the few other people in his life who knew bits and pieces also tried to reason it out, but Joel knew that without living it you could never really understand.

Hope had grown up in a loving home with a father who doted on her. Not every day was easy, of course. She'd lost her mother to cancer when she was a young girl, but Hope never worried about having food or running a drill about how to escape the police. She loved her dad. Joel had seen the bond. It bordered on overprotective, but it beat strong.

"I assure you that if Dad had known I would use my abilities to work for any government agency or a team that helps governments, he likely would have shot me on the spot." That was the threat—*disappoint me and you're dead.*

Hope froze. "Why do I think you're not kidding?"

"If only." She'd moved in closer, which put her head back in the line of fire, so he shifted her to the side again. "You need to stand away from the window."

She looked at him and then to that spot outside that seemed to capture her attention. Through the driving rain and storm that had whipped up right when it looked as if it would taper off, she'd focused in on that area.

"What is it?" he asked.

"You know about trajectories, right?"

If this had anything to do with his dad, Joel lost the track on how. "Sure."

"One of the ways I perfected my aim in archery was

to track the trajectory of my arrow. First I played with my stance and did all this math to figure out the proper draw length, and then I got this fancy computer program. Point is, I figured out I was starting out too high and then the drop off…" She smiled. "You should see your face."

"You have to admit this is an odd conversation in light of being trapped in a cabin and all." He put his body in front of her and brought up the binoculars to scan the area.

"True, but the bottom line is Lance's entry wound is higher than the exit." She drew a diagram in the condensation on the window. "I felt Lance get shot. We were on the ground and the bullet came from above, so the angle isn't a surprise, but it's off."

Something had clicked together in her mind. He could see the light go on and hear the growing excitement in her voice. The energy bouncing off her was contagious.

But he still wasn't sure about her point. "That leads you to believe what?"

"I think the shots came not just from someone standing above Lance but from someone in the trees. The trajectory is that steep."

The comment hung there. Even Cam looked up from finishing off Lance's arm. Jeff was the only one who'd missed the discussion. He was too busy trading places with Charlie as he came out of the bathroom in a set of clean clothes that looked exactly like the dirty ones he had just shed.

Hope's intelligence focused all the pieces. As usual, she found a way through the confusion and came up with a reasonable explanation. She was smart and sharp and didn't hide it.

He loved that about her. Of course, he loved pretty much everything about her.

Still, he wanted to make sure they were on the same page. "So you're saying this guy is sitting up in a branch shooting?"

"I think it's a good possibility the shots came from there, but that doesn't answer every question."

"Okay."

"If I'm right about the position, the shooter should have been able to pick us off one by one because we were all truly vulnerable." She stabbed her finger against points in the diagram on the glass. "That leaves us with a bigger problem."

That's what they needed. More problems. "Which is?"

"Neither Perry nor Mark is the athletic scaling-trees type."

Joel hadn't met either man, but he totally trusted her view on this. He could climb and she could probably do it faster than he could, and that was saying something. That didn't mean two businessmen who spent most of their time sitting behind desks had a chance at getting up there. There was a slight possibility that one of them, or one of the men in the cabin, pretended to be clueless and really had sniper tree-climbing skills, but Joel doubted it.

"We're talking some random guy out here shooting for fun." Joel glanced at Cam. His grim expression mirrored Joel's thoughts—that was the absolute worst case scenario. A pure risk and someone they couldn't get a handle on.

Lance made a strangled sound but didn't say anything.

"Unfortunately, the theory leads to more questions. I mean, how would the random guy get down without you or Cam seeing him?" She pointed to the open space outside as she asked.

Joel had that exact question. There were possible explanations, but none of them proved all that convincing.

Cam and Joel were trained. They were on high alert. Even as worrying about Hope getting hurt occupied part of Joel's mind, Cam stayed fully focused.

"It was raining and we were being shot at," Cam said from across the room.

"And you stood out there like a human shield." Hope stopped whispering and went back to her normal voice. "All I'm saying is if someone wanted to kill you, someone with the level of skill to balance in a tree with a gun and then sneak away unseen by two covert agents, he would have killed you."

Charlie stopped running the towel over his wet hair. "What are you guys talking about?"

Hope ignored the older man and talked to Joel. "All the advantage goes to the person in that position. If that were you, you'd hit the target without trouble."

"So would you." Joel knew that was true because she was the most competent woman he'd ever met.

"Where does that leave us?" Cam asked.

Joel fought the temptation to handle the issue now. He just needed the weather to give him a five-minute shot at testing her theory. "With lots of questions and something to do as soon as the storm breaks."

Her eyes narrowed. "Which is?"

"Go out there and look around."

TWO HOURS LATER the rain had morphed into a steady fall, but the dark sky gave way to white and the wind died down. While Charlie watched from the porch with a gun in his hand, Hope ventured outside with Cam and Joel.

They fought to have her stay behind, but she refused. Because she threatened to follow them the minute they stepped outside, they gave in and brought her along.

They trudged along on either side of her until they

walked a few feet into the wooded area and well within shouting distance of the cabins. Both men had guns and she carried the binoculars but had a gun and her knife within grabbing range.

Cam shifted into the lead as they got close to the tree they'd staked out as the best contender for climbing. "Remind me again why we're doing this?"

"A hunch." That's all she had, but she'd calculated all the angles and run through all the alternatives, and this was the only one that made sense.

"Seems like a dangerous hunch."

"Not if Hope is right." They stopped at the tree and Joel tapped his palm against the bark.

"Which is why I get to be out here, too." No matter what they thought, she didn't plan to stand around and watch. "I'll climb."

Joel snorted. "No way."

"You two are better to guard and I can—"

Joel broke her concentration when he snatched the binoculars and flung them around his neck. Next came the standing jump where he grabbed the lowest branch, which wasn't all that low. The move stretched him out and had his T-shirt riding up and showing off his flat stomach. With an impressive pull-up, he was up and gone in a matter of seconds, leaving her sputtering.

Cam laughed. "He's fast when he wants to be. He's also smart enough to know you're likely better at that than he is and he had to beat you to the punch."

Joel's voice reached them from above. "Maybe less talking since we could be wrong about this and have a guy stalking us even now."

That reality check had her back teeth knocking together. She'd pushed the fear out, insisting she could handle this...somehow.

With that warning, Cam backed her up against the tree and put his body in front of hers until no part of her was exposed. The bulletproof vest Joel made her wear before he opened the cabin door gave her added protection.

If someone came shooting, Cam would go down and she'd have a shot. The mere idea of that had her stomach flipping around.

She cleared her voice and looked up. Beads of rain fell, hitting her face and running under her hood and into her hair. "See anything?"

From this position she spied a flash of blue jeans and the bottom of Joel's hiking boots. His voice sounded distant and the rain muffled every sound.

"It would help if it stopped pouring." That grumble came through loud and clear.

Cam kept watch as his back pressed into her chest. "Take that up with another department."

Joel shifted and she could make him out as he balanced on a branch. He faced deeper into the woods.

She pushed the panic out of her mind. Others might wobble or slide off. Not Joel. He could probably live up there if he had to.

His arms went up and she knew he was taking a look around. "I want a pair of those binoculars."

"We'll get you a pair," Cam said.

"Hold on," Joel called out.

"What?" She looked up and Cam joined her.

"There's something in the trees about thirty feet out."

Hope's body threatened to break into a full shake. She clenched her hands into fists to keep from fidgeting and shifting around. "A person?"

"A rigging of some kind."

She shook her head as the constant thudding of rain

against her jacket had her talking louder. "I don't even know what that means."

"A platform and a gun set-up to fire either at specific times or via remote." Cam spared her a quick look before he went back to checking out the area around them. "A human might not be pulling the trigger now, but a human built the rigging."

"So we're back to everyone being a suspect." She didn't know if that was good or bad. With the businessmen as suspects she at least knew something about her potential attacker.

A rogue sniper terrified her. That suggested someone with skill and put Joel and Cam at greater risk because she knew they would shield the rest of them with their bodies if it came to that. The thought of watching Joel go down almost drove her to her knees.

"Move." A loud whoosh followed the warning. Joel shouted as he dropped out of the branches and landed with a slight bend of his knees as if he'd been practicing the move his entire life.

She heard a thud and saw the binoculars land in the mud. Adrenaline pumped through her as she spun around, looking for the danger that had set him off.

The forest blurred in front of her. Joel grabbed Cam's shoulder and turned him toward the cabins while Joel shoved her behind him and brought up his gun. The men took up positions behind two trunks and faced in the same direction, this time toward camp.

Despite the dizzying few seconds, she stayed locked behind Joel with her fingers slipped through his belt loop.

"Hands up," Joel yelled in the direction off to the side of the far cabin.

She peeked around his shoulder and saw trees and branches and sheets of water. Nothing moved and no sound came. She was about to ask what was happening when a smaller tree bent. The wind didn't take this one. A shadow moved.

"Come out or we fire." Joel pushed her deeper behind the tree as he motioned for Cam to take the far side. "You have three seconds."

She shifted and looked out from the other side of the tree. Then she saw it. The shadow, clearly a large figure, stumbled. "Joel, I think—"

"One…"

"An animal maybe?" Cam asked.

"Two."

Without a sound, the figure dropped. A man's torso fell into the clearing with the rest left behind in the woods. Arms outstretched and a familiar green polo shirt. The rain pounded his face, which was turned toward them.

She started to rush out, but Joel caught her arm. "Wait."

Cam's shoulders fell as he lowered the weapon. "What the—"

But she knew exactly who it was. "It's Perry."

Chapter Nine

They'd informally shared her town house and slept to-gether more times than he could count, but when he stepped into Hope's confining cabin that night he still felt about three sizes too big. "At least it smells better in here than it did ten minutes ago."

She glanced over at him and smiled. "Who knew a candle could help that much?"

The men had cleared out, with Charlie taking the cabin on one side of hers and dragging Lance and Jeff along with him. Cam was looking after their newest patient, Perry, next door while keeping the first watch on the camp.

The man hadn't roused long enough to answer even one question. The nasty gash on the back of his head suggested a fall or a hit. Joel was betting on the latter.

They had gotten it bandaged, and Cam had agreed to wake him up in a few hours for a concussion check. Other than that, all they knew was Perry had the same clothes on when he stumbled back into camp that he had worn the night of Mark's fight with Hope.

Every time Joel started to think they'd all walked into some big work argument between Perry and Mark, the reality of that gun rigging would strike. Joel just couldn't see either man having the skills for that, never mind

the equipment. Hope said she had done a bag check…
of course, Mark got a gun through, so maybe it wasn't
impossible.

Joel took one last sweeping look out the door, then
shut it behind him. The rain still fell, but the wind no longer whipped through the trees. He toyed with the idea of
loading everyone up and heading for the helicopter, but
the darkness and memory of the uneven ground stopped
him. Last thing they needed was another injury.

"Still nothing from Perry?" She wadded the old sheet
and blanket into a ball and threw them on the floor.

"He's out cold." Trying hard not to think of the bed
and her in it, and failing miserably, Joel walked to the
farthest point from her.

He should help her strip and remake the bed after
they'd laid Perry out there. His clothes had been caked
with mud and his shirt soaked with blood. But that side
of the room spelled trouble. Even with the danger spinning around them, Joel wanted her and his self-control
was going down for the count.

She froze in the act of unzipping her sleeping bag and
spreading it over the bare mattress. "Any chance we could
lose him during the night?"

Joel decided to go with the least panicked version.
"Cam is staying with Perry. We're worried about a concussion. His head is pretty banged up."

"Maybe he got lost and the exposure—"

"No." Joel couldn't let her think that. Not when he
needed her on guard for the worst-case scenario. "Something slammed into his head. Either he fell or he got hit."

Her expression hardened. "Where's Jeff right now?"

"Jeff, Charlie and Lance are bunking together." Joel
understood her narrow-eyed reaction because he also had
suspicions about Jeff. Though the evidence pointed to-

ward Mark as the attacker, something wasn't right with Jeff. Something Joel couldn't nail down. "I want someone with weapons knowledge in each cabin. I don't know if I can trust Charlie, but I trust him more than Jeff."

She dropped onto the bed and balanced a hand on the mattress on either side of her trim hips. "When can we leave?"

This he could handle. Simple emotionless conversation. Joel didn't like the idea of Lance and Perry being hurt or Mark being on the loose, but getting them out of there alive gave Joel something to concentrate on... instead of thinking about her. "I'm not sure if we can move Perry. Without medical help, I can't really assess how bad off he is, and I don't want to drag him around and cause more damage."

"So we're going to live here now?"

"Hardly." Joel bit back the wave of heat hitting him. She sat there in thin sweats and an even thinner tee, looking vulnerable, and his mind started flipping back to them as a couple. He cleared his throat and forced his mind to clear. "A group will go to the helicopter. If we can rig some sort of gurney, we may be able to carry Perry out and all go to the clearing."

She frowned. "With a sniper out there?"

"First thing tomorrow I'll check that station in the tree. I'm guessing I'll find a jerry-rigged weapon and no space for a human shooter." He sure hoped that was the case.

The scenario would at least give them a direction. Someone on foot with a gun could easily pick them off one by one as they lumbered along dragging Perry on a slab.

There was a nightmare thought. A rigged gun had a limited attack range. A human on foot spelled real danger.

"And that means we can walk through the woods."
She rubbed her hands together until the skin turned red.

"I think we need to take the risk." He walked over
and sat next to her. "Speaking of which, you were pretty
impressive today."

"I got lucky."

He slipped his hand over hers and stopped her fidgeting before she rubbed her skin raw. "I'm thinking your
climbing skills and all those years of archery helped."

"I'll give you the archery."

"Not the climbing?"

She shrugged. "I stick with normal climbing now."

"Why?" He knew the story because he'd never stopped
watching over her, making sure she was okay.

Part of the story anyway. He could tell from the nervous energy that she kept part of it trapped inside her and
it needed to come out.

"A burst of sanity?"

His thumb rubbed over the back of her hand, and his
thigh touched hers. "Hope, this is me. I know how much
you love climbing. I've been along with you, seen your
face."

"To be fair, I'm a fan of almost anything that happens outside."

He wasn't buying it, refused to let her dismiss this.
"You excelled at taking groups up. Your dad didn't like
it, but it was a good living."

"Until it wasn't."

The monotone voice tugged at him. "What piece am
I missing?"

"The accident." Her free hand brushed over their
joined ones. "Come on, you talk with my dad, right?
You know about this."

Joel had read the news articles about it and gotten the

basic information from her dad. Joel knew it was a horrible accident—not her fault—but it didn't sound like she did. "I know you took a group up Mt. Rainier and bad weather rolled in."

She sighed and her shoulders fell. "Two men died, Joel."

"You're not responsible for an unexpected snowstorm, Hope."

"But I am the one responsible for knowing when to turn around." She loosened her grip on his hand.

"Wait a minute." He held on, even squeezed her palm until she looked at him again. "I read the file—"

"What are you talking about?"

He refused to be derailed by the rising anger in her voice. "You've tracked me, at least a little, because you know I live in Annapolis. Well, I know what you've been doing since we broke up, and the point is you trained that group and when something happened, a guy panicked and took his friend down the mountain with him."

"We should have—"

"The other people in the group said you insisted everyone go down. You followed your own rules and didn't screw around. The guy ignored you."

"It was as if he expected me to chase him up the mountain."

"Not to speak ill of the dead, but his ego took over. That's on him, not you." Joel had watched her struggle with male stupidity more than once in her work. She had all the skills and knowledge, but you put a bunch of guys together and sometimes a certain type would show off. Add in how pretty she was and some guys underestimated her.

Joel never did. She was stunning and fierce…and he

loved her as much today as he did when he had walked out. Maybe more.

"All he had to do was turn around and slam his ax into the ice." She whispered the words, lost in whatever mental image played in her head. "He was tied to his friend and they both raced down the slope and…"

"Listen to me." Joel's hand went into her hair and he turned her to face him. "I deal with danger and guilt all the time. I know the difference between negligence and horrible tragedy. You lived through the latter."

"It destroyed my love of climbing."

He leaned in and kissed her because he couldn't stand not to right then. "It's too soon to know that."

"I just wanted to start over, find something else I loved, and now this." She tucked her head under his chin.

"Also not your fault."

The vanilla scent of her shampoo and smell of her skin had his mind blanking. He had to close his eyes to stay in comfort mode and away from whatever mode it was that had him wanting to push her back into the sleeping bag.

"The comment is funny coming from you." Her hand pressed against his chest, and her fingers toyed with the neck band of his T-shirt. "You take on the weight of everyone else's sins and let them define your life."

"That's not true." He wouldn't let that be true.

She lifted her head then and stared at him with those big brown eyes. "You left me because of things that have nothing to do with us."

She kissed his chin. Let her fingertips dance over his cheek.

"Hope, don't—"

"You love me." She pressed her fingers to his lips.

He kissed the tips. "Always."

"Yet we're not together."

"My feelings and reality are two different things." The mantra played in his head, but his body and his heart rebelled. The need for her kicked strong enough to knock him over.

Being this close to her, holding her, seemed so easy. Made him doubt everything he believed about how his life should go. How he should stay alone rather than risk dragging someone else into his life.

Bottom line was he could easily become his father one day. The old man had been normal once, or so their old neighbors said. But at some point, he'd lost it. Joel worried every day he'd travel down the same road.

No, he was right. They couldn't make this work. "We're never going to agree on this."

"How about this?" She swept her lips over his, gentle and quick.

His temperature spiked and somewhere in his brain an alarm bell rang. "What are you doing?"

"Wow, it really has been a long time for you, hasn't it?" Her sexy smile promised a sleepless night.

It also smashed through his control with the destructive crush of a bulldozer. "This is a bad idea."

"Then let's do something bad." She slid out of his arms and fell back against the mattress with her hair spilling over the small pillow.

Maybe if he kept saying her name his brain would have time to restart. "Hope…"

Having none of it, she pulled him down on top of her. "You want me. I want you."

He balanced his weight on his elbows and stared down at her. "What we feel is deeper than that, and sleeping together could mess it all up."

It took every last bit of his strength to get the words out. He didn't mean them and hated saying them.

Her arms wrapped around his neck, and her body slid against his. "Do you honestly think our relationship could be a bigger mess than it is?"

"We broke up." But he had nothing left. No way to fight her.

"And neither of us has moved on." She treated him to a lingering kiss. "Do you want me to move on, Joel?"

Hell, no. "You need—"

"You."

The next kiss didn't brush or linger. It burned. Her tongue touched his and her hot mouth had him reeling.

When he lifted his head again he could barely breathe and his brain stuck on permanent misfire. "I have exactly one condom."

Her eyebrow lifted. "I'm a little surprised you have even that."

"Call it wishful thinking, but when I knew I was coming to you—"

"Go get it." She whispered the command against his mouth.

He scrambled out of the bed and grabbed the wallet out of his pocket. After a second, he dropped it on the floor.

Before he could climb back onto the bed, she was there, sitting on the edge. Her fingers went to work on his belt, then his zipper. The screech echoed through the quiet room as she lowered it.

Her hand covered him and her breath blew across his boxer briefs. Looking down and seeing her hair, feeling her soft hand on his erection, proved to be too much. The last of his common sense fled as he threw the condom on the bed and pushed her back.

Hands roamed everywhere. His, hers, it didn't matter. His shirt came off and then hers. It wasn't until he saw her bare skin and the sweet shadow between her breasts that he forced his body to slow down, to savor.

He skimmed his fingers over the smooth skin of the top of her breasts, then slipped a finger inside the edge of a plain white bra. At that moment, the sexiest bra he'd ever seen. With a teasing flick over her nipple through the material, he heard her gasp.

"I can't forget you." His mouth went to her neck as he said the startling truth in a gruff voice.

"Don't."

He felt the tug of his pants and felt them slide down farther on his hips, freeing him. Her hand slipped past the elastic band of his underwear and then she was on him, skin against skin, and he had to grind his back teeth together from ending this too soon.

"I want you." He told her right before he kissed her, not giving him a chance to take it back or her a chance to question.

His lips crossed over hers as the heat rolled through him. A signal went off in his brain. Protection…it was there somewhere. His hand patted the bed, searching for the condom. Adrenaline pounded him and he was about to rip the sleeping bag apart to find it when she picked it up and held it in front of his face.

"Looking for this?"

He didn't say anything. Couldn't. He plucked it out of her hand and tore through the paper. His body was on fire now. He had to have her, to sink into her again.

Desperate to make it good for her, he ran a hand over her stomach and hit the band of her pants. Yeah, those had to come off. He didn't waste a second as he stripped them down, taking her bikini bottoms with them and throwing the rumpled ball to the floor.

Then she was naked and open, her legs falling to

the side to make room for him between them. When he dragged a finger through her heat, her back arched off the bed.

She was wet and ready. She didn't pretend shyness. He could read the need on her face and see the excitement in the pink hue of her skin.

It was all the invitation he needed. Rolling the condom on, he fit his tip to her and pushed. His body plunged into hers as it always had, with a tightness that made a groan rumble up the back of his throat.

The night fell away and the closeness of the other cabins didn't matter. He was back inside her as he'd fantasized about for so long. And he wanted it to last. He stilled, enjoying the feel of her tight body around his.

She pinched his shoulder. "Joel, move."

But his body had already taken over. He pressed in and pulled back out. A steady rhythm gave way to a frantic beating of his blood. Her nails dug into his shoulder as she whispered his name in his ear.

He kissed her, touched her, made love to her as the driving need took over. Tension coiled inside him. The building started in every limb. That's what she did to him. Destroyed his intentions and stole control over his body.

Unable to hold back, he slid a hand between them and touched her. A slight circle with his finger and her head pressed back. When her mouth dropped open he covered it with his, thinking to catch those delicious gasps he loved so much as she found her release.

The orgasm slammed into him a second later. His body let go and his shoulders shook until he thought they wouldn't hold him. With one last push, he surrendered.

His last thought was that he hadn't taken the time to pull his pants off.

Chapter Ten

An alarm buzzed beside her head, breaking into Hope's delicious dream. She thought about throwing it at the wall.

When her eyes opened and she adjusted to the overhead light and darkness outside the window, it all came rushing back. Joel's arm across her stomach. His breath against her neck. The memories of the kissing and touching. Making love with him, feeling him over her. Rolling around after and his cursing once he remembered they only had one condom.

She'd wanted another morning after with him for so long. It was somewhere around three and not yet sunrise, but this was close enough.

Through the waves of anger and hurt all those months ago and every day since, she knew they'd get back to this emotional place. That they weren't over. The real question was how long they could stay in this holding position.

The temptation to hide under the blanket and forget the world and the horrors outside the cabin rushed over her. She hated to wake him, but that was the deal. One person on guard duty, and Cam had been handling that for hours.

Now, deep into the night, rain still pinged against the cabin and the alarm on his simple black watched sounded a second time. No question about it, it was Joel's turn to stand guard.

"I want to stay in bed with you." Joel mumbled the comment into her hair.

She had to smile at the grumbling. "Cam would kill you."

The man protected for a living and could shoot anything, track anything, catch anything, yet he hated waking up. It had always been that way with Joel. Morning came and he whined and groaned and tried to get her to stay in bed beside him.

He'd concoct elaborate scenarios just to win another ten minutes. When that failed, he'd start kissing her, and he'd always won the bed battle once that happened.

"Trust me, Cam would understand." Joel lifted up and balanced over her on one elbow. "He can't believe I let you get away the first time."

"Me either."

She hadn't said the words last night because she wanted him to accept the risk and tell her first, but she did love him. They'd said it before and it didn't stop him from walking out. She had no idea if it would matter now. The not knowing made her want to knock some sense into him.

His mouth opened, then closed. It took another few seconds before he said anything. "I walked into that one."

"And, technically, you left me."

He groaned and sat up. "On that note, I'll get out of bed now."

Naked and not even a little shy about it, he threw his feet over the side of the bed. He wiped his face with his open hand but didn't cover his body. Just looked around the floor.

"I'm going to regret this a few hours from now when

I'm trudging through the forest dead on my feet," she said as she gathered the lone blanket against her bare skin and sat up. "Now I just have to find my clothes."

He glanced over his shoulder at her. "What are you doing?"

"Coming with you."

This time he stood up. "You are not."

Her body flushed at the sight of him. He was long and fit, and the idea of crawling back into bed and pulling him in there with her nearly won out. But they needed to keep moving and get ready to head out.

She had no idea what would happen between them back in the real world, but she knew she'd be safer there. "I'm not staying in this cabin alone."

"I will be right outside. Guard duty consists of sitting on the porch with a gun and shooting anything or anyone I don't recognize."

She spied his pants at the end of the bed, underwear still lodged in them, and lifted the bundle up to him. "And you won't be out there alone."

He took the pants and just as quickly dumped them on the floor. He reached for her arm instead and tugged her to her feet, closer to him.

With his arms around her waist, he leaned down and kissed her. Sweet and warm but not demanding.

He smiled when he lifted his head. "Did I ever tell you how beautiful you are?"

All the time. Joel wasn't one to hide his feelings. He'd told her repeatedly that he loved her and how much he wanted her. His expression would get all heated when he looked at her, and his breath would catch when he stripped her. The man knew how to convince a woman with words and actions how beautiful he found her.

He just didn't know how to stick around.

Rather than fight and ruin a perfectly good moment, she leaned into him. Her arms went to his neck and she brought him down for another kiss. "Yes, but feel free to say it again."

This kiss rumbled through her. When she thought he'd pull back, he deepened it, crossing his mouth over hers until a wave of dizziness hit her.

She ended it before poor Cam started banging on the door. "I like the way you use your mouth to make an argument. Very interesting, but I'm still coming with you."

"I figured as much." Joel smacked her butt and winked. "Get dressed."

When they stepped out on the porch five minutes later, Cam was already standing there with his fist raised as if about to knock. His gaze passed from Joel to Hope.

Cam swallowed a smile. "I can take another shift."

"Okay." Joel turned back into the cabin.

Hope ignored the flush of heat hitting her cheeks and grabbed him. "Joel, no."

"Fine." He stepped outside with a hand on her lower back and pulled the door shut behind them. "Anything happening out here?"

"Shuffling over there." Cam pointed at a shadowed spot to the far left of the cabins. "When I went to check it out I met a raccoon family."

Joel blew out a long ragged breath. "They know anything about the shooter?"

"If so, they're not talking." Cam yawned.

Joel shook his head as he grabbed Cam's flashlight. "Go to bed, you lightweight."

Hope took two steps off the porch and glanced around, looking for anything that might have changed from the nights before the retreat went haywire. Same logs and campfire area.

The front porch lights of each cabin remained off as Joel ordered. Turning them on would cast the world just a few feet out in total darkness, and that was too risky. So, they went with limited lighting and depended on their vision to adjust.

The night was still and the rain had slowed to a drizzle, so she lowered her hood. She could hear the dripping of water off the leaves. The soft ping of raindrops hitting the ground usually comforted her. Tonight it had an odd shiver shaking down her spine.

Something wasn't right. She'd spent so much of her life outside and could pick up on the strangeness of a moment. Her father joked she was one with nature, whatever that meant. Really, she had mentally catalogued the sights and sounds…and smells.

She turned around and the men stood right behind her. In her haze she hadn't heard them move.

Joel frowned. "What's going on?"

The scent. That was it. "Do you smell that?"

"I smell rain," Cam said.

Joel leaned past her in the direction of the cabin Cam was temporarily using and where Perry recuperated. "No, she's right."

Memories of her father's powerboat from when she was a little girl. The sharp scent she smelled every time she filled the tank of her car. "It's gasoline. Fire."

Joel was already running, with Cam right behind. They were shouting orders but she couldn't pick up the words as they got lost in the forest in front of them. They ran toward Perry's cabin.

Joel hit the door first. He reached for the knob and drew his hand back fast. Bending down, he rammed into the wood with his shoulder and it slammed open, bouncing against the inside wall.

He disappeared. Never hesitated. Never called for help. He just slipped in, stuck on hero mode like always.

Through the doorway she could see the orange flames licking up the inside back wall, and her heart shredded. Heat punched her in the face as smoke curled out of the opening and into the dark sky.

She tried to get her legs to move, but a sharp scream cut through her consciousness. It took another second to realize it came from her. Then Cam was in front of her with his hands on her shoulders.

He gave her a small shake. "We need water."

She grabbed fists full of his shirt and pulled. "Joel." His name ripped out of her.

"I'll get him, but I need water."

The comment refused to register in her brain. Every cell screamed at her to rush in that door and hunt Joel down. "What?"

Cam put a hand on her cheek. "Hope, listen to me. We need to put this out before it spreads. It could take out all the cabins and us with it."

The cloud of confusion hovering around her cleared. Sparks caught on the breeze and drifted up into the sky in bright flashes of light. "There's a hose in the kitchen cabin. It's hooked to a well, but—"

"Go bang on Charlie's door. Wake him and everyone else up. We need all bodies on this."

A load roar had her looking past Cam into the cabin. She could make out a figure moving around. Her fingers tightened on Cam's shirt. "Get Joel out of there."

"I promise." He turned her toward Charlie's cabin. "Go."

Time blurred as she raced to the far cabin. Every step took forever, as if her legs weighed a thousand pounds each, and she yelled as she ran. By the time she hit the steps, the door opened and Charlie stood there in a white tank and shorts.

She ran right to him. "Fire!"

His eyes widened. "What?"

"We need everyone."

She didn't stay around to explain. She took off again. Her feet slid in the mud and she skidded across a patch of slick grass. Her balance faltered and her arms waved.

Out of the corner of her eye she saw a shadow looming near the doorway of the burning cabin. With her concentration gone, she slipped and fell, catching her weight on one arm before hitting the ground on her butt.

"Hope, are you okay?" Lance was right behind her, dragging her back to her feet with his hand under her arm.

His strength stunned her. The mild-mannered guy nearly picked her up with one hand. But her attention was on the scene in front of her. Joel staggered onto the porch with Perry hanging across his shoulders. Relief had her knees buckling. She would have fallen back to the ground if Lance wasn't holding her.

Joel got to the steps and flames shot up around him. The fire crackled and there was a loud bang from inside the cabin.

Hope needed to get to them. She took a step and ran into Jeff. He stood there, holding a blanket and staring blankly into the flaring orange.

Snatching it out of his hands, she rushed forward. She met Joel halfway down the stairs. The fire followed them. In a blind panic, she threw the blanket over Perry's body and patted out the flickers on his back and sleeve.

At the bottom and a good fifteen feet away from the porch, Joel dropped to his knees. He rolled Perry off him and onto the ground. Joel followed a second later as he hacked and his body shook.

She slid down, ignoring the way the ground soaked her jeans and the residual pain from her knee injury. "Are you okay?"

A second coughing fit stopped whatever Joel was about to say. Slapping his hands against the ground, he turned around and got up on his hands and knees.

The noise plus the crackling of the fire drowned out his words. She looked up at him. "What?"

He put his hands over his mouth like a funnel. "Where are Charlie and Cam?"

Then she remembered the hose and the danger. Perry hadn't moved and Joel's skin was warm to the touch. Soot stained his forehead and she saw a hole in the back of his shirt where she guessed a spark had hit him.

"We need to get this fire out." She got up, thinking to grab Lance, until she felt a hand on her leg.

Looking down, she watched Joel use her for balance as he struggled to his feet. His chest caved from coughing, but his grip was strong. "We need a hose," he said over the shuddering cough.

"Cam is getting it." She pushed Joel farther from the fire and toward Jeff and cleaner air. "Lance and I will go."

Joel was already shaking his head. He pointed at the far side of the cabin. "We all go."

"What about Perry?" Lance asked as he stared at the still body.

"He's dead."

The sharp words stabbed into her. They'd lost Perry. It would have been Joel, too, if he'd stayed in the cabin another minute or two. Even now she heard wood break as the roof shifted.

She only shook herself out of the nightmare when

Joel started moving. She reached for him just as she saw Cam and Charlie come around the corner with a hose and buckets.

Joel straightened as his coughing abated. "Everyone move."

"It won't reach," Cam called out the problem as he yanked on the thick hose dragging behind him. "We have to get this fire out now."

Charlie motioned to Lance and Jeff. "You two come with me and get the barrels."

She had no idea what that meant. Desperate to do something, she stood by Cam and Joel on the side of the fiery cabin and took over the job of spraying water. The hose was heavier than she'd expected and slipped through her hands twice, sending water shooting up and soaking her.

With a tighter grip, she tried again. This hose was nothing like one she'd seen in gardens. It was thicker and heavier. Heaving it under her arm, she aimed the stream at the flames peeking through the cabin wall.

As the flames grew, crashing thundered around them. The fire raged and more beams fell. More than once Joel and Cam stomped out small fires that jumped the cabin and took hold on the forest floor.

"Figures it's not raining now," Cam said.

Joel headed for the porch again. "We can't reach around to the front door and I need to get water in there. If I can get higher…"

When he eyed up the roof her gut twisted until she thought it would explode inside her. "No."

Cam sided with her and grabbed Joel just as he started to move. "No way. It's caving in. You'll go right down into the fire. Honestly, it will tick me off to have to go in after you."

"We don't have a choice."

"Shove something into the side. Make a hole." She screamed to be heard over the mix of fire and banging and water.

Both men stared at her.

She tried again. "Crash it in if you have to, just make an opening wide enough for me to get the water in."

This time they moved. After a quick look around, Joel motioned to the impossible-to-move logs they used as a seat around the fire pit. They each took an end and pulled.

She saw the strain on their faces and shaking in their arms. Somehow they carried it over to the cabin's side. Heat pulsed off the building in waves. Sweat rolled down her back, and her face felt on fire, like the worst, most intense sunburn ever.

On a count of three, with the muscles on their arms bulging from the staggering weight, they heaved the heavy piece of tree trunk at the wall. She waited until that exact minute and hit the buckling wood with a blast of water.

At first nothing happened. She held her breath and kept shooting the water. Then the crashing started. With a series of booms and thuds, a beam buckled. The roof side closest to them caved in and took a chunk of the wall tumbling down with it.

One minute she saw peeks of fire through the wall. The next it flared right in front of her. Scorching heat licked at her and then her back hit the ground.

The breath knocked out of her and the world went dark for a second. When she opened her eyes again, Joel's body pushed her into the mud as fire flashed over their heads.

Men yelled all around her. Over Joel's shoulder she saw Cam grab the abandoned hose and Charlie and Lance heave what looked like some sort of white powder at the fire. The joint hit had the flames lowering by a few feet.

She knew they weren't safe and the whole thing could explode. She searched her memory for anything incendiary inside the cabin and couldn't think of a thing.

Without another word, Joel helped her off the ground. In a line, working together, they all kept at the flames and doused any fires caused by sparks before they could burst into a new disaster.

No one mentioned how it could have started or pointed fingers. They were too busy trying not to be consumed by it.

TONY COULD FEEL the clock ticking as if it had been wound and placed in his brain. Connor had thrown his weight around and gotten Rafe all riled and demanding action. Now search parties had been set up. On Connor's orders, they were planning a hike to the campsite, rain or shine. Connor threatened to take a helicopter in even if it was raining.

Control had shifted and Tony no longer held the reins. After all the plotting, all those tedious hours of setting this up just right, one stupid woman had brought it all down. She didn't play the role he'd assigned her. Add in Connor and his group and it all fell apart.

Tony had planned this from the beginning. Step in, turn Baxter around and become its savior. When the sales numbers had come back soft, he'd waited. Then he'd seen preliminaries for a second quarter worse than the first and panicked.

He knew the work was there for Baxter. Piles of money just waited to flow his way, but he had to get the division in line with expectations. He had to dig more, push his staff harder. He needed time and bought it.

Then people got nosy and he had to regroup. The retreat had been the perfect way to settle things down. An accident and the game could reset.

Instead, Tony shoved pages into the shredder at four in the morning. His wife had called twice. She spent most of their weeknight dinners complaining about his long work hours.

Never mind that he worked around the clock for her. For the things he could give her and buy for her. That he had won her with his checkbook and the big house.

His trophy wife was slowly turning into a regular annoying one. He wanted pretty and obedient and understanding. A woman to wear on his arm and show off at the club. A blonde he'd enjoy in bed. One who would cause envious glares from his business associates. He'd had that for less than a year, and now he had the whining.

The shredder buzzed and the paper pulp dropped in the can underneath. He had a batch here and more at home. With his problem gone and the evidence erased, he could put the system back together again. The board might back off in deference to whatever was happening at the campground.

Tony could get his needed time, but it all depended on Connor not sticking his nose where it didn't belong. Making pages disappear and fudging numbers was one thing. Taking out a guy with a background in special ops was another.

No, Tony had to pull the plug. Shift the blame to another member of the executive staff. Plant the seed and focus the guilt elsewhere.

The idea came to Tony. If Mark was missing, maybe there was a reason he'd walked away, disappeared. Guilt. He'd played with the books to improve the look of his performance. He caused it all, did it all.

The more the idea spun in Tony's brain, the more he liked it. Turn Mark into the guilty party and then sit back and act surprised.

Tony pressed the button and stared at the stack of documents left in the file. He needed to spend his time recreating paperwork and making the trail. It would lead right back to his trusted vice president.

That meant Tony had to hold on to the money he'd syphoned off. Keep it hidden for now. Take everything underground until Connor and his team crawled back out of Baxter's business. The sooner that happened, the better.

Chapter Eleven

Hope had no idea how long they worked. Spraying the water, smothering the shorter bursts with blankets. They ran through all fire retardant Charlie had, but not before the flames had receded to a manageable level. It could have been an hour or minutes, but finally Cam waved them all back and went in with the hose to extinguish the last of the fire.

Exhausted, she dropped to the ground and sat. Some of the men joined her, and Joel sat by her side with his legs out in front of him and his shoulders slumped.

No one spoke as they studied the burnt-out char that once had been a cabin. Smoke still hung in the air and they all took turns coughing. The red sky had given way to a soft gray. Hope knew that meant sunrise wasn't that far away.

Jeff was the first to say anything. He sat with his legs bent and feet on the ground as he dragged a stray stick through the mud. "So, what, Perry woke up long enough to set a fire?"

Lance shrugged. "Could be guilt."

It never dawned on her that Perry could have done this. Last she knew he was unconscious. She was about to point that out when Joel squeezed his hand over her knee.

"He was missing. Mark's still missing. Maybe the two

of them had a fight and something happened." Lance rubbed his hand over his wound. "Perry's the type who couldn't live with it if something happened, even by accident."

"An autopsy will tell us," Cam said as he returned with Charlie from turning off and replacing the hose.

Nearly hitting Lance, Jeff threw the stick. "How are we going to get one of those out here?"

"He means later." Joel stood and put a hand down to help her up. "We're putting together something to carry Perry's body. Once we get a bit more light, we can leave for the open field."

The plan sounded like heaven to her, so she started mentally preparing a list of things they needed. Two items of guilt piled on her, pushing her down into the cloying mud. The baggage, the loss of Perry, it all stacked up on top of the guilt from Mt. Ranier.

Mark was her responsibility and he was still lost. He could be the cause of all this, but he could also be a victim. Celebrating walking out of there while Mark stayed behind filled her with a blinding uncertainty.

"Take only what we need. Someone can come back for the rest later." Like, after they figured out who did what and when and tracked down Mark. In the scheme of priorities, "things" didn't matter.

They had all started moving when Jeff broke in again. "What about the sniper?"

"We'll go a different way." Joel grabbed Hope's knife off the ground and handed it to her.

She had no idea where or when she had dropped it. Likely in the middle of all the bucket carrying and blanket smothering, but who knew?

"Won't the sniper, or Mark, or whoever this is, just follow us?" Jeff's voice rose an octave as he talked.

"No." Hope knew about the riggings and had a good idea where Joel's head was on this.

Perry didn't start that fire because he was unconscious, which meant it was likely one of the people standing here did. She could rule out three and didn't want to take her chances with the rest.

"No offense, but I'm not just going to believe your gut. Or his." Jeff pointed at Joel.

For the second time since they'd met, the men were in a standoff. Joel was taller, younger and fitter. This battle would be no contest, but Jeff didn't seem to realize that fact.

She did. "Jeff, this isn't a good idea."

But he talked right over her. "That's what this is, right? You think you can somehow dodge a bullet."

Joel waited, letting Jeff's agitated comment ring in the air before responding. "Are you done? If so, let's move."

Lance raised a hand. "I'm in."

"I have some stuff I need to grab, and some food and supplies, just in case, but so am I." Charlie left right after he made his informal vote.

"Want to stay out here and take your chances, Jeff?" Joel nodded at the blanket that now covered Perry's body. "Because he's coming along."

Jeff shook his head. "No, we should—"

"Enough arguing. Rain or shine, we're moving. There's a helicopter and a radio and our team."

"Team?"

Joel talked right over Jeff's shout. "The storms stopped. We're down to light rain, and I say we can at least get out of this area and to somewhere safer and warm."

Cam nodded. "As the pilot, I agree."

"This plan is insane," Jeff said.

She had taken just about enough. She stepped in between Joel and Jeff and stared the businessman down. "We've been shot at, there's been a fire, Perry is dead and Mark is still missing. Staying here is insane."

"We'll deal with all of this once we're at the helicopter," Joel said.

"I have two tents." She was sure she had other supplies, but those came to her first.

Joel's expression stayed blank as he glanced at her. "For what?"

"In case we can't take off and need to set up in the open field."

"I can't believe this." Jeff turned around in a huff. He faced the shadowed forest, then started pacing.

"Again, you're welcome to stay here." Joel caught Jeff's arm and stopped the march. "But we're leaving."

"Fine," Jeff said through clenched teeth.

Hope didn't realize she was holding her breath until Jeff finally said the word. Relief and fear and a few emotions she couldn't name swept over her. She vowed to sleep for a week after this was over…if it ever ended.

But first they had to survive it. "Let's get ready to move out."

THE SUN HADN'T risen, but Joel was already out of patience. The lighter sky made it possible to dodge upturned branches and other potential hazards on the forest floor. He took the lead with his weapon ready. Cam brought up the rear. The responsibility fell to Jeff and Charlie to carry the sleeping bag with Perry inside.

Hope guided their new path. Using her GPS, she veered off the rough trail campers used to lead them to the open space where the helicopter sat. They knew from experience there were weapons rigged and ready to shoot that way. Worries about those riggings being everywhere had Joel constantly looking into the trees and tripping over whatever he missed on the ground.

"Why don't we go the way we know?" Charlie asked through labored pants.

"Because the shooter might also know that way." Joel didn't even want to share that much. He kept his tone clipped and angry, hoping to end the discussion.

"But we could end up anywhere."

"We're fine." Hope kept her gaze on the GPS as she shifted them through overgrown branches and around felled trees.

"Doesn't feel like it," Jeff mumbled as he shuffled his feet and grumbled about the weight of the sleeping bag.

"We could probably do without the whining." Joel decided he could go a lifetime without that.

"You're not the one carrying a dead body for miles."

"A mile." Hope made a tsk-tsking sound. "Don't exaggerate."

Joel felt safe smiling because no one could see him but Hope and she was looking off to her left, deep into the forest. "Would you rather no one check for snipers?"

Next time anyone asked him to head out and help babysit a bunch of weekend warriors, he'd find something else to do. Unless it meant being with Hope. He'd always choose the option that led to her.

It would shred him into pieces to leave her again. Sleeping with her guaranteed that, but he had been a dead man before that anyway. He saw her and he lost his mind. He spent time with her and he started thinking impossible things. For about the billionth time since he'd met her, he wished he was a different man from a different background.

"I can help." Lance slid his pack off his good shoulder and held it out to Hope. "Can you take this?"

"Sure." She grabbed it with her free hand. Never mind the fact that she already had one strapped to her back.

Joel tried to do the calculation. He stopped when the number got too high. At this rate she could be dragging more than she weighed.

He reached over and took Lance's pack from her. "I'll take it."

"I'm a big girl, Joel. I can carry a second bag."

Not that he let that stop him. If one of them was going to carry two bags, it would be him, not her. "Unlike Jeff, I totally believe in your skills."

"Uh-huh." She was squinting and didn't seem to be listening. Not her style at all.

He crowded in closer and leaned down to whisper in her ear. "You okay?"

"Not really."

He tried to keep one eye on her and the other on the area ahead. A second of lost concentration could cost them all. Still, he needed her on her game. "Do you need to stop for a—"

"We left Mark behind."

There it was. The blame he knew she was shouldering. Her eyes were big and sad when they stared up at him. The pain he saw there nearly broke him. "Don't take that on."

Confusion mixed with the rest. "What?"

"The guilt."

She visibly swallowed as she looked away. The ground thumped beneath them as they continued to walk. "He's my job. I guaranteed his safety and promised to bring him home."

"And I'm an expert at this sort of thing. Trust me, if there's blame to be had here, other than to Mark for wandering off in the first place, it goes on my shoulders."

"Why?"

"I was sent to make sure something like this didn't happen, and it did. On my watch."

Her steps faltered as her foot hit a loose root. "You always do that."

"What?"

"Take on everyone's pain."

He knew it wasn't true. If anything he shied away from emotional connections. He kept a cool head and a distance. The combination made him good at his job. And lousy at his relationship with her.

"I can handle it." He'd been trained to shoulder the responsibility.

In his father's world, the men had to step up and do what had to be done. Most of what the man said was a convoluted mess of craziness, but Joel internalized the need to step up and he wouldn't apologize for that.

"So can I," she said.

Joel pitched his voice even lower. "I know, but I don't want you to."

It was killing him not to touch her then. He could hear the buzz of conversation behind him, most of it complaining from Jeff. They were not alone.

"We need to head to the right. There's a better path over there," Charlie called out from near the back of the pack.

Hope shook her head. "That swings us too far over."

"It's the best way," Charlie insisted.

She kept her focus on the GPS screen. "We're fine. We're not far now."

"I'd rather trust Charlie on this since he owns the campground. *He* knows these woods," Jeff said.

"This time Jeff's right," Charlie agreed.

Joel wasn't in the mood to encourage their ramblings.

He heard Cam settling everyone down, which was good because Hope kept frowning.

"Look to your left." She looked straight as she said the words. "Don't draw attention, but look. What's that about thirty feet out by the small hill?"

"A mound of dirt and leaves." Her eyesight was perfect. Joel questioned his because he had to narrow his gaze, homing in on the spot she indicated. "All stacked under a lean-to."

He also saw something red. A piece of material, maybe. The storm had blown apart someone's hiding place, and there was no question something was buried under there.

"Maybe the wind pushed it all up there during the storm."

If she needed to believe that to get through the next few hours, he'd let it happen. "Is that what you think?"

She nibbled on her bottom lip. "What are you thinking?"

That she might have found Mark and, if so, the man was not their attacker. Only bad news no matter how you looked at it. "You don't want to know."

"We should look."

"I can't spread any more panic." Joel caught her hand when he thought she'd peel off and check out the site on her own. "Note the coordinates on your GPS and move us to the east so the others don't see."

"Do you really think—"

"Get us to the clearing as fast as you can, but take us out around this site."

Before she could say anything else, Joel dropped back, hanging along the right side of the group and hoping to bring their attention with him and away from the find on the left. He answered one of Lance's questions, though

Joel would never be able to remember what he'd said if someone asked him later.

He drew next to Cam, impressed at the clip Hope had them moving in now on the rough terrain. After working with him, Joel didn't have to clue Cam in to the existence of a problem.

Cam kept his gaze straight and dropped his voice low. "What's wrong?"

"Behind you to the left, thirty or so feet."

"The pile." Cam nodded. "Want me to check it out?"

"Do you need to?" They had had the same training, had seen many of the same things.

Cam took a second to study it. "Probably not." Joel was about to rejoin Hope when the concern in Cam's voice stopped him. "Be careful up there. I don't like you in front of this group."

That made two of them. "Watch my back."

"Done."

About ten minutes later they broke through the thick cover of trees and hit the edge of the woods on the opposite side from where he'd gone into the forest when they first arrived. The open expanse of the clearing stretched in front of them. The helicopter sat shining despite the overcast morning skies.

Joel brought the group to a halt under the cover of the final line of trees and scanned the area.

The space provided the perfect place for an ambush. Anyone could be hiding anywhere. A weapon could be pointed at them right now.

Lance dropped his side of the makeshift gurney and double-timed his steps as if he was running to freedom. Cam caught him in mid-stride. "Hold up."

"What?" Lance's gaze bounced from Cam to Hope.

She gave him a shaky smile. "It's going to be okay. Just be patient."

Joel didn't feel the need to sugarcoat it. "We don't know who else is out here, so do not move."

Charlie's head came up. "Wait a second."

With Cam's help, Charlie and Jeff lowered the sleeping bag the rest of the way to the ground.

Lance kept shifting his weight back and forth as if he was ready to bolt. "So we're going to just stand here?"

"What's the plan?" Charlie asked at the same time.

Joel had met more grateful rescuees before. Then again, he'd had some with even bigger attitudes. The protection business wasn't always an easy gig. "As Hope said, patience."

Cam stepped up. "I'll go."

No way was Joel letting that happen. If anyone ran out there, it would be him. He'd dragged Cam along on this gig, promising a quick stop, and ended up dropping him into the middle of a disaster. "We're not sacrificing you."

Charlie threw up his hands. "Someone has to get out there and call for help."

"You're clear of the trees. Can't you use your sat-phone?" Hope asked.

"It's on the helicopter." Not the best topic as far as Joel was concerned.

When they first left the helicopter, he figured he'd be right back. When they came a second time, he was more interested in the gear and extra guns. He'd screwed up, and Cam gave him crap for it.

Not that the sat phone would have been of any use until right now anyway. Like hers, his needed a clear shot at the sky, and between the trees and the weather, he hadn't had that for two days.

"I'm going." Cam slipped off his pack. "Cover me."

He took two steps and a shot rang out. His body went down. Hitting the ground on his stomach, he didn't move.

Hope gasped and the men started shouting. Joel refused to lose it. A single shot and a spiderweb of broken glass on the helicopter windshield. That put the shot high and likely from the direction of the old location.

Still, his voice shook as he called out, "Cam?"

"What?" He didn't move as he answered.

Joel let the relief wash through him. As expected, Cam had fallen more out of training and experience than anything else. "It's the rigging."

"You sure?" Cam put his palms against the ground and pushed up enough to glance back at Joel. "I'd really hate for you to be wrong here."

Hope shook her head. "But no one is standing over there to trip it."

"There could be another one on this side." Joel looked behind him, trying to find it.

"What are you two talking about?" Lance asked.

The other men wore similar confused expressions. Joel understood the frustration and need to know, but this wasn't the time. And if his suspicions were correct, one of them might already know.

"I'm getting up." Cam shifted as he spoke.

Joel wasn't about to leave him out there unprotected. He pushed into the open, breaking the tree line and glancing back into the forest. He scanned the area for movement as well as riggings, just in case.

Nothing spiked his radar. "Go."

He heard the pounding of feet and saw Cam race past him at full speed. Jeff jumped back and Hope tried to catch him. Cam ceased his momentum with a rather large tree. His hands hit the bark and his feet stopped.

Hope went right to him, running her hands over his back and arms. "Are you okay?"

Cam glanced at Joel. "Fine."

"What is that?" Jeff cowered as a thwapping sound split through the otherwise quiet morning.

The helicopter cleared the trees and headed for the clearing. There was enough room to land, but it would take some skill. Good thing the Corcoran Team had plenty of that.

"The cavalry." Forget panic. Other than the rain finally stopping, this was the first good news they'd had in days.

"Your team?"

The hope in her eyes nearly did Joel in. "Yeah."

The helicopter kicked up wind, and the noise drowned out all other sounds. The trees around the open space swayed and the grass flattened. It felt like forever before it touched down and the propellers slowed.

Joel took one step into the clearing and held up a hand. After a few more minutes, the helicopter wound down.

Connor leaned out and yelled. "What's wrong?"

Joel appreciated the boss's caution. "We just took fire. Could be a rigged weapon."

Connor nodded and then moved back inside for a second. When he came out it was with guns up and two men helping. Joel recognized one—Corcoran's second in command, Davis Weeks, a man Joel would serve beside and trust with Hope's safety any day.

When they ran across the area without another shot being fired, Joel figured it was safe. He met Connor with a handshake about ten feet from the edge of the clearing. "About time you got here."

"I had to break about a dozen laws and ignore the screaming from the guy at a nearby airport and a police chief to get here." Connor hitched his thumb in the other guy's direction. "Davis came along to fly the plane and we picked up a ranger."

Joel knew they could all fly but didn't question the extra man. Only issue was getting them all out, but that was Connor's problem. "Thanks for that. Both of you."

Connor slid his gun back into the holster. "I almost hate to ask, but who's in the bag?"

"Better yet, who's the woman?" Davis asked.

"Perry, one of the Baxter executives." Joel motioned for the rest of the group to join them. "And this is Hope Algier."

Davis smiled at Joel. "Her father is not happy with you."

"He's the one who sent me out here."

"We'll talk about how you spend your vacations later." Connor walked past Joel to welcome the group.

Davis leaned in. "And we'll definitely talk about the woman."

Chapter Twelve

Hope barely made it to her town house that night before falling over. She'd gotten to know Connor and Davis as they kept up a steady stream of mindless chatter on the helicopter ride out of the forest. They talked about a debriefing but gave her a day's reprieve on having to sit through it. Apparently she had paperwork to fill out and questions to answer.

They promised they'd take care of the inevitable search for Mark and investigation into Perry's death. She was grateful, but there was so much information to take in. It all welled up until it threatened to choke her.

At one point she had to concentrate on her breathing to keep from putting her head between her knees to calm down. And she wasn't the scare-easily type.

She always held it together. Or she had done so until her life fell apart in the double whammy of losing Joel and losing her climbing guide career.

Back at the airport hangar, when Joel had announced the coordinates she'd marked off in the forest and suggested it could be a grave site—presumably Mark's— her stomach had dipped. She'd known what he thought when they were out there. Hearing the stark truth as he delivered the news to his colleagues sliced through her.

When the cavernous room had started to spin away

from her, Joel had held her hand and told her everything would be fine. But it was Davis with his photos of his pregnant wife that took her mind off all the death.

The big man seemed to be totally in love. He grinned as he pointed and his voice picked up with excitement. Hope found his happiness contagious.

The talk also filled her with a strange sadness. A longing for what she feared she'd never have. She couldn't exactly move on and start a new life when she was still stuck in the old one. The main part of which was rummaging around in her kitchen right now.

"I take it you're staying here tonight?" she asked as she sat down across from him.

Joel froze with his hand on the open refrigerator door. "I don't want to drive back to Annapolis."

Never mind that the rest of his team found somewhere to sleep in the DC area. He hadn't even asked. Just drove her to the town house and settled in.

Truth was he was here and she wasn't about to kick him out. Didn't even want to try. "Fair enough."

He shut the door and came around the kitchen island to where she sat on a high barstool. Her bare feet dangled off the footrest. She'd showered and changed into clean clothes, consisting of a thin T-shirt, which had his gaze skipping to her breasts every few seconds, and plaid boxer shorts.

She'd chosen the outfit on purpose. To entice him. Some men loved to see women in tight skirts or sexy lingerie. Joel preferred the fresh, down-home look. Put on something he could tunnel his hands under, maybe no underwear and just a hint of the bare skin beneath, and he lost his cool. Happened every time.

She wasn't the only one who showered. So had he, but

he'd used her downstairs bathroom instead of the one in her bedroom upstairs.

The restraint surprised her. She had half expected him to pull back the curtain and step in with her. Not that she would have objected, though the dressed version was pretty nice and smelled pretty good, too.

Damp hair, faded jeans and a white tee that slipped over him like a second skin. Looked like he also knew how to entice.

Right now he did it by stepping into the space between her legs. He didn't touch her. Didn't have to. The place was small enough for her to feel his presence in every room, even though he hadn't lived there in months.

The end unit had two bedrooms and a small office. The entire place could fit into the guesthouse at her father's place, but the size was perfect for her. She liked cozy and her oversize sectional sofa that dwarfed the rest of the family room. The shelves loaded with books and the collection of mismatched coffee mugs she collected from her travels.

Her dad liked shiny knickknacks and marble floors. He had money and enjoyed spending it. She didn't begrudge him the wealth or the power. It didn't define him. Certainly didn't say anything about him as a dad, and he was a good one. Overprotective with a tendency to butt in, but his heart was in the right place. He wanted her happy and insisted Joel was the man for her.

She didn't disagree.

Joel stood in front of her now and slid his palms up her shorts, skimming his fingers underneath to touch bare skin. "Do you want me to leave?"

There was no reason to play games. They loved each other and hurt each other. It was a vicious cycle, but one she couldn't break. "No."

"Is it too forward to say I have condoms in my duffel bag?" He kissed her cheek, then his mouth traveled to her ear.

She tilted her head to give him greater access. The man could kiss, and when he kissed her there her body trembled with excitement.

Her hands came up and she held on to his upper arms for balance. "More wishful thinking?"

"Just good planning." He said the comment and it vibrated against her skin.

Her eyes, already half closed, popped open again. She pulled back, almost breaking contact, and stared at him. "I don't get it."

"Davis put them in there when he packed the bag."

The married man with a pregnant wife was carrying condoms? "I don't know what to say to that."

"They were totally for my benefit. He got the briefing on you."

The conversation was sucking some of the life out of the seduction scene. "Meaning?"

Instead of answering, Joel dipped his head and kissed her, and the seduction was back on. The rush of longing hit her so hard she would have fallen off the stool if his hands weren't on her hips.

Even with the adrenaline and danger gone, she still craved him. The feelings kicked into high gear when she'd convinced herself they'd fade.

When he lifted his head, she traced a finger over his bottom lip. "Nice."

"He knows...they all do now, my whole team..." Joel kissed her nose. "...what you mean to me."

Her heart flipped. Actually felt as if it had torn loose and performed a perfect somersault. "Which is?"

"Everything."

And that was it. The doubt fled and the need for self-preservation wavered. He had given her the words that broke open the gates and made her want to try again.

She knew in her soul he believed them, felt them. She hoped he'd follow through this time, but reality nipped at her on that one.

But none of the "what ifs" and "what about tomorrows" mattered right then. His fingers brushed the insides of her legs to her upper thighs, and his hot mouth pressed against hers. She wanted him—over her, with her, inside her.

"Come upstairs with me." She whispered the plea against his mouth.

The kiss deepened and the room spun. One minute she was on the barstool and the next he stood with her body wrapped around his.

She linked her ankles and let her legs ride low on his hips. His erection pressed against her, and his deep breathing filled her head. When he walked, taking them across the room, the movement barely registered.

Somehow he got them to the couch. He stood hovering over it, without ever breaking the contact of their mouths or stilling his hands as they traveled all over her back.

When he sat down, her knees pressed into the couch cushions on either side of his hips. Her fingers went into his hair as his hands slipped under her shirt and up her back.

"I'm happy you were at camp." Her lips pressed against his throat.

His head tipped back. "I hated the idea of you out there without me."

"It's my job."

He cupped her cheeks with his palms and looked deep into her eyes. "I want you safe."

Her hand trailed down his flat stomach to his lap. She could feel the heat pounding off him and into her. His erection pressed against the notch between her legs and he kept shifting, driving in closer.

When he moved again, she unbuttoned his jeans. He hadn't bothered with a belt and as she lowered the zipper, she knew he hadn't put on underwear either. How very practical of him.

Her hand slid over him, and her mouth brushed over his. "Take me to bed."

Hands clenched against her outer thighs. "I thought you'd never ask."

IT WAS AFTER nine as Tony walked to the head of the conference room table and sat down. His men had experienced days of difficulty and hardship. Their numbers had been shaved from four to two. They wore the horror of the experience on their faces. Both Jeff and Lance were pale and drawn. Neither gave Tony eye contact.

He suspected they wanted to go home and forget everything that had happened. He couldn't exactly blame them. He wanted to erase the past few days from his memory, too.

On his orders, both had been checked out at the hospital at length. Despite the ordeal, they were healthy physically. But he wanted to assess the emotional part. He also needed to know what they knew.

Everyone wanted to interview them, from the police to the park rangers to Connor to the press. Tony wanted to secure them and lock them away, but he knew that wasn't practical. As it was, he had managed to buy a little time, citing their raw state. But the clock was ticking.

He knew he'd lose the battle when it came to Connor.

The man appeared to take the lead on the entire investigation, and no one in the police department or any federal agency objected or tried to push the man aside. He walked in and they stepped back.

As suspected, Connor and his team were trouble. Hope and this guy Joel were the worst. Their names kept coming up, so Tony placed the blame for his pounding headache and the twisting in his gut solely on them.

But he had to deal with that later. Right now he had more bad news to deliver. The kind of news that broke men, or at least started them on a vigilante crusade. Tony didn't want any part of either of those things. He needed these two healthy and indebted to him. Supporting him.

"After they got you out, search and rescue found a body in the woods." The news, though expected, still had stunned Tony when Connor called to tell him.

With everything that had gone wrong, this part had gone as planned.

Jeff slumped forward, balancing his elbows on the table. "What?"

"Mark."

Lance shook his head. "Did Perry do it?"

"We think so." Or that was the story that worked best for this new scenario Tony had concocted.

Mark was supposed to have an accident. Walk off into the woods and fall off a mountainside or fall and hit his head. The fact that he was buried under a pile of leaves made that tough to sell.

"Perry wouldn't hurt Mark." Jeff looked to Lance. "Right?"

Last thing Tony needed was these two teaming up and

exchanging stories. "You need to know the rest. After you left camp, I discovered some financial irregularities."

Jeff dipped even lower in his chair. "What does that mean?"

"It looks like Mark was inflating his numbers to make the new division look like it was performing better than it was." The evidence now supported the claims. Notes and files, all backdated and slipped into computer back-ups using earlier dates. It paid to have a staff of tech experts who passed on their expertise. Tony had learned a thing or two over the years.

"That explains the information I collected," Jeff said.

Tony forced his expression to stay neutral. "What are you talking about?"

"Inconsistent performance in one of our divisions, the newest. I thought it might be an aberration but wanted to get at the issue in case the dip in productivity and revenue was a signal of things to come."

"You didn't come to me with this?" Tony couldn't keep the menace out of his voice. He knew that when Lance glanced up and his eyes narrowed.

"I talked with Mark about marketing strategies we could use to stabilize the numbers." Jeff frowned. "I thought he had talked about that with you."

That answered that question. Tony worried Mark had shared the information he compiled with other members of the staff. Looked like Jeff was the source and went to Mark, who listened to the concerns but didn't play his own hand or express his suspicions about what was going on. Mark ran to Tony, never mentioning Jeff, and everything rolled downhill from there.

The poor decision-making by Mark to take credit for Jeff's findings and keep the matter quiet made it easier for Tony to lay the trail. He placed a few more tracks now. "The real problem is the reason behind the instability."

Lance stopped tapping his hand against the table long enough to stare. "What do you mean?"

"It looks as if Mark had created a pretty elaborate scheme. He set up false client accounts and funneled money into them. The initial moving of money showed up as a down quarter in performance when, really, he was pocketing portions of money we received. He tried to cover everything up with inflated numbers after the fact, making it look as if he'd saved the division, but it was too late." When Tony realized he was swiveling his chair back and forth, he stopped. He needed calm and reassurance right now. The nerves rattling inside him couldn't show.

Lance shook his head. "That can't be right."

"I'm afraid it is." Tony rushed to dispel any thoughts of questioning him. "The only logical explanation is Perry found out and paid for his loyalty to this company with his life."

"I can't believe this," Jeff said.

"You're lucky it wasn't you. My guess is you were next." Tony thought back to the last document he had created. "I guess that explains why he sent me the memo asking for the corporate retreat. To get all of you out there and provide cover as he hid his hand in this."

"But then who killed Mark?" Lance flattened his hand against the table and leaned forward as he talked.

He still wore the sling from the injury he'd sustained in the woods. Something about a sniper or a rigged gun. Tony didn't know about any of that but planned to find out.

Tony shrugged. "My guess is Perry."

That was the new plan—implicate both men. Invent

a scenario where they turned on each other. Mark lost in his lying and Perry trying to get at the truth. It played well, and Tony found it easier than continuing to hide the losses.

He could spin this into betrayal and vow to fix the corporate tendency that led to it. Overhaul the whole reporting process and means of calculating overhead.

In the end, the ruse could streamline the company and preserve the bottom line. And that would secure his position and the bonuses he needed.

But Lance didn't appear to be buying the story. The lowest man on the corporate leadership ladder kept shaking his head, skepticism apparent on his face. "This is going round in circles."

"The important thing is we're back on track." The man would need convincing, and Tony vowed to do just that. But not today. They all needed to stand down and get some breathing room on this. Tony also needed to handle Connor and the Corcoran Team, which looked like it could be a full-time job. "These men's families deserve to believe in them. We'll walk a careful line, clean this up and move on."

"The board is in agreement with that strategy?" Jeff asked.

"We'll work it out. Everything will be legal and transparent, but respectful to the dead." As soon as he had a report to present Tony would start that process.

The board, reeling from the loss of two executives, wasn't pressuring him for anything other than answers about their deaths. The financial issue wasn't on their radar. He'd put it there but in his own way. The way he needed it to look.

"In the meantime, you two should take a week. To the extent you need any assistance in terms of counseling or additional medical issues, Baxter will, of course, cover everything."

"Thanks," Jeff said, but Lance stayed quiet.

They'd all had enough for one night, and the next few days would be rough. There were funerals to plan and a story to spin out. "Now go home."

With a minimum of shuffling, both men got up. They exchanged thank you's and shook hands before he sent them out the door. Tony gritted his teeth through the entire spiel. He wasn't accustomed to explaining anything to anyone. He gave orders and people followed them. Now with Mark gone and the information buried with him, Tony could get back to the business of running Baxter.

Through the glass door, he saw Lance and Jeff head out for the night. Tony waved and smiled even as the cell in his jacket pocket buzzed for the fourth time in less than a half hour. He knew who was calling. Knew and ignored it because this was the one problem he hadn't counted on.

Tony glanced at the cell screen. He recognized the number because it had popped up all day. The texts, the voicemails. If his unwanted partner was trying to create a discoverable trail, he was doing a great job. The covert part of their relationship seemed to be confusing the man at the moment.

Tony would explain and set it straight, but not now. He needed a few minutes of quiet to think.

The man would come calling soon. And Tony would be ready.

Chapter Thirteen

The next morning Joel watched Connor do the two things he did every day—sit at the head of a conference room table and pour coffee. Only today, the table wasn't his table, and neither was the business. This office space and all the resources they needed were on loan from Algier Security, but that didn't seem to faze Connor or make him look any less in charge.

He poured a cup for Hope, then dropped the pot on the tray in front of him, leaving Davis and Joel to fend for themselves. After a night in Hope's bed, making love with her, holding her, Joel didn't need the kick.

But Connor was a caffeine addict. Could put away a pot in an hour and keep going back all day. Joel often wondered if he slept.

Since Connor's wife had moved out and he refused to talk about why or where she was, Joel doubted it. Connor still wore his wedding ring and referred to Jana all the time.

At first he insisted she was visiting a relative, but as the months dragged on it became obvious the marriage had imploded. He didn't even bother to try to explain anymore.

Joel chalked it up to one more example of how a relationship couldn't work long term with this job. Everyone agreed Jana and Connor were the perfect couple. Smart, focused, dedicated to each other and the work. And now she was gone.

"Your father is letting us use his office as our satellite office," Connor explained to Hope.

She smiled over the rim of her mug. "Sounds like Dad."

"He's on the way back home and not happy he got stuck because of weather and couldn't be here to meet you." Joel knew because he'd had two long, yelling phone calls from the man already this morning. The second ended with an order to marry Hope and be done with it.

With all his power and money, Rafe Algier had a very basic agenda. He wanted his only child safe and he wanted her with Joel. Both options worked for Joel except that he couldn't figure out how to make the second stick without endangering the first.

As if she had read his mind, she slid her hand under the table and rested her hand on his knee. "I'm fine."

The simple touch sent fire racing through him. That's all it took. "I'll make sure you stay that way."

"On that note…" Davis looked at his watch for the tenth time since they'd all gotten there a half hour ago and gotten the video feed hooked up to the Corcoran Team offices. "I'm thinking I should move out to headquarters. I'll coordinate from Annapolis. Use our resources and Joel's impressive computer programs to get through all the information we've collected."

"I'd ask you not to touch my stuff, but—"

Davis nodded. "I'm going to anyway."

"When is your wife due?" Hope asked.

"Lara." Davis smiled as he said her name, just as he always did. "And she's a little more than five months along."

"He doesn't like to be away from her." Joel knew he was stating the obvious, but he did it anyway.

"True, but I also want to be back in our office, helping Pax and Ben analyze the data." Davis winked at Hope. "Being with my wife is just a huge bonus."

"Who are the other men you mentioned?" Hope's hand slid off Joel's leg.

He put it back on his thigh again. "Members of the team. There are a few others who mostly work with Cam, but they're on enforced leave right now."

"Enforced?"

"I demanded they take some downtime because they travel all the time," Connor said. "Cam happened to be available and can fly, so he headed out to drop Joel off with you."

"Which didn't go so well for me," Cam pointed out as he slipped into the room and took the seat next to Davis.

"Okay then." She exhaled as she took another sip of coffee. "I think I'm caught up now."

"I'm sure we'll lose you a second or third time," Cam said. "Sorry I'm late."

"Why are you?" Joel asked.

"Checking the helicopter." When Connor started to talk, Cam waved him off. "It's fine and the front window is being fixed. We'll be able to use it as soon as you're ready."

Joel wanted to ask what for, but Cam looked at him and gave a small shake of his head. Whatever the mission was, it looked like it was off the books for Connor. That only intrigued Joel more.

Hope wrapped her hand around her mug. "At the risk of ruining any image you may have of me as a smart person, let me ask what could be an obvious question. Why do you need an office here at all? Why not just head home now that I'm away from the campground?"

Home. The word knocked around in Joel's brain. It meant leaving her. "The job isn't over."

True, it was an informal one, but Rafe made it clear Corcoran had been hired to figure out what went wrong on the retreat. He wanted answers and some assurance his daughter would not be put in jeopardy again.

Joel wanted the same thing, and Connor didn't even blink at the request. He might have lost his wife, but he was deadly loyal to the team. If one of them needed something, Connor stepped in.

The light in Hope's eyes dimmed a bit. "I still can't believe Mark is dead."

Joel squeezed her hand. "Thanks to you spotting him, we were able to recover his body quickly."

All of the men nodded. Davis looked more than a little impressed. Joel wondered what he'd say if he knew about all of her skills.

"Forensics teams are swarming all over the place," Connor said.

Cam half stood up and reached across the table for the coffeepot. "Why aren't we there?"

"Jurisdictional nonsense, but we get a look at everything. Raw data, samples whatever we need."

Davis chuckled. "You convinced the police to do that?"

Connor smiled. "I can be very persuasive."

Some of the building tension that came with talking about tough subjects seeped out of the room, but Hope continued to frown. "I still don't get the outpost here."

"Baxter is in town and I want to be where Tony Prather is right now." Connor's smile grew, as if he relished the idea of going to battle with this guy. "Let him know I haven't forgotten him or the promise I made to solve this mystery."

"Plus we have two murders and an explanation that's half-as—"

She chuckled over Davis's sudden stoppage. "Yes?"

He cleared his throat. "Let's go with unbelievable."

Cam nodded. "Nice save."

"The Perry versus Mark fight Tony is trying to sell doesn't hold together." Connor scanned the notes in front of him. "How could Perry start the fire in his condition and why would he?"

Joel filled in the blanks in case she didn't follow the jumping conversation. As a group they sometimes talked in shorthand and forgot to cut that out when others joined in. "We all know Perry was out of it. Cam checked on him about ten minutes before you smelled gasoline, and the guy was out cold."

"So, supposedly Perry sprang up and was oriented and stable enough to go find gas, which he hadn't used up until then, pour it all over the cabin, light the match, then lie back down and go to sleep." Cam snorted. "I don't think so."

Davis shrugged. "The police buy it."

Hope's mug hit the table with a sharp whack. "Come on, really?"

"Tony Prather tells a good story. The man is a natural salesman, after all," Connor said.

"He didn't do anything for me. And this is the same executive who didn't go along on the executive retreat even though he set it up?" She added an eye roll to the end.

"Wait, go back." Connor stilled. "Tony insists Mark is the one who wanted the retreat."

"That's not what Tony told me when we talked about what he wanted on this job." She took out her cell and started scrolling. When she landed on a specific email, she turned the phone and showed Connor. "I asked why he wasn't coming along and he gave me some excuse about not being able to take time away from running the company but said it was necessary for everyone else for morale and team building."

"The guy is slippery." Connor finished reading and then passed the cell phone to Davis. "Tony didn't want to send out a search team and didn't seem all that concerned about Mark or motivated to get out there for a rescue."

"A great guy all around." Davis slid the phone back to her.

She put it in front of Joel and returned her hand to his knee. "But why do all of this? The executive retreat is a lot of trouble."

"With a lot of moving parts." That's the point Joel didn't understand.

If you wanted to get rid of an executive or pit two against each other, there had to be easier ways. Out in the forest the control vanished. There was the human element, plus weather and animals and accidents. The list went on and on.

Connor rested his elbows on the table and reached over to refill his already empty coffee cup. "I think we're looking at the oldest reason in the world—money."

She groaned as she rubbed her eyes. "I was afraid you'd say that."

"With the help of a skeptical member of the board who didn't want Tony hired in the first place, Ben has been back at Corcoran headquarters digging through the Baxter records. He's had access to notes and files and reports so boring your head would spin," Davis explained.

"How'd he get stuck with the job?" she asked as a smile tugged at the corner of her mouth.

"Newest member." Joel had been in that unenviable position and celebrated when someone came in after him.

He was no longer the new guy, though he often felt that way. Still getting his footing and learning along the way. He knew the basic skills coming in and could match, or beat, any of them at shooting and tracking, but strategies and tactics were a different skill set. Connor and Davis excelled at those.

"And he's former NCIS, so he's used to government crap." Cam waved his hand in the air. "Business crap is about the same."

Hope shook her head and mumbled something about men acting like boys. "Tony is pursuing the Mark-as-bad-guy story, I take it."

"As far as Tony is concerned, the case is closed."

She never broke eye contact with Connor. "But you disagree."

"Definitely." Davis took the question. "We're going to rip his company apart, look at every piece of paper and check out whatever angle we can find."

"We think Tony is at the heart of it all," Joel said.

"Then he needs to pay." Her hand clenched his thigh. "How can I help?"

Davis laughed, this time full and open. "I like her."

"Apparently she can shoot a bow and arrow, too," Cam added.

Connor's eyebrow rose. "That's impressive."

They didn't know the half of it. She could guide them all and outhike them. They were in shape. The job demanded them to be, but she had stamina that beat them all. Joel was man enough to admit that…and then there was the part where he found it more than a little sexy.

Cam spun his mug around on the table, letting the bottom clank as it turned. "And she managed to date Joel without killing him."

"Amazing." Davis shook his head as his voice filled with awe.

Talk about a mood killer. Joel stepped in to end the conversation before it got completely out of hand. Last thing he needed was this group rapid-firing questions at her about his love life. "That's enough."

"In case you're wondering, he dumped me." This time she moved her hand and put it on the table where everyone could see it.

Yeah, that was definitely enough of this conversation now. Joel knew they were one step from him losing all control over it. "Can we not have this discussion right now?"

Davis's mouth still hung open. "No way he dumped you."

"I didn't believe it either," Cam said.

Connor's expression suggested he thought Joel needed serious counseling. "Always thought you were smarter than that, Joel."

"I'm starting to wonder." Joel mumbled the response before he could think twice about it.

If Hope caught it, she let it slide because she was already off to another topic. "There's one more thing. The… What did you call them, riggings? There's no way any of the men on the trip set those up."

Davis eyed her up, the appreciation growing with each passing second. "That leaves a rogue angry person or—"

"Charlie." Joel dropped the one name that kept kicking around his head.

The man blended into the background and didn't cause trouble. He also knew the area and could have hooked up the riggings and set the whole thing up. The question was why.

"My dad vetted him. Except for some financial issues due to down business like almost everyone else these days, he was fine." When a slap of silence hit the room, she looked around at each of them. "What?"

And there was the answer to Joel's question. "Money."

Davis blew out a long breath. "His background is a place to start. We'll run through it all again."

The room erupted in action. Connor started shuffling papers and Davis reached for the laptop. Even Cam grabbed a file and started looking through notes. Except for Hope's shell-shocked expression,

Joel loved this part of the team operation. They had a mission and a direction. From here they could spin it out, look over everything and run through scenarios.

"Look for recent payments." Connor handed Davis a paper with a list of items on it. "See if anyone is helping Charlie pay his bills."

Hope finally snapped out of it. Her expression morphed from blank to furious. Those cheeks turned pink and she clenched the mug with enough force to break it in her hands. "I trusted him. He was out there with a gun, right with us."

"Kind of makes you want to punch him, doesn't it?" Cam asked.

Joel reached over and took the cup out of her tight grip. "Stand in line."

Chapter Fourteen

Tony slammed his car door and walked to the designated meeting spot. He passed other cars in the parking area under the Whitehurst Freeway and kept going until he hit the gravel spot at the far end, away from the bulk of the foot traffic.

It was the middle of the afternoon and traffic whizzed by. Georgetown was a mass of tourists and students. People talked and screamed as they fought for coveted parking spaces and swarmed in a large swath from the waterfront to M Street, where most of the stores and restaurants sat.

Charlie had insisted they meet or he'd start spilling everything he knew. Tough talk for a man with all of the blood on his hands.

After taking the last few steps with his dress shoes clicking against the pavement, Tony stopped. This close to the water the fish smell hit hard, but Tony didn't plan to be there long.

Have his say, issue his threat and go.

Charlie leaned against the driver's side door of his dark truck as he glanced around, looking at everything but Tony. The dismissal made Tony regret ever making a deal with this guy.

Tony didn't wait for small talk. After a quick look

around to test for privacy, he jumped in. "We agreed not to contact each other right now."

Charlie dropped his cigarette on the ground and stomped it out with the heel of his hiking boot. "Yeah, well, a lot of our plans got mixed up."

"Which is why it's even more important you lie low and keep quiet." If he refused to do that, Tony would have to make a new plan, one that included taking Charlie out.

The man was older but still fit. One of those guys who could fall anywhere in a twenty-year age range and grizzled from all of his time outdoors.

The choice of Charlie made sense at the beginning. The man needed money and Tony needed a particular expertise. One of the tech guys mentioned his uncle in terms of providing an extra hand for moving storage data. Talked about the man being discreet and taking odd jobs. How he was a loner and very private.

Apparently the nephew should have added ruthless extortionist to the list. Charlie had information and thought holding it over Tony's head was the answer.

Never mind Tony was smart enough to cover his tracks and divert the trail away from him. He even added in a bribery message from Charlie to suggest the old man made it all up for a big payday and Tony was nothing more than a victim.

He definitely covered his bases. Even now, he had a signal blocker and a gun with him for protection to keep Charlie from getting the jump on him. In a battle of his word versus the loner's, Tony would win. He made sure of that. No one would blame him for killing a crazy stalker if attacked.

Charlie crossed his arms and legs as he leaned back against the door. "You've been ignoring me."

"I'm letting the heat die down." That was only half a

lie. The other had to do with moving the money out and burying a paper trail.

"Interesting comment in light of Perry's death."

"You didn't have to touch him." Tony shook his head. "Fire, what were you thinking?"

"It was a clever solution."

"It was sloppy and makes the Mark story we're trying to sell—"

"We're?"

"—harder to swallow."

Charlie just stared for a few seconds before saying anything. "Perry came along when I was moving Mark's body."

The man failed to do anything right. Charlie was told to stage a fall. They'd gone over the plan several times. No trouble. Moving bodies where anyone could stumble by was not in the instructions.

Tony tried to hold on to his patience and keep the advantage. "Why were you touching it?"

"You wanted an accident. I was trying to stage one." Charlie shrugged. "I looked up and saw Perry and had no choice but to hit him."

"Then you make it look like a joint accident. Like they went after each other or something. You don't leave the guy alive." Tony clamped his mouth shut as soon as the words were out. He was a businessman. A legitimate one. He didn't engage in this nonsense.

He'd pushed the guilt out. Mark and Perry were decent workers and deserved better. But the idea that his plans had gone this far off course was the one thing Tony couldn't take. Find the wife, get the job, make the money. Easy.

Baxter had seemed like the right place to make his mark. Until it wasn't and he had to reform it in the image he wanted. He had never expected the collateral damage, and that it kept growing to include Hope and Charlie just made Tony want out faster.

"That woman you picked caused that problem," Charlie pointed out. "She went looking for Mark. Practically jumped out of bed and went on the hunt the next morning. I had to think quick, and that meant hiding the bodies."

It all came down to Hope Algier. Tony thought putting his executives in a novice's hands would mean a smooth-running plan with an easy scapegoat. She wasn't watching and someone got hurt. It had happened to her before, so people would believe history repeated itself. She would be busy finding her way and getting used to the job while Charlie went to work.

The exact opposite had happened.

But that didn't explain everything. "Even so, you left Perry alive."

"That was a miscalculation."

Two men were dead and Charlie viewed it as a math error. Tony started to wonder if Charlie was more sociopath than loner.

Treading carefully was the only answer. Tony bit back the frustration whipping through him and did just that. "You need to back off."

"I want my money."

Tony waited until a group walked past. They were a good thirty feet away, but he wasn't taking chances, regardless of how low they spoke. "We can't move money around right now."

Charlie groaned as he pushed off from the truck and stood up. "We made promises to each other, Tony."

"And I will fulfill mine." Tony had perfected the art of lying. Wearing a blank expression while delivering a sentence devoid of any bit of truth. All those years turning companies around, swearing he was there to help and then recommending a full-scale reduction in force, had hardened him, but the skills came in handy now.

"I'm in it for the cash."

"Go back to the camp—"

"You're not in charge here." Charlie slammed a hand on Tony's chest and kept him from walking away.

Tony stared down at the hand and dirty fingernails, then back to Charlie's face. Tony didn't aim for neutral this time. He wanted Charlie to know his disdain, to feel his hatred. "This is my plan."

"It stopped being your plan when you sent Hope Algier out there for me to handle."

When Tony saw a couple headed their way, he shoved Charlie's hand away from him. "She should have panicked, called for helped and all of this would have been fine."

"She's an expert with connected friends."

The other thorn. Between Hope, Joel and Connor, Tony had his hands full. He couldn't decide if the answer was to remove the problems or ignore them. Not feed the beast. Charlie didn't need to know about the conflict.

"I'll take care of the Corcoran Team." Tony meant that as a vow. He didn't know how he'd do it, but he would.

"You keep saying that, but I don't see any evidence of you resolving anything."

They continued to talk at a near whisper as the couple turned and crossed the street. No one looked their way, but people walked by on the other side of the street. That was too close for Tony.

He pivoted until his back leaned against a freeway post and faced away from the street. "The timing is wrong."

"Not for me." Charlie reached into his open truck window.

The move had Tony shifting to inch his hand closer to his gun. "I have to settle my business issues first."

Charlie pulled out a new pack of cigarettes as his gaze slipped to Tony's hands, then to his suit jacket pocket. "I don't care about those."

"Listen—"

"No, you listen." Charlie tapped the end of the pack against Tony's tie. "You have one day to get my money. Then I take care of a loose end and leave."

"What loose end?" There had been enough death as far as Tony was concerned. They already had too many facts to cover and too much evidence to hide.

Then there was the bigger problem. Charlie had proved his lack of skills. Two times and Tony might be able to evade trouble. He could cover up and create backstories. A third was pushing their luck. If he moved into the spotlight one more time, Connor would never let this go.

"Hope Algier."

And touching her all but guaranteed trouble. Rafe would bury anyone who messed with his daughter. Charlie had already warned Tony that she was sleeping with Joel and the guy had a severe protective streak.

No, she had to be off limits. "She is too connected."

"She can die like anyone else."

"You don't understand." Tony leaned in and pitched his voice low. "This team, what you said about Joel and his relationship to this woman...you have to let this go."

"No."

Tony's back teeth slammed together as he stood up straight again. "Charlie, we've got to be smart about this."

"I agree. Get smart."

"What does that mean?"

Charlie unwrapped the cigarette pack and dropped

the plastic enclosure on the ground. "Get my money and then get out of my way."

"I don't want Connor and his team on my tail."

Charlie opened the door to his truck. "Then do what you're told."

"BINGO." JOEL LEANED back in the leather conference room chair and rubbed the back of his neck.

"Want to clue the rest of us in?" Cam stopped just before taking a sip from a water bottle.

Joel glanced at Connor at the head of the table and Hope beside him. "Line of credit."

Hope smiled. "I love when you just say random words."

It only took a few hours and numerous calls by Connor to obtain information he shouldn't have been able to nail down. He excelled at convincing powerful and connected people to turn over personal information in the name of protection. In law enforcement, at utilities, it didn't matter.

Joel didn't know how, but Connor had the private numbers of officials and a direct line to government agencies. With Joel's tech help, the whole team had access to databases with firewalls no one should be able to breach. But they did.

As a result, financial documents, phone records, every credit card statement imaginable and even electric bills— seven years of Charlie's life—were spread out on the table in front of them. "Charlie had two mortgages on the camp, right?"

"Both of which are overdue." Connor leaned back in his chair. "There's no hope of salvaging the place absent a big payday. It's possible it hasn't happened yet."

"He also has another line of credit. One he carries at

an astronomical rate. At first it looks like a credit card and I don't see any loan documents to support it, but he just paid it in full." Joel passed the document showing the paid-off line of credit to Hope, who read it before slipping it to Connor.

"He made the payment three weeks ago." She shifted the bank documents in front of her. "There's no record of money going through his bank accounts, personal or business."

"It had to come from somewhere," Cam said.

"I'll put Davis on this." Connor glanced at his watch. "He should be back at the office by now."

"He better be." Cam snorted. "He left hours ago."

Connor shot Cam a you've-got-to-be-kidding look. "I assume he stopped by to see Lara before heading to the office."

Joel understood the temptation. For almost a month after he left Hope, he'd still drive to her house, thinking to check in. The habit almost broke his will.

The one time he saw her coming home, he'd sat in his car for hours and waged a mental battle about whether to get up and knock on the door. After the need tore him apart he decided going in and out of her life was worse than leaving. But he'd blown that theory over the past few days.

"So how does any of this help?" Hope pointed to the almost negligible balance on the older man's business checking account. "He still can't keep the campground with this income. He can't charge enough to cover insurance and operating costs."

Cam scoffed. "Having two deaths out there isn't going to help business."

"Maybe we caught him at the beginning of a new

career." Joel didn't know if he should be happy about that or not.

A shiver shook her. "Killing for hire? That's a horrible thought."

"Now we have a way to apply pressure." Joel slipped a hand under the table and linked his fingers through her cold ones. He tried to absorb the chill and the trembling.

Her other hand covered their linked ones. "If he killed Mark and Perry, don't we want to turn him over to the police?"

"We want Tony Prather to go down, too," Connor said in a soft voice.

"It makes sense he's involved. I'm not sure I'd bet my life on it yet, but it's more logical than Perry starting that fire." She made a grumbling noise. "I talked with Charlie several times and never suspected."

"Neither did we," Cam said.

Joel had to choke back the fury clogging his throat. He'd had the guy right there, right next to him out in the woods, and didn't pounce. He didn't know whether Perry could have been saved there at the end because he was in bad shape thanks to the injury and exposure, but Joel would have tried. It looked like Charlie had stolen that chance.

"We're paid to notice." But it was the *what could have happened* that had fury twisting in Joel's gut. "The bigger issue is how he put you in danger."

She tightened her hold on him. "Why would he want me dead?"

"I think you were a pawn." Connor delivered the news like he did everything else—straightforward and calm. "He underestimated you."

Cam clasped his hands behind his head as he chuckled. "I'm thinking people tend to do that."

Not Joel. He knew better. And he didn't find any of this funny. "Tony's going to pay for all of this."

"Again, you mean if he's involved," she said.

Joel had moved on to plotting the guy's takedown. "Uh-huh."

"Sounds like we have a plan." Connor picked up his cell. "Then let's get to work."

Chapter Fifteen

Exhaustion threatened to drop her by the time she got back to her town house that night. Her father insisted he see her before she headed home. Then his connection got delayed and they settled for looking at each other through a computer screen while he sat in an airport lounge somewhere. He ended the conversation by vowing to never travel halfway around the world and hours from an airport again.

She hadn't even found time to unpack from the campground. Her duffel bags and bow case, along with the arrows inside, sat on the floor right next to the front door. She needed to move them or she was sure to trip. If only she had the arm strength to lift more than a bottle of water at this point.

Before she could get from the foyer to the kitchen to get one, Joel wrapped his arms around her and pulled her body tight against his. "You okay?"

"A little shaky." Not that she needed to tell him. He must feel her shivering.

Ever since learning about Mark and seeing the evidence for murder pile up, her head had been spinning. So much danger and pain. The idea that money caused it all made her switch between wanting to double over and needing to hit something.

Not that she'd never experienced heartache or loss, but she'd been luckier than most in life when it came to the essentials. She got that. Her father had money and never withheld it or affection. She never worried about having food or shelter or being loved.

Joel missed all of those things and still she didn't know a better man. He didn't think the world owed him. He didn't try to gather all the "things" or believe only money mattered.

Now if she could just get him to understand loving her meant being there for her. Always.

He kissed the side of her neck. "You're tensing up."

"It's been a rough day."

"Hey." He turned her around until his lips hovered over hers and her body slid against his. "It's going to be okay. We'll get Tony and Charlie, if they're the ones behind this."

The poor guy thought the camp and all the horror there caused her reaction. It surely contributed to where her mind had gone. Confronted with so much death, she wanted to grab on to life and not let go.

But the sadness stealing over her came from him. From not knowing if there would ever be a "them" again.

She played with the second button from the top of his long-sleeve shirt, opening it and slipping it back through the small hole again. "We need to talk."

"No good conversation ever started that way." His smile faded as fast as it came. "Wait, you're serious?"

She couldn't be this close and hold her ground. She needed space for this conversation. Heck, she hadn't even planned to have this discussion now. But coming back and having all of her emotions back up on her drove her.

She pulled away and stepped back a few feet. "What are we doing?"

He frowned and his gaze traveled up and down her body, as if he couldn't understand what was happening. Maybe that was part of the problem.

"I think we should get some sleep." He paused after each word.

She recognized the tone. He knew something was coming and mentally prepared for the hit. Usually at this point, he shut down. He suggested sex or talked about needing a walk. Dodged and ran, his well-practiced M.O.

Suddenly she had to know the answer to the question that had plagued her from the moment he stepped off that helicopter—would this time be different?

Having him pull away wasn't a game she could keep playing. He left and she'd waited for him to come to her. Now he was here, likely because her father begged him or, worse, paid him.

"Joel, come on." She was surprised at the strength in her voice.

"Please don't do this." All the color left his face. "Not now."

"When then? Two months from now when you come back for the third time? Next year when you stroll back in for the fourth?" The words sliced through her. She could see the cycle repeated forever. Didn't even have to close her eyes to envision it because she's already lived through the first round.

He wiped a hand through his hair as he spun around and headed for the family room. He started to sit on the couch but stopped and paced instead.

His movements wild and his usual control fading, he turned to her. "Can't we just let this be it for now?"

The question pounded her. She didn't even know how her heart kept beating. "I don't even know what 'this' is."

His hands clenched at his sides. "I missed you."

The longing in his voice tugged at her, but she would not go to him. Too many times this argument ended with her giving in. Not this time. "I know."

"I love you."

"I know that, too." That was what made this so hard. He wasn't a jerk. He wasn't afraid to tell her what he felt. Maybe it would be easier not to know because being this close and not being able to push their relationship across the finish line destroyed her. "I love you, too."

"My life…" He closed his eyes right as a cloud of pain crossed his face. He dropped onto the couch with his elbows balanced on his knees. "I live with danger. Hell, I need danger."

"You protect people."

"You can phrase it however you want, but the bottom line is I thrive on the adrenaline. I'm not a sit-on-the-couch-for-days guy." He stared at the ceiling. "You know this."

"I know your past doesn't matter to me and your personality doesn't scare me." Not even a little.

She saw the man he was, all they could be together. If anything, knowing he survived such hardships, overcame so much, to become so decent and loving made him even more special.

His head dropped and went into his palms, but he stayed silent. Debating how to give comfort without getting sucked in, she slid in next to him and lowered his hand. A few seconds ticked by before he looked over at her.

"I know you're not your father." She brushed her lips over his hair. "You are nothing like him."

Joel trapped her hand between both of hers. "Yet."

"Ever."

He slipped his fingers through hers and held on tight. "I get antsy. Staying still makes me jumpy."

"Do you want to date other women?" She had to swallow several times to keep the ball of anxiety from racing up her throat.

"What?" He made a face as if he'd tasted something truly awful. "No, of course not. This isn't and has never been about needing other women. I only need you."

The wonderful things he said made the inevitable end so much more staggering. "Then explain it to me."

"It's like this wild thing inside me. I went to DIA, a job I thought I'd love, and got restless. I worked for your dad and left."

The lump in her throat refused to move. "You left me."

He lifted her hand and kissed the back. "I've hated every second without you."

The conversation kept spinning and she had no idea how to make it land. She went with the question that circled in her head. "Do you plan to leave Corcoran?"

"No." Fast and sure, he didn't even hesitate.

That wasn't a surprise to her. Watching his easy manner with Cam and Davis, seeing how Connor led, it all convinced her Joel had found a home with the team. He'd found friends. Even if he denied it, he'd found normal.

He might talk about being a loner or an outcast, but they accepted him and he didn't show any signs of bolting. Whatever it was that made him twitchy when he thought about a forever relationship with her was silenced when it came to work. A certain calm washed over him.

She was happy for him to have found a home of sorts, but jealous it wasn't with her. "Do you want to end this—whatever it is—with me so you can find something else? Maybe something better?"

"There's nothing better." He shifted, getting even closer to her. "You have to believe that."

She wanted to. "Oh, Joel."

"It's not a line."

"I know." She trailed the back of her fingers over his cheek. "That's the point. You are with the one woman who understands you."

"It's not that easy."

She tried one last time to make him understand how evenly matched they were, despite their very different backgrounds. "I love having a home base but crave the outdoors. Life isn't about comforts for me. It's about nature and hiking."

"And climbing."

If she wanted him to face a demon, she needed to stare one down, too. "Yes, that."

"Will you try it again?"

Right now she'd say anything to get through to him, but she didn't want to lie. The deaths on the mountain that day had stayed with her. The ones at the campground probably would too. So much responsibility and so much failure.

With him she could get through it. He just had to jump first. "Will you stay with me?"

"Your need to be outside and the anxiety that gnaws at me are not the same thing. Your love is healthy. Mine grew out of a strange sickness handed down from my father."

"But you're a grown-up now."

"I get that."

"Then the only other explanation for your behavior, your decisions, is you're a coward." Not in life and at work, but he was when it came to her.

He dropped her hand. "Excuse me?"

He didn't move but she felt the chill as sure as if he'd doused her with ice water and walked away. To keep from grabbing him back or begging him to listen, she got up. The couch was too small and the room was too close.

In the past few minutes the walls had pressed in. This place, her sanctuary, fell over her like a cage.

She knew the word would prick at him. Strike at all he believed about himself. That's why she'd used it. He needed a wake-up call. If this was their last chance, and she was pretty sure from the ache around her heart it was, she intended to use every weapon to win the battle.

Her breath escaped in hard pants as she struggled to find the right words. "You have a woman standing in front of you who loves you. Loves all that you are and believes in who you've become."

He stood in front of her. "Hope, look—"

With a raised hand from her, he stopped talking. "We love each other. We certainly don't have any problems in the bedroom."

"Definitely not."

"Yet you push me away." The memory of every word, every excuse, hit with the force of a hard slap. "What can that be but cowardice?"

His jaw tightened. "Let's find a new word."

"I'd prefer if we found a new way to do this."

"Meaning?"

She took the final step and walked right off the emotional cliff. "You have to go."

"You mean for tonight?" His eyes narrowed as if he never dreamed she would draw the line.

She had to own that. Somehow, in some way, she gave him the impression he could always crawl back.

To be fair, that was their unspoken deal. She told him she'd be there while he figured out what he needed. He told her to move on. The final words hanging between them from last time strangled them now.

"If you can't get your act together, forever." She rubbed her hands over her bare arms, but her skin refused to warm up. "I can't do this. I can't love you and wait, which is exactly what I've been doing."

"Your father said you were dating." His chest rose and fell in hard breaths.

Tension snapped between them and choked most of the air out of the room. When she looked at him she saw a mix of anger and resignation in his dark eyes. His mouth stayed in a flat line and every muscle stilled.

She didn't know if the final warning or the idea of her with someone else put him in this place, but the loving man who wanted to go to sleep had disappeared. The hardened fighter remained.

"Those were fix-ups and dinners when I got tired of my father begging me to try." She wouldn't lie because that's not how she lived her life. This wasn't some silly game. "I don't know what he told you but I've barely kissed another man."

Joel's head shifted forward. "Barely?"

"I am here, Joel. I am yours forever. There is no one else and never will be if you reach out and take what I'm offering." Her fingernails dug into the skin on her arms as she threw down the final gauntlet. "But I'm done running after you."

He held out his hands. "What does that even mean?"

There was no way he couldn't know. She didn't engage in word games. "This time you have to come after me because I'm done being the only one trying to keep us together."

His hands dropped to his sides. "I never meant to hurt you."

"But you do. Every single time." Time after time, so many nights alone and desperate for him.

He winced.

She didn't back down.

Taking small steps, because that was all she could muster, she went to her front door. The knob felt heavy in her hand as she twisted. She would have thought she was trying to pull hundreds of pounds when she drew it open.

"Goodnight, Joel…and I'll hope it's not goodbye."

He didn't say a word as he walked past her into the dark night.

Chapter Sixteen

The next night, twenty-four hours after the love of his life had escorted him out of her house and his world exploded, Joel stood at the far end of a tree-lined road filled with mini-mansions and driveways loaded with expensive cars. They were tucked back in on a construction lot. The frame for a massive house loomed behind them, and a trash bin hid Connor's SUV.

In this neighborhood, parked cars and strange men walking around would be noticed. This was the kind of place where most houses had a live-in maid and the police on speed dial. No soliciting and certainly no gawkers.

They couldn't see Tony's house from this position, but it sat around the corner. As Joel would expect, Tony had bought the house at the end of the cul-de-sac on a double lot. From the pictures, with the white columns and three stories, the sprawling place looked big enough to be a school.

Joel grabbed his Kevlar vest out of the backseat of the truck. Concentrating on the straps and his weapon, he tried to push Hope's face out of his head. The pale cheeks and sunken eyes filled with pain.

He had done that. He had put her there.

He'd seen her cry exactly twice in all their time together. Both times he caught a glimpse as he walked out the door, never intending to return. Both times, the dev-astated look rammed into his gut until he moved his hand and checked for blood.

The first time nearly killed him. He feared this time would finish the job.

He tried to focus on the task in front of them—Tony. Finishing this off was the last thing Joel could do for her. Guarantee her safety.

Then he had to walk away. No checking up. No com-ing back. No answering her father's calls. Any contact resulted in wounds and the bleeding didn't stop.

"Tell me again about the intel." When neither Cam nor Connor answered, Joel glanced up. The concern was right there on their faces. He hated that, too. "Well?"

Cam held his gun in front of him, but instead of a weapons check, he stared. "You okay?"

More like smashed in little pieces. "I just want to run through the plan one more time."

Connor shut the driver's side door of the truck. "We've had eyes on the house."

Because there were exactly three of them in town, Joel didn't know what that meant. "Who?"

"Davis and Ben rigged something from back at head-quarters using security cameras and I have no idea what else."

Joel did. He knew because he had created the program that snaked into private systems and everywhere else it shouldn't be. "Trade secrets."

Cam frowned. "What?"

"That's the name of my program. Ben's been helping me with the design and implementation." The guy's tech background proved helpful. He claimed to have limited knowledge, but combining their interests had created something with great promise in the field of surveillance.

"That's likely it then." Connor took out his cell and showed them a photo of the house one last time. With another swipe of his finger, he brought up the schematics and blueprints they'd all memorized, complete with a security system overlay. "Charlie came in about a half hour ago. The security system has been off since."

"He went in through the front door?" That struck Joel as something partners might do. Seemed they finally connected the dots on who had set the whole camp scene up and why.

"Only after making a lot of racket," Cam said.

Connor shook his head. "Tony might have had some concern he was coming because the wife left hours ago and hasn't been back. I'm guessing he sent her away."

Two men. A big house. Corcoran in control of the security system. Joel liked the odds and, because he hadn't liked a damn thing all day, it was a relief to stumble into some good news now. "What's the plan?"

Connor leaned against the truck's hood as his gaze toured Joel's face. Whatever Connor saw made him scowl. "What happened yesterday that has you snapping and stewing?"

No way could Joel handle this now. He doubted he could handle it a year from now. "Nothing."

Connor didn't let it go. "We need your head in this."

"It is." Joel vowed to close off his feelings and concentrate on the task at hand.

He knew all too well how to block his emotions. He'd call on those long-ago learned skills and drag them out now. Maybe they'd finally be good for something other than destroying his life.

Cam exhaled. "Hope—"

"Is not a topic I'm going to discuss." Shutting the conversation down, not mentioning her name, was the only way to get through this.

Cam and Connor exchanged glances, but Cam was the one to speak up. "I guess we have our answer."

With a click Connor set his gun down on the hood. "We can stand down and—"

"I want this guy. Both of them." This much he could do. Joel would not leave until the job was done. Then he could slink back to Annapolis and figure out how to regroup. "It's the only way I'll know she's safe."

"Then you'll leave her again." Cam's eyebrows lifted in question. "Right? That's what you're saying."

"Last time." Connor put a hand on Joel's shoulder. "Are you in a place to help us? Cam and I can go in and Davis can book it up here. At this time of night it won't take long to drive back from Annapolis. We can go back to the hotel and—"

"I'm fine."

Cam scoffed. "Yeah, you sound it."

"How about if I punch you? Will that prove it?" Yeah, knowing Cam's reputation Joel would regret it later. But blowing off some of the energy pinging around inside him would feel good at the moment.

"Go ahead. If that's what it takes for you to get your head out of—"

Connor held up a hand. "Okay."

"Are we going to talk or move?" Joel asked, hoping to get the conversation back on work and out of his private life.

Connor's eyes narrowed as he assessed Joel again. "We're heading in."

"Happy that's resolved," Davis's voice boomed over the mics they all wore. Tiny silver discs in their ears that kept them connected. They called it the comm. "For now."

Joel remembered the entire conversation and swore under his breath. "How long have you been on the line?"

"We all are—me, Pax and Ben—and as the three members with women, we'll talk to you about your idiocy later. Maybe let Cam knock some sense into you," Davis warned.

And they would. Joel planned to dodge that meeting. "Lucky me."

Connor picked up his gun. "Move out."

HOPE HAD GOTTEN as far as her couch. She thought about taking a shower. Dreamed about crawling into bed and not coming out for months. Instead, she slouched down on the couch and curled into a ball.

That's what you did when your world crashed down around you and scattered into a million unfixable shards. You cowered.

She curled tighter into a ball with her feet tucked underneath her as she berated the choices she'd made tonight. This time she had no one to blame but herself. She could have played the whole scene better. Waited until morning, after they had gotten some sleep and some distance from all that had happened.

She could have doled her concerns out in short bursts to Joel instead of laying it all on the line. So many decisions and all of them seemed wrong in hindsight.

The goal was to force Joel to step out of the blackness that surrounded him and into reality. Talk about a miserable failure.

For someone who insisted she didn't play games, she certainly had done so tonight. She'd given him an ultimatum, something she vowed never to do again.

After so much death she thought he'd choose a life with her. At least fight back and insist they find a way, or that he have some time. But, no. He fell back on the old excuses and insecurities.

Her head dropped against the couch cushion and she snuggled in deeper. Her gaze fixed on a point above the fireplace. Not a photo or anything concrete. Just a spot.

She sat unmoving for what felt like hours. Her muscles ached and her head pounded from the crying. Her cheeks were dry now because she had nothing left. Not even the energy to get up.

Just as her eyes closed, she heard a gentle tap at the door. Her head shot up and she tried to remember if she'd set the alarm when Joel left…Joel.

The idea of seeing him, of him coming back, had her up and sprinting.

Somewhere at the back of her head, a bell clanged. All those lectures from her father about being careful. Joel's insistence that her place be outfitted with the best security system on the market. The warnings jumbled together as she hit the foyer.

The green light blinked on the alarm, meaning she'd typed in the code at some point and turned it off. She pressed a hand against the door and went up on tiptoes to peek out.

The wood caught her in the forehead. A slam and a crack followed by a blinding pain and spots floating in front of her eyes.

Her body reeled back and her socks slid on the polished hardwood floor. She threw out her arms to catch her balance, but the move only made her more tipsy. The room spun and darkness closed in at the edges of her vision. She had to shake her head to clear out the ringing.

When she heard the soft click, she looked up. Charlie stepped inside and closed the door behind him.

He smiled. "You need better locks, but thank you for making my job easier and turning off the fancy alarm. That I couldn't break. Well, not without some serious help."

His presence was so out of context. She didn't know what time it was or what was going on. "What are you doing here?"

He grabbed her arm and dug his fingers into her skin until she felt the bite and sting of his pinch and let out a soft gasp. She struggled to pull away, but he tightened his hold and started twisting.

"Good evening, Hope." He dragged her in closer until his breath brushed over her cheek. "You and I are going to have a little talk."

The rattling in her brain stopped long enough for her to blink out the cobwebs. "You're supposed to be back at the campsite helping the police."

"I'm done with law enforcement."

Of course he was. That's what happened with criminals and she had no doubt that's exactly what he was.

The truth washed over her. "You're Tony's partner in all of this."

"Was." Charlie smiled. "Now I'm your nightmare."

Chapter Seventeen

They entered Tony's house through the back gate as planned. Waiting to hear the distinctive click before going forward, Joel stood with his fingers wrapped around the handle. Once the noise came, he twisted and they slipped through the entrance usually reserved for gardeners.

Crouching, they jogged in the planned formation with Connor in the lead and Cam and Joel falling into a triangle behind him. Each one wore protective gear and blended in with the trees and darkness. Their shoes tapped against a patio as they moved by the building the plans referenced as a pool house.

Joel glanced up and locked on the motion sensor light by a hammock. When it failed to switch on, he knew Davis was working the controls from Annapolis like the expert he was. He heard what they heard and saw what they did through small cameras implanted in their helmets.

Joel often sat in that chair and orchestrated from a distance. Even though it reduced the chance of taking a bullet, the task was much harder than it looked.

Lights shone along the whole back of the house. A wall of windows stretched across most of the bottom floor. Joel could see every stick of expensive furniture and a kitchen usually reserved for magazine spreads. He silently wondered if Tony ever ventured into it.

The one thing Joel didn't see was people, no one on any floor, though the top one stayed eerily dark.

Connor motioned for them to peel off and take their positions. He took the middle area and headed for the double doors off what looked like a dining room. Cam went left toward the garages and Joel took the right, aiming for a side door that led to something called a mud room. He assumed that meant a laundry or closet or something. Davis, who was knee-deep in renovating an old house, had tried to fill Joel in but he didn't listen to the particulars.

Pivoting around the outside furniture on the back patio and what looked like a heater, Joel hugged the hedge line. He skated away from the area just outside the doors, preferring the staggering darkness. Let Connor figure out how to stay unseen with spotlights hitting his head.

The darkness of night bothered others, but Joel had trained to let his other senses run wild. Even now the smell of orange hit him, likely from flowers or a tree.

Slipping around the house took Joel out of the line of sight of the others. He could no longer see what they were doing or assess their progress. But because Davis hadn't reported a problem over the comm, Joel assumed there wasn't one.

The door was right where the plans said it would be. He reached up and turned the knob. It rattled in his hand but didn't budge. The sound bounced around the quiet night and Joel pressed his back against the wall, ready for an attack from any direction.

Wincing, he waited for a shrill alarm to sound. None came. He counted that as a win and let out the rough breath he was holding.

The rule was radio silence. That meant limited talking and almost no communication back to headquarters unless an emergency arose. Headquarters could talk all they wanted, right into your ear, but Davis was a pro. He knew that broke concentration and he stayed silent.

His breathing filled the line. Then a voice, no louder than the breath that came before, sounded over the line. "Open."

Joel reached up again and this time it turned. He held up the prearranged "go" signal in front of the helmet cam.

Keeping the opening as small as possible so as not to gain attention, he slid inside. The side of the door scraped his back but he ignored the slice.

Balancing on his haunches, he listened for any sound. This was a big house and the men could be anywhere. Good news was Davis reported only two people in the house, or such was the case a half hour ago when they did their check. They'd been watching ever since and no one else had come.

Music or talking would help guide him, but Joel didn't pick up anything. He heard the soft hum of the refrigerator and the usual creak now and then that all houses let out. Nothing that sounded like arguing or negotiating. Unfortunately. Looked like Tony was going to be unhelpful to the end.

Standing taller, Joel walked past the washers—two of them, because that seemed necessary for two people. He waited at the door and when he failed to pick up footsteps or any other sliver of movement or noise, he crossed into the next room.

This time he heard a sound. A thumping, loud and steady. It came from the area above his head. To sink through the floor and radiate through the house, it had to be pretty obvious upstairs.

Shifting around the long marble counter, he grabbed a small knife out of the collection in the block. Never hurt to have an extra weapon. The size, easy to tuck into the edge of his glove, gave him one more advantage. Or so he hoped.

In front of him loomed several doorways. He could see into a large room with a television. He closed his eyes and thought about the plans. He needed to go deeper into the house and find Tony's home office. If that didn't work, Joel would head for the stairwell.

But the thumping kept grabbing his attention. With a brief look around, he skipped the downstairs check and headed for the bottom of the stairs. Cam met him there. He pointed up and Joel knew they shared the same idea.

The double height of the entry let them study a wide area, but not every angle. The steps curved, so the top landing wasn't fully visible. Someone could be hiding, but Joel bet not.

Tony sat at a desk all day. He didn't plan attacks. The one he had tried to handle ended up with two men dead and too many questions. Joel doubted that went as hoped.

Careful to stay to the side and not to hit a creaky spot, they trailed each other up the stairs. Joel took the lead and kept his attention above them. The responsibility for scanning the area below and calling out about danger fell to Cam. Joel couldn't think of another man he trusted more with his back. Cam spent most of his time traveling, but they stayed in touch. The trip to the woods had only cemented their trust.

A huge chandelier hung over their heads, and the stair railing shone like it had been polished for days without stopping. There was one benefit to such an over-the-top house. Everything had a place. There wasn't any clutter and the plush carpet silenced their steps.

Nothing moved as they climbed, but the steady thumping grew louder as they reached the top. Though he tried, he couldn't place it. Not a weapon or any machine he recognized.

At the top, Joel stopped for a second to get his bearings. The master bedroom consisted of nearly a thousand square feet, more than the size of his last apartment, and sat to his right. He turned the corner and headed there. Cam followed right behind.

The door at the end of the hallway was open. Joel could make out something scattered all over the floor. Clothes, maybe. Papers, certainly. He knew there was a large sitting area in there in addition to the bedroom and bathroom.

He and Cam took positions on either side of the wide hall and stalked with their backs against the walls and their guns aimed in that doorway. Joel caught Cam's attention and glanced down at the floor. Cam looked, then shrugged. Whatever was going on in there stumped both of them.

The floorboard under Cam's feet creaked and the thumping cut off. That meant the end to their covert advance. One more step and the boom of gunfire started.

Both Joel and Cam dropped down. Joel crawled on his elbows, shooting as he went. Cam took the higher position but still kept low.

They pushed forward, emptying their magazines as they went. Bullets flew and artwork crashed off the walls. Something made of glass exploded near Joel's head and he ducked to avoid the shards.

Plaster from the walls kicked up and curtains bounced and shredded. Joel could hear crashing and shattering as their bullets slammed into all the furniture in the bedroom.

A mix of dust and smoke swirled around them. He

sniffed for gas, because that seemed to be Charlie's specialty, but only smelled the sulfuric scent of gunfire.

A noise registered over all the banging. They stood just outside the doorway when Joel signaled for Cam to cease firing. It wasn't hard to make out the yelling now. Loud and male and near hysterical.

"No, stop!" The chant came from inside the room.

Joel didn't buy the surrender. He braced his body against the doorframe. "Come out."

"I can't." The thumping came in quick succession that time.

Cam asked what it was, but Joel didn't have a clue. "Why can't you walk out there?"

"I'm down."

Cam shook his head. Joel didn't believe it either, but a standoff in a shredded hallway wasn't his idea of a smart use of time. Not when they only heard one voice and there should be two.

"It's Tony Prather." Davis had voice recognition software on his side and a pretty good memory. If he said this was their guy, Joel believed him.

"Where's Charlie?"

"Gone."

A soft thud, almost hidden, sounded behind them. Cam spun around but dropped the weapon again when Connor's head popped up at the top of the stairwell.

"Who's in there?" he asked.

Joel repeated what he knew. "Tony."

Connor stepped around the worst of the debris, but small piles crunched under his feet. "I was in the office when I heard the shots."

"Help me." Tony's plea sounded softer and breathy that time.

Joel started inside but Connor held him back. "Tony, this is Connor Bowen. Where is Charlie?"

"He left." Tony's voice filled with panic. He groaned and something fell.

Connor looked to Joel, then Cam. "Believe him?"

"No," Cam shot back.

Connor nodded. "Let's go in and get him."

All three walked into the room with Connor in the lead. Broken furniture and clothes littered the floor. Papers and dust were everywhere. It looked as if someone had taken a wrecking ball to the place. Not a simple glass anything remained intact. Gunfire had shredded the comforter and curtains.

Joel recognized some of this as their work. But not all. Someone else needed to take credit for the opened drawers and the empty bag on the bed.

One thing was missing—Tony.

Filing in, they opened doors to massive closets and a room with boxes in it that Joel couldn't even identify. If it was a closet, it was a big one. To the right, Joel spied shoes. He snapped his fingers to get his teammates' attention. They all stopped and aimed.

"Come out, Tony," Connor said in a stern voice. "This is over."

"Can't." The guy practically cried now.

Joel recognized the tone as one of defeat and pain. He motioned them forward. The sight that greeted him would stay in his head for a long while. Tony slumped on the floor with blood soaking his shirt.

He balanced against the sink cabinet with his legs in front of him and his hands limp at his sides. It looked like someone had taken a knife to him and enjoyed it too much.

Tony's head lolled to the side. Joel followed the line of

his body to his foot. He jammed his heel against the door to another closet and it slammed against an inside wall.

A phone sat a few feet from his foot and just out of reach. Joel could only assume Tony was trying to reach it and kept moving his foot when the rest of his body failed him.

Connor squatted down in front of the seriously injured man and took his pulse. The guy's eyes were open but glassy. He was fading, and they had minutes only. Even then Joel doubted help could get there in time.

Connor glanced up at Cam. "Call for medical."

"Is anyone else here?" Joel thought about the report of his wife leaving and hoped they got that right.

Tony shook his head but didn't talk.

Cam talked low in the background and Connor went to work trying to stem the flow of blood from Tony's chest. Dropping to his knees, Joel took up the position on Tony's other side. He grabbed a towel off the counter and pressed it against the man's stomach. It stained with red almost immediately.

Tony's eyes closed on a hiccup of breath. Joel worried they'd lost him.

"Hope."

Joel leaned in. "What did you say?"

His heart clunked and Connor's hands froze.

Tony's head drifted farther to one side. "He wants her dead."

Joel grabbed the man's shirt in his fists to shake him awake again. This was about Hope and he didn't care what he had to do to hear the message. "This isn't the time for your bullshit."

Tony panted and his chest jumped up and down as he forced out words. "Charlie thinks she ruined everything."

Panic flooded through Joel as he sank back on his

heels. He couldn't think. Couldn't breathe. He'd spent so much time walking danger away from her and here she was, alone with a nutcase on her tail.

"I'll call and warn her," Cam said.

Joel's entire world froze. He could hear Cam speaking and Davis saying something over the comm, but the sounds muffled and mixed until nothing made any sense. It was as if someone had fired a gun right next to his ear and taken out his hearing.

Joel looked at his boss. "Connor?"

"Take Cam." Connor held out his hand and Cam dropped the phone in it. "I'll wait for the ambulance."

A question finally pushed into Joel's brain. "Did you reach Hope?"

Cam shook his head.

"He's going to kill her." Tony panted through the words but his eyes closed. His body became boneless as his hand fell open at his side. "I want him to fail."

HOPE FORCED HER mind to stop racing. She needed to stay calm. A madman stood in her home and her alarm system was off. Joel wouldn't be rushing in to help her. She didn't even know if he was still in town.

That left only a few options, the main one being to scream her head off.

Something flashed and a cold hardness pressed against her throat. A knife. "Don't try to be a hero, Hope. We've all had enough of that from you."

"I didn't—" She inhaled as the blade broke skin.

"One sound and I will cut you. Deep this time, whether I slice you or throw it at you. Do you understand?"

"What do you want with me?" Her voice wavered, but she had to keep him talking while she thought of a new plan. The front door was the best candidate.

"You ruined everything."

Charlie being here made no sense. He should be running. "I was just doing my job."

He shoved her against the couch and she fell deep into the cushions. Before she could bounce up again, he sat on the coffee table across from her. A second later he held her wrist in his grasp with the knife hovering right there.

He tapped the flat side against her skin. "Mark was supposed to disappear, but you had to go looking."

"Yes." She tried to pull away, but Charlie only tightened his hold.

"I told you Mark was blowing off steam and to let it go." Charlie shook his head and treated her to an annoying hum. "You never listen."

"But you killed him."

"That was the deal." He waved the knife in front of her face this time. Back and forth. "Pay off the mortgages and in return I helped Tony with a little problem."

"Mark was a human being, not a problem. And Perry. Was he just an afterthought?"

Charlie made a face as he stood up. "So many questions from the spoiled little rich girl, but I'm not going to play along. I'm not one of the men you have wrapped around your finger, like your daddy and Joel."

She watched Charlie move around her apartment, touching photographs and stopping at the front door to hit the lock button. The system chirped and the red light came on.

As if that would stop her if she had a clear shot to the outside. She would run and scream and he would have to track her down. She would go out fighting.

But she might be able to entice him with something he needed. "I have money."

"That's why this will look like a burglary turned rage-filled attack turned fire." He walked into the kitchen and grabbed a towel. "You die and I take some items and cash."

She bolted for the exit. He was on top of her before her hand hit the knob.

He smashed her into the door hard enough for it to shake on its hinges. Then he grabbed her around the waist and threw her. Her legs went out from under her. She put out her hands to stop her fall but landed in a sprawl on the foyer floor by his feet.

Her elbow hit the hardwood with a crack. Every part of her ached and her head throbbed. She didn't even remember it slamming into the floor, but it must have.

"That's enough of that." He crouched down in front of her. "Want to know what happens next, Hope, the expert hiker and climber?"

"Joel will be here any minute."

Charlie laughed at her. "I was outside and saw him go. He left you. Looked pretty happy to be gone, if you want to know the truth."

"That's not—"

"Ran to his car to get away from you instead of staying the night. What guy does that?"

She pushed that hurt out of her mind and concentrated on survival. Joel would want her to kick and bite and do whatever she had to do to survive. "He will come back."

"Not tonight. He's busy with Tony."

A new horror spilled over her. More bodies. More death. "What did you do?"

"My partner got greedy. Now he's dead." Charlie took the lighter out of his pocket and lit the kitchen towel. The fire swallowed one end in a second. "The trail leads to me returning to camp. Joel will go there, only to get the call there's been an accident."

Fear swelled inside her. She'd battled back flames at the campsite and it had taken all of her strength. Seeing even this small fire twisted her stomach in knots. "You didn't do so well with that before."

"This time it's foolproof. You die and the town house burns down." He stood up and threw the burning rag on the couch. The cushion lit with fire almost instantly. "I think Joel will get the message, don't you? He may have stopped one fire, but he'll be too late for this one. See, I made sure to be on the security cameras at Tony's house. I slipped out the side, but he'll think I'm still there, and in a house the size of Tony's without help, Joel will be there for a while."

The fire crackled and she heard a whoosh. She knew she had mere minutes. And Charlie would want her dead before the fire took hold and raced through her house. "You'll never get away with this."

"If I wanted to stick around, you're right. But see, I have the money Tony planned to hide and now I can leave. Let the banks have the campground. I don't care."

"Just go." The new attack made no sense. He was free. He could run.

"I've decided you need to be taught a lesson first." He stepped away from the fire.

She didn't hesitate. Crawling on her hands and knees, she headed for the bow case. She'd never get off a shot, but her arrows were clipped inside and the pointed end could cause some damage. The hard thumps rattled through her and jarred her from head to foot as she went.

Her hand had just hit the case when Charlie's foot appeared in front of her face. He stepped on her hand and she screamed.

"I warned you." He used a scolding voice.

It only emboldened her. Finding energy she didn't

know she had, she made a fist and punched the fleshy part right above his knee straight on and with all her might. It buckled and he doubled over, almost going down. The move took his weight off her hand and she made another lunge.

Smoke billowed around her and fire raced up the walls in long lines. She ignored it all and reached for the latch. She fumbled but got it open just as something stabbed into her hip. The sharp pain had her flinching, but she fought on.

Throwing the lid open, she ripped an arrow from the lid and spun around. Charlie crawled up next to her thigh with his knife raised. His chest shook from coughing, but all she saw was the madness in his eyes.

She had one shot and she took it. Gripping the arrow, she stabbed it right into his shoulder as hard as she could. He screamed and the knife fell to the floor. She thought about searching for it, but the thick smoke clouded her vision.

She looked up. The door loomed in the distance. She thought she'd fallen near it, but it wavered and blurred in front of her.

She tried to crawl, but her strength abandoned her and she crumpled to the floor.

Somewhere over her she heard a crack. The noise sounded familiar. She remembered it from the cabin and feared the ceiling was caving in.

Then a rush of warm air poured in and swept over her. She heard her name. In her cloudy head, she thought the voice sounded like Joel's. She tried to call out, but her throat refused to work.

As the world went hazy, strong arms slipped under her. Fearing she'd slipped into a dream, she forced her eyes open and saw a line of flames headed her way.

But there was someone else in her dream. She lifted her hand, expecting to touch air.

Her fingertips hit warm skin. Reality punched through her.

Blinking, she forced her vision to settle and touched the face swimming in front of her. "Joel?"

"I'm right here, baby." His voice sounded harsh and faster than usual. But he sounded real, like he was actually there.

"It was Charlie." An illusion or not, he needed Joel to know. The desperation to get the words out broke free.

Then she was floating. Her feet had almost left the floor when a hand clamped over her ankle and tugged her back.

The jolt revived her. Joel held her. They were in danger.

She looked down the length of her body and saw Charlie's furious face. She turned to warn Joel about the knife, but she saw Joel's gun.

He tucked her head against his shirt and brought her body in close to his. The roar of the shot broke through the thunder of the fire. It boomed in her ears and she rushed to cover them.

After one sharp crack, all pressure was gone from her legs and Joel stumbled back. Freefalling, she tried to get a sense of where the flames were and realized they raged all around them.

She heard people talking and the wail of her alarm before she smelled fresh air. When her back hit the grass, she believed she'd finally slipped into that welcoming dream. Before she could settle in, the coughing started. She turned her head and hacked as the scent of fresh grass filled her head.

After a few minutes she lay back down. She tried to

gulp in breaths of fresh air as the realization hit her—
she was alive. Which meant...

Joel's face hovered in front of her. "You're going to
be fine," he said.

She thought she heard Cam and a neighbor. Sirens
screamed in the distance and all around her. None of it
made sense. It was so dark and she'd lost track of time.
"What's happening?"

"You're safe."

She saw it all now. She sat cradled in Joel's arms as
people rushed around them and Cam repeated something
to Joel, something she couldn't understand. For some reason she needed to tell him one more thing.

She grabbed on to Joel's shirt and tugged him closer.
"I love you."

Then the world went black.

Chapter Eighteen

Joel would never forget that moment. The SUV had screeched to a halt in front of her place and the whole first floor was aglow with orange flames. He searched the crowd that had gathered, looking for her and shoving people aside without thinking.

When he didn't see her, he rushed to the door. Cam grabbed his arm and told him to calm down, but Joel was desperate. Filled with panic, he kicked and the door slammed open then the alarm went off.

The gun. The knife. The blood. It was all so much to take in.

The sound of her voice as she'd told him she loved him was playing in his head now. Even as he sat by her bedside at the hospital and the loudspeaker squawked, he remembered her final vow of love.

The smell of disinfectant slammed into him. At least the dragging numbness had worn off. He rubbed his thumb over the back of her hand and stared at the crisp white sheet pulled up to her chest.

He'd come so close to losing her. If any one thing had gone wrong he would have lost her. The traffic had worked for them thanks to some stoplight maneuvering by Davis. Cam drove fast enough. The door gave on the first kick.

Knowing about Charlie's wound, Joel also knew she'd saved herself. That was his woman. Strong, confident and fierce. The only bad news was the guy would live.

Tony wasn't so lucky. Charlie had unleashed on his former partner, leaving him no chance for survival. Remembering the state he was in, Joel thought it was probably a miracle he had made it until they had found him.

Cam stuck his head in the doorway. "Is she awake?"

"Not yet." Joel took in Cam's ripped and bloody clothing and wondered why someone hadn't taken one look at him and called the police.

Of course, they were crawling around but Connor handled them, as always. Cam looked as if he'd been dragged by a truck. Joel guessed he looked even worse himself.

"Where's Connor," he asked.

"Still talking with Hope's dad."

Talk about taking one for the team. The older man had yelled at Joel via cell phone during the entire ambulance ride to the hospital. He promised revenge if Joel didn't get his act together and treat his baby girl better.

Joel didn't blame the guy. He'd done a pretty lousy job of protecting her. The one thing he excelled at was leaving, and tonight doing so had almost cost her life.

He didn't know what kind of husband he would be. Hell, he wasn't sure he even ranked that high on the boyfriend scale, but he wasn't letting her go. Not again. He'd had a glimpse of life without her and he'd rather be selfish and hold her tight.

"At least he's back in town," Joel said, remembering the worry in her dad's voice.

"He's not happy about any of this."

Joel looked at her still form and a new wave of anger crashed over him. "That makes two of us."

The nurse came in wearing an official badge and drag-

ging a tray behind her. The only way for her to get by
Connor just outside the door was to be pre-approved by
Corcoran.

More than one doctor commented on the overabun-
dance of caution. It was nothing compared to the contin-
gent of police assigned to watch over Charlie one floor
down.

The nurse nudged him away from Hope's side. "I need
to check her bandages."

He held his ground. "I'll stay."

"You should step outside." The woman was five-feet-
nothing and she stared him down like she would take
him out.

He thought about arguing until he saw the smile on
Cam's face and conceded. "Fine."

Joel waited until they stepped into the hallway to tell
Cam what he should have said hours ago. "Thank you."

He brushed a square of what looked like part of a
curtain off his upper arm. It could have come from anywhere since they'd been fighting all night. "For what?"

"Everything." Joel didn't even know how to put his
gratitude into words. "I know you were supposed to be
on vacation."

"Fighting fires is more interesting." Cam clapped Joel
on the shoulder and nodded. From Cam, that was a huge
show of emotion. "Besides, I was going to fly anyway."

It was the way he said it that had Joel questioning.
"Where?"

Cam glanced at their boss where he passed back and
forth a few feet away in front of the nurse's station. "That
was up to Connor. He asked me to take him to Jana."

Now, there was news. "What?"

"He stayed to help you instead."

"Because I recognize a man in love." Connor stepped up and stared Joel down. "Do you?"

The conversation left Joel speechless. Connor back together with Jana, or trying to be. Davis and Lara. They gave him hope.

Cam groaned. "Don't do it, man."

Lost in his thoughts, Joel lost track of the conversation. "What?"

"Don't give a list of excuses why it won't work with Hope."

Before Joel could answer, Connor launched into a speech. "One thing you might want to remember is that not being with her in this case made her vulnerable."

"Okay, but—"

"I'm not saying that to make you feel guilty, because this wasn't your fault, but being away from her didn't make her safer." Connor wound down long enough to exhale. "You're not your dad."

"I know." For the first time, Joel believed it. Unlike his father, he fought for other people. He believed in people. He possessed a sense of humanity.

Hope had told him so many times. Having a woman like her love him should have clued him in. She wouldn't waste her time on a dangerous loser. He got it now.

"No, you don't, but if you give that woman a chance she'll show you." Connor's comment came out almost as an order. "Be half as smart as I think you are."

Cam nodded. "Or her father will kill you."

"It doesn't matter what he thinks." It really didn't. It was great to have his support and his blessing, though right now he was pretty displeased, but Joel didn't need her father's opinion. He had Hope and she believed in him, even when he didn't believe. That meant more than anything else.

"Joel, come on."

He held up his hands. It was either that or listen to these two try for the next two hours to convince him of something he already knew. "I'm saying that because I already know living without her isn't an option."

Cam threw up his hands. "There, was that so hard?"

"Actually, I think the hard part is ahead of him," Connor said.

Cam barked out a laugh. "I hope she makes you beg."

HOPE SLOWLY AWAKENED. She saw the white ceiling and heard the beep of machines. She closed her eyes and mouthed a little thank you. She wasn't dead.

A deep male laugh had her turning her head. One she recognized and savored whenever she heard it. Joel sat in the chair next to her bed looking all rumpled and scruffy and far too delicious.

When their eyes met, he stood up and came to the side of the bed. Bending down, he slipped an arm over the top of her head. "No, you're not dead."

"You wouldn't let that happen."

"Never." His fingers danced across her skin. "But we should really thank your quick thinking."

That's not how she remembered it. "You pulled me out of the fire."

The memory played in her head. She'd thought it was some weird dream, but it wasn't. His strong hands and words of encouragement. The firm grip and the gunshot. Her ears still rang from that, and a high-pitched ringing sounded as if in the distance. She knew from experience on the shooting range that that would eventually go away.

His fingers slipped into her hair. "You saved yourself. I was just there for the ending."

The word cut through her. She closed her eyes to beat

back the pain as a new series of memories hit. Him leaving and her crumpled in a ball on the couch.

"Hey." His thumb rubbed over her forehead. "It's okay. Charlie can't hurt you now."

He had the wrong nightmare, but she opened her eyes anyway. "Is he dead?"

"No."

In a way, the news was a relief. She wasn't responsible for killing the man, and this one would've been on her. No accident. She'd stabbed him and had meant to… and would do it again.

But the idea of him being out there and alive in society made her stomach twist. "Did you catch him?"

"Pretty easy to do after you hobbled him."

She smiled at that. "I'm not sorry."

"Me either. I just wish I'd been there a minute or two sooner."

She wished he'd never left. Now that the thought was in her head, she wouldn't think about anything else.

"Are you leaving?" The question burned her throat, but she forced it out.

Looking into those eyes, all soft and sweet as he stared at her, broke her resolve. She wanted to take back everything she'd said to him at the house and call him back to her on whatever terms he wanted. The expression was the very definition of love. She had no idea how this man could continue to bring so much pain.

"No."

The word clashed with her thoughts. "What?"

"I've walked out on you twice." He leaned down and placed a small kiss on her nose, then pressed one against her lips. "I'm so sorry I hurt you."

Tears pushed at the back of her eyes. She refused to let them fall.

"You break my heart." She had told him so many times how much she loved him. This time she wanted him to understand how much pain he inflicted.

"Never again."

She tried to move her head, and the bed flipped around on her. Apparently she had a head injury. At some point she would have to take stock of all the bumps and bruises and figure out why her hip ached so much.

Then she'd deal with her town house and not having a place to live. Right now the combination of it all was too much to handle.

Especially when she was trying to grab hold of this conversation. "What are you saying?"

He snuggled in closer, careful not to jostle her or move the pillow. His face rested right above hers, and those dark eyes were as clear as she had ever seen them.

"My father wouldn't have put aside his own needs and tried to rescue you." Joel kissed her on the mouth, short and quick. "He wouldn't love a strong woman like you." This time the kiss lingered and heated. "He wouldn't work for a place like the Corcoran Team. I am not him, nor will I ever be."

Her heart jumped. It was as if she nodded off to sleep and woke up to him spouting the things she'd been telling him forever.

But he wasn't spitting the words back. He believed. She could feel the confidence radiate off him.

"The fire convinced you?" If so, she might set up a permanent bonfire in the middle of her kitchen. On second thought…

"You did." He smiled at her. One of those sexy smiles that had her toes curling. "You wouldn't love a man not worth loving."

Her fingers slid through his. "Exactly."

"You certainly wouldn't stick around waiting for him to wake up."

Just like that, all the pain fell away. The loneliness and anger evaporated and the gut-wrenching fear vanished.

The strength in his voice and his unwavering eye contact would have convinced her if the kisses hadn't. He wasn't playing a role and nursing her through an injury or, if she guessed right, injuries. This was a man with staying power. The man she'd been hoping to see forever.

She raised their hands and kissed the back of his. "It's as if you read my mind."

"I love you more than anything." His eyes grew serious. "I would walk away from my job, from civilization for you. Ask me for anything and I'll give it to you."

Right about now that sounded fine with her. All the death and danger rang in her head. She'd leave that behind in a second if it meant a lifetime with him.

"Hell, I'd move to a suburb for you." He scowled as he said it.

She believed it and burst out laughing. The vibration moving through her had her grabbing her side when a shot of pain hit her. "Now, that's love."

He frowned as he reached for the nurse's call button. "You okay?"

Hope stopped him with a touch of her hand. "I am now."

"Don't doubt my feelings for you. Ever." He nuzzled her cheek. "Those have never wavered. Even when I lost my way and my mind, I loved you."

From this man, it was a vow that meant everything. "I know. It's part of what gave me hope that we could work through it."

"There's been no one else since the day I met you."

He buried his mouth in her neck. "There won't be anyone else ever."

This time she let the tear fall. It ran down the side of her face.

When it rolled onto him, his head popped up. He caught the second one with his thumb before it hit her cheek. "What's this?"

"Happiness."

He toyed with her fingers, touching each one. "I know I've failed you in the past."

Rather than hold back, she went for it all. "I want a future."

A huge smile lit up his face. "That I can make happen as soon as you get out of this bed."

"I mean—"

"As soon as I convince you I'm staying, because I am, I'll propose. We'll do it right. Your father will eventually forgive me and give his blessing."

"Joel." His name came out as a breath. She'd say yes right now, and so would her dad, but she sensed Joel needed to do it his way.

He wanted to prove something to her. She already believed, but she certainly had no trouble with the idea of being wooed.

But they did have a more practical problem. "I think I need a new house."

She didn't think about all she'd lost. Those were things. Today she'd gained so much more.

"I was hoping you'd look for one with me. In Annapolis." He was handing her everything yet he sat there looking sheepish.

"A future marriage proposal. A new town. A man I love with a new attitude." She slipped her arms around his neck and planted a long kiss on his mouth. One that said something about her intentions once she got out of this bed. "A woman couldn't ask for more."

"Actually, I have two favors."

His eyes sparkled as he said it, so she didn't worry. "Uh-huh."

He finally sat down on the bed next to her. The mattress dipped and he rubbed a hand over her stomach, making her forget about any pain. "Just for a while…"

The man was drawing this out and making her crazy. "Yes?"

"No camping and no fires."

She laughed. "Deal."

* * * * *

Luke stepped in front of her, holding his finger to his lips again to tell her to be quiet.

She flung her arms around his waist and gave him a tight hug before stepping back. The look of surprise on his face had her feeling foolish. But then he pulled her close and hugged her, and leaned down with his lips pressed close to her ear.

"Glad you're okay, too, but you should have stayed upstairs in the closet. Or better yet," he whispered, "you should have gotten out of here and hid in the woods."

She shook her head and pulled back. "I'm not leaving you here alone. So you'd better figure out a way to include me in your plans."

His brows lowered. "You promised."

"I know, and I'm sorry. But it wasn't a promise I should have given."

THE BODYGUARD

BY
LENA DIAZ

Published in Great Britain 2014
by Mills & Boon, an imprint of Harlequin (UK) Limited,
Eton House, 18-24 Paradise Road, Richmond, Surrey, TW9 1SR

© 2014 Lena Diaz

ISBN: 978 0 263 91359 0

46-0514

Harlequin (UK) Limited's policy is to use papers that are natural, renewable and recyclable products and made from wood grown in sustainable forests. The logging and manufacturing processes conform to the legal environmental regulations of the country of origin.

Printed and bound in Spain
by Blackprint CPI, Barcelona

Lena Diaz was born in Kentucky and has also lived in California, Louisiana and Florida, where she now resides with her husband and two children. Before becoming a romantic suspense author, she was a computer programmer. A former Romance Writers of America Golden Heart® finalist, she has won a prestigious Daphne du Maurier Award for excellence in mystery and suspense. She loves to watch action movies, garden and hike in the beautiful Tennessee Smoky Mountains. To get the latest news about Lena, please visit her website, www.lenadiaz.com.

I dedicate this book to abused women everywhere. It's not your fault. It's NEVER your fault that someone else chooses to hurt you. You deserve a life without fear. Please, don't wait until it's too late. For information or help, visit The National Domestic Violence Hotline at www.thehotline.org. (The website has a quick escape option in case your abuser monitors your internet activity). Or call 1-800-799-SAFE(7233) or TTY 1-800-787-3224.

Chapter One

The monster sat across the breakfast table from Caroline, looking deceptively handsome in a dove-gray, thousand-dollar suit that emphasized his broad shoulders and the bulging muscles in his upper arms. The tanned hand that flicked the page on his electronic tablet was elegant, strong, with perfectly groomed nails.

They should have been talons.

Talons would have warned people who didn't know Richard Ashton III that those hands were lethal, especially when they were clasped into fists.

He skimmed through the latest stock-market figures, then looked pointedly at the untouched food on Caroline's plate.

In spite of the worry that had kept her awake most of the night, the worry that had nausea churning in her stomach this morning, she picked up her fork and took a bite of egg the cook had prepared exactly to Richard's specifications. She dabbed her napkin on the corners of her mouth as he'd taught her, before training her face into the carefully blank expression she'd learned was the safest.

His brows lowered. "You're getting too thin, Caroline. That displeases me."

She stilled, her fingers curling against her thigh.

"I—I—I'm sorry, Richard."

Calm down. He hates it when you stutter.

She fought back the fear that so often jumbled her words. "I'll eat everything on my plate. I promise." She took another bite of egg.

Tiny lines of disapproval tightened around his eyes.

Her stomach twisted. What had she done? She raced through a mental checklist. Her hair was neat and curled to drape over one shoulder in the style he preferred. She'd painstakingly applied the makeup he'd selected for her, natural looking but polished. She held her napkin in her left hand in her lap, her fork in her right, no elbows on the table. What had she missed?

"Don't look so alarmed," he chided her. He cocked his head, his eyes narrowing. "Or have you done something that requires further instruction?"

"No, no, no, I've been good. I don't…n-need another l-lesson."

Stop it. Calm down.

"Don't stutter, Caroline. It's unbecoming of an Ashton to stutter. Tell me, why aren't you eating enough?"

Her hands went clammy with sweat and shook so badly she almost dropped her fork. Desperation had her scooping another forkful of eggs into her mouth. As she chewed, she smiled across the table at him, trying to placate him.

He shook his head. "You're being rude. I asked you a question, and now your mouth is full. You're making me wait for an answer."

Stupid, stupid, stupid. She should have answered him first and then taken a bite. She swallowed hard, forcing the lump of eggs down her tight throat without taking the time to chew.

"I'm so sorry," she rushed to assure him. "I didn't

mean to be rude. I w-wanted you to be proud that I was obeying, that I was eating." She wiped her moist hands on her pants.

"I'm still waiting for an answer."

She blinked. What was the question? What *was* it? She couldn't remember. He'd said something about her being too thin, and then he'd said—

"I asked why you aren't eating enough." His voice was clipped, harsh.

"I'm s-sorry. I guess I'm just…tired. Not hungry."

One of his elegant brows arched. "And why, *exactly,* are you tired?"

She grasped for an excuse, anything but the truth—that she'd lain awake most of the night, going over her plans, trying to build her courage.

"I—I don't know. Perhaps I worked too hard in the garden yesterday. I *am* a bit sore."

The slight reddening of his face had the blood draining from hers, leaving her cold and full of dread. He would take her comment about being sore as an accusation against him, a complaint. Because, as he frequently reminded her, it was always *her* fault when he was forced to teach her a lesson, *her* fault he had to punish her.

"You've worked in the garden plenty of times without being sore." His voice lashed out at her like a whip. "I'm more inclined to believe you're complaining that you forced me to teach you a lesson yesterday."

She dropped her gaze, her pulse slamming in her ears. A whimper bubbled up inside her, but she couldn't let it escape. Crying was undignified. Ashtons did *not* cry.

"Look at me when I'm speaking to you," he demanded.

"Please," she whispered, trying to appeal to the man he *used* to be, the man that must surely still be there, somewhere, hidden deep inside, the man she'd loved once, so very long ago. "Please, Richard. It was a…poor choice of words. I'm sorry."

He plopped his napkin on the table and stood. "Yes, it certainly was, a very poor choice." He stalked to her chair.

She shrank back and hated herself for it.

The cook walked into the dining room, smiling a greeting at Richard, ignoring Caroline, as she'd been ordered to do. As they'd *all* been ordered to do. The staff knew Richard was the perfect, loving husband saddled with an unbalanced wife who made his life miserable—a wife who was to be ignored, for her own safety, lest she get too worked up. A wife who must never be allowed to leave the estate without her husband, except for her once-a-week errands, which were carefully timed and reported upon so Richard could immediately come to her aid if she became confused. Only Richard knew how to handle her, how to take care of her, how to keep her calm, or so they all believed.

At times like this, Caroline almost believed the lies herself. After all, she had to be insane to have stayed with the devil as long as she had.

"Mr. Ashton, good morning to you. Can I get you anything else, sir?" the cook asked.

His face smoothed out and he returned her smile. "Yes. Please let Charles know I'll be leaving a bit later than planned." He circled his fingers around Caroline's wrists and pulled her to her feet, smiling the entire time. "Have him bring the car around front in exactly one hour. Mrs. Ashton and I would like to…talk."

He added a wink that had the cook blushing and assuming exactly what he wanted her to assume—that he was a loving husband intent on loving his wife.

"Very good, sir." She hurried out of the room.

Richard's grip on Caroline's wrists turned crushingly brutal.

She gasped and tried to pull her hands back. "Please, you're hurting me."

He immediately let go, frowning at the red marks he'd left. "Later, you will change into long sleeves. I won't have someone misinterpreting anything they might see. Now, come along. Apparently yesterday's lesson was insufficient."

He put his hand on the small of her back. She tottered on shaking legs toward the winding marble staircase in the two-story foyer.

She could endure this. She could get through this. She could survive this.

Those three sentences went through her mind over and over, like a prayer, giving her the strength to climb the stairs with her husband at her side, towering over her, like a prison guard leading an inmate to the death chamber.

At the first landing, he caught her shoulders, turned her around and kissed her. She was so stunned she forgot to pretend to respond. He broke the kiss and pressed his lips close to her ear.

"Close your eyes, Caroline. Kiss me back."

She saw the reason then for his pretend affection. A maid had entered the foyer below. This was part of Richard's game, making others believe he was devoted to her. Appearances were everything to an Ashton.

His lips touched hers again. When the hard ridge of his erection pressed against her belly, she shuddered with revulsion. His arms tightened painfully around her bruised side where he'd kicked her last night. She fervently hoped he'd taken her shudder for passion instead of disgust, or her lesson would be more severe than usual.

He led her to the master bedroom at the end of the hall.

As he closed the thick, soundproof double doors behind them, she reminded herself again that she'd endured his lessons many times. She could survive one more. She had to. Because after today, she would be free. After today, she would never see Richard Ashton III again.

He yanked her long hair, jerking her backward, twisting her neck at an impossible angle. She sucked in a sharp breath, loathing and despair boiling up inside her. His eyes darkened with the anticipation she'd grown to dread, even as he shook his head like a teacher bitterly disappointed with his star pupil.

She knew what he would say next, the same thing he said every time he "instructed" her, the same thing he would tell her when he plunged into her bruised and battered body to slake the lust that always consumed him after giving her a lesson.

"I love you, Caroline. I do this *because* I love you." The disappointment in his voice might have been convincing if it weren't for the anticipation that had his mouth curving into a feral smile.

His eyes narrowed when she didn't rush to say what she was supposed to say.

Perhaps it was the knowledge that this was the last time she'd ever have to endure his touch that made her brave. She glared at him, refusing to give him the words he wanted.

He grabbed her upper arms, his fingers digging into her with bruising force.

The pressure made her cry out. Unwelcome tears pricked the backs of her eyes. "Please, stop."

"Say it!" His fingers dug harder, like the talons she'd pictured earlier.

Her vision blurred.

"I love you," she choked out, despising him all the

more for the coward he'd forced her to become. But she would say the empty, meaningless words a thousand times if it would stop the blinding pain. "I love you, I love you, I love—"

"And?" He shook her, snapping her teeth together, making her bite the inside of her cheek. The metallic taste of blood filled her mouth.

"I—I'm...s-sorry."

He abruptly let her go. She staggered back. A wave of dizziness sent her wobbling to the nearest piece of furniture in the expansive room, the four-poster bed. She clung to one of the thick posts. The pain that lanced through her upper arms made her cry out again.

His nostrils flared. He stalked toward her, shedding his clothes as he approached, his arousal stiff and heavy, an unyielding sword to wield against her. She cringed against the bed as the monster's perfect hand coiled into a fist.

Chapter Two

Another wave of nausea hit Caroline. She clutched the edge of the receptionist's desk and drew in deep breaths, fighting the dizziness that had plagued her since she'd dragged her aching body out of bed this morning. Richard's "lesson" yesterday had delayed her plans by a full day. But nothing would stop her this time. She'd just have to fight through the pain.

"Mrs. Ashton, are you okay?" The receptionist hurried around the desk, her youthful face mirroring concern.

"She's fine." Leslie Harrison, the Harrison part of the law firm of Wiley & Harrison, admonished the other woman. "I'll escort Mrs. Ashton to her car."

"Yes, ma'am." The receptionist resumed her seat, aiming a resentful look at her boss's back.

"Leslie, I'm actually not feeling all that well. Perhaps I should sit down for a moment."

"Come along, Caroline. You'll feel better when you get out of this stuffy office into the fresh air." She leaned in close. "It's just nerves." Her voice was low so no one else would hear as she escorted Caroline outside the busy lobby. "You're taking a huge step today. Besides, you don't have a minute to waste if you're going to get to the new house before your husband discovers you're missing."

Caroline gave her a shaky smile. "I'm sorry. You've gone to a lot of trouble to help me. I don't mean to sound ungrateful." She clicked her key fob and unlocked the black Mercedes S600 sedan Richard had chosen for her. Not for the first time, she wished he would allow her to drive something simpler, less pretentious.

Leslie held the car door open. "No worries, dear. I'm happy to help. Remember, go straight to the new house. No stops along the way. Promise me."

"I promise."

Leslie smiled and stepped back as Caroline eased into the driver's seat.

A few miles down the road, another wave of dizziness hit. A sharp cramp shot through her belly. She yanked the wheel, pulling to the shoulder of the road amid a flurry of honking horns as other drivers swerved to avoid her.

Sweat popped out on her forehead in spite of the cold air blasting out of the air-conditioning vents. She tried to sit as still as she could, willing the dizziness and pain away. Being sore the morning after one of Richard's lessons wasn't unusual. But for some reason it was so much worse today. It must be nerves, as Leslie had said. She'd been plotting her escape for months. And now that she was actually going through with her plan, the stress was making her sick.

She worried her bottom lip with her teeth and clutched her cramping belly. Richard's extra lesson had almost ruined everything, making it physically impossible for her to do her Wednesday chores. But this morning it was Richard who insisted that she couldn't be lazy two days in a row. He'd ordered her to get out of bed to take care of the errands she'd skipped yesterday. Her eagerness to do his bidding had pleased him. What he didn't realize was that he'd given her a gift by ordering her to go.

After breakfast she'd stood at the door and waved goodbye to her husband for the last time while Charles pulled the Rolls-Royce around the circular driveway. Richard closely watched her through the rolled-down window in the backseat. His suspicious gaze had her clutching the doorway, worried she'd done something to give away her plans. But the car hadn't stopped, and Richard continued down the road toward his office.

Careful not to do anything that might trigger a call from the household staff to her husband, she'd stuck to her usual weekly itinerary of going to the dry cleaner's and then to the lawyer's office. The difference this time was that instead of dropping off her clothes with Richard's at the cleaner's, she'd only dropped off Richard's. She kept the small bag of her clothes and toiletries she'd carefully packed to begin her new life. Using the dry-cleaning trip as her excuse, she'd been able to carry her bag out of the house without tipping off the security guards that something was different.

After the cleaner's, she drove to the lawyer's office to deliver the accordion of tax receipts and documents to Leslie and to supposedly collect any papers Richard needed to review or sign. Of course, this week, there would be no return trip to give him anything. She wasn't going back.

Since he could have ordered any number of people to perform both chores every week, Caroline assumed her errands were some kind of test. So she'd always been careful to go straight to the cleaner's, then straight to the lawyer, then straight home.

The clock in the dashboard had her hands tightening on the steering wheel. Leslie had warned her not to make any stops. She didn't have time to sit on the side of the highway, no matter how much she hurt. In exactly twelve minutes, the security detail would notify her husband she wasn't home. Richard would call Leslie and ask when Caroline had left. Once he realized she hadn't gone straight home, he'd leave the office and go searching for her.

She lifted a shaky hand to her brow. Dear Lord, what was she doing? What had made her think she could escape? She debated turning around and racing back home. But even if she managed not to get pulled over for speeding, she'd never make it in time. How would she explain being late?

If she told the truth, that she'd been sick and had pulled over, he probably wouldn't believe her. But even if he did, he'd accuse her of complaining again. It was her fault that she felt bad, and she shouldn't make him worry or have to come check on her just because she couldn't accept the consequences of her actions. He'd feel compelled to "instruct" her again.

She clenched her teeth. She was already one huge mass of bruises. Everything hurt. Endure another lesson? No, she couldn't, she just *couldn't.*

Protection. She needed protection. But who could protect her? She had no friends, no family—not in Savannah, anyway. And her parents wouldn't exactly be pleased to find out she'd left her wealthy husband. They'd be worried the monthly checks Richard sent them would stop.

Who else, then? Leslie was the only person she ever dared to speak to outside the house, unless she was with her husband at some function. And since her duty at those functions was to cling to his arm like a decoration and not leave his side, she never had the opportunity to foster any friendships.

But she couldn't ask Leslie to outright defy Richard by harboring her. Leslie's law practice depended on Ashton Enterprises' lucrative account. Jeopardizing Leslie's income wasn't fair, especially after everything the lawyer had already done to help her. No, she'd started down this path. She had to see it through. So, what, then? What *could* she do?

The idea of going to the police flitted through her mind but was quickly discarded. She'd seen the shows on TV. The cops couldn't do much until *after* a crime was committed, except maybe tell her to get a restraining order. And what was the use of a flimsy piece of paper against a man as rich and powerful as Richard Ashton III?

Not that a judge would believe her and give her a restraining order in the first place. Society worshipped and adored Richard. To them, he was a generous humanitarian who donated millions every year to charity and supported the campaigns of just about everyone holding office in Savannah right now, including the sheriff of Chatham County. No, going to the police wasn't an option.

Then how could she protect herself? Richard's idea of protection was a twenty-four-hour guard at the house. Maybe that was what she needed: her own guard, someone who would be loyal to *her* and only her.

She drew her hand across her damp brow and used her car's voice-command center to search the phone book for "bodyguards in Savannah, Georgia." She selected the first company that popped up in the search results and set the GPS to direct her there.

IF HER ROYAL HIGHNESS—Kate Middleton—had materialized in the offices of Dawson's Personal Security Services, it would have surprised Luke Dawson far less than the woman who'd just stepped through his door: Caroline

Ashton—beautiful, platinum blonde, wife of billionaire businessman Richard Ashton III.

Luke couldn't say what designers had made her tasteful silky tan skirt and matching blazer, or the tiny, shimmering handbag hanging off her shoulder. But he did know her clothes were expensive—and totally out of place in the cramped, dusty office that normally catered to hookers looking for protection from their pimps, or small-business owners needing protection when they got behind with their bookies.

Obviously, she was lost.

He glanced at the only other person in the room, his office manager, Mitch Brody, sitting a few feet away. Mitch shrugged, indicating he didn't know what was going on, either.

Luke waited for their guest to say something, but she simply stood in front of his desk as if she was waiting for permission to speak—probably some quirk of the superrich. He shoved his chair back and offered his hand to shake.

"I'm Luke Dawson. And that's Mitch Brody. What can Dawson's Personal Security Services do for you, Mrs. Ashton?"

Her blue eyes widened, providing a stark contrast to her pale complexion. Was she surprised he knew her name? Didn't she realize *everyone* in Savannah knew who the Ashtons were? The "perfect couple" was plastered on the front pages of the local gossip rags at least once a week, and their annual Christmas party was the event of the social season, rivaling the acclaim of the infamous parties held by Jim Williams back in his heyday. Or at least, that was what Luke had *heard*. His name would certainly never appear on the Ashtons' Christmas party's prestigious guest list.

She swayed slightly, as if caught in a daydream, before stretching her manicured hand out to shake his.

His hand practically swallowed hers, and he felt a shudder go through her. What the hell? She pulled her hand back, but not before he noticed something flash in her eyes, something he'd seen too many times in his line of work not to recognize it.

Fear.

Was it possible she was here on purpose, and that she needed help? That seemed so unlikely as to sound ludicrous, but Luke's internal radar sounded a warning. Rather than show her to the door as he'd been tempted to do the moment she'd walked in, he rounded his desk and picked up a stack of folders from the one guest chair he owned.

He frowned at the lint on the dark green fabric. Normally he wouldn't give it a second thought, but Caroline Ashton was far too sophisticated to sit on a dirty chair.

"Give me a minute and I'll find something to cover the seat."

"No, no, please. Don't go to any trouble on my behalf. This is fine."

She sat before he could stop her.

He raised a brow in surprise and leaned back against the edge of the desk, his legs stretched out in front of him as he waited for her to explain why she was here. But again, she seemed perfectly content not to say anything. She simply looked up at him with a polite, blank look. He wondered again at the foibles of the wealthy.

"Mrs. Ashton, how can we help you today?"

"I n-need t-to…" She squeezed her eyes shut for a moment as if she was in pain. "I need to hire a bodyguard."

Her nervousness had him studying her more closely.

"I figured you came in here by accident and needed directions."

Her thick lashes dipped down to her lap, as if keeping eye contact was too difficult.

"I'm not lost. I need protection."

Her words, and the desperate quality of her voice, had those alarms ringing in his head like church bells on Sunday. Still, he didn't want to offend her if he'd misunderstood—because surely a billionaire's wife didn't really need Luke's protection.

"Mrs. Ashton, it's no secret that your husband has a contract with Stellar Security, one of the best security firms in Georgia, one of my biggest competitors." He glanced at Mitch, who'd gone stone-faced as soon as Luke mentioned Mitch's former employer. Mitch hated Stellar Security, but since he'd never explained why, Luke could only go by his own personal dealings with the other firm.

"I wish I could tell you my company could do better," he continued, "but honestly, I don't have the resources the other firm has. I have five bodyguards, besides myself. Stellar has dozens. If someone's bothering you, I can call your husband's security guys and talk to them for you."

She shook her head, her eyes widening. "No, don't call them. They're the last people I would trust."

He frowned. "Why wouldn't you trust them? They work for you."

For the first time since coming into the office, she seemed to really focus on him. The blank look evaporated, replaced by a look of startling clarity and intelligence, as if she'd been playing a role earlier and she'd decided to drop all pretenses.

"No. They *don't* work for me. They work for my husband."

Few people surprised Luke Dawson anymore, but

Caroline Ashton had just given him a sucker punch. Was it possible she was afraid of her *husband?* If something… bad…was going on between them, Luke would have expected rumors in those gossip magazines. At the very least, he'd expect to hear something in the bars when he and his security friends bantered about their clients and the crazy things they sometimes did. But he'd never heard a whisper of anything bad about the Ashton couple. Not one.

He *had* heard the exact opposite, that Richard Ashton III was practically a saint, in spite of his wife being a bit…needy, to put it kindly. She was said to be nervous, high-strung, but her husband was the epitome of tenderness whenever they were seen together. He was always at her side, seeing to her every whim.

Luke studied her face. Her skin tone was even, her makeup accenting her natural beauty, not thick like women wore when trying to cover bruises. Long sleeves covered her arms—no clues there. But her legs, at least what he could see beneath her modest, below-the-knee skirt, were long and sleek, without the hint of a bump or a bruise. There was *nothing* about her appearance that made him think she had valid reasons to fear her husband.

With everything he'd heard about the Ashtons, he *should* believe she'd come here, like so many women before her, planning a divorce and hoping to use the "abuse excuse" to take her husband for everything he was worth. That would make sense, except for one thing.

The fear in her eyes is real. He'd bet his autographed Tom Glavine baseball on it.

Still, just in case he was wrong, he proceeded as he would with any other client, probing for the facts.

"Let me guess. You're getting a divorce, and you want a bodyguard until the divorce is final."

Her eyes widened again. "I haven't filed yet, but that's my intention, yes. I've rented a house outside of town. I'm on my way there now. I just need someone to stay with me until things are…settled."

That admission sent a flash of disappointment through him. Maybe he was wrong about the fear in her eyes. Maybe she *was* just like those other women, the ones who would tarnish their husbands' reputations with ugly lies so they could profit financially when their relationships went south.

"You need a bodyguard right now?"

"Yes."

He straightened away from the desk. Regardless of the kind of person she was, he couldn't afford to turn away a paying client. He had too many unpaying ones to allow that luxury and keep his business afloat.

As for going on assignment right now, that wasn't a problem. He kept a go-bag packed at all times with his clothes and extra ammunition. Since Luke needed to keep his hands free while guarding a client, Mitch would load the bag into the car while Luke escorted the client outside. Standard operating procedure, and so routine he didn't even need to remind Mitch, who had already jumped out of his chair and grabbed the go-bag. He stood waiting beside Luke's desk with the strap over his shoulder.

"We can leave right after you sign a contract and pay a retainer fee," Luke said. "Do you want to take your car or mine?"

Her cheeks flushed a light pink. "Mr. Dawson, I mean no disrespect, but you're a bit…small. Is there someone else you could assign to help me?"

He stared at her in stunned amazement. Mitch shook his head, obviously as confused as Luke was.

Luke crossed his arms over his chest. "Mrs. Ashton, in all my thirty years, no one else has ever called me small. I'm six foot three and weigh two hundred twenty pounds. I'm not bragging when I say most of that is muscle. It's just a fact, a necessity of my occupation. I was a champion boxer in high school and college. I'm extensively trained in self-defense. I carry a concealed weapon, am a crack shot and I know just about everything there is to know about guarding people. I assure you, I'm more than capable of protecting you."

She politely cleared her throat, not looking all that impressed with his speech. "Have you ever met my husband?"

"Not in person, no. But I've seen pictures of him." He leaned back against the desk again and braced his hands on the edge while he waited for her explanation.

"Richard is a very…large, strong, determined man. He can be…dangerous. He's extremely… If he were to… I just…" She let out a deep sigh. "I need to know that you would be safe if…*when*…he comes looking for me."

This time, there could be no doubt that the fear in her voice, in her expression, was real. It was palpable, a living, breathing thing, constricting around her, ready to choke her into submission.

She twisted her fingers together. The diamond ring glittering on her left hand sparkled beneath the fluorescent lights. The center stone had to be four carats, easy. It could have paid the rent on Luke's office *and* his house for a full year, with money left over.

But that wasn't why he decided he had to convince her to hire him.

He had to convince her to hire him because whether

the threat against her was real or imagined, she *believed* it was real. But even more important than that, he'd never met any clients before who were more concerned about their bodyguard's welfare than their own. A person like that deserved his protection, because he was one of the best. And regardless of who she was, she deserved something he sensed she hadn't had in a long time: someone who would look after her, someone to take her seriously, someone who would be her ally.

He waited until her haunted gaze lifted to his before answering.

"Mrs. Ashton, your husband may be a tad taller than me, possibly even brawnier. But fighting isn't all about size. It's about training, experience, strategy. I don't have the slightest doubt I can handle him in a fight…if it comes to that. The best strategy is to avoid a fight if at all possible. But if you hire me, I'll guard you with my life. I will do everything I can to keep you safe. And I'll make sure your husband never gets anywhere near you again. That's a promise. And I never, *ever* break a promise."

Unshed tears brightened her eyes, inexplicably making Luke want to pull her close and hold her until the fear subsided and the shadows in her eyes disappeared.

"Thank you," she whispered, her voice shaking with obvious relief, her throat working as if she was struggling not to cry. "Thank you so much."

Chapter Three

Caroline sat in her car in the circular driveway of the blue-and-white one-story cottage. She'd lived in a mansion for over five years. Before that, she'd lived with her parents about three hours from Savannah in the same house since the day she was born. But this plain, simple structure already felt like the home she'd never really had.

Because she wouldn't be sharing it with Richard.

A tap on her car window made her start. But it wasn't her husband's angry visage glaring at her through the glass. It was the concerned face of Luke Dawson, who'd hopped out of the car as soon as she'd parked. She'd apparently zoned out, lost in her memories, and her fears, and forgot about him. She pressed the button and lowered the window.

"Mrs. Ashton, we need to get inside. You're sitting out in the open here."

"Of course. I'm sorry. Should I pop the trunk for our luggage?"

"No…I'll get our bags after you're safely inside the house."

She rolled the window up and opened the door.

He reached for her hand. She hesitated, bracing herself not to jerk away when his much larger hand closed around hers. But when he touched her, to her surprise and relief, she didn't feel nausea or dread. Unlike her husband's touch, the warmth and strength in Luke's hand made her feel something she hadn't felt in years…safe.

She smiled up at him, but he was too busy scanning the yard and street out front to notice. As she stood, another sharp pain shot through her belly, making her wince. She was glad Luke hadn't seen that. It had been difficult enough to admit to a stranger that she was afraid of her own husband. It would be beyond humiliating for Luke to even suspect the extent of her cowardice over the years, to learn just how much she'd endured, all because she'd been too weak to stand up for herself.

A warm breeze filtered through the trees overhead, stirring his lightweight leather jacket. She'd wondered why he wore a jacket in the summer, but now she knew: to conceal the gun holstered on the hip pocket of his jeans. She'd never been this close to a gun before and had always assumed it would terrify her. But the sight of his weapon was actually reassuring. Richard might laugh at her puny attempts to deflect his blows, but even her husband wasn't immune to the ravages of a well-aimed bullet.

Luke stayed at her back as she walked the short distance to the front stoop, but as soon as she unlocked the door, he rushed her into the foyer and flipped the dead bolt behind them.

His mouth tightened into a thin line. "No security alarm?"

"Not yet. I only rented the house a little over a week ago." She rubbed her hands up and down her arms. "We've never had one at the mansion. Richard didn't like the inconvenience of having to worry about using a keypad if he decided to step outside at night."

"You didn't need one at the mansion because the estate

was gated and had security guards watching it 24/7. I'll get someone out here today to install one."

He gently pushed her aside as he opened the hall-closet door, apparently searching for intruders. Next, he glanced through the archway to their right into the family room, then back down the hallway to their left. "Stay here while I check the bedrooms."

He disappeared down the short hall. It took him less than a minute to search the two bedrooms and bath. Then he was back at her side in the foyer.

"I assume the kitchen is through the family room?" he asked.

"Yes, through that other archway." She didn't bother to add that this was her first time seeing the house in person. Leslie had handled everything for her: helping her find the house, arranging for the lease, getting the key. Caroline had only seen the house online and knew the layout from the virtual tour. There was never a chance for her to physically go to the house. Richard would never have let her out of his sight long enough for that.

Luke headed into the family room, which had a panoramic view of both the street out front and the fenced backyard. The long, narrow style of the house was one of the primary reasons Caroline had chosen it. When Richard eventually discovered where she was—and she didn't doubt that he would—she wanted to see him coming. And with both front- and rear-facing windows in most of the rooms, she'd always have an exit nearby so she could flee if she had to.

After looking behind the couch and the few other places big enough to hide someone, Luke continued into the kitchen.

A moment later, the sound of his deep voice carried to Caroline, in a one-sided conversation she couldn't quite make out. He must be talking to someone on the phone. Obviously there wasn't anything to worry about if he could take the time for that.

She wiped her brow, surprised to find it damp with perspiration. The inside of the house was nice and cool, both from the air conditioner and because of the majestic, Spanish moss–dripping oak trees that hung over the roof, shading it from the merciless summer sun.

Maybe she was catching a cold, or the flu. That would explain why she was achy all over, even in places where Richard hadn't hit her. She dropped her purse on one of the end tables that had come with the furnished cottage and headed toward the kitchen. When she stepped into the entryway, she froze.

On the far side of the room, Luke was talking to someone on his cell phone. But on the white tile floor at his feet, lying in a pool of blood, was Richard Ashton III.

The room began to spin. Richard had found her already. How? It was a trick. It had to be. Any second now he would jump up and point an accusing finger at her. Then he'd teach her another lesson. Her eyes widened as she stared at him. The blood. *No, no, no.* The blood was soaking into his favorite Italian suit—the suit he'd worn the day they met. He'd *kill* her if that suit was ruined.

She took a step toward him, then stopped. She started shaking. Someone called her name. Her world tilted. Everything went black.

LUKE SHOT AN aggravated glance at the balding Chatham County police officer sitting across from him in the E.R. waiting room. "I've already told you all this, Detective Cornell."

"Then tell me again. You said you've never met Mrs. Ashton before today?"

"That's right."

"What time did she arrive at your office?"

"About 9:10."

Cornell wrote something on the old-fashioned little spiral notebook he carried. "And she was in your office how long?"

"Ten minutes, give or take. She wanted to hire a bodyguard. She signed a boilerplate contract, gave me a retainer—"

"How much?"

"How much what?"

"How much was the retainer?"

Luke shook his head. He was never big on patience anyway, but answering the detective's relentless questions had destroyed what little patience he had.

"My standard fee for a full-time assignment, two thousand a week, plus expenses."

The detective whistled. "Sounds steep."

"You get what you pay for. Look, I want to check on Mrs. Ashton."

"There's no point in checking with the nurse again. Once a doctor has time to examine her, we'll be updated about why she fainted."

Luke laughed without humor. "She didn't just 'faint.' There's something wrong with her. I couldn't wake her up. And there were bruises on her wrists, bruises that looked like handprints. Do you know how hard someone would have to squeeze a woman's wrist to leave marks like that?"

"You think her husband hurt her?"

"Don't you?"

He shrugged. "You think she was justified in killing her husband?"

Luke stilled. "You don't seriously think she's the one who killed him."

"She's the wife. She's the first person I'll look at."

"Richard Ashton was already dead when we arrived at the house. And if she's the one who killed him, why would she hire a bodyguard?"

Detective Cornell slid his notepad and pen into his shirt pocket and sank back against the unyielding hard plastic chair as if it was the most comfortable of recliners. "Sounds like a good defense, something that might give the jurors reasonable doubt. Pretty smart, if you ask me."

"Do you know the time of death yet to see if she has an alibi?"

"No. And that's the main reason I haven't arrested her."

"That, and the fact that she's unconscious, I suppose." He couldn't help the sarcasm that crept into his tone.

Cornell smiled as if amused by Luke's statement. "Yep. There's that, too."

Luke stared at the exasperating police officer. Part of him thought the detective was latching on to the easiest explanation, but another part of him agreed with Cornell. If Caroline Ashton was abused, as Luke believed, she might have planned her revenge. She may have used Luke and his company as part of that plan so someone would be with her when she "discovered" her husband's body.

That possibility didn't sit well with him. But he'd signed a contract, and he'd given her his promise. He was duty-bound to protect her until the contract expired this time next week, or until she released him from that promise.

"There's another angle to consider," Luke said. "The killer's target may have been *Mrs.* Ashton. After all, it was her house. The killer could have been waiting there for her, but the husband showed up. The killer may have felt cornered, so he shot Mr. Ashton and ran off."

The detective pursed his mouth. "I won't dismiss that out of hand. But it's not high on my list of probable scenarios."

It wasn't high on Luke's, either, but he was trying to keep more of an open mind than the jaded policeman across from him.

"I've got to make a call." Luke shoved out of the hard, narrow chair he'd stuffed his body into for over two hours while waiting for a doctor to see Caroline Ashton.

He hurried outside the waiting area and turned his cell phone on. When Mitch answered his call, Luke didn't waste time on small talk. "Have you found out anything?"

"Sure did. I called a buddy of mine who works for Stellar Security. He said they keep a log of everyone going in and out of the Ashton mansion, right down to the minute. And Mr. Ashton keeps a GPS tracker on his wife's car. Can you believe that? I have a printout of every place she went this morning, with the exact times."

A GPS tracker sounded invasive, controlling, which made Luke's suspicions about abuse even stronger. Wouldn't it be ironic if Richard Ashton's attempt to keep a tether on his wife ended up proving her innocence? "Go ahead. Tell me."

"Mr. Ashton left the house at 7:55. His wife left fifteen minutes later. She drove directly to a dry-cleaning company and stayed there for ten minutes. After that, she drove across town to Wiley & Harrison, again without making any stops along the way, arriving at precisely 8:40."

"Wiley & Harrison, the law firm?"

"One and the same. Her visit at the law office lasted

twelve minutes. After that, she headed down Highway 80, pulled over and stopped for fourteen additional minutes."

"Any clue why?"

"You'll have to ask her that."

"Okay, then what."

"You know the rest. She drove straight to our office, arriving at 9:12, hired us, and you followed her to the cottage, arriving at 9:47. You placed the 911 call four minutes later."

Luke considered what Mitch had said. "I haven't been told an official time of death yet, but Richard Ashton's body was still warm when I checked for a pulse. From what you just told me, there's no way she had the opportunity to kill him."

"Doesn't look like it."

Some of the tension went out of him. It was only then that he realized how much he'd hoped Caroline Ashton was innocent. He was normally an excellent judge of character, a skill that helped immensely in his line of work. From the beginning, Caroline had seemed kind and caring, as evidenced by her concern about whether he might get hurt protecting her. She didn't strike him as the type of woman who could murder someone, even if they deserved it.

"Thanks, Mitch."

"You bet. You need me to follow up on anything else?"

"Not right now. Just keep the office going. I'll call you later."

He headed back into the waiting room. When he updated the detective about what he'd found out, disappointment flashed across the policeman's face.

As if noticing Luke's puzzlement, Cornell gave him a lopsided smile. "I'd hoped for a quick open-and-shut case. The coroner called while you were outside. He said the victim was killed within an hour of when the body was discovered. I already confirmed Mr. Ashton arrived at his office at 8:30 and left again at 8:45. His limo driver said he dropped Mr. Ashton off at the cottage, per his instructions, twenty minutes later. That would have been about the same time Mrs. Ashton arrived at your office. If everything you just told me checks out, she didn't have the opportunity to shoot her husband."

"His limo driver dropped him off? And left him there?"

"Apparently. I've got another detective interviewing the driver right now to find out more. I'm also sending someone over to your place of business to take a statement from this Mitch guy, the one you said can vouch that Mrs. Ashton was there this morning."

"Mr. Dawson?" a voice called out. "Detective Cornell?" A doctor stood in the entrance to the waiting room, looking around at the various groups of people. Luke and Cornell both rose. The doctor hurried to them and introduced himself.

"Is Mrs. Ashton okay?" Luke asked.

"I'm hopeful for a good outcome. She's in recovery now."

"'Hopeful'?" Luke said. "'Recovery'? You had to operate?"

"She was bleeding internally, from a ruptured spleen. If she hadn't gotten here when she did, she might not have made it."

"Do you know how she was injured?" Cornell asked.

Luke shook his head. The answer was as obvious as the bruises on Caroline's wrists.

The doctor's jaw tightened. "I've got a pretty good idea. Follow me."

He led them through the double doors and turned left

down a brightly lit hall, stopping at a door marked Recovery. Inside, he brought them down a row of curtained-off enclosures to the last one at the end. He pulled the green curtain back to reveal Caroline Ashton, asleep, looking pale, vulnerable, her small body lost in the middle of the hospital bed. An IV tube ran from the back of her right hand to a bag suspended on a pole. A blood-pressure cuff was wrapped around her other arm. The monitor behind the bed beeped and displayed numbers and graphs as it tracked her vital signs.

The doctor waved to the bruises on her wrists.

For once, the detective wasn't smiling. He hadn't seen the bruises earlier, as Luke had. The sight of them now had his mouth pressing into a hard, thin line.

"I won't disturb her to show you the other bruises," the doctor said, keeping his voice low. "But I can tell you, there are plenty of them, across her abdomen, her back, her side, in places typically covered by clothing. Unless she was in several violent car wrecks recently, there's only one obvious explanation. Someone beat her, viciously, repeatedly, over a period of several days, based on the coloration of the bruises. But that's not half the story."

He crossed the small space to a computer monitor on a rolling cart. After typing a few commands, he turned the screen around to reveal an X-ray.

"This," he said, pointing to the screen, "is a healed hairline fracture on her right forearm. It was probably broken a few years ago." He punched another button to reveal a new picture. "And this is another fracture, on her other forearm. Again, it's healed, a relatively old injury, probably within the past eight or nine months." He turned the monitor back around. "I could show you more scans, but they all show the same thing—a history of injuries. None of them were compound fractures, meaning they weren't bad enough breaks to cause lasting damage or require setting. Which is probably why whoever did this to her was never forced to take her to a hospital. But those injuries should have been stabilized with a cast to aid in healing and to reduce her pain."

Luke flinched and looked down at the bed. How could someone do that to another person? Especially a woman. And especially a woman as small and delicate as this one.

"How do you know no one took her to a hospital?" Cornell asked.

"Because as soon as I saw the scans, I had my assistant call the Ashton house and talk to the staff. None of them were aware of any trips to the hospital and never saw her in a cast. We also verified that none of the hospitals in Savannah ever listed Mrs. Ashton as a patient. Either she wasn't treated for these injuries at all, or she was treated out of town, or possibly seen in a private office by a doctor who didn't know her history of other injuries. If a doctor only saw her once, for one fracture, he might not have had any reason to suspect domestic violence. But this last time, her abuser went too far, ruptured her spleen, nearly killed her. But that's still not the worst of it."

Luke's head whipped up. "What could possibly be worse?"

"Mrs. Ashton is septic. She's on IV antibiotics and will be moved from Recovery to Intensive Care soon."

"Why is she septic?" Luke asked.

"Because she was recently pregnant. I suspect she lost the baby during a beating, and she never had medical treatment. I performed a D & C to scrape out her uterus. If she's lucky, she'll respond to the antibiotics."

"And if she isn't lucky?" Cornell asked, his notebook out again.

"She could die."

A nurse came into the room and whispered something to the doctor.

"I have to check on another patient, gentlemen," the doctor said. "I'll be back in a few minutes."

After the doctor left, Cornell flipped his notebook closed.

"I'm keeping Mrs. Ashton at the top of my persons-of-interest list."

Luke stared at him incredulously. "After what the doctor just said? You'd pursue her as a suspect?"

"Regardless of what her husband did to her, she didn't have the right to kill him. She should have reported the abuse."

"It's not that easy and you know it. I've seen enough domestic-violence cases to know people feel trapped, with nowhere to turn. Or they kid themselves into thinking the abuser is sorry, that he'll change his ways. Or worse, they blame themselves. Getting out isn't as easy as you would think from the outside looking in."

"Regardless, she's a billionaire's wife," Cornell said. "She wasn't exactly hurting for money. She could have left him. She *did* leave him. She wasn't trapped."

Luke ground his teeth together and reached for Caroline's hand. Her skin was burning up, pale, almost translucent. He couldn't begin to imagine the pain she'd suffered. Did she even know she was pregnant? Did she know she'd lost a baby?

"In the waiting room," Luke said, "you agreed she couldn't have killed him."

Cornell's gaze flicked to where Luke held Caroline's hand. "I agreed she couldn't have shot him. But that doesn't mean that she doesn't know who did. Her husband was a billionaire. That gives me a billion reasons she might be involved in his death somehow. And the evidence the doctor just showed us is pretty convincing. What better motive to kill her husband than because he'd abused her and caused her to miscarry?"

His argument was sound. But Caroline had come to Luke asking for his help, and here she was in a hospital bed fighting for her life. She needed someone else to fight for her now. Since no one else was volunteering for the job, that someone might as well be him.

"Do you even know if she'll inherit?" he asked. "If not, that blows your billion-reason theory away."

"Not yet. I called the husband's law firm. His lawyer is going to send me a copy of the will." The detective looked at Luke's hand on Caroline's again. "Tell me, Mr. Dawson. With her resources, how hard do you think it would be for Mrs. Ashton to hire someone to kill her husband?"

Luke wanted to deny the possibility but couldn't. What Cornell said made sense. If Caroline had finally decided enough was enough, she had all the resources to make it happen.

Chapter Four

Luke shifted in his chair, bracing his forearms on his knees as he watched the doctor and nurses on the other side of Caroline's hospital room. She'd responded well to the antibiotics and was already out of the Intensive Care Unit. Now the doctor was lightening her sedation to bring her out of her deep, healing sleep. For the first time since the discovery of Richard Ashton's body, Luke was going to be able to talk to Caroline. He looked forward to seeing her open her eyes, but he also dreaded the pain she might suffer if she hadn't known about the baby.

All but one of the nurses left the room. The remaining nurse sat in a chair beside the bed. The doctor spoke to her in low tones before approaching Luke.

"It won't be long now," he said. "Nurse Kennery will stay and monitor Mrs. Ashton until she wakes up, but I don't expect any problems."

Luke rose and shook his hand. "Thank you, Doctor."

He nodded and left the room.

Luke started toward the bed to check on Caroline, when the door opened again.

A rail-thin woman in a coal-black suit jacket and skirt hurried inside, her high heels clicking against the hard floor. She stopped when she saw Luke, her brows rising.

"Who are you?" she demanded.

He positioned himself between her and the bed. "Who are *you?*" he countered.

If anything, her brows arched even higher. "Leslie Harrison, Mrs. Ashton's attorney and friend. I know you aren't family, so again, who are you and what are you doing in her room?"

"I'm a friend," he said, not seeing any reason to tell her otherwise.

She snorted. "Caroline doesn't have any friends."

"I thought you were her friend."

Her lips compressed.

"Interesting friend," he continued. "She's been in the hospital for several days and this is the first time I've seen you here."

She opened her mouth to say something, but a moan from the bed stopped her.

The nurse rose from her chair to check on the patient.

Caroline's face tightened as if she was in pain, but her eyes remained closed.

Deciding the game of one-upmanship wasn't worth playing, Luke introduced himself. "I'm Luke Dawson. Mrs. Ashton hired me as her bodyguard. I was with her when we discovered her husband's body."

A look of surprise flashed across the lawyer's face. "She hired a bodyguard?"

"Yes. Apparently, she realized she was in danger. But apparently...you didn't? Did you know about the abuse?"

The only change in her expression was a subtle tightening of the tiny lines at the corners of her eyes.

She did know.

"How long?" he demanded.

"How long what?"

"How long did you know she was being beaten by her husband? And why didn't you report him to the police?"

"None of this is any of your business," she snapped. "Get out, Mr. Dawson. I'm the closest thing in this town to family that Caroline has, and I assure you if I have to call Security, they'll take my side—someone who has known her for years—over the side of a man she hired a few days ago. I'm her attorney and the executor of the late Mr. Ashton's estate. I have every right to be here. You have none. I repeat, get out."

The nurse looked back and forth between them. Behind her, Caroline's brow furrowed again, and her lips whitened. She was obviously in pain. The tug-of-war between Luke and the lawyer was distracting the nurse from taking care of her.

"All right," Luke said. "I'll go. For now. Just make sure that when you speak to Mrs. Ashton you warn her not to talk to the police without a criminal attorney present— not a civil attorney like yourself. The police are investigating her as a suspect and could misconstrue anything she says."

"I assure you, I don't need your advice about how to take care of my client." Leslie swept past him to the nurse and peppered her with questions.

Luke reluctantly left the room. He might have lost this battle, but he wasn't leaving Caroline alone for long. He'd never met Leslie Harrison before, but he didn't get good vibes from her. And her lack of concern for her alleged friend showed in the fact that she hadn't visited or called since Caroline had been brought into the emergency room. She didn't strike him as the kind of friend Caroline needed right now.

He took the elevator to the first floor and went outside to use his cell phone. The man he needed to talk to wasn't someone he spoke to very often. In fact, it had been years since the last time their paths had crossed, so he had to call a few friends to ferret out the unlisted number. Finally, he programmed it into his phone and pressed the call button.

The phone rang twice. Then, "Alex Buchanan."

"Alex, this is Luke Dawson."

"Luke." His voice mirrored his surprise. "Tell me you're not calling me to bail one of your clients out of jail again. I hung my hat up on that kind of work years ago."

"Not this time. I'm at Memorial University Medical Center visiting a friend. Are you still a practicing attorney, or are you retired?"

"I keep my license active, but I only take cases for family or friends."

"How about friends *of* friends?"

"Depends on who they are and what kind of trouble they're in. Who's your friend?"

"Caroline Ashton."

The phone went silent.

"Alex? You still there?"

"I'm here."

"Well? Will you help or not?"

A deep sigh sounded through the phone. "Bring me up to speed while I dust off a suit."

THE NURSE HELPED Caroline hobble from the bathroom to the bed. The pain in Caroline's belly was much better than before, so she wasn't about to complain at the sharp jolt that shot through her when the nurse helped her swing her feet up onto the bed. She drew several shallow breaths until the twinge passed, then collapsed against the pillows.

"Are you sure you're ready for your friend to come back inside?" the nurse asked, patting Caroline's hand and looking at her with concern. "The doctor's visit really seemed to wear you out. If you want to rest a bit, I can make sure no one bothers you."

She shook her head. "No, I'm okay. Please tell Leslie she can come back in now."

"Very well. She's in the waiting room. I'll tell her. But if she overtires you, or if the pain gets worse, press the call button."

"I will. Thank you."

The nurse left. A few minutes later the *tap-tap* of Leslie's heels sounded outside the room. The door opened and she burst inside, with three men following her.

Caroline clutched the sheets as Leslie and a stranger she'd never met moved to her left side, while the remaining two men—Daniel and Grant, her husband's brothers—caged her in on the other side of the bed.

"Leslie, I don't understand," she whispered. "Why are Daniel and Grant here?"

"Our brother is dead," Grant sneered. "We have a right to find out what happened."

Leslie's lip curled with distaste. "Unfortunately, they were in the waiting room, demanding to see you. When Detective Cornell and I headed here, they followed like lapdogs."

Grant looked as if he wanted to leap across the bed and take a swing at Leslie. Daniel's face turned a light shade of pink, as if he was embarrassed at his brother's behavior.

The man beside Leslie held up his hand. "Quiet, everyone. Mrs. Ashton, I'm Detective Cornell with Chatham County Metro P.D. If you're feeling up to it, I have some questions for you." He glanced at the others, the look on his face showing displeasure. "Your family insisted on coming in with me, but I can ask them to step outside.

Or, if you prefer," he said, his voice sounding grudging, "I can wait in the hall until you speak to them privately."

"No." She winced at how loud her voice sounded in the small room. "That is, I'd prefer not to have these other men here, if that's okay."

"We're not going anywhere," Grant said.

"Yes. You are." Luke Dawson's deep voice rang out from the open doorway. He strode inside and stopped at the foot of Caroline's bed, frowning at Cornell and Leslie before looking at the other two men. "You heard her. Out."

Grant drew himself up, but even so, he was still an inch shorter than Luke and not nearly as broad. "Our brother was murdered," he snapped, aiming a glare at Caroline. "And we have the right to hear what *she* has to say about it."

Luke moved so fast it stole Caroline's breath. One minute he was standing there, calmly eyeing Grant. The next minute he had Grant's arm wedged up between his shoulder blades. Grant's face was bright red, but he didn't seem to be able to move.

"Let me go, you stupid rent-a-cop," he gasped.

"I'll let you go—outside." Luke raised a challenging brow at Daniel, daring him to intervene.

Daniel glared at Luke before heading to the door. Luke followed, pushing Grant ahead of him. The door softly closed behind them.

Cornell pulled a plastic chair to the side of the bed and sat. "I take it you aren't close to your brothers-in-law?"

Caroline shook her head. "No. I definitely don't consider them…family. And I assure you, the feeling is mutual."

The door clicked back open and Luke hurried inside, stopping at the foot of the bed again.

"Mrs. Ashton, if you don't want me here, I'll wait in the hallway." He looked pointedly at the detective and Leslie. "But I thought you might want one ally in your corner, something you seem to have little of at the moment. I also strongly urge you not to say anything to Detective Cornell without a lawyer. A *criminal* lawyer, not a civil one."

Leslie pursed her lips but didn't say anything.

"Cornell isn't here with your best interests at heart," Luke continued. "He considers you a suspect in your husband's murder."

Caroline blinked at the detective. His face reddened, telling her Luke's words were true.

"I'm not your enemy," Cornell explained. "I simply want to know what happened. But first, I'd like to offer you my condolences on the death of your husband."

She shivered and rubbed her hands up and down her arms. Even though she knew Richard was dead, hearing it out loud didn't make it seem real. She kept expecting him to pounce at her from behind the curtains, or stride out of the bathroom and laugh at her for thinking she could ever escape him.

"Thank you, Detective."

"Have you had a chance to speak to your doctor yet?"

"Yes," she whispered. "He was here a few moments ago."

"Then you know he suspects your husband abused you, that he's the reason for your fractures, bruises, your ruptured spleen…your miscarriage?"

She winced and automatically moved her hand to her belly. "Yes. He told me."

"Is it true? Did your husband beat you?"

She blanched, her face growing hot. She'd never wanted

anyone else to know about her shame. Until a few days ago, no one did. No one but Leslie.

"I don't want to talk about this."

"It's the elephant in the room," Cornell continued. "It can't be avoided. You hired a bodyguard, Mr. Dawson here. Why did you hire him?"

She glanced at Luke. "I knew my husband would be angry that I'd left him. And I didn't want to have to deal with an argument. I wanted someone who could confront him, if necessary, and save me from the ugliness."

"Are you denying your husband hurt you?" the detective asked.

She twisted her fingers in the sheets. "I don't—"

"Don't say another word," Luke said. "You need a criminal defense attorney before you speak to the police."

Leslie patted Caroline's hand. "The sooner she answers the questions, the sooner this will all be over and she can put it behind her. Perhaps it would be best if you waited outside, Mr. Dawson."

"Not a chance."

"No," Caroline said at the same time. She pulled her hand back from Leslie's. "I'm sorry, but I feel…better with Mr. Dawson here. Detective Cornell, all I can tell you is that I didn't kill my husband. I don't own a gun. I don't even think Richard owned one. There was no need, not with a security firm watching over the house. And regardless of what Richard did or didn't do, I never wanted him dead."

"I agree it appears you couldn't have killed him yourself, based on the timeline of events and the witnesses to your whereabouts. But that doesn't mean you didn't hire someone else to kill him."

Her mouth fell open. "Why would I do that?"

"Your husband was quite wealthy. Maybe you figured you wouldn't get much if you divorced him." He cocked his head and studied her. "Was there a prenuptial agreement limiting how much you would get in a divorce?"

"Yes. There was. But I didn't care. I was leaving my husband, regardless of the money."

Cornell didn't look impressed by her statement. He scribbled something in his notepad. "I think when you decided to leave your husband, you didn't want to lose the money. You called a friend, maybe a lover, offered him a portion of the estate if he'd help you stage your husband's murder to make it look like you had nothing to do with it. Who helped you?"

She laughed bitterly. "A friend? A lover? My husband made sure I had no one, Detective. I didn't make a move that he didn't know about. I couldn't even leave the house without him."

"Obviously that's not true. You left without him Thursday morning."

She rolled her head on the pillow. "The one thing my husband allowed me to do on my own, the *only* thing he let me do, was run two weekly errands—taking our clothes to the dry cleaner's and bringing his papers to his lawyer's office, to Leslie's office. That's what I was doing. That's how I left without him knowing I was taking off."

"'Let' you?" the detective asked. "Are you saying you were a prisoner in your own home? Did you resent your husband for controlling you that way?"

"That's enough." Luke said. "Mrs. Ashton, again, I strongly urge you not to say another word without adequate legal representation."

The door flew open. A tall man in a business suit stepped into the room. His coal-black hair had tiny streaks of silver, but that was the only thing that hinted at his age. His blue eyes were still vivid, piercing, as they swept the room and landed on her.

"And just who the devil are you?" Leslie demanded.

Luke looked relieved to see the other man.

The man ignored Leslie, nodded at Luke. He stepped to the side of Caroline's bed and smiled down at her. "I'm Alex Buchanan, a defense attorney with one of the best records in the state of Georgia. Mr. Dawson called me about your situation. And from where I stand, you look like you could use my help." He pulled a dollar out of his suit-jacket pocket and handed it to her.

"What's this for?" she asked, automatically taking it.

"I figure you probably don't have any cash with you here in the hospital. If you'd like me to represent you, you can give me that dollar as my retainer."

Leslie scoffed.

Cornell's mouth curved in grudging admiration.

Caroline looked at Luke. "You think I need help?"

"I know you do. Alex really is the best. I recommend that you hire him."

She held the dollar out to the handsome man smiling down at her. "You're hired, Mr. Buchanan."

He took the dollar and slid it back into his pocket. "Excellent. Detective Cornell, miss," he said, looking at Leslie. "I need a moment alone with my client."

"I'm not leaving unless he does," Leslie said, pointing at Luke.

Alex smiled without humor. "Yes, you are. You're both leaving. But Mr. Dawson stays. Three days ago, someone killed my client's husband. And if she'd arrived at the house a few moments earlier, she could have been killed, as well. Mr. Dawson is her bodyguard. He's not going anywhere."

APPARENTLY, CAROLINE LOVED GARDENS. Luke had done his best to find one for her so she, Alex and he could talk without anyone overhearing them. The closest thing to a garden the hospital had was a spot in a small, empty waiting room on the first floor that looked out a group of windows to some flowering shrubs.

Not that it really mattered. Caroline wasn't paying attention to the view. She sat in her wheelchair staring at Alex with the same confusion Luke felt.

"I don't understand," she said.

Luke shook his head. "Neither do I. Maybe you should explain one more time, Alex. How, exactly, am I supposed to protect Caroline when I won't even be in the house with her?"

"Mrs. Ashton already has a contract with a security company to guard the mansion. Stellar Security has an excellent record. There's no reason to believe they can't take care of her without your help."

"If you truly believe that, then why am I even here?" Luke asked.

"To protect Mrs. Ashton."

Caroline's brow furrowed and she shared another look of confusion with Luke.

"See, that's the part where you lost me earlier," Luke said.

Alex smiled. "Forgive me. I'm not explaining this very well. Based on my current understanding of the case, we only know one thing—that someone murdered Mr. Ashton. We don't know if the killer wanted to kill him, or if Mrs. Ashton was his true target, or if it was simply a burglary gone wrong with no real connection to either of the Ashtons."

"I hadn't thought of that," Caroline said.

"I'm sure Detective Cornell has, but he confronted

you earlier to shake you up, to see your reaction. Right now, everyone has more questions than answers. What I want to do is keep the status quo, keep the variables as close to normal as possible. That will make it much more obvious if someone has changed their routine, or if they act differently. By returning to your usual routine, it will be easier to judge people's reactions, easier to point out if someone seems a bit...off."

Luke tapped the table. "And I'm supposed to sit in my car and watch the mansion? What good does that do?"

"It allows you to become invisible. No one is going to pay attention to you outside, but if you're inside, everyone acts differently and it will be much harder for Mrs. Ashton to pick up on any changes."

"Please call me Caroline, both of you. And as far as your plan, Alex, I agree it will be fairly easy for me to spot any changes that way."

"I'm concerned about your safety," Luke insisted.

"There's no reason to believe Mrs. Ashton's...that is, Caroline's security company that's already in place can't continue to protect the mansion. Stellar Security has an unblemished reputation."

"You're right. They do. Caroline, as much as it galls me to admit it, you probably don't need me anymore."

She reached for his hand. From the way her eyes widened, it appeared she was just as surprised at her action as Luke was, but he didn't pull away. Instead, he threaded his fingers with hers.

Some of the tension went out of her and she gave him a tentative smile. "It may not seem like I need you, but I do. The mansion has never been my home. No one there is my friend or cares one whit about me. While I'd prefer that you be inside, with me, just knowing you are watching over the place will give me comfort. That is, if you don't mind."

He considered the hours he'd be spending sitting in his car. He wouldn't be able to run the air conditioner all that time, not without overheating the engine, which meant *he'd* be the one overheating. That thought should have had him wanting to end the contract and go back to his office. But it didn't. For some reason, he couldn't bear not being there. He wanted, needed, to make sure she really was safe.

"If that's what you want, then I'm happy to stay on the case, in whatever capacity you and Alex think makes sense."

She smiled and pulled her hand back.

Luke sorely missed the feel of her delicate hand in his, which surprised him again. Everything about Caroline and his reactions to her surprised him.

Alex raised a brow at the exchange but didn't comment on it.

"What about Leslie?" Caroline asked Alex. "You mentioned earlier you had concerns about her."

"I do. Tell me, how did you end up renting the cottage where your husband was killed?"

"Leslie helped me find it on the internet."

"Did she know what time you were supposed to arrive on the day you were moving in?"

"Well, yes." Her eyes widened. "You can't be suggesting she had anything to do with Richard's death."

"Not suggesting," Alex said. "Just exploring the facts. She knew where you were going and what time you'd be there, so you have to consider she could have planned the murder expecting you to discover the body. She may have wanted you to look guilty."

Caroline shook her head. "No, that's not what happened at all. Leslie had nothing to gain from Richard's death. And she couldn't have known what time I'd be at the cottage because I changed plans after leaving her office. I hired Luke. Then I went to the house."

Luke exchanged a look with Alex. From the expression on Alex's face, Luke realized they were both thinking the same thing. Luke shifted forward in his chair. "Caroline, you changed plans, but Leslie didn't know that, did she? What exactly did she think you were going to do after leaving her office?"

Her lips compressed into a tight line. She obviously didn't appreciate where the conversation was going. "She was just looking out for my safety. She didn't want Richard to find me. We both agreed I would go directly to the rental."

"And if you had done that," Luke said, "you would have arrived right about the time your husband was shot. It sounds to me like you wouldn't have had an alibi if you had done what your lawyer expected you to do."

The resentment on her face faded as the truth hung in the air between them.

She swallowed hard. "Leslie did stress that I needed to go directly to the cottage, that I shouldn't stop anywhere. But that doesn't mean she had anything to do with Richard's death. You're suggesting she might have wanted to frame me. What would she gain from that?"

Alex shook his head. "I have no idea. But we need to look at all the possibilities. I have other concerns about Miss Harrison. She's a tax attorney, but she still took the same oath I did. She knows that protecting her clients is her first priority. And by allowing you to speak to the police without a criminal-law attorney present, she displayed incredibly poor judgment, at the least. I'd like you to be careful around her until the investigation can clear her of any involvement. You can still keep her in your normal routine, but don't sign anything or agree to anything without vetting it through me first. See if she does anything to raise red flags with you."

"Okay, but I can tell you there's no reason to be concerned. Leslie is the only friend I have. She's the one who helped me get the cottage and helped me plan leaving my husband."

Alex crossed his arms. "How long did she know about the abuse?"

Caroline's gaze fell to her lap. "About six months."

Luke cursed.

Alex looked as if he wanted to do the same, but he refrained. "As a lawyer, it was Miss Harrison's obligation to help you. While she may not have been legally bound to report the abuse like a doctor would be, she's ethically and morally bound to do so. I assure you, her turning a blind eye—even if she helped you later on—would not look well for her if she came up for review before the bar."

"I don't want her to get in trouble," Caroline said. "Whether you agree with her methods or not, she's the only one who ever tried to help me, the only person who ever seemed to notice there was anything wrong. Without her, I would never have figured out how to escape."

"How long was the abuse going on?" Alex asked.

Her face went pale. "Years."

"Then why now? After all that time, what made you decide it was time to leave?"

"The baby," she whispered. "As soon as I realized I was pregnant, I decided I had to figure out a way to get out of there. I couldn't risk bringing up a child in that environment. I may have been weak and a coward when it came to myself, but I couldn't do that to a child. I started making plans that same day." She closed her eyes. "But before everything was finalized, Richard…taught me one of his…lessons. The cramping, the bleeding…I knew I'd lost the baby. I was so ashamed. I couldn't allow myself to risk getting pregnant again, risk the life of another child."

Luke took her hand in his. "Stop talking like that. You aren't weak, or a coward. You were in an untenable situation. I understand the cycle of abuse. I've seen it over and over. It's not easy to get out. Your abuser plays a mind game on you, slowly wearing you down until one day you don't even know how you got in the place where you're at. It's not your fault. None of this. It's Richard Ashton's fault. And you didn't kill your child. He did."

Unshed tears made her eyes bright. She gave him a watery smile. "Thank you."

He squeezed her hand in answer.

Alex frowned. "I'm sure Miss Harrison has filed your husband's will with the courts by now, but I'm new to this case and don't have the particulars. Can you give me a summary? Who are Mr. Ashton's beneficiaries?"

"His brothers and me."

"Split equally?"

"No. For some reason, Richard decided to leave me the bulk of the estate. He left five million to each of his brothers, but everything else goes to me."

"Did he get along with his brothers?"

"More with Daniel than Grant, but he fought with both of them off and on over the years. Daniel hasn't been to the house in quite some time, but I don't know if he and Richard were fighting or not. Grant comes over more often, but his visits usually end in some kind of argument. He and Richard seem to have…issues. They came to blows on occasion. Richard was definitely the type to hold a grudge, so maybe that explains why he didn't leave much—relative to the entire estate, of course—to Grant.

But I thought Richard and Daniel had a better relationship overall. I don't understand why he left Daniel so little."

"Forgive me," Alex said, "but I have to ask because you can bet the police will. If you'd divorced, was there an agreement in place about what you would have received?"

"Yes. Two hundred thousand dollars a year, for life. I was never worried about the money. Trust me, that kind of money would have been plenty."

"A jury might feel differently. That's a drastic change in lifestyle for someone who's used to being in a mansion, married to a billionaire." He shrugged. "Those are the facts. We'll just have to deal with them."

Luke leaned forward in his chair. "Let's get back to the plan for how to keep her safe until the killer is caught. I'm all for assuming she's as much a target as her husband. I'd rather be too cautious than to let down my guard. First thing to consider—what do we do about the funeral for Mr. Ashton?"

Chapter Five

It nearly killed Luke being outside Caroline's inner circle, relying on Alex's instincts that she'd be safe with her usual bodyguards, at least for now. But he did as Alex had suggested. The plan the defense lawyer had put in place seemed solid. And Alex had hired a private investigator to dig into everything on the side to bolster Caroline's defense, if that became necessary, and also to try to find out the identity of the killer.

The investigator was also digging into Leslie Harrison's past to see if she had anything to gain by either framing Caroline, or by having her killed along with Richard if Caroline had arrived at the cottage when Leslie expected her to that day.

Luke watched the hospital entrance from his 1997 Ford Thunderbird parked between two tall SUVs that made it less likely anyone would notice him. Not that they would anyway. Few people stopped to admire his olive-green, beat-up car, which was exactly how he wanted it. This was his work car, built like a tank, dented and scratched from run-ins when the people he was protecting his clients from decided to come after him instead. He even had several spare tires in the trunk instead of the traditional "one," prepared for the next time someone decided to slash his tires.

But worrying about some pimp coming after him wasn't on his mind today. Caroline was. She was being released from the hospital. And her husband's funeral was being held today. Alex had advised her to go to the funeral, whether she wanted to or not, saying it would look bad if she didn't attend. If things didn't go her way and she ended up in court, accused of orchestrating her husband's murder, her not being at the funeral might poison the jury against her. So here she was, about to leave the hospital and having to pay homage to the man who'd put her there in the first place.

The idea made Luke sick and wish he could bring the bastard back from the dead and kill him himself.

The parking lot around him was filled with media vans. As soon as the Ashton Rolls-Royce pulled up the circular driveway to the front of the hospital, reporters converged on them like a swarm of mosquitoes.

His cell phone vibrated on the seat beside him. He glanced at the screen, then put it on speaker. "Hey, Mitch."

"You still at the hospital?"

"Sitting out front. The Ashton limo just drove up. She should be out soon. Are you in position?"

"I've got the best spot in the cemetery picked out. Not close enough to the party to be obvious, but close enough to observe and photograph everyone who shows up. I'm starting to like this P.I. stuff. You might have to expand the business and make me lead detective."

"Guess that depends on how well you do today. I'd say don't make a scene taking pictures, but with the media horde that will be there, you aren't going to stand out anyway. Alex will have someone there taking pictures, too. Between the both of you, if Alex's theory that the killer will be there is true, we'll at least have him or her

on camera and be able to start a list of potential suspects."
He shook his head at the crowd of reporters trying to get
past the police line at the hospital for a better angle for
their cameras. "Then again, counting the press, we'll
probably have hundreds of people to look into."

"Doesn't bother me at all. Like I said, I'm enjoying
this. It's a heck of a lot better than sitting in the office
all day."

"Speaking of which, who's looking after things while
you're playing amateur sleuth?"

"Trudy."

Luke squeezed the bridge of his nose. "You've got my
business being watched over by a hooker?"

"Ex-hooker. She's gone respectable, trying to make a
living with her feet on the ground for a change."

"Since when?"

"Well…playing office secretary might be her first real
gig, but I think it's great for us to give her a start toward
a better life, don't you?"

Luke rolled his head on his shoulders, trying to relieve
the growing knot of tension. He was all for helping the
less fortunate, but not at the expense of his livelihood.

He was about to set Mitch straight when the passenger
door to the limo opened and one of the Ashton-estate security guards got out. The hospital doors swished open.
Out came Caroline Ashton, looking extra pale in a con-
servative black dress, being pushed in a wheelchair by
a nurse. Beside her was her so-called friend Leslie Harrison. A bevy of security guards surrounded them both,
preventing any of the reporters from getting near her.
Luke had to admit that he was impressed with how Stellar Security had handled the situation.

"I've got to go. They're helping Mrs. Ashton into the
limo. After the burial, get those pictures straight to Alex."

"You got it, boss."

Luke ended the call and eased out of the parking lot, keeping well back from the Rolls-Royce and the caravan of press hounds sniffing in its wake.

HUNDREDS OF PEOPLE who'd worked for Richard at his various companies turned out for the viewing at the funeral home. Caroline tried to be gracious as she sat up front and accepted their condolences. But it was hard to smile and listen to so many people who had such wonderful stories to tell about her husband, when she'd seen so little of that warmth as his wife.

By the time the viewing was closed and everyone had filed out except the funeral director and security guards, and, of course, Leslie—who didn't seem inclined to ever leave her side—Caroline's nerves were stretched so tight she thought she might start screaming like the madwoman so many people believed her to be.

"Caroline, we should go now or we'll be late for the burial," Leslie said.

Leslie's worries seemed silly with the coffin sitting a few feet away. They couldn't hold a funeral without the guest of honor.

She hadn't gone near the coffin with everyone else there. At first, she had assumed she wouldn't want to, but now, knowing this was the last time she'd ever see him, she had the sudden urge to do so.

"I'd like a few moments alone, please."

Leslie frowned. "But we need to—"

"I need a few moments alone," she repeated and looked pointedly at the security guard closest to her.

Leslie's brows rose, but she got up as the guard stopped in front of her. She gave Caroline an irritated look and left the room.

Once all the guards were gone, she sat for several moments, trying to gather her courage.

A whisper of sound had her turning her head. Luke Dawson, dressed in a black suit, moved up the aisle and sat beside her. He put his hand on the wooden bench seat, palm up, an unspoken offer of friendship and support. She didn't hesitate. She put her hand in his.

"I'd hoped you'd come," she said.

"I gave you a promise that I'd keep you safe. In spite of what Alex recommends, I can't seem to stay that far away from you." He inclined his head toward the coffin. "If you want me to leave, I will."

Her hand tightened on his. "No. I'm glad you're here. Would you mind…standing with me?"

"Whatever you need." He helped her to her feet.

She was still wobbly and weak. She would use the wheelchair later, at the graveside service, but right now—with the coffin open—it was almost as if her husband could still see her. She knew it didn't make sense, but she didn't want to use the wheelchair here so she wouldn't look weak in front of him.

Luke's strong arm was her rock to cling to as she slowly approached the coffin.

She stared down at the man she'd married, and a shiver ran through her. Luke placed his arm around her shoulders and drew her against his side. Somehow that action helped stave off her panic and allowed her to do what she really wanted to do—face the monster and say goodbye to the man the monster had once been, the man she'd fallen in love with.

Tears coursed down her cheeks. "I'm sure to someone like you, just knowing about the awful things he did to me, you can't imagine why I'd cry. But he wasn't always the man you've heard about. When I met him, he was my savior. He took me from a life of poverty, from an unhappy home, and gave me a fresh start. He was so handsome, and strong, and his smile…I felt it all the way to my heart. I truly, deeply loved him, before…before he…changed."

Luke gently stroked her upper arm. "You don't owe me, or anyone else, any explanations."

The lack of judgment and condemnation in his voice dramatically highlighted the differences between these two men. Where Luke treated her with respect and tried to build her up, Richard had only sought to break her down with his constant criticism and humiliating lessons.

She blinked back her tears. Crying wouldn't soothe the hurt deep in her heart, or heal the ache for the man he'd once been and the man he'd ultimately become. Only time would do that—or, at least, she hoped so.

LUKE STOOD WELL back from the group of mourners and security guards and police officers, the latter there mostly to keep the press from mobbing the graveside service. A dark green tent covered the casket and the thirty or so white folding chairs that were all occupied, with many mourners standing at the edge of the tent, spilling onto the green grass.

Luke stood in the cover of oak trees, scanning the crowd, watching for anything that didn't seem right. Normally he performed bodyguard services right beside the person he was guarding. Watching over Caroline long-distance didn't sit well. It didn't sit well at all. But, again, the guards with Stellar Security seemed to be doing a good job of keeping everyone back and keeping a ring of their men around Caroline. If the killer was here, and wanted to get at her, he'd have a tough go of it.

Satisfied that Caroline was being well protected, he

scanned the crowd to find Mitch. There, on the top of a knoll, separated from the closest group of media hounds by about ten feet, Mitch snapped pictures with a big grin on his face. Luke wryly wondered if Mitch had found his true calling in life. He certainly never looked that happy at the office.

Using his binoculars to search the crowd, Luke located Alex and was surprised to see him standing beside Leslie Harrison. The two of them had no love for each other. Maybe Alex was trying to get in Leslie's good graces to extract information from her.

Screams sounded from the crowd. Luke focused on the tent. He couldn't find Caroline. Panic squeezed his throat. But then he saw her being carried in the arms of one of her guards, with the rest of the guards circling her, guns drawn, ready for any threat. As soon as she was in the car, the caravan of security vehicles raced away.

Another scream rent the air. Luke whirled around, urgently searching for the other people he knew. He located them, one by one—first Leslie, unhurt, running toward the parking lot. Then Alex, at her side, using his tall, muscular frame to protect her. One more person to find. He scanned back and forth over the area where Mitch had been just moments ago.

A small crowd had gathered on a slight rise. Luke zoomed in, trying to see why they were all looking down. He sucked in a sharp breath. It was a body, deathly still, blood seeping through his shirt. A camera lay like a forgotten trophy beside him. *Mitch.*

No! Luke drew his gun and tore off in a sprint, desperately offering up a prayer as he ran.

AN HOUR LATER, Caroline sat with Alex on one side of the table in the interview room at the police station, while

Luke sat alone on the other end, stone-faced, pale, his lips drawn into a tight line. Cornell sat in the middle.

"I'm very sorry for your loss, Mr. Dawson," Cornell said.

Luke gave him a curt nod.

Alex clasped Luke's shoulder, expressing his sympathy in silence before dropping his hand.

"I'm sorry, too," Caroline whispered.

Luke's dark gaze fastened onto hers. "I know. It's not your fault." His eyes narrowed. "You realize that, right?"

She looked away.

"Caroline?" he repeated, his voice raw but insistent. "You're not the one who stabbed him. It's not your fault."

She nodded, since he seemed to be waiting for an answer.

"Did Mr. Brody have family we can notify?" Cornell asked.

A pained expression crossed Luke's face. For a moment Caroline thought he was going to break down. But, instead, he straightened his shoulders, as if to brace himself against giving in to his grief.

"No. He was homeless when I met him. No family, no education to speak of. I'm all he had." His last sentence came out a stark whisper.

Caroline's guilt nearly choked her. Luke had taken Mitch in and given him a new life. And now—because of her—his friend was dead. She twisted her hands together in her lap.

"There will be an autopsy, of course," Cornell said. "But the cause of death is obvious. Someone stabbed him in the back. He bled out. As far as a burial—"

"Give the coroner my contact information," Luke said. "I'll make the arrangements."

"Very well. I know this is a tough time, but did any of you see anything?"

All three of them shook their heads.

"Okay. We'll examine the pictures from his camera. Maybe something will come of that. We don't actually know if this is related in any way to Mr. Ashton's murder, but I have to believe it's a strong possibility. Mrs. Ashton, are you sure you've never met Mitch Brody before?"

She glanced at Alex. He nodded, letting her know it was okay to answer.

"Not until last Thursday, when I picked Dawson's Personal Security Services out of the phone book."

"Okay. At this point I recommend that each of you be extra careful. Until we figure out what we're up against, everyone is a suspect. Watch your backs."

Chapter Six

Caroline paused at the front door to the mansion. A sense of foreboding swept through her. She couldn't shake the horror of Mitch being killed earlier today. She hadn't really known the man, but he'd been there because of her. His death was her fault.

No. His death was *not* her fault. She had to stop blaming herself and putting herself down the way Richard had always done. The person to blame for Mitch's death was whoever had stabbed him. She had to remember that. Richard had made her feel guilty for everything and had made her doubt her own sanity. No more. She was taking control of her own life, her own self-worth.

Still, she hesitated to go inside, in spite of the puzzled looks the security guards and Leslie were giving her. All she could picture in her mind was how strong and virile her husband had been. It was almost impossible to accept that he wasn't going to greet her at the door. She could easily imagine his outrage over her being so late in coming home, over her trying to escape. Of course, in front of others, he'd pretend to be happy to see her. He'd likely kiss her and hold her close. But in private, once the bedroom doors shut, he'd be all too eager to teach her another "lesson."

She shuddered and protectively wrapped her arms

around her middle, although it wasn't even slightly cold in the humid heat that engulfed the house.

Leslie put her hand on her shoulder. "Are you okay? Are you in pain?"

Caroline stared at the woman she thought of as her friend, looking for some sign that she really *wasn't* her friend, that she might have had something to do with Richard's murder as Alex and Luke had theorized.

"Caroline?" Leslie's brows drew together.

"No, I'm not in pain." Caroline hated that she had these doubts about the woman who'd done so much to help her. "I was just...thinking."

One of the security guards opened the door and stood back for them to enter.

She braced herself, then stepped into the foyer with Leslie at her side, only to be greeted by three maids and the cook. Or rather, they greeted Leslie and ignored Caroline. Which was just as well because she didn't want to deal with their red-rimmed eyes and sniffles. Richard was beloved by the staff, and it looked as if they were taking his death hard.

The security guards locked the door and melted into the house as they always did, somewhere out of sight but ready to help when needed—except, of course, when Caroline had really needed help, when Richard was around.

The household staff gathered around Leslie, whom they'd all met on numerous occasions, and offered her their condolences, completely ignoring their employer's widow, who just so happened to now be their *employer*.

Suddenly it was all too much. The miscarriage, two severe beatings in two days, finally escaping Richard only to find him murdered, winding up in the hospital with sepsis and having emergency surgery, and then for young, innocent Mitch Brody to be killed at the cemetery—all of it had her nerves stretched to the snapping point.

Someone was either trying to kill her or pin her for murder. And after everything she'd been through, it was so unfair. Well, she wasn't putting up with "unfair" anymore. She'd taken a huge step escaping Richard. Now it was time to take another huge step, to set her house in order. Because now this house was *hers*. Not Richard's. Not the staff's. And it was high time they treated her with the same respect they treated everyone else—starting now.

"Karen, Missy, Natasha, Betsy," she said, enjoying the startled looks on the other women's faces. They weren't used to being addressed by her directly. They probably didn't even think she knew their names. "I appreciate your condolences and that you all miss my husband, but life must go on. Your time is best spent performing your duties. Betsy, will you please arrange for my belongings to be moved out of the master suite into the main guest bedroom?"

Betsy looked from Leslie to Caroline. "I, um… Ma'am, why would you want me to do that?"

Caroline fisted her hands at her sides. She shouldn't have to explain to this woman who'd treated her as if she didn't exist for the past five years that her husband had repeatedly beaten and raped her in the master bedroom and she would never, ever step foot in that hated room again.

"If you have a problem following my orders, then I suggest you look for employment elsewhere." She looked in turn at all four women, who were huddled together as if they thought she was crazy. "That goes for all of you. Things are going to change, starting today. I refuse to be invisible in my own home any longer. I'm your employer. If you can't live with that, you are welcome to leave."

She brushed past the women, her shoulders straight

and her head held high, pretending a confidence she was far from feeling. She stepped through the nearest doorway, then abruptly stopped and pressed her hand to her throat. The enormous wood-paneled room at the front of the house looked out over the circular driveway. The view was unfamiliar because she'd only caught glimpses of it before. This was Richard's office, a room he'd forbidden her to enter. She could look through the doorway, on those occasions when her husband needed to speak to her, but she could never step inside. She turned around, intending to leave, but Leslie and the others were in the foyer staring at her.

She straightened her spine. "Leslie, are you coming or not?"

"Um, yes, of course." She clutched her purse and followed Caroline into the room.

Caroline raised a brow at the women in the foyer.

They scurried away, like chickens running from a fox. She grinned, pleased with the image. It was nice to be the fox for a change, instead of the chicken. She shut the door with a decisive click.

Her smile died when she saw the look on Leslie's face. "What? Did I do something wrong?"

Leslie set her purse on a decorative table and sat on the couch in the grouping at one end of the room. A massive walnut desk sat on the other side, next to the wall of windows. Caroline steered clear of the desk and sat in one of the leather wing chairs beside the couch.

"Not wrong, exactly," Leslie said. "I just don't think you should bait the staff and talk about changes so quickly after Richard was killed. You're still on the potential-suspect list. We wouldn't want anyone to get the idea you were glad Richard is dead."

"Is that what you think? That I'm glad he's dead?"

"Aren't you?"

She thought back to Alex's warning to keep everything the same as much as possible, to flush out anyone who might act out of the ordinary. But in spite of his recommendations, she couldn't pretend to be sorry. She was tired of being invisible in her own house.

"I'm glad I don't have to be afraid anymore. That's what I'm glad about. But I would never take comfort in someone's death, not even Richard's."

"Admirable of you, my dear. Just be careful not to give anyone the wrong impression."

Caroline bit her lip. "I suppose I did come on a bit strong." She shook her head. "No. I'm not sorry I took charge. I've been living like a turtle afraid of its own shell for too long. I'm determined not to live that way anymore. I've been given a second chance. I'm not going to waste a single minute of it."

She crossed to Richard's most prized possession, his sacred desk. She plopped down in the leather chair that practically swallowed her up and crossed her arms on top of the meticulously polished surface. Unable to suppress a childish urge, she pressed her palm against the dark wood, leaving a smeared print.

Leslie's brows rose and she crossed to sit in one of the two chairs in front of the desk. "This sounds ominous. What do you intend to do, exactly?"

Caroline laughed, and because it felt so good, she laughed again. "I don't know. I suppose, to start, I just might fire the security firm that Richard hired. Yes, I think I will."

Leslie's eyes widened. "Why would you do that?"

She clasped her hands tightly together on the desk, her mood plummeting as the recent past pressed down upon her.

"I haven't told you half of what I went through living here with Richard. And I have no intention of sharing those details. But suffice it to say, I was a prisoner, and the security company was my jailer. They reported every movement I made."

"I understand your resentment, but again, I don't recommend that you be hasty. There are a great many Ashton properties the security company takes care of, and numerous businesses."

"I hadn't thought of that."

"Of course not. You aren't used to the world of finance and business. There's a lot to consider." Leslie took some stapled papers out of the side pocket of her purse and set them on the desk. "If you'll sign the first and last page, I can take care of the details for you, and all you'll have to worry about is what kind of clothes you'd like to go shopping for or what kind of vacation you might want to take." She smiled brightly and set a pen on top of the papers.

Caroline picked up the pen and read the heading on the first page. "'Power of attorney'? I don't understand. Why do you need this?"

"Just a formality. It allows me to continue to conduct business for Ashton Enterprises without you having to sign papers every week."

The doubts that Alex and Luke had planted in her mind about Leslie suddenly became too glaring to ignore. Something wasn't right.

"But Richard signed papers every week. He didn't give you one of these forms, did he?"

Leslie waved her hand. "No, but we both know how controlling he was. It was entirely unnecessary for him to sign papers all the time when I could have done it for him. You can avoid all that by simply endorsing this one.

I'll have Linda put her notary stamp on it back at the office to save you a trip."

Had this been Leslie's goal all along? While Caroline couldn't see her friend as a murderer, she wasn't blind to the ambition and greed the lawyer never bothered to conceal. Had Leslie planned to get Caroline to sign over control of a billion-dollar enterprise? Had she planned on Caroline being in jail and desperate at the time, so that she wouldn't think twice about signing?

Caroline set the pen down. She glanced past Leslie to the closed door, every muscle in her body going tense. She forced the safe, blank look onto her face that she'd used so many times when trying to hide her feelings from her husband.

"This is all new to me, like you said. And I want to make sure I get everything right. Will you bring me up to date on all of the Ashton holdings so I know what's what?"

Leslie frowned. "Why on earth would you want me to bore you with those details? I'll take care of everything for you."

Caroline clenched her hand beneath the desk and glanced at the door again. She forced a smile. "Have I done something to annoy you, Leslie? You sound…aggravated."

Leslie's frown smoothed out and her lips curved into an answering smile. "Of course not. I'm just worried about you. If you want to dig into the boring details of the businesses, then by all means. I'll gather the necessary reports to bring you up to speed."

"That would be nice, of course. But I'd like to start with something smaller, just the household accounts. I want to know what expenses we have and how to pay the bills. After all, that's something I need to take care of, right? And I'll have to get the banks to put me on Richard's checking accounts, savings accounts, things like that. The monthly allowance he gave me in my own account won't be sufficient to pay the costs of running this place, like the staff's payroll."

"Again, that's something I can take care of. If you'll sign—"

"Leslie. I'm not going to argue about this. It's important to me. I want to learn what I need to know to run my own life, without someone else running it for me."

Leslie pursed her lips. "Of course. I wasn't considering everything you've gone through, and that having control over such mundane things might be important to you." She reached for the papers.

Caroline pulled the papers away and slid them into the top desk drawer. "I'll keep the papers here and think about signing. Okay?"

Leslie glanced toward the drawer, not looking at all pleased. For a moment, Caroline wondered if she was going to lunge over the desk and try to grab the papers. But finally Leslie snapped her purse shut.

"I'll get what you need from the bank as well as the house account information. It will take a day or two. With it being Sunday, the bank's not open, of course. I can come back on Wednesday. I should have everything together by then."

Caroline shoved out of the chair and walked Leslie to the door. "Wednesday sounds perfect. We can have lunch out back by the pool. Wear something casual. It will be fun."

"Fun." Leslie frowned again. "I've never seen this side of you, Caroline. I must say, it's going to take a bit of getting used to."

When the front door closed behind Leslie, Caroline slumped against the wall. She ran a shaking hand through her hair and stood for several minutes until she felt calm enough to go back into Richard's office.

No, *her* office. She went inside and stood at the floor-to-ceiling windows. She closed her eyes and leaned her forehead against the glass. The energy she'd had earlier seemed to desert her now. She was tired, so tired, and the day was only half over. She had so much to do, like telling Alex and Luke about the documents Leslie had tried to get her to sign.

"Excuse me, Mrs. Ashton?"

She turned at the sound of the head maid's voice. "Hello, Natasha. I'm sorry if I was a bit...abrupt earlier."

The maid gave her an uncertain look, as if she wasn't sure Caroline was going to run shrieking from the room tearing at her hair.

Caroline sighed. "Was there something you wanted?"

"Oh, yes, ma'am." She held out a small stack of envelopes. "The mail. I usually place it on Mr. Ashton's desk, but I...wasn't sure where you might want it."

Progress already. The maid had actually asked her preference rather than ignoring her and going about her business.

Caroline smiled and took the mail. "Thank you. I feel as if I've been sleepwalking around here for quite some time. I haven't really been aware of the routines you and the others go through. I apologize for not paying attention. As clean and well run as this household is, it's obvious the staff does an amazing job."

The woman stood a little straighter and her smile reached her eyes this time. "Thank you, ma'am. I'll be sure to share your compliment with the others. They'll appreciate it, very much. Is there anything I can do for you?"

"No. And, please, continue to put the mail on the desk

each day as you always do. This is my office now. I'll read the mail in here."

Natasha bobbed her head and backed out of the room, closing the door behind her.

Caroline crossed to the desk. She was about to sit, when she thought better of it. Richard's chair was far too big for her and it still smelled of the spicy cologne he favored, the cologne she'd once loved but had grown to hate.

Tomorrow, she'd have one of the maids throw the chair away or give it to charity.

She tried to scoot one of the guest chairs behind the desk instead, but it was too heavy. And pushing it across the plush carpet made her incision hurt. She gave up and plopped down in the guest chair right where it was, on the opposite side of the desk from where Richard must have sat when he was in the office.

The mail contained bills and a few letters from people whose names Caroline didn't recognize, addressed to her.

Surprised someone would send her anything, since she never received any personal mail, she opened the first one. The letter was short but touching, an expression of sympathy from someone who'd worked with her husband. Caroline appreciated the sentiment, even if her own opinion of her husband was a hundred-eighty degrees different than theirs. She'd have to make a point of getting some thank-you notes so she could respond.

The second letter was much shorter than the first. And right to the point. Caroline pressed her hand to her throat as she read it then read it again. She set the note down and opened the drawer where she'd put the papers Leslie had wanted her to sign. When she finished reading them, she was shaking so hard the pages were making rattling noises. She let them flutter to the top of the desk and put her head in her hands.

LUKE STRAIGHTENED IN the driver's seat of his beat-up Thunderbird, parked beneath one of the centuries-old oak trees lining the street next to the Ashton mansion. With Mitch's death so raw and fresh, he wanted nothing more than to drown his grief in a bottle of tequila. But that wouldn't bring Mitch back, and it wouldn't catch whoever had murdered him. Luke figured his best shot at catching the killer was to keep working the Ashton case. Which was why he was sitting outside Caroline's house, instead of getting drunk like he wanted. That and the fact that he was too worried about Caroline's safety to leave. The mansion took up an area the size of an entire city block at the outskirts of Savannah. And there was definitely something strange going on inside. The front door might as well have been a revolving door as often as it had been used since Caroline had gotten home from the funeral.

First to come in was Caroline with her lawyer, Leslie Harrison. After the lawyer left, the place was quiet for another hour. But that was when things got interesting and a bit crazy. Over a dozen men from Stellar Security came in and out of the front door, as if there was some kind of meeting going on inside. That had certainly piqued Luke's interest and had him craving to go up the front steps and knock on the door, in spite of the agreement that he was supposed to hang back. But he waited in the car, taking photos and recording everyone who came and went. Security guard after security guard exited the house until he suspected there weren't any left inside.

Was it possible Caroline had fired them?

Why would she do that? Alex wanted her to keep

everything status quo. Caroline definitely needed protection right now, at least until her husband's killer was caught. If she'd changed her mind and wanted Luke's company to protect her, the problem was that he was the only one available. His other men were all out on assignment.

A bead of sweat slid down the side of his face. Even in the shade it was probably close to ninety degrees. He debated turning the car on to run the air conditioner for a few minutes. But he'd probably feel even hotter once he had to turn it off again.

His phone vibrated on the seat beside him. When he saw who was calling, his gaze shot to the front windows of the mansion. Sure enough, Caroline stood at the glass with a cell phone pressed to her ear, looking right at him.

He picked up the phone. "Is everything okay?"

"No, Luke. Everything is *not* okay."

Chapter Seven

Caroline had insisted that she and Luke have dinner before she told him whatever it was that had shaken her up so much. He didn't know why she'd insisted on waiting, but he sensed she was near the breaking point and needed a few moments of "normal" in order to cope. That was the only reason he didn't press her. That, and the fact that neither of them had eaten since the funeral, and he figured it would do them both some good.

But the wait was driving him crazy. He needed to *do* something to catch Mitch's killer instead of sitting here doing nothing. His frustration with the delay was compounded when Caroline entered the sunroom at the back of the mansion carrying a tray of sandwiches and drinks. He jumped up from his seat at the small café table and hurried to take the tray from her.

"Shouldn't the cook, or maid, or whoever works for you, bring this in here instead of you carrying it through the house? You were only released from the hospital this morning."

Her face flushed and she took a seat while he set the tray in the middle of the table.

"I suppose you're right," she said. "I hadn't even thought to ask. It will take a while for the staff, and me, to get used to doing things differently now that Richard is gone."

He frowned. "'Differently'?"

"Please, have a sandwich. And some iced tea. I'm sure it must have been horribly hot sitting out in that car."

Her overly bright smile and evasive answer told him far more than she realized, and confirmed what he'd suspected when she'd opened the front door herself and ushered him inside. The staff basically ignored her. Luke couldn't imagine Richard answering his own door. A butler or maid would have done that for him and would have seated the guest, then arranged refreshments.

Rather than embarrass her by pointing out what to him was obvious—that she should fire every last one of the idiots who supposedly worked for her—he quickly finished off a half sandwich and emptied a glass of blessedly cold tea. Caroline ate very little, probably because she was so focused on her manners.

Her back was ramrod straight, her left hand in her lap holding her napkin, which she daintily wiped at the corners of her mouth after every bite, whether she needed to or not. He also noted that she didn't look at him and mostly kept her eyes downcast.

Curious to see what she would do, he propped his elbows on the table. He was pretty sure that was a big no-no according to fancy etiquette rules.

Caroline's gaze flicked toward him, widening, but she quickly looked away. She took another sip of her water, then dabbed at her mouth with the napkin.

Testing her again, he pushed his plate of food away. "That was a delicious dinner, thank you."

Sure enough, she immediately stopped eating, even though her plate was mostly full.

"You're welcome. Is there anything else I can get you?"

He sighed and sat back. "I'd really like to know what got you so spooked. What's going on?"

Her lips pressed together and she stared out the windows at the sparkling pool behind the house. "Do you know how to swim?"

He followed her gaze, not sure where she was going with this. "Yes."

"Is it fun? I always thought it would be. Fun."

"You own a pool and you don't know how to swim?"

She shook her head. "It was Richard's pool, not mine. And, no, I don't know how to swim. My husband always said he was worried I'd burn too easily out in the sun because of my pale complexion." She tapped the arm of her chair. "But that's not the real reason he didn't want me to know how to swim."

"What was the real reason?"

"Fear. Richard liked to invent new ways to control me, to make me afraid. I always figured one day he'd use the pool to teach me one of his lessons. I'm sure he would have, eventually. He just never got around to it."

Luke scooted forward in his chair. "Tell me about these lessons."

She shook her head. "No. That's not something I'm going to share."

"But you *are* sharing, aren't you? You're telling me little bits and pieces of your life, how your husband controlled you and allowed—or perhaps encouraged—the servants to pretty much ignore you from what I've seen."

She bowed her head. "Yes."

"If you don't want to talk about it, why share even some of it?"

Her mouth curved into a harsh smile. "Because I'd hoped that I'd never have to admit the truth to anyone. I'd hoped to keep my shame to myself. Earlier this year, for the first time, I shared a tiny part of what was going on with someone I thought I could trust."

"Your husband's lawyer, Leslie Harrison."

"Yes."

"Did something happen earlier? When she was here?"

She stared at the pool for a moment before answering. "You and Alex were right to doubt her." She rose from her chair. "I'm ready to show you why I called you."

Luke scrambled out of his chair and hurried after her. She led him through the maze that was the mansion, to the front room just off the foyer. He barely had time to realize it was probably her husband's office, when she picked up some papers from the massive desk. She handed an envelope to him.

"Read this first."

The short missive inside was written in carefully printed block letters.

I KNOW YOU KILLED HIM. I KNOW THE WILL IS FAKE. YOU WON'T GET AWAY WITH THIS.

"How did you get this?"

"One of the maids brought it in. From the looks of the envelope, it came through regular mail."

"When?"

"Today, I guess. The maid brought it to me shortly after I got home."

He placed the letter and envelope back on the desk. "We need to call Alex and Detective Cornell."

She laughed bitterly. "Why? So they have more evidence that makes me look guilty?"

"No. So they have more evidence that someone is trying to hurt you, that you're the target."

She grew very still. "What do you mean?"

"I mean that it's most likely the killer sent that note. He's trying to threaten you, scare you. Maybe that's why he killed Mitch. But frightening you isn't his only goal. He wants to torture you, by making you look guilty."

"Well, if that's true, goal accomplished."

He started to round the desk toward her, but she held up her hand. "Wait. That's not all. Leslie tried to get me to sign something earlier today. I thought it was a simple power of attorney, and I told her I wanted to take control of my own affairs now, that I didn't want to give up control to her, but I would think about it. She tried to take the document back, but I put it in the drawer. She was fairly nervous about that. After I received that letter—" she waved toward the note he'd just set down "—I took a fresh look at what she wanted me to sign." She pointed at some papers on another part of the desk.

Luke picked them up, saw the top page was, as she'd said, a typical-looking power-of-attorney form, but then he read the second and third pages. He set the documents down.

"I can see why she was nervous and didn't want you to read the rest. Did she really think you would sign over a huge portion of Ashton Enterprises to her? And make her a voting board member?"

"Apparently so. And the way I've allowed everyone to trample over me for the past few years, I shouldn't be surprised that she thought she could get away with it. Everyone tries to control me or profit off me in some way." Her blue eyes lifted to his. "Except you. You haven't tried to take advantage of me, to push me around. You're the first person who has really listened, and cared enough to look out for my interests. I never would have thought to hire Alex if it weren't for you. And I probably would have signed that paper Leslie gave me if Alex hadn't warned me about being extra careful and holding no one above suspicion."

Tears gathered in her eyes. "And what do you get in return for helping me? Your friend is killed."

Without stopping to think about how she might react, he moved around the desk and gently pulled her toward him, holding her close. At first, she stiffened, but then she melted against him. He reveled in the feel of her softness molded to his hardness and rested his chin against the top of her head.

He told himself he was holding her to make her feel better, but he realized that wasn't the whole truth. Holding her made *him* feel better. For the first time since losing his friend, he felt some of the tightness in his chest begin to ease. He selfishly held her, using her as his lifeline, a balm to his troubled conscience.

"I lost a good friend today," he whispered against her hair. "But I know Mitch wouldn't want either of us to wallow in guilt over his death. He'd want us to work together and find justice."

When she didn't say anything, he pulled back and looked at her. "It's not your fault."

"My brain knows that, but my heart is having a lot harder time with it."

She moved out of his embrace and wrapped her arms around her waist. "What do we do now?"

He resisted the urge to pull her back into his arms, just barely.

"For one thing, I think you should fire Leslie."

Her face paled and her eyes took on a haunted look. "I know. I will. But not today. That's not an easy conversation, especially after she helped me escape Richard. I owe her so much."

"You don't owe her your company, your wealth, and that's what she tried to take. She basically tried to steal it from you, hoping you wouldn't notice."

"You're right. And I will take care of it, just not today."

He didn't like that, but it was her decision to make. "I recommend you don't wait too long. She knows too much about you and your holdings, enough to be dangerous if she can't be trusted, which she's proven she can't." He waved at the letter and the power-of-attorney document. "Are you going to call Alex and Cornell?"

She blinked at him. "You're *asking* me?"

"Of course. I'm not going to try to order you around. You're a full-grown woman." The look of astonishment on her face made him realize what she'd been thinking—that Richard would never have asked her. He would have told her.

Luke stiffened. "Caroline, don't confuse me with your late husband. I would never hurt you, would never try to control you or dictate your actions. Richard Ashton and I are nothing alike."

Her face turned a light shade of pink. "I see that. I'm sorry. I'll try not to confuse the two of you again. Maybe it would make it easier if you'd quit calling me Caroline. That was Richard's preference, not mine. My maiden name was Caroline Bagwell. My friends, my parents, always called me Carol. But Richard thought it sounded too common, so he insisted on calling me Caroline."

Humbled that she would put him in the same category as her friends and family, he smiled. "Carol. It's a beautiful name."

She returned his smile with one of her own. "Thank you." Her smile faded, replaced by a look of worry.

"Is there something else?" he asked. "Something you haven't told me?"

She briefly closed her eyes, and when she opened them, they looked so haunted his heart ached for her.

"After Leslie's visit, and getting that letter in the mail, I searched Richard's desk. I knew he kept his most private papers in those drawers. I guess I just didn't want any more surprises, no more secrets. So I went through all his documents."

She pulled the bottom drawer open, lifted the first piece of paper out and handed it to Luke.

He scanned the short letter, from a private-investigation firm, dated two months earlier. Then he met her tortured gaze and waited.

She sighed and admitted out loud what she already knew. "We need to call Alex and Detective Cornell."

CORNELL FINISHED PUTTING the documents into evidence bags. He sealed them and wrote something across the front in permanent marker before sliding them into his suit-jacket pocket.

Carol sat behind her husband's desk while Alex, Cornell and Luke sat in chairs they'd pulled up to the other side. Carol had to admit Richard was right about one thing: the large desk that dominated the room gave someone a sense of power and control. She decided right then and there that she was going to keep it, and that she would stop thinking of it as Richard's desk. It was her desk now.

"Mrs. Ashton," Cornell said. "That letter from the investigation firm makes it clear your husband suspected Miss Harrison was stealing from him. He was working with that company to entrap her with false documents and information they were feeding her during your weekly visits to her office. It's also clear he was going to fire her soon and provide the evidence he'd gathered to a prosecutor to press charges. Do you have any reason to suspect that Miss Harrison was aware of this, prior to your husband's death?"

She shook her head. "No, I didn't know anything about it until today."

Alex tapped the desk. "Depending on what types of traps the investigator was setting, Miss Harrison may have realized something was 'off' with the documents. She may have been suspicious and figured out what was going on."

"If so," Cornell said, "that gives her motive. I imagine if she lost the Ashton account, she'd be in serious financial trouble. And of course she'd be in danger of losing her license, even if she wasn't found guilty in criminal court. Those are powerful motives for murder." He jotted some notes on his notepad. "What about the anonymous note? Miss Ashton, do you have any reason to believe the will that was filed with the courts was fake as the note states?"

"No. I know my husband drew up a will right after we got married, making me the primary beneficiary. I didn't know the details, of course. And if he changed the will later on, I have no knowledge of it. But Richard wouldn't have told me about it if he had."

He pursed his lips and considered. "It does seem odd that he would only give his family members five million each and give you the rest, with…everything that went on between you two. Seems reasonable that he changed the will later to cut your portion much smaller and give more to his brothers. Do you know if his brothers have much money?"

"They both own their own businesses and live in expensive homes. Not as grand as this one, but certainly not cheap by any means. I'd say they're both doing extremely well without their brother's money."

"Millionaires?"

"I believe so, yes."

"It must have galled them that their brother was a billionaire. Maybe they assumed he'd leave the estate split equally if he died. They would have been shocked when the will was filed and they didn't get much, relatively speaking."

Luke leaned forward in his chair. "You think one of them killed Richard?"

"We've been looking at them all along as potential suspects, but I think we need to dig harder and see what shakes out."

"What about Mitch?" Luke asked. "Have you gotten anywhere with that investigation? Are you convinced his death is related to Ashton's?"

"I'm keeping an open mind on a link, but investigators on both cases are sharing information since it seems highly likely both murders were performed by the same killer. Unfortunately, I don't have anything new to offer you." He turned to Carol. "Have you thought of anyone else who might have wanted to harm your husband?"

"Or harm Caroline," Alex added from his chair on the other side of Cornell. "We haven't established who was the target, her or her husband."

Cornell frowned, obviously not caring for that reminder. "I haven't made up my mind on anything. I'm exploring all possible angles. Mrs. Ashton? Did your husband—or you—have any enemies?"

She shook her head. "Actually, just the opposite. Everyone loved Richard. They thought he was an extraordinary humanitarian." She couldn't help the bitterness that crept into her voice. "I suppose, from the outside looking in, he was. He certainly gave an incredible amount of money each year to charities. As for me, I don't see how I could have made any enemies. I barely know anyone."

"What about your attorney, Leslie Harrison?"

"She's not an enemy right now. I consider her a friend—or I did, until I read that document she left. I imagine the friendship will be over tomorrow, when I fire her. But, honestly, I can't count her as an enemy, at least not as someone who might have wanted to harm either me or my husband."

"It's getting late," Luke said. "I think the more important consideration right now is how to protect Carol."

Alex's brows rose. "'Carol'? Not 'Caroline'?"

"It's what I prefer," she said.

"Carol," Alex corrected himself. "As for protection, I thought there was a team of security guards watching over the mansion, but I didn't see anyone when we drove up."

She cleared her throat. "I fired them—at least, from watching this house. They still handle security for the rest of my husband's—the rest of *my* holdings."

"Any particular reason?" he asked.

She glanced at Luke before responding. "They were my jailers for years. I suppose I wanted to take off my shackles and cast them aside."

Alex's eyes widened, but he didn't say anything else.

"You still need security," Luke said. "Even if nothing was going on, a mansion like this needs a show of security to dissuade would-be thieves. And until we find your husband's killer, you need to assume it's possible the killer was targeting you and therefore you need to be protected."

She looked pointedly at him. "Fine. Then I'd like to hire you instead, permanently, to stand guard over this house."

"While I appreciate the faith, all my guys are still out on other assignments." His mouth tightened. "Not to mention the office is in chaos without Mitch to direct everything."

"I'm sorry for your loss," she said again, offering him a watery smile. "If you need to cancel our contract, I'll understand. But if there is any way for you to keep me as a client and stay here as my personal bodyguard, I'd appreciate it. I can give you money to hire someone to watch the office, and to hire more guards so they can watch the house."

"I'm sure we can work something out, but it will take time. Of course I'll stay to protect you, but I can't do it alone. The house doesn't have a security alarm. And a house this size has dozens of entrance and exit points. Without a full security staff right now, it's not safe."

"Couldn't you get an alarm company to wire the house, like you said you were going to do at the cottage?"

"Yes, but it's after seven o'clock at night, on a Sunday. It will take days to adequately wire this house. That's not something that can be done before tonight. I've got another recommendation. And you're not going to like it."

"What?"

"I think you should rehire Stellar Security, at least until the alarm system is installed and I have a chance to hire some more guards and bring them in."

She bit her bottom lip.

"I agree," Cornell said. "You can't stay here without more guards."

"Then I'll leave. I hate this house anyway. There are no good memories here. I have no intention of living here long-term again. I can go somewhere else."

Alex leaned forward, resting his arms on top of the desk. "The simplest, safest thing for tonight would be to get Stellar Security to send their guards back here. If you don't want to stay, you can plan where to go tomorrow. But tonight, I'd be more worried about you trying to figure out a new place that's safe and arranging all the details. You just don't have enough time for that."

She rubbed her hands up and down her arms. "All right. I'll call Stellar and ask them to guard the house again. But tomorrow I'm moving out."

A LITTLE OVER two hours later, the staff of security guards from Stellar Security was back in place as if they'd never left, with one notable exception—Luke.

Per Caroline's—Carol's—request, he accompanied her everywhere she went. He would have recommended that he stay glued to her side anyway, but having her suggest it made everything smoother, and made him feel good that she trusted him and seemed to derive strength and confidence from his presence.

When she'd spoken to the head of security on the phone, after Alex and Cornell had left, she had tentatively reached for his hand. He took the gesture for what it was. She needed his support, someone to help her find the strength she'd forgotten she had inside her all this time.

But once the security guards arrived, she hadn't needed to hold his hand anymore. He could see her blossoming, coming out of her shell, like a phoenix rising from the ashes. And it amazed him how different she seemed already, less than a week after her husband's influence over her had been severed. Looking at her now, he couldn't imagine she would ever allow another man to control her the way Richard Ashton had. And it made him wonder how she'd gone from the strong woman before him to the timid, insecure woman he'd met that day in his office. Thank God her husband hadn't been able to completely kill the strong woman inside her. Hopefully, in time, she'd learn to smile far more often than she did now and have a happy life. Lord knew she deserved it.

After accompanying him on a tour of the house so he could verify the doors and windows were locked and that there were sufficient guards posted, she led him to the massive winding marble staircase in the two-story foyer. They'd passed it several times today, but she'd never seemed to notice it, as if she was avoiding it. But it couldn't be avoided any longer. It was time for bed. And now, as she paused at the bottom of the staircase and looked up at the next landing, he couldn't miss the telltale shaking of her hands.

He edged closer to her side and did what she'd done earlier: he offered her his hand.

She entwined her fingers with his. "I shouldn't be scared to go up these stairs, but I can't help picturing him up there, waiting, watching, ready to punish me for thinking I could escape him."

"He can't hurt you anymore, unless you let him."

Her mouth tightened. "That's the problem, isn't it? I let him hurt me for so many years. How could I have been so weak, so cowardly, for so long?"

He gently pressed his hand beneath her chin, urging her to look at him. When she did, he leaned down and kissed her forehead. Her eyes widened.

"What was that for?" she whispered.

"A reminder."

"About what?"

"That you're an intelligent, beautiful, strong woman. You faced a monster in this house every day, a man who was over twice your size and used his size to intimidate and hurt you. And in spite of that, you did what few women could have done in your position. You survived. You didn't let him destroy you. Look at what you did today. You made some tough decisions, like deciding to fire someone you had once thought of as a friend, and rehiring the security company because you knew it needed to be done. A coward couldn't have survived what you have and wouldn't be getting stronger every day like you are." He squeezed her hand and gestured toward the second-floor gallery. "Tell me what you see."

Her gaze followed his, up the stairs, pausing on the middle landing, then higher as she looked left and right down the gallery with its doors opening off it.

"I see fear, and misery, and pain," she whispered.

"Do you know what I see up there?"

She shook her head.

"I see a white marble railing. Behind it, I count five wooden doors, with thick, carved molding around them. I see red plaster walls—"

"Burgundy," she said, her voice halting.

"Okay. I see burgundy plaster walls, some little wooden tables with shiny tops."

"Granite tops." Her voice was stronger this time.

"Expensive, pretentious shiny tops." Out of the corner of his eye, he noticed her lips curve into a tiny smile. Encouraged, he continued. "And on the walls of the pretentious gallery are paintings. Most of them are of other buildings or animals, a few portraits here and there. And smack-dab at the top of the stairs is some alleged artist's really blurry, wretched attempt at painting an outdoor scene, but it looks more like a picture taken out of focus."

She let out a burst of laughter. "It's a Monet! And it probably costs more than this entire house."

He cocked his head. "Hmm. Can't say that I see the appeal."

She cocked her head as well, mimicking him. "Honestly, I don't see its appeal, either." Her eyes danced with laughter as she smiled up at him.

Unable to resist the impulse, he brushed her hair back from her forehead.

Her smile faded, but she didn't look upset that he'd been so familiar. Instead, she looked puzzled.

"I should be afraid of you," she said.

He stiffened. "I would never, ever hurt you."

"I know. I'm not sure how I know, but I know. You're a large, muscular, incredibly handsome man."

He grinned. "Good to know."

"That wasn't a compliment. Big men, handsome men, scare me. Normally. Because I expect them to be like my husband. But you're…different. You make me smile. And you make me feel…safe."

She turned back toward the stairs. Her eyes were still full of shadows, but she squared her shoulders, and her mouth tightened into a determined line. "Let's do this."

THE HOUSE WAS DARK, silent. The live-in staff had retreated to the wing on the opposite side of the estate hours ago. And Carol was asleep in the guest room next to Luke's. So what had woken him?

He slid out of bed, yanked his jeans on and shoved his gun into the back of his waistband. Moving as quietly as possible, he rushed through the open doorway that joined his room with Carol's. She was lying in the middle of the bed, looking like a fairy princess in her diaphanous, long, white nightgown, her golden hair splayed out on the pillow around her like a halo. The door from her bedroom to the hallway was still locked. If he'd heard something in his sleep, it hadn't come from this room.

He hurried back to his own room and eased the door to the hall open. Wall sconces along the gallery spaced about every twenty feet gave off a dim glow, like expensive, crystalline night-lights. Just enough light to change the pitch black to a muddy gray, to reveal images, shapes, but little else. Enough light to keep someone from stubbing their toe on one of the decorative tables that lined the hallway, or to keep them from stumbling against the marble balustrade and taking a nasty fall to the foyer two stories below.

He waited, listening intently, watching. But he didn't see or hear anything. He thought about going downstairs to check on the guards, but that would mean leaving Carol upstairs alone. Not an option. Instead, he pocketed the door key to his room and locked the door closed behind him to prevent anyone from going inside and getting to her that way. He quietly made his way to the end of the gallery, listening at each door, then quickly searching each room until he stood in front of the double doors that led to the one room he hadn't searched. The master bedroom.

Earlier, when Carol had led him upstairs and pointed out the guest rooms where they would both stay, she'd waved toward the end of the hall and announced that was the master bedroom. But she hadn't looked at it, and she'd quickly turned and gone into her own room after saying good-night.

Now he stood in front of the elaborately carved double doors, carefully turned the knob, then eased one of the doors open. The room was surprisingly well lit, as if the former occupants didn't like the dark. Dim light filtered from wall sconces spaced throughout the room, much like the ones in the gallery.

He edged farther inside. Everything was neat, nothing out of place. The four-poster bed in the center dominated the expansive room. He didn't think he'd ever seen a bed that large and imposing. The man who slept in a bed like that had to feel as if he was king of the world. And the woman who had slept there had to have felt as if she was…lost.

He forced thoughts of Carol away. He needed to focus, search the room. Then get back to his own. He moved into the adjoining bathroom, with its sunken tub and walk-in, glassless shower. He'd always considered his own master bathroom to be rather large, but he could have fit two of them in here.

He headed back into the bedroom and stopped. Something was off. Out of the corner of his eye, he realized a door that had been closed when he entered the room was now open. He clawed for his gun but he was too late. A dark shape launched itself from the closet. Luke twisted, slamming his shoulder into his attacker's sternum.

The man grunted with pain and staggered back, knocking over a delicate decorative table. A vase on the table fell to the marble floor and crashed, sending shards of glass flying across the room, pinging against the walls.

Luke lunged forward, but before he could throw a punch, his prey scrambled out of the way and took off in a dead run for the double doors. Luke ran after him, drawing his gun as he dashed through the open doorway onto the gallery.

"Hold it. Freeze or I'll shoot," Luke yelled.

The man skidded to a stop and slowly raised his hands. As he turned around, the door to Carol's room opened. She faced Luke, not seeing the intruder. She stepped into the hallway.

"Get back in your room," he shouted as he raced toward her. He couldn't shoot with her between him and the intruder.

The seconds seemed to drag by as everything happened at once.

Carol turned around.

The intruder grabbed her and yanked her in front of him. The glint of a knife winked in the light from one of the hall sconces. He held it to her throat.

Luke skidded to a stop just a few feet away.

The man had one hand manacled around Carol's waist, the other holding the knife at her throat. He crouched down behind her so Luke couldn't get a clear shot at him. His face was covered with a ski mask. He slowly backed toward the stairs, pulling Carol with him.

"Let her go," Luke demanded.

Carol whimpered and clutched the arm at her throat.

"There's no way I'm letting you out of this house with her," Luke said. "And there's no way you can get down the stairs without me getting a clear shot at you at some point. Your only hope is to let her go."

The man stopped. "If I let her go," he rasped, his voice sounding oddly forced, strained, "you'll just shoot me."

In a heartbeat. The man had signed his death warrant the second he held a knife to Carol's throat.

"Not if you don't hurt her," Luke lied.

The man backed a few more steps down the hall.

Luke followed relentlessly, his gun out in front of him.

Suddenly the man backed up against the baluster. "Drop the gun or I toss her over."

The blood drained from Luke's face. He hesitated.

The man lifted Carol a few inches off the floor.

She gasped, her eyes rolling white with fear.

"All right, all right. Don't hurt her." Luke knelt down and placed his gun on the floor.

"Kick the gun away from you," the man ordered.

Luke kicked it behind him, away from the intruder.

"Now back up."

He weighed his options.

The intruder lifted Carol higher.

Luke swore and backed up several feet.

The man lowered the knife from Carol's throat and peered at Luke over her shoulder. The face-off by the baluster seemed to stretch out forever, but only a few seconds had really gone by when the intruder heaved Carol up over the banister.

She screamed as he slapped her hands around the top of the railing and let go, leaving her hanging on all by herself, her feet dangling over the two-story drop, as he raced for the stairs.

Chapter Eight

Luke charged forward as the intruder raced away from him. The man had been smart, forcing Luke to make a choice between catching him and helping Carol.

There *was* no choice.

Luke lunged for the railing and leaned over, grabbing Carol beneath the arms and hauling her up and over. He fell back with her to the gallery floor, holding her in his arms. She buried her face against his chest, shaking uncontrollably, tears hot and wet against his skin.

Below them, the assailant raced across the foyer and out the front door, disappearing into the night.

LUKE CROUCHED DOWN in front of the couch where Carol was sitting, wrapped in a heavy terry-cloth robe, her face almost as white as the wall behind her.

"Are you sure I can't get you something? Aspirin? A drink?"

She shook her head but didn't say anything.

He sighed heavily and sat beside her. "I can call a doctor. Maybe you'd like something stronger, to take off the edge. Something to help you sleep."

She shook her head more forcefully this time. "No. No drugs. I don't want to go to sleep. Not here." Her eyes turned pleading. "Please," she whispered, "take me somewhere else. Anywhere. Somewhere safe."

His heart felt as if it was breaking as he looked at her mournful face. "I will. In a few minutes, okay?"

"Okay." She sank back against the cushions.

The house blazed with light now and was full of security guards and police officers, as well as the cook and two of the maids. They were the only live-in servants and had been roused from their rooms on the other side of the mansion by Cornell and his men. But they hadn't seen or heard anything that might help with the investigation. So, now they were busily laying out an assortment of refreshments for their unexpected visitors.

Cornell spoke in the corner of the family room to the guards' supervisor, who looked angry enough to kill someone. He'd already lambasted the entire staff for allowing the intruder inside, but now that they knew how the intruder had gotten in, Luke almost felt sorry for the guards. Almost.

The intruder had ambushed the guard at the front door and left him bound and gagged in the bushes, hog-tied with no hope of getting himself freed. He'd done the same thing to two other guards, leaving the front totally clear for him to sneak on in. Which just proved Luke's original theory, that the mansion required a security alarm, a high-tech one that was tamper-proof, or as close as possible to one.

When Cornell finished with the supervisor, he hurried to Luke. He glanced uncertainly at Carol, before motioning for Luke to step away with him.

As soon as Luke started to get up from the couch, Carol started to get up to follow him. He glanced at Cornell, shook his head, then sat back down.

"You might as well say whatever you need to say in front of her," Luke said.

Cornell dragged the coffee table closer and sat on it facing them. "Okay, here's where we stand. Other than your basic description of a white man, at least six feet tall, a hundred ninety pounds, wearing dark clothes, I've got nothing to go on. And since the grass out front is so thick, I don't even have a shoe print. I need another angle to figure out who this guy is. What I need to know is why he was here." He looked at Carol. "Mrs. Ashton, it seems likely the intruder was after you, since he went to the master bedroom. But if he was going to kill you, he could have just tossed you over the banister instead of making sure you were clutching the top rail before he took off."

"Or he knew if he hurt her I'd kill him," Luke said. "He may have been trying to kill her but had to change his plan to make sure he survived the night."

"If that's the case, then perhaps he went into the master bedroom looking for something besides Mrs. Ashton. Can we go up there together? See if something is missing?"

"All right," she said, her voice soft but steady.

She moved like a wraith through the living room, but this time she didn't cling to Luke's hand. She walked with dignity, somehow having pulled herself together for the task at hand. Cornell and Luke followed her up the staircase and down the long hall to the bedroom. Everything was quiet, like a church, until she pulled the doors open. Then the steady buzz of crime-scene investigators talking as they dusted for prints and searched for forensic evidence assaulted them.

Luke exchanged a startled look with Cornell.

Carol must have noticed the look, because she half

turned. "The room is soundproof," she said. Her mouth twisted bitterly. "So no one would hear my screams."

She went inside, leaving Luke and Cornell shaken and staring after her.

"I wish that bastard was still alive so I could kill him," Luke said.

Cornell's mouth lifted in a half smile. "Honestly, I'd probably be right there with you. The guy really was a class-A bastard."

They entered the suite and stood back, watching Carol slowly make her way around the room, weaving among the investigators as they collected evidence.

She seemed to wander in no particular pattern, stopping to open a drawer, or a jewelry box, or one of the three closet doors. Luke watched her closely, a suspicion growing inside him. If anything, her search was almost too random, as if she was trying to make sure no one paid her any particular attention or realized she was looking for something specific.

"I'm going to chat with the team lead and see if they've found anything," Cornell said.

Luke nodded but didn't take his gaze off Carol.

When she turned toward him, he looked off to the side, pretending interest in the tech nearest to him, dusting the top of a chest of drawers. A few seconds later, Luke looked back toward her. She opened a drawer in another chest and reached her hand all the way in. She felt around, then her eyes widened, and she felt around again. Whatever she was searching for obviously wasn't there.

She briefly shut her eyes as if in pain, then closed the drawer.

Luke averted his gaze.

Carol crossed the room and stood beside him.

"Anything missing?" he asked.

She wrapped her arms around her waist and shook her head. "No. I'm going back to the guest room to lie down for a few minutes."

Disappointment flashed through him that she didn't feel she could confide in him. "Hang on a second." He waved one of the security guards positioned at the doorway over to him. He read the tag on his shirt and addressed him by name. "Mrs. Ashton is going to lie down. Go with her and stand guard outside the door."

"Yes, sir."

Carol glanced uncertainly at Luke, obviously confused that he wasn't the one who was going to watch over her.

"I'll be there in a couple of minutes," he said. "I need to ask Cornell a few questions."

Some of the worry went out of her, but she still didn't look happy about trusting her care to one of the security guards.

Luke's supposed questions for Cornell were just a ruse to get Carol to leave. He waited until she was out of the room and he heard the guest-bedroom door close down the hall before hurrying to the chest of drawers she'd been so interested in. He pulled the same drawer open that she had opened earlier and reached inside. The drawer was empty, which struck him as odd since the rest of the chest contained clothes. But what would have been at the back of the drawer that she'd been searching for?

He felt all four corners, then pressed against the back of it. Still nothing. Then he turned his hand palm up and felt along the top. His fingers brushed against cold metal and a tiny cord. What the heck?

He straightened, pulled the entire drawer out of the chest and set it on top of the bed. The drawer was empty, but he'd expected that. The metallic object was attached to the chest itself, above the drawer.

Cornell crossed the room, his brow furrowed. "You find something?"

"Maybe. Give me a hand?"

Together, they lifted the chest and moved it about a foot away from the wall.

"That's enough," Luke said.

They set it down and bent to examine the back of the dresser. The little cord Luke had seen came out a hole in the back and went into the wall.

Cornell raised a brow. "What is that?"

"Got a flashlight?"

"Always." The detective pulled a penlight out of his suit-jacket pocket and handed it to Luke.

Luke shined the light into the cavity now exposed without the drawer covering it. He reached in and un-clicked the object he'd found and pulled it out.

"Is that what I think it is?" Cornell asked.

"If you're thinking it's a camera, yeah. It is." Luke examined it. "Looks like it's motion activated."

They both glanced at the bed, which was where the camera had been pointed. There must have been a small gap above the drawer that gave the camera a clear view to the bed.

"Sick jerk," Luke swore.

"You won't find an argument here."

Luke pressed the side of the little camera and opened it. "Looks like there was a video card in here, but it's gone."

"I can't imagine the intruder broke in to get his jollies watching videos of a married couple in their bed."

"Me neither. I think he was after something else."

"I'll tell the techs to be on the lookout for a video card. Maybe Mr. Ashton had put it somewhere else and the camera was empty." He shook his head. "These cases get stranger and stranger the older I get."

"If there was one camera, there may be more," Luke said.

"Understood." Cornell headed to one of the techs.

Luke set the camera on top of the chest of drawers. The more he learned about Richard Ashton, the more he despised the man. He would have liked to believe the camera really was empty, that Ashton hadn't used it to record whatever he did with Carol in this room. But Luke was willing to bet that wasn't the case.

The real question was—who else knew about that video card? Did the intruder know? Had he removed the card after getting whatever it was he wanted from the bedroom so no one would have the video of him?

To answer that, he needed to confront Carol. And that was not a confrontation he was looking forward to.

A LIGHT KNOCK sounded on the guest-room door. Carol drew the quilt up to her chest.

"Who is it?"

"Luke. Can I come in?"

She sat up and scooted against the headboard. "Come in."

He stepped inside, shut and locked the door behind him. Normally she'd have thought he was being a little overcautious, locking the door when there were dozens of police officers and security guards right outside. But after tonight, she wasn't sure there was any such thing as being "too careful."

He perched on the edge of the bed, one leg on the floor, the other bent at the knee resting on top of the mattress.

"I know about the camera."

She sucked in a breath.

"Sorry. I shouldn't have been so blunt."

"No, no, that's okay," she said. "That's one of the reasons I trust you. You're honest, straightforward. I know what to expect around you. And believe me, that means a lot." She shoved her hair out of her face, belatedly wishing she'd taken the time to brush it or braid it. "Now you know one of my secrets. My husband liked to film everything that went on in the bedroom."

He reached out his hand, palm up, and waited.

That was something else she liked about him. He didn't grab for her hand or try to do anything she didn't want to do. He was patient, calm, and let her make the choice. And he seemed to understand how much she craved human contact, no matter how small, after so many years of only being touched by a monster.

She blinked back unexpected tears and threaded her fingers with his.

"You wanted to get the video card when you went into the bedroom," he said. "Did you find it? Did you bring it in here and hide it somewhere?"

"No. I didn't. Yes, I looked for it. I had forgotten about it earlier. The camera has been there so long, I quit paying attention to it years ago. But when I saw everyone in the bedroom, I remembered. I didn't want my shame to end up as fodder for the police in their squad room, or worse, to end up on some internet site for everyone to see."

"Your shame?"

She glanced longingly toward the door.

"Carol, you don't have to tell me anything you don't want to. But if there's anything at all that you can think of that might explain why someone would break into the house and go into the master bedroom, let me know."

"The only thing I saw that was missing was the video card. So…I have to think that was the reason for the break-in. But other than showing…how Richard…hurt me, there wouldn't be any point in taking the card. What value would that be to anyone?"

He stared at her for a long moment, his mouth tightening. "I wish I could take away the hurt, roll back time somehow and spare you from whatever he did to you."

She lifted his hand and kissed the back of it. "Thank you. You really seem to care. I don't know why you do, but I… It means the world to me. It's been so long since anyone…cared."

"I want to hold you, Carol. Will you let me hold you?"

His request startled her so much she dropped his hand.

He winced. "I guess not. Sorry. I thought—"

She put her hand on his again. "I would like that very much."

He raked the covers down and slid underneath them, fully dressed. He put his arm around her waist and pulled her close, her back to his chest.

"I told you earlier I'd take you somewhere else tonight, but it's only a few more hours until dawn. There's a security guard right outside the door. And once the police leave, there will still be a dozen guards throughout the house, working in pairs this time. If you're okay with waiting, we can both rest for a little while and figure out a new plan in the morning. Are you okay with that? Staying here until morning?"

In answer, she snuggled into the pillow, content to have his arm around her. With Richard, the arm would have felt like an anchor, pulling her under, drowning her.

But with Luke, it was a protective circle, making her feel safe, cherished, as if—for once—she actually mattered.

As SOON AS Carol woke the next morning, she took care of a task that she'd been dreading, but that she knew had to be done for her to move forward. She called Leslie and fired her. Leslie hadn't taken the news well, and the call had turned ugly.

After that, Carol had straightened her shoulders and informed Luke she was going to pack and leave. Her destination? Anywhere but the house where she'd lived for the past five years. No, correction—she'd told Luke four-and-a-half years. For the first six months of her marriage she and Richard had lived in a smaller house about an hour outside of Savannah.

Which was where they were going right now.

Luke was still shocked she wanted to go to a home she'd shared with her late husband, but while driving there in his beat-up old Thunderbird—which he'd insisted on taking rather than her car since hers had a GPS tracker on it—she'd told him a lot more about her past. She'd explained how she'd met Richard when she was a struggling waitress. He'd taken her from a life of poverty to a life she never could have imagined.

That first six months, Carol had explained, had been pure bliss. They'd been happy, until their first fight. It was over something silly, something she couldn't even remember now. It wasn't the argument that stuck in her mind. It was Richard's reaction to the argument. He'd been absolutely livid that she disagreed with him. His eyes had darkened to almost black. His face had turned a bright red. And then, so quickly she didn't have time to even comprehend what he was going to do, he'd slammed his fist into her jaw.

He'd seemed just as horrified as she was after he hit her, but everything changed that day. At first she'd been too shocked, and too busy nursing her bruised jaw, to even contemplate leaving him. And then he'd spent the next two weeks doing everything he could to make it up to her. He'd apologized over and over, waited on her every need and sworn he would never, ever hurt her again. She'd believed him, even if she was a bit wary.

But the honeymoon was officially over, and the magic of their lovers' hideaway was destroyed. Both of them knew it, even if they didn't admit it. Richard purchased the mansion in town and they moved. They'd never returned to their hideaway. But he hadn't sold the house. He had a service come in once a week to clean it, and stock it, just in case they ever wanted to go there on vacation or for the weekend. But they never had. Which was why Carol was certain no one would ever think to look for her there.

Luke parked his car under a tree a short distance from the house, where it wouldn't be easily noticed from the road. He hadn't been keen on the idea of going to one of Richard's holdings, but the place did look deserted and they hadn't passed anyone on the two-lane road for the last half hour. They certainly couldn't have gone to *his* house since he was in the phone book. And it wasn't exactly a secret that he was her bodyguard. Maybe this would work out.

He went around to the other side of the car to open the door, but Carol didn't wait. She opened it herself and met him at the trunk. He popped the trunk open and grabbed their bags, which only had a few days' worth of clothes. He'd had her ditch her larger bag back at the mansion and pack a smaller one with a shoulder strap like his to keep his hands free.

He kept an eye on the road as they hurried up the walkway to the two-story house that, although nowhere near as big as the mansion in Savannah, was still considerably larger than average.

Carol punched a code into the electronic keypad to unlock the door.

"That's unusual," Luke said.

"Maybe for most people, but not for Richard. He insisted on keypads instead of physical keys for properties he rarely visited. It made it easier for him to be spontaneous without having to worry about finding the property manager to get the keys."

"From what I've read of him in the papers, he didn't strike me as the spontaneous type."

She hesitated. "He wasn't always the man you read about in the papers. But you're right. At least for the bulk of our marriage, he wasn't spontaneous. He was much more…controlled."

Luke immediately regretted saying anything about her husband. Yes, she'd brought him up first, but it was Luke's comment that put that spark of hurt, that flash of fear, back in her eyes. He sensed there were many more layers of pain inside her, and every once in a while one of those layers would reveal itself. He just hoped she'd be able to talk it all out someday, and then maybe she'd start feeling whole again. Richard had hurt her so much in life. Luke hated that the man had the power to continue to hurt her in death.

She led the way inside the foyer to the two-story family room in the middle of the house. It was surprisingly dust free, but then again, if a property-management company was coming in once a week to clean the place, it made sense. Especially with no one living there to make any messes.

"Let's check the kitchen," Carol said. "If the manager keeps it stocked with fresh groceries like he's supposed to, I might be able to whip us up something for breakfast. That is, if I can remember what I used to know about cooking."

She started forward, but he stepped in front of her.

"I need to search the house first, make sure there aren't any unwelcome visitors hanging around."

Her mouth tightened at the reminder that they might not be safe, but she didn't argue.

"This place is too big for a quick search. You'll need to come with me so I'm not worried leaving you down here by yourself, okay?"

"I wasn't looking forward to being left alone, so that's fine with me."

He gave her the keys to his car and pulled out his gun. "If anything happens to me, I want you to promise you'll run. Get out of here. Don't try to help me and don't stop for anyone until you're in a public area surrounded by other people. Promise?"

Her back stiffened. "I'm not going to be a coward and run away. I can help. If nothing else, I can knock someone over the head with a lamp or something."

"No way. I don't want to risk your getting hurt." From the mutinous look that flashed across her face, he knew she wasn't going to do as he said. He decided to go for her main weakness—her soft heart. "Let me put that another way. If you're in the way, or if I have to worry about you while I'm trying to fight for my life, the distraction could get me hurt or killed."

She crossed her arms. "You're just saying that to make me feel guilty."

"Is it working?"

She rolled her eyes. "Yes. Fine, I won't get in the way. I'll go for help."

"Thank you." He waited, trying not to laugh, knowing her impeccable manners wouldn't allow that comment to stand on its own.

"You're welcome," she said between clenched teeth.

He waited until he turned around to smile. "Let's check upstairs first."

Had he really thought this house was smaller than the one in town? From the front, it appeared smaller. But there seemed to be just as many doors upstairs as at the other house, with just as many places to hide. The only good thing was that there wasn't an open banister across the upstairs hallway where someone could be thrown over. He forced the unpleasant reminder of Carol's near miss out of his mind and continued the search through the bedrooms and bathrooms.

Carol followed along, her fingers occasionally tracing some small object, as if reliving a memory. A good memory, from the dreamy, faraway look in her eyes. That should have made Luke happy, to know that she had some good memories from the early part of her marriage— heaven knew, she deserved and needed some good memories—but he wasn't nearly as selfless as she was. And he was okay admitting, to himself at least, that he was jealous of those early memories.

When he was satisfied no one was lying in wait for them upstairs, they headed down the second staircase, at the end of the hall, that led directly into the kitchen downstairs. They made a complete circuit of the first floor and ended up back in the foyer.

"Satisfied?" She set the keys he'd given her on the half wall by the door.

"Satisfied."

"Then let's eat. I'm starving." She led the way through the family room to the adjoining kitchen and went straight for the refrigerator.

"Remind me to send a thank-you note to the property manager once this is all over," she said. "He's definitely keeping the place clean and stocked with groceries. We have fresh milk and eggs and everything I need to make omelets. Do you like omelets?"

"Sure. I could just eat cereal, though. No one has to go to the trouble of cooking. And you sure don't need to wait on me." He located what appeared to be the pantry, next to the refrigerator, and opened the door to look for some cereal.

Carol's soft hand on his stopped him.

"I know I don't *have* to cook for you. That's why I want to. Okay?"

He saw the truth in her eyes, so he closed the pantry door. "How can I help?"

"Just sit down at the island and stay out of my way."

He laughed. "I'm starting to like this new Carol, Commander Carol," he teased.

"Commander Carol. Hmm. I could get used to that."

She hummed a low tune as she cut up some peppers and ham then whisked the ingredients together in a pan over the gas stove top.

As she cooked their breakfast, Luke set a pot of coffee brewing and poured them some orange juice. He was used to eating his meals off paper plates and using disposable forks and cups, but he figured she was used to an entirely different style of living, so he rummaged through the cabinets and drawers and set the table the way his mother had taught him years ago.

Carol slid a perfect-looking omelet onto his plate and

a smaller version onto hers. "I probably would have used paper plates and plastic forks, myself. Less to clean later."

He laughed. "Me, too. I just figured…"

She straightened, her smile disappearing. "That I was a snob?"

"No, not at all. I figured you were used to…better. That's all."

She put the pan in the sink and sat on the barstool across from him. "Sorry. I'm being overly sensitive. It's just that…I played a role for so long, pretending to be someone I wasn't. I'm only just now beginning to remember the real me again."

They ate in silence, but it was a comfortable silence. When they were done, they both cleaned the kitchen. Luke wiped his hands on a paper towel and tossed it in the garbage.

"That was the best omelet I've had in ages," he said.

She grinned. "I'm surprised they came out so well. It's been ages since I last cooked."

"When?"

"At a diner, a few hours west of here, in a tiny town called Chester. That's where I lived…before, with my parents."

He shook his head. "Don't think I've heard of Chester."

"Not many people have. It's basically a blip on State Road 126, in Dodge County. Most of the few hundred people who live there commute to work in bigger towns or they work on farms."

"What did you and your parents do?"

"They were short-order cooks at a diner. I was a waitress most of the time, but my father taught me to cook when things were slow."

"You met Richard there," he said, urging her to continue.

"Yes. He was traveling on business, back when he used

to drive himself places, before his businesses exploded into the stratosphere and he went from well-off to rich beyond imagination. I was nineteen. He was twenty-nine, handsome, funny. The first time he came into the diner, he was lost. I gave him directions. The next time he came in specifically to see me. Less than a year later we were married. And for a little while, he really was my white knight." Her lips twisted. "Who am I kidding? He was never a white knight. He didn't change after he married me. He was already the man he would always be. He just hid it well and I was too blinded by his money and his handsome face to see past the facade."

She crossed her arms and leaned back against the sink. "Maybe coming here was a mistake. I'm surrounded by memories, wallowing in the past. Did my husband and I have some good times? Yes. We did. Most of them in this house. But that ended a long time ago. I'll never understand why he treated me the way he did, or why I took it for so long, but the only way I'm ever going to move forward is to truly put my past behind me. And I can't do that until my husband's killer, until Mitch's killer, is caught, and I can begin a new life—not a life of hiding out in the country, either."

He winced at the reference to Mitch. He hadn't allowed himself to grieve for his friend, not yet. He needed to keep his emotions locked away so he could focus on his primary duty: keeping Carol safe.

He pushed himself away from the sink and faced her. "What are you saying?"

"I'm saying I'd like to leave. Let's go somewhere else, somewhere without my husband's ghost hanging over us. And once we're there, I want to call Detective Cornell and Alex Buchanan and find out what's going on with the investigation. I'm a wealthy woman, Luke. I can hire any number of private investigators. I've been sleepwalking and cowering through this entire ordeal instead of thinking for myself. Not anymore. I'm going to throw all my resources into catching this killer so I don't have to hide and cower ever again."

"Sounds good to me. We'll figure out another place to stay once we're on the highway."

They headed through the family room again and into the foyer. Luke picked up their bags and settled the straps over his shoulders. He was about to open the front door, when he glanced at the half wall where she'd left the keys earlier.

The keys weren't there.

"Carol, run!" He let the bags drop to the floor and whirled around.

Something hard slammed against the side of his head. White-hot agony spiked through his skull. Carol's screams echoed through the room as Luke dropped to his knees.

Chapter Nine

"Run, run, run!" Luke yelled as he wrestled with the man who'd walloped him with the baseball bat in the foyer.

Carol took off as fast as she could through the family room. Leaving Luke behind was one of the hardest things she'd ever done, but she remembered what he'd told her about being a distraction. He'd made her promise that if something like this happened, she wouldn't try to help him—she'd try to escape instead.

She zipped into the kitchen and raced up the back staircase to the second floor. The sounds of fighting continued behind her, which gave her hope that Luke might be okay if he was able to continue to wrestle with the man who'd attacked him—the man with a ski mask on, the same man who'd been in the house in Savannah last night, and most likely the man who'd killed Richard and Mitch. But how had he known she would come to this house? And why did he want to kill her, too?

She prayed that she and Luke would survive long enough to get the answers to those questions.

Bam! A gunshot echoed through the house. Carol froze in the middle of the upstairs hallway. Where had the shot come from? Behind her in the kitchen? Or ahead of her down the main staircase? She waited, being as still and quiet as she could while she listened for another sound to tell her who had fired that shot and where they were. But no more sounds came from belowstairs.

She inched her way down the dark hallway. With all the doors closed upstairs, the only sunlight that filtered in was from the staircases, leaving the long hall almost pitch-black. She could turn on the lights but she didn't dare. Instead, she tiptoed down the wooden floors toward the front of the house to peek down into the foyer.

When she reached the stairs, she flattened herself against the wall and carefully leaned around the corner.

A hand clamped over her mouth. Another hand yanked her backward against a hard, warm body. She bit down on the finger pressed against her lips.

Her attacker jerked against her but didn't remove his hand. Instead, he cupped it so she couldn't bite him again. He pulled her back, away from the stairs in spite of her struggles and into one of the bedrooms. He eased the door shut behind them.

He spun her around, moving his hand to keep it over her mouth as his other hand now cupped the back of her head so she couldn't get away. She looked up into a pair of chocolate-brown eyes and slumped in relief. Luke.

She pulled his hand away from her mouth, wincing when she saw the clear impression of her teeth on his skin. "I'm sorry," she whispered, but he was already crossing to the window.

He pulled the heavy draperies back and looked down.

Carol rushed to him. "There aren't any balconies on this house," she said, keeping her voice low. "And a brick porch extends the entire length of the back. There's no way out through these windows."

He dropped the curtain back into place. "What about the front windows?"

She shook her head. "Pretty much the same. If we're

lucky, we might drop onto one of the shrubs, but they're not exactly soft, either." She frowned and feathered her hand across the side of his head, where his dark hair was matted with blood.

He ducked away and hurried to the door.

"You need stitches," she said. "Do you have double vision? Are you hurt anywhere else? I heard a gunshot, but I—"

He held one finger to his lips, signaling her to be quiet.

She nodded, letting him know she understood.

He opened the door and peered into the hallway.

A knife suddenly glinted in front of Carol's face as a hand wrapped around her from behind, holding the knife at her throat. She sucked in a breath.

Luke jerked around, his brows lowering in a thundercloud when he saw the man holding Carol.

"How did you get in here?" Luke demanded.

"That doesn't matter," the man rasped in Carol's ear, his voice oddly distorted as if he was purposely trying to change it. "What matters is that I've got her. And I'm not letting her go until I get what I want."

Luke took a step toward them, but stopped and put up his hands when the knife bit into Carol's throat.

"Ease up," he said. "Don't hurt her."

"If you don't want her hurt, then keep your distance."

Luke straightened and adopted a bored look. "What do you want?"

"I want her to admit what she's done."

"I haven't done any—"

"Shut up." He jerked her hair.

She gasped and strained against him, trying to ease the pressure on her scalp.

"You're a murderer," he said in his thick rasp. "I know you had Richard killed. The only question is—who's your accomplice? Who's the one who actually shot the gun so you wouldn't have to dirty your own hands?"

"That other door over there," Luke said, waving a hand toward the door at the back-right corner of the room. "That leads to a bathroom, right? A bathroom that leads to an adjoining bedroom? That's how you got in here."

"Yeah, so? What does it matter?"

"It matters a lot. It tells me you know this house just as well as Carol does. And it explains how you knew the security code to get in the front door. The only question is—which brother are you? Daniel or Grant?"

Carol gasped.

The man behind her swore and pulled his hand away from her throat. He shoved her toward Luke. She stumbled forward. Luke grabbed her and pushed her behind him, blocking her with his body as he faced the other man. Luke slowly backed up, pushing her along with him.

The man standing on the other side of the room wasn't holding the knife anymore. He must have tucked it into his clothing somewhere. But in its place was a gun— Luke's gun. He must have gotten it away from him in the struggle downstairs.

"You seemed tougher at the hospital," Luke said, still backing up, "when you weren't sucker punching anyone with a baseball bat or holding a gun on them. Why don't you put the gun away, take off your mask and face me like a man, Grant."

The man cursed again. He yanked the ski mask off. Sure enough, Grant stared back at both of them, his face mottled red and furious. But he didn't lower the gun.

"How did you know?" he demanded.

"It was a guess. I figured I had a fifty-fifty chance of being right." Luke stiffened and looked off to his right, toward the open bathroom door. "What the hell is he doing here?"

Grant jerked around toward the bathroom.

Luke yanked the bedroom door open and lunged through the doorway into the hall, pulling Carol with him.

An angry shout told them Grant wasn't too far behind. He'd fallen for Luke's distraction but not for long.

"In here." Luke opened a door and shoved Carol inside. But instead of following her, he closed the door, cocooning her in the darkness of the hall closet.

Carol froze at the sound of his footsteps pounding on the wooden floor of the hallway. She squeezed her hands so hard the nails bit into her palms. Why hadn't he come with her? She knew the answer. He was making himself the target, giving her a chance to get away.

A shout sounded down the hallway. A shot rang out, sounding impossibly loud in the narrow confines of the closet. More footsteps pounded against the floor, running past the closet. What was happening? Was Luke okay? Was he hurt, shot, bleeding?

The image of her late husband lying dead on the kitchen floor of the cottage filled her mind. But instead of *his* face, she saw *Luke's* face, cold and pale.

No! She had to help him. She twisted the doorknob, determined to find Luke. But she hesitated. He'd been emphatic about her not trying to help him if something happened. He'd made her promise to escape if at all possible, to go for help. It wasn't as if she could just call the police. Her cell phone was in her purse, which was downstairs in her overnight bag. Luke had his phone, or at least she thought he did. But would he get a chance to use it? Or had it broken during the struggle with Grant in the foyer?

What were her options? Driving Luke's car was out. She didn't have the keys. But Richard kept a car out back in the garage in case he ever visited the house. The keys would be in the garage, too, hanging in the cabinet with the same code to unlock it that was used for the front door. If she could make it out of the house without being seen, she could drive to town and get help.

The image of Luke lying on the floor, bleeding, flashed through her mind again. All her adult life she'd made the wrong choices. She'd chosen the wrong man. She'd believed he was sorry every time he hurt her and she kept giving him chance after chance to change, until everything went so far she was too scared to even try to leave. And now here she was, faced with another choice. If she did what Luke had asked, she might be able to get help. But the nearest town was thirty minutes away. Round trip that was an hour, plus the time to find help, and the time to run to the garage and sneak out the car. If Luke was hurt, could he last an hour, or longer?

She squared her shoulders. That wasn't a chance she was willing to take. She knew this house. Every inch of it. She knew all its secrets, every connected room, every little alcove or storage place. There were panels in some of the walls both upstairs and down that no one would know about if they hadn't been shown. She could well imagine Richard giving Grant the code to get into the house in case he ever wanted to get away or use the house for vacation. But there was no way Richard would share all the little secrets the house contained. Which meant she had an advantage over Grant.

As she inched the door open, the uncertainty and fear she'd felt earlier were, amazingly, gone. She'd made her decision. And for once, she knew it was the *right* decision. If she died today, she would die as a strong, brave woman who was willing to risk everything to save a good man. That was far better than living the rest of her life wondering if she could have done something to help Luke.

She poked her head out the door and looked up and down the dimly lit hallway. She listened intently, searching the shadows, but no sounds alerted her to anyone close by. No shadows separated themselves from the doorways or alcoves where decorative tables sat. Time to be brave. She yanked her heels off and discarded them in the closet. Barefoot, she could run across the wood floor upstairs and the tile floor below without making a sound. She hurried out of the closet and rushed toward the back stairs. She figured those would be safer because only someone in the kitchen would see her on those stairs, and then only once she got to the bottom. The front stairs were too exposed and could be seen from most of the main rooms on the bottom floor.

She crept down the stairs, carefully listening for sounds of anyone who might be waiting for her. But everything was quiet. Too quiet. Where was Luke? And where was Grant?

When she reached the last step, she looked around the kitchen. Empty. She hurried to the doorway that led into the family room. Again, she paused, looking out at the massive room, but she didn't see anyone. Where had they gone?

Across the room she could see the foyer. With the front door standing wide open. Was it a trick? Was someone watching her even now, baiting her with the open door, the promise of escape?

Where are you, Luke? Are you okay?

She ducked back into the kitchen, debating her next steps. A weapon. She needed a weapon, something to defend herself with, or Luke, if it came to that. She ran to the butcher-block holder on the countertop and pulled out the biggest knife she could find. From tip to tip it had to be at least twelve inches long. The thought of wielding it against someone had her stomach twisting. She put the knife back and selected a smaller one, one that she could conceal the way Grant had. She would use it if she had to, but only as a last resort.

She slid the knife blade beneath the sleeve of her blouse and held the hilt in her palm. For the most part, the weapon was hidden, but she could pull it out quickly if needed. Then she pulled a small cast-iron skillet out from a cabinet. About five inches in diameter, it wasn't too heavy for her to hold, but it could do some serious damage if she had to swing it at someone's head.

That sickening image had her almost putting the skillet down, but she reminded herself there was someone else needing protection this time. It wasn't just about her. She had to be brave, and if that meant she had to hurt Grant, then that was what she'd have to do.

She crossed to the doorway again and looked into the family room. This time, she heard something. A taunting voice, low, familiar. And then a scream, quickly cut off. She blinked in confusion. The scream had sounded familiar, too. And it had sounded like a woman. Was someone else here?

She stepped into the family room. Movement to her left had her spinning around, holding up the skillet.

It was snatched from her grasp as Luke stepped in front of her, holding his finger to his lips to tell her to be quiet.

She flung her arms around his waist and gave him a tight hug before stepping back. The look of surprise on his face had her feeling foolish. But then he pulled her close and hugged her back. He leaned down and pressed his lips close to her ear.

"Glad you're okay, too, but you should have stayed upstairs in the closet. Or better yet," he whispered, "you should have gotten out of here and hid in the woods."

She shook her head and pulled back. "I'm not leaving you here alone. You'd better figure out a way to include me in your plans."

His brows lowered. "You promised."

"I know, but it wasn't a promise I should have given."

He obviously didn't like to hear that. He looked as though he was about to argue with her, when another noise reached them. It sounded like angry words, again, in a low, ominously familiar tone, followed by a loud thump, as if someone had been hit.

"Where's it coming from?" she whispered.

He pointed to the door at the end of the family room, one that led into a room next to the foyer.

He set the skillet down on a nearby end table. "I gave Grant the slip a few minutes ago and was going to come upstairs and get you. But then I saw him go into that room."

"The study," she whispered. "He's got someone else in there. A woman. He's hurting her. We can't leave her here."

His mouth thinned. "I know. Try to stay out of the way, okay? Can you at least promise you won't jump out in front of a gun or something?"

"I'm not an idiot."

He grinned. "No, you're not an idiot. You're beautiful, maddening and utterly adorable, but never an idiot."

She grinned back.

They hurried along the edge of the wall so the occupants of the study couldn't see them. When they reached the doorway, Luke motioned for her to stay there.

She nodded, content to trust that he knew what he was doing. If she saw an opening to help, she would. But he didn't need to know that. After all, she didn't want to distract him, as he'd said earlier.

Another scream sounded from inside the room, oddly muted, though.

She pressed her hand to her throat.

Luke's jaw tightened and he looked into the room. He stiffened, then hurriedly disappeared through the doorway.

Carol waited, but when he didn't immediately return, she crept forward and peeked inside. When she saw what Luke had seen, the knife she'd been holding concealed in her left hand fell from her numb fingers and clattered to the marble floor.

LUKE HAD JUST reached the chair where Grant was sitting, when he heard the sound behind him and knew Carol had come into the room. His heart broke for her, but at the same time he couldn't help her, not yet.

Grant didn't move in spite of the noise Carol had made. Instead, he held his head in his hands and wept. Luke rushed around the edge of the chair and grabbed the gun that Grant had placed on the end table. Grant lifted his head and gave him a bleary-eyed look.

"Go ahead," he rasped. "Shoot me. It doesn't matter now."

"Where's your knife?" Luke demanded, pointing the gun at him.

Another scream sounded from the tableau playing on the big-screen TV at the end of the room. Luke winced and forced himself not to look. He'd already seen more than he'd ever wanted to see when he entered the room.

"The knife," he prodded. "And for the love of God, turn the TV off."

Grant fumbled on his left side for the knife he'd apparently tucked into the cushion.

A whimper escaped from Carol.

Luke couldn't stand knowing what she was seeing. He couldn't wait for Grant to find the remote, either. He turned his gun and fired at the TV. The screen cracked and went dark, a burning smell rising through the room. Luke didn't care if the entire house burned down. At least Carol wasn't seeing the recording of herself anymore, being beaten and raped by her former husband.

Grant handed the knife to Luke. "I'm sorry, Caroline," he called out. "I didn't know. Why didn't you ever say anything?"

She crossed to the TV and took the video card out of the player beneath it before facing him. She clenched the card in her fist. "It was my shame, my burden, to share or not to share. And neither you nor Daniel ever made a secret of your dislike for me. I had no reason to think you would believe me, or help me, if I told you about Richard."

He wiped his eyes that were still streaming tears. "You were a waitress. We thought you married him for his money. But that doesn't mean we wouldn't have helped you if we'd…" He shook his head. "I didn't know. And after Richard was killed, I assumed you were behind it, that you'd paid someone to kill him. And once I heard about the will, I figured you must have switched the wills so you'd get all his money."

"Why did you break into the house back in town last

night?" Luke asked, risking a quick glance at Carol to see if she was okay. She was pale, but holding her own.

"I broke in because I knew Richard had those recorders all over the place. He was always paranoid like that. I was going to get the cards and watch them to see if any of them showed Caroline talking to someone about killing Richard, or talking about the will." He shook his head. "But it doesn't matter now. I don't care that you killed him. He deserved it for what he did to you. God, I'm so, so sorry." He covered his face with his hands again.

Carol's face had gone ashen as he spoke. "What other recorders?"

Luke held the gun on Grant and crossed the room to stand by her. "Answer the question."

Grant wiped his eyes and collapsed against the back of the chair. "Richard showed me one of the recorders once, a long time ago, at his office. He was trying to catch someone he thought was guilty of sharing corporate secrets with one of his competitors. He joked that he should use them at home, too, to make sure the staff wasn't helping themselves to the silver when he wasn't around. When I was visiting the mansion once, I searched the guest room I was in just to see if he was serious, and I found the camera hidden in the top dresser drawer—just like the camera hidden in his desk drawer at work. I always figured he had them in every room after that."

Luke reached out his left hand. Carol threaded her fingers with his and he gently squeezed.

"Carol isn't the one who had your brother killed," Luke said. He felt more than saw Carol's gaze on him. "I don't need to see the recordings to know that."

"Thank you," she murmured.

He nodded. "Grant, my phone's broken. Do you have a phone?"

Grant reached into his back pocket.

Luke stiffened. "Slowly."

Grant carefully pulled out the cell phone.

"Put it on the coffee table in the center of the room and then sit back down."

Grant did as he was told. When he was a safe distance away, Luke picked up the phone and handed it to Carol. "Will you call 911?"

She made the call, gave them the address, then sat on one of the couches with Luke, facing Grant.

"I think you made up that story about thinking Carol was behind your brother's death," Luke said. "*You're* the one who killed him. And you killed Mitch. Did you come here to kill Carol, too?"

Grant's eyes widened and he vigorously shook his head. "No, no, no. I swear. I would never hurt anyone. I didn't bring a gun with me here. I only took your gun away so you wouldn't shoot me."

"Right. And those were warning shots you fired at me."

"They were! I only came here to talk. I wanted the truth from Caroline."

"People who want to talk don't break into other people's houses and hit them over the head with a baseball bat."

His face flushed red. "I just wanted to overpower you so I could get your gun away and make you both sit down. I admit, I probably went about it the wrong way. But you have to understand. I thought she'd killed Richard, or had him killed, so I was afraid for my own life, too."

"I'm not buying any of this," Luke said.

"I am." Carol's soft voice called out beside him. "Grant has always been impulsive, and he's not much better than me at making the most well-thought-out, reasoned choices." She smiled sadly. "I also know you loved Richard deeply, even though you were both at odds with each other so much. You must have been overcome with grief thinking I had something to do with his death."

"You're being far kinder than I deserve," Grant said.

"I agree." Luke kept his gun trained on the other man.

"To be honest," Carol said, "I was half convinced you might have been the one who'd killed him."

"Me?" Grant's face reddened again. "Why would you think that? I loved Richard."

"I know, but you two argued so much."

He twisted his hands together. "We argued about money, a cardinal sin in his opinion. Money meant everything to him." His mouth tightened. "Even more than family."

Luke had had enough of Grant's whining and Carol's feeling sorry for him. The man had held a knife to Carol, twice. Even now there was a small smear of blood on her throat where his knife had pricked her. And his stunt on the balcony could have killed her if she'd let go before Luke could pull her back up. Grant didn't deserve her sympathy. He deserved a fist in the face, just for starters. "You said something about a will earlier. What were you talking about?"

The look Grant gave Carol wasn't anywhere near as sympathetic as it had been earlier. If anything, he looked bitter, angry, as if he'd hold that knife to her neck again if he got another chance.

Luke motioned with his gun, catching Grant's attention. "Don't look at her. Look at me, and answer my question."

"Why don't you ask her? She may have killed Richard, she may not have. I don't know. And I don't care anymore after watching that, that…" He waved at the broken

TV. "But it's not fair that she switched Richard's will. It doesn't matter how mad he was at me, he wouldn't have left me only five million dollars. And he didn't have any reason to be mad at Daniel and only leave him five million, too. I want to know where the real will is. The one that was filed with the court is fake."

Carol shook her head. "I don't know anything about a new will. All I know is that Richard drew one up shortly after we got married and I assume that's the one that was filed with the court."

"Why do you care about the will?" Luke asked. "You and your brother are both millionaires."

"Daniel's a millionaire, but not me. My money's all tied up in my company. In case you hadn't noticed, the economy has been rough for the past few years. I'm close to bankruptcy. And my daughter is ready to start college. Five million dollars is a Band-Aid. We're going to lose everything."

Sirens sounded outside the window, getting closer.

Grant's fingers tightened on the arm of his chair.

"Don't even think about it," Luke warned.

Grant cursed and sat back.

Carol had grown quiet. Once again she'd been put through more than anyone should have to bear. All Luke wanted to do was hold her and assure her that everything would be okay. But it would be a lie. Because he wasn't at all sure that it would be. Someone had murdered Richard Ashton. And someone had killed Mitch. Was that person Grant? Yes, probably. But if there was even a remote possibility that Grant was innocent, then the culprit was still out there, and Carol's life was still in danger.

The sirens stopped in front of the house, their lights flashing through the windows behind the ruined TV.

"I'll let them in." Carol crossed the room. She stopped

at the doorway and glanced down at the video card in her hand. She looked around, as if searching for something, and then held her hands up. It looked as if she was trying to bend the card in two, but she wasn't strong enough.

A rapid knock sounded on the front door. "Police. We had a 911 call from this address. Open up."

"Give me the card," Luke urged. "I'll destroy it for you." He wasn't sure if he was telling the truth or not. He didn't want to look at the video, and certainly didn't want anyone else to, but what if it contained evidence that would prove the identity of the killer?

Carol hurried to him but hesitated as she started to hand him the card. "Promise me you won't look at it and that you'll destroy it the first chance you get."

Guilt squeezed his throat, making it tight. He didn't want to give her his word when he wasn't sure yet what he was going to do. He didn't make promises lightly. And she didn't deserve to be lied to.

She frowned. "Luke?"

He cleared his throat, self-loathing nearly choking him. "Promise."

The look of relief that crossed her face had him silently cursing himself.

She handed him the card.

He shoved it into his pants pocket as she rushed out of the room to let the police inside.

Chapter Ten

It took over an hour to sort out things at the house and for an EMT to stitch the wound on the side of Luke's head. He refused to go to the hospital, saying he was fine and that he wanted to keep guarding Carol until the police determined whether or not Grant was the killer.

When Luke and the police escort ushered Carol into the police station back in Savannah, the dull hum of noise quickly faded to an almost eerie silence. And when Carol saw one of the local gossip papers sitting on a table in the lobby area and saw her picture on the front page, she knew why. The caption underneath read DID WEALTHY, ABUSED SOCIALITE FINALLY GET HER REVENGE?

Luke's hand at her back tensed. He'd noticed the paper, too. Their eyes met and he shook his head, as if trying to tell her not to worry about it. She smiled, both to reassure him and to give the impression to anyone watching that she didn't care what others thought of her.

"In here." The police officer pushed a glass door open and waved them into an office. "Can I get you anything to eat or drink while you wait for Detective Cornell?"

Since the officer was looking at Carol, she shook her head. "I'm fine. Thank you."

"How long do you think Cornell will be?" Luke asked. He sat beside Carol in front of Cornell's desk.

"Depends on how the interview goes. As long as Ashton is talking, Cornell won't leave the room. You sure you want to wait?"

"Yes," they both said at the same time.

The officer left, closing the door behind him.

"Actually," Carol said, rising from her chair, "I wouldn't mind a moment in the ladies' room to freshen up."

Luke stood, too, and stepped to the door.

She put a hand on his arm. "I can handle this without you. We passed the ladies' room two doors down. And the place is crawling with police officers. I'll be perfectly safe."

He didn't want to let her leave without him, but she insisted.

"All right. But if you're gone more than a few minutes, I'm sending a policewoman in there after you."

"I'll keep that in mind." She smiled again and headed out.

Luke stood in the hallway outside Cornell's office watching her. She gave him a small wave and went into the ladies' room.

Once inside, she quickly saw to her needs. Then she pulled her cell phone out of her purse to take care of the real reason she'd wanted a moment of privacy. Since meeting Luke she'd been as honest as possible with him, except for keeping the details of her relationship with her husband as private as she could. But this one time she knew she couldn't make this call in front of him because he would have argued and tried to stop her.

The phone rang twice, then a man's deep voice answered. "Hello?"

"Hello, it's me, Carol Ashton."

"Is everything okay? Luke called me earlier and told me what happened at the house in the country."

"Yes, yes, we're both fine. Actually, we're at the police station. Cornell took Grant Ashton to an interview room and he's talking to him right now."

"Good. I hope Ashton tells Cornell everything."

"I don't."

"Excuse me?"

"That's why I called. I don't want Grant telling Cornell *anything*. I need your help."

HALF AN HOUR LATER, Cornell stepped into his office and greeted Carol and Luke before sitting behind his desk. "Looks like we've got our man."

"He confessed?" Luke asked.

"Sort of. He admits he's the one who broke into the Ashton mansion here in town the other night and left Mrs. Ashton dangling off the balcony."

Carol shuddered at the memory and gripped her hands together in her lap.

"He also said he moved the GPS tracking device from Mrs. Ashton's car to your Thunderbird because he figured if Mrs. Ashton went anywhere she'd be with you."

"How did he know where the tracker was in the first place?" Luke asked.

"I get the impression he and his brother Richard used to be quite close. He knew a lot of his secrets." Cornell glanced at Carol and his face turned a light shade of red. "Apparently not all of them, though. He insisted quite emphatically that he didn't know what your husband... did to you, or he would have tried to help you."

"I believe him," she said. "I didn't realize back then that he would have helped, or I might have told him. But after seeing how upset he was earlier, I do believe he would have tried to stop my husband."

Cornell folded his arms on his desk. "He mentioned a

video, and that Luke shot the TV at the country house to stop the video. But no one found a DVD or video card. Do either of you know what happened to it?"

"What else did he tell you?" Luke asked, avoiding the question.

Carol shot him a grateful look.

Cornell studied both of them, obviously debating whether to press the issue of the missing video. Finally, he said, "Grant gave us details about how he tracked you to the house in the country. He insists he only did so because he was convinced Mrs. Ashton had arranged for Richard to be killed and he wanted a chance to confront her about it. He swore he never meant to hurt either of you."

Luke pointed to the side of his head where he had a brand-new row of stitches. "I'd like to offer evidence to the contrary."

"Noted, I assure you. The gist of what he said was that he wanted to confront Carol both about the murder and about his brother's will. He's convinced there's another will somewhere and that Mrs. Ashton knows where it is."

"Did Grant say anything about killing Mitch?" Luke asked.

"He insists he had nothing to do with that, or his brother's death. His financial difficulties are a strong motive for him killing his brother. He assumed Richard would bequeath him a substantial part of his fortune, and he was bitterly surprised when that didn't happen. As for Mitch, we haven't come up with a motive yet but the evidence supports the possibility that Grant killed him."

Carol straightened in her chair. "What evidence?"

"One of the people at the cemetery remembered seeing Grant and Mitch arguing before the service started.

Grant was apparently upset about Mitch taking pictures. I don't know whether there was more to it than that, or whether that would be enough to make Grant turn violent. But from what we're gleaning from other interviews with Grant's friends and known associates, he has a temper and tends to act without thinking first. Plus, he's known to carry a pocketknife. The coroner said a small knife, like a pocketknife, was used to kill Mr. Brody."

Luke winced.

Carol offered him a sympathetic smile before turning back to Cornell. "I thought you said Grant might be Richard's killer. It doesn't sound to me like you have any evidence of that."

Cornell smiled and put his hands behind his head. "That's because I saved the best part for last. You told me at the country house that Grant and Richard argued quite a bit. I was able to subpoena Grant's credit-card records and already got a hit that puts a whole new light on things."

He sat forward, resting his arms on his desk. "The morning of Richard Ashton's murder, Grant Ashton filled up at a gas station…two miles from the cottage where Ashton was murdered. Lucky for us, that station is brand-new, with state-of-the-art electronic video surveillance. They keep their recordings on a hard drive, which means they can store them for months without running out of space and writing over them again like some of the cheaper equipment does. I've got someone on the way there right now to review the recordings from the morning of the murder. I think we all know who we're going to see on that video."

He pushed himself up from his chair and straightened his jacket. "Now, if you'll excuse me. I think I've let my subject stew long enough. I'm about to go get that confession."

A knock sounded on the door.

"Come in," Cornell called out.

A police officer opened the door and stood back. Alex Buchanan walked in wearing a suit and holding a briefcase.

Luke and Carol stood.

"I didn't know you were coming to the station," Luke said. "Did your investigator find something out about the case?"

"Unfortunately, no."

"Then why are you here?"

He glanced at Carol before crossing to Cornell. "I've been notified that you have a client of mine in custody and that you're interviewing him without his lawyer present. I'm here to stop the interview and confer with my client."

A look of confusion crossed Cornell's face. "But the only person I'm interviewing right now is Grant Ashton."

"He's my client."

"He hasn't asked for a lawyer," Cornell insisted.

"A family member hired me to represent him."

Cornell crossed his arms across his chest. "Oh? Who? His brother, Daniel?"

"That information is confidential."

Cornell argued with Alex about having the right to know who was trying to make things so difficult for him.

Luke wasn't paying attention to either of them. Instead, he was intently watching *her.*

She cleared her throat. "Gentlemen." When Cornell continued to shout, she cleared her throat louder. "Detective, Alex, please. I think I can clear up this...misunderstanding."

Cornell gave her an aggravated look. "Oh? And how can you do that?"

"I'm the family member who hired Alex."

CORNELL'S PREVIOUSLY COOPERATIVE attitude ended the moment Carol told him she'd asked Alex to represent her brother-in-law. He ushered her and Luke out of his office and ordered them to wait down the hall in a conference room while he and Alex went to see Grant.

Once inside, Luke shut the door and pulled a chair out for Carol. He crossed to the other side of the table, but rather than sit, he flattened his palms on the table and leaned down toward her.

"What was that all about?" he growled.

She calmly picked up her purse and stood. She was all the way to the door before he realized she was actually leaving. He rushed around the table and caught up to her in the hallway.

"What are you doing?" he demanded.

"Leaving."

He rolled his eyes. "Yeah, got that. *Why* are you leaving?"

Her knuckles whitened from where she gripped her purse so tightly. "I spent nearly five years cowering from a man who used his size and strength to intimidate and hurt me. Those days are over."

She tried to move past him.

He reached out toward her.

She flinched and backed up.

Luke froze, his hand in midair. The anger drained out of him as understanding dawned. "Carol, I was just going to fix your purse strap. It's about to fall off your shoulder."

Her face flushed and she grabbed the strap just as the purse started to fall.

Luke took a step back to give her some more space. "I thought you knew I would never hurt you."

Her blue eyes rose to his and he was shocked at the anger that flashed in them. "Yes, I do know that. Because I won't let you, or any man, hurt me. Ever. Again."

He scrubbed his jaw with his hands. "I'm sorry. I don't know what else to say. Was I using my size back there to intimidate you? Yeah, I guess I was. My size is an asset in my line of work. I use it to my advantage automatically, without even thinking about it. But I never should have done that with you. It won't happen again."

She glanced uncertainly past him.

He held his hand out toward the door. "We need to talk. Please."

The seconds ticked by like minutes and Luke was worried he'd screwed up beyond her ability to forgive. How could he have been so stupid, knowing her past? If he could kick his own ass he would.

She took a step toward the conference room but stopped at the sound of footsteps.

Alex Buchanan turned the corner and headed toward them. "Are you two leaving?"

Luke raised a brow and waited for Carol to make that decision.

"No, we were just going back into the conference room," she said.

"Mind if I join you?"

"Of course not."

Luke would have rather had a private conversation with her, but since he didn't have a choice, he followed the two of them back into the room and closed the door.

Alex leaned his forearms on the table. "Grant gave me permission to share what he and I discussed, but you hired me, Carol. Do you want me to share the information in private or can Luke be included?"

"Of course he can be included. Please, tell us what you found out."

Carol's quick agreement to include Luke had some of his earlier worry fading.

"Okay," Alex said. "But first, I'm curious to know why you hired me in the first place. You never really explained that on the phone."

"The phone? When did you have a chance to call him?" Luke asked.

Her face turned a light pink. "I wasn't with you every single minute since we got to the station."

Luke frowned, then enlightenment dawned. She'd called Alex from the bathroom. He grinned but decided to stay quiet so he wouldn't embarrass her further.

"I hired you because it was the right thing to do. Grant isn't the killer—"

"You don't know that," Luke insisted.

"Yes. I do. I've known Grant for a long time. And while I may not know a great deal about his personal life and what makes him tick, I do know one thing for certain. When he gets upset, he lets everything out. There's no holding back. He doesn't know how to be clever or coy. Back at the country house, his emotions were raw. He was telling the truth when he said he didn't kill Richard. It isn't right for him to be railroaded into prison. And it especially isn't right that his wife and daughter should suffer, either."

Luke watched her intently. "I notice you haven't said anything about your other brother-in-law during all this time. Do you feel Daniel's innocent, too?"

She frowned. "Honestly, I have no idea. Daniel is more…self-contained than Grant. He's always treated me politely, respectfully. But he didn't come to the mansion very often. I really don't know that much about him except that he's not married. Daniel and Grant are in many ways opposites. With Grant, you know what you're getting. With Daniel, he's all manners and self-control." She rubbed her hands up and down her arms. "Richard was very controlled, too. I guess that's one of the reasons I can't come to any conclusions about Daniel. They seemed so much alike."

"Well, Cornell is looking into both of them," Alex said. "He was excited, hoping he'd caught his man earlier, but he's keeping an open mind and making sure his team explores every possible lead."

"What all did Grant tell you?" Luke asked.

"He reiterated what he'd already told Cornell. He basically admitted to breaking into both houses and assaulting both of you."

"I don't want to press charges for that," Carol said.

Luke cursed.

Alex shot him a warning look. "That's for you to discuss with Cornell. It would be a conflict of interest for me to talk about that. I will, however, tell you that Grant's main hang-up seems to be about the will. He's convinced the will that was filed was fake and that his brother wouldn't have left him only five million dollars. He wanted me to try to get a search warrant for the mansion. He's convinced the will is hidden inside."

"Would a judge go along with that?" Luke asked.

"Highly unlikely, and that's what I told Grant. Unless he has some kind of proof, no judge will want to get embroiled in that kind of mess. When I told him that, he got upset and said he should hire Leslie Harrison to represent him. He said Leslie represented Richard in a dispute with the IRS last year and won. He figured if she could beat the IRS, she could get a judge to look into the will. I reminded him Harrison isn't a criminal lawyer. I also told him if she was his lawyer I wouldn't be. I've never cared much for Miss Harrison and how she does business and I don't want to be associated with her professionally."

Carol frowned. "What's he going to do?"

"I don't know. He's in an odd state of mind right now, hard to reason with. I think he knows more than he's telling. I know you want me to protect him, but he's his own worst enemy. Hopefully my warnings to him to not say anything else to Cornell will sink in. I'll come back in the morning and talk to him after he's had a chance to sleep on everything."

Alex stood to leave. "Oh, I almost forgot. Cornell said to tell you that you're free to go. His lead detective wanted to discuss the investigation with him and he wasn't sure how late he'd be. He'll call you if he has more questions about what happened today."

"Thank you, Alex," Carol said. "For everything."

"My pleasure." He shook their hands and left.

Luke sat back in his chair and considered Carol. "We've had an incredibly full night and day. Any idea where you want to go this time? As your bodyguard, I'm advising you not to go to any of your husband's holdings, no matter how much you believe no one knows about them. And I think we need to pick up a rental car just to be sure no other GPS trackers are hanging around."

"I'll leave the destination up to you this time. I'd like nothing better than one night without worrying about some madman finding me. But first, we need to stop at the mansion here in town."

"To get more clothes?"

"No. To get Richard's will."

Chapter Eleven

It was late afternoon by the time Luke and Carol arrived at the mansion, or at least, arrived a block away and parked on a side street while they surveyed the mass of news vans and reporters surrounding the estate.

"Good grief," Carol said. "The press has never been this bad before."

"Murder sells." He glanced at his watch. "We're five minutes early. Are you sure you want to go in there? We can leave right now, rent a car, hole up in a hotel somewhere."

"A hotel hardly seems like the place to hide out. I'd think the paparazzi have lookouts all over town. A hotel is one of the first places they'd expect me to go."

"Not if you're in disguise."

"Hmm. Maybe. But the point is moot for now. Because I'm not going anywhere but the mansion. I have to find that will."

"You've been secretive about the alleged will since dropping that bomb on me back at the police station. I think now is a good time to explain why you're suddenly so sure there *is* another will."

"It just makes sense. The more I think about it, the more I'm convinced that Richard would never leave his fortune to me, not after the first six months of our marriage, at least. I wasn't…important to him as a person. I was an object, his property, to control. He wouldn't have wanted to risk leaving his legacy to me. He wouldn't expect I'd be intelligent enough or capable enough to keep his businesses on the right track. He would have left the bulk of the estate to his brothers. Which means, there must be another will inside, in his papers somewhere."

"Possible, but he had Leslie as his personal lawyer on retainer. Why not file the will if he went to the trouble of drawing up another one?"

"Good question."

"I'm not sure I understand why you'd want to find the will, assuming it exists."

"What do you mean?"

"You're a billionaire. If what you say about an alternate will is true, you could lose everything. Why would you risk that?"

"Because it wouldn't be right. If the money belongs to someone else, they should have it."

"We're talking about Grant and Daniel here. Grant tried to kill you—"

"Allegedly."

"He held a freaking knife to your throat. Twice. He left you dangling off a balcony."

She winced. "Okay. Good points."

"And Daniel hasn't exactly come around to check on his beloved widowed sister-in-law after news of Richard's treatment of you leaked to the press. Neither of them seem particularly deserving of a massive change in fortune. On the other hand, you lived through hell and deserve every penny."

She looked out the windshield. "I can see where you might feel that way. But it's not like I could ever enjoy the money, knowing what I went through to get it. Don't you see? Everything I have reminds me of Richard." She held up her carefully manicured nails. "He dictated the color of my nail polish and how long my nails should be." She grabbed a handful of her long hair and held it up. "I'm a natural brunette. I never wanted to be blonde, but Richard wanted my hair this color. These clothes—" she waved her hand toward the silky pantsuit she wore "—these clothes were all chosen by Richard. All I want is to resolve this case so I can be safe once and for all. And then I want to go away somewhere, anywhere, someplace that doesn't remind me of him. If I buy another house, or new clothes, I'm buying them with his money. How will I ever truly escape him that way?"

Luke gently pushed her hair out of her eyes. "I always seem to say or do the wrong thing around you. It's none of my business what you do with the money or how you choose to live your life. You don't owe me any explanations."

She took his hand in hers. "You've been nothing but kind to me. You don't deserve to be lambasted for asking an obvious question." She shook her head. "But I just want to make sure the rightful owner of the money gets it. I want to be done with it so nothing ever comes back to haunt me later. I want to be free."

"You will be. Soon."

"I hope so. Too much has happened too fast. I just want to search the obvious places in the mansion to see if I can find a will. And then I want to get out of here. We can go wherever you think we'll be safe and won't be bothered by the press."

"Okay. Leave that to me. This won't be the first time I've had to sneak a client out from under watchful eyes and take them to a safe house." He glanced in the rearview mirror. "Here they come. Get ready. As soon as the press realizes what's happening, they'll be all over us."

She clutched her purse in her hand and grasped the door handle. "I'm ready."

A black Suburban pulled up beside them per the plan. Another one pulled up behind them. The doors popped open and half a dozen Stellar Security guards jumped out, surrounding Carol as she got out of the car.

Just as Luke had predicted, the press saw the Suburbans and started running toward them, aiming their cameras in their direction.

Carol hopped into the lead truck and it took off toward the mansion. Luke cursed and tossed the two bags that contained his and Carol's clothes into the back of the second truck and jumped in.

"Hurry up," he growled as the woman he was supposed to be guarding pulled farther away.

CAROL SLID THE bottom drawer of Richard's desk closed and plopped down in his leather chair. She'd searched every place she could think of for another will but hadn't found anything. At this point, she was inclined to think maybe Luke was right. Grant was just desperate for funds and had convinced himself the will that had been filed was a fake.

Luke walked into the office and propped himself on the edge of the desk. "I searched the master bedroom like you asked, top to bottom. Nothing. Even the wall safe is empty."

"Empty? It wasn't locked?"

"No. I pulled on the door handle and it opened right up. I assumed you'd given Cornell and his men the combination when they searched the room the other day and they didn't relock it." He frowned. "You didn't?"

She shook her head. "No. I don't even know the combination. But Richard put papers in that safe all the time. I find it hard to believe he would have left it unlocked. And I've never known it to be empty."

Luke pulled out his cell phone. "I'll update Cornell. See if he dusted the safe for prints. If he did, and didn't get any besides Richard's, I'll ask him to send a crew out here again and dust every inch of the thing. And then we're getting out of here. Is there anything you need if we don't come back for several days?"

"No. My bag from when we went to the country house has everything I need."

"All right. Wait here. I'll make that call, and then I'll arrange our escape from the press."

LUKE HURRIED OUT of the room and waved down one of the housemaids. He made his request and a moment later she came back with an envelope and a sheet of paper. He thanked her, explained what he wanted to do to get Carol safely out of the house, and she ran off again to do what he'd asked.

He was going to call Cornell, but first he had two other calls to make. And since he didn't want anyone to overhear him, he hurried to the little glassed-in garden off the back of the house that Carol had shown him a few days ago during the house tour. There was a fountain in the middle of the garden that splashed and made enough noise that he felt confident no hidden cameras or spying servants would hear his conversations.

First, he called Trudy at the office. She commiserated with him over Mitch's death, which made him feel guilty because he hadn't thought much about Mitch with everything else that was going on. He didn't have time to grieve for his friend right now, so he forced the emotions aside and gently brought Trudy back to the task at hand. He explained what he needed in detail and had her repeat it back to him. Satisfied she would give his message to his men so they could set his escape plan in motion, he hung up and made his second call.

To Alex.

Guilt gnawed at him again as he waited for Alex to answer. What he was about to do would horrify Carol if she ever found out. He'd made a promise to her, and he'd assured her he never broke his promises. And up to this point, he never had. But after what she'd told him about the safe, he knew they were on borrowed time.

Whoever was behind Richard's death had also managed to break into the house and empty Richard's safe without anyone knowing, which meant the killer was most likely someone Carol knew and quite possibly trusted. It was Luke's duty to keep her safe, which meant—in this one instance—he needed to break his promise, because it very well might mean that he would find out the killer's identity.

"Alex Buchanan," the voice answered on the phone.

"It's Luke. I have to make this fast. First, can you ask your investigator to look into Stellar Security?"

"Okay. What's he supposed to look for?"

"Anything suspicious, anything to do with the Ashtons. I'm getting a weird feeling about Stellar. There have been too many security breaches with them supposedly in charge."

"All right. You said 'first.' What else did you need?"

"A huge favor. I'm going to leave something for you in a van later today. The keys will be under the front bumper in a hide-a-key box. I'm leaving you an envelope under the driver's seat." He gave Alex the address of where the van would be.

"Okay. And what am I supposed to do with this envelope?"

"I'm hopeful you can examine the evidence inside it and let me know if you can figure out who broke into the safe in the Ashtons' master bedroom. I have a feeling whoever broke into the safe is Richard Ashton's killer."

"And just what is this evidence that you want me to look at instead of the police?"

Luke glanced around to make sure no one had come into the garden. Then he reached into his pocket and pulled out the video card Carol had given him back at the country house.

Chapter Twelve

An hour later, Cornell's CSI team was upstairs dusting the master-bedroom safe and the wall surrounding it, just in case they'd missed any prints the first time. Moments later, a housemaid and one of the Stellar Security guards—dressed in Carol's and Luke's clothes—ran out front to the circular driveway and hopped into the Rolls-Royce, sandwiched between two black Suburbans.

The caravan took off and barreled onto the street.

Just as Luke expected, the press made a mad dash to follow, and soon most of the news vans were racing after the decoy.

Some of the reporters remained, perhaps to ensure their counterparts hadn't been fooled. But they expected the wealthy socialite would leave the mansion in luxury, driven in one of the estate's expensive cars. They didn't pay attention to the pretty young housemaid and coarsely dressed gardener who left by way of the servants' entrance a few minutes later, walking hand in hand down the sidewalk.

When Luke and Carol in their disguises rounded the corner of the next street a couple of blocks over, another Stellar Security truck was waiting for them. They jumped in and rode in the truck a couple of miles away. Then the driver pulled over next to a dark blue Dodge Charger.

"Are you sure you want to do this, ma'am?" the driver asked. "Our company is more than capable of providing the security you need." His disdainful look wasn't lost on Luke.

Luke shrugged. "Up to you, Carol. They've done a smashup job so far." He didn't bother to temper the sarcasm in his voice.

She shook her head. "No, thank you. We're sticking to our original plan."

She got out, and Luke followed with their bags. Another security guard got out of the Charger and tossed the keys to Luke. He and Carol got inside, but as soon as the security van turned the corner, they hopped back out. They ran across the street to the parking garage on the corner and ducked inside.

"Where is it?" Carol asked.

"Two rows over, the white van on the end."

They hurried to the van and Luke grabbed the hide-a-key from under the front bumper. He slid open the side door behind the driver's seat, tossed in their bags and helped Carol inside. The windows were tinted dark just as Luke had insisted when he'd called two of his men to help him arrange the second half of the escape plan, unbeknownst to Stellar Security. He and Carol changed their clothes, using the clothing his men had gotten for them—T-shirts and jeans.

Carol finished putting her hair into a ponytail, then grinned as she ran her hands over the soft jeans covering her legs. "Richard would have been appalled to see me wearing something so…common."

Luke smiled, her restored good mood infectious. "That doesn't seem to bother you."

"Nope. Not one bit."

Not content with just one car change, Luke drove them

a few more miles outside the historic district of Savannah and they traded cars again. This time they drove a black Camaro.

A few minutes later, with Carol in disguise so no one would recognize her, they signed in at the Hyatt Regency just off River Street as Mr. and Mrs. Carl Johnson.

CAROL WAS LAUGHING when they ran into their hotel suite. "That was so much fun. No one knew who I was! We walked past that reporter in the lobby and he looked right through me."

Luke smiled and set their bags beside the couch. "You should smile more often."

"Yes. I should!" But her smile faded when he took a straight-backed chair from the table in the kitchenette and propped it under the doorknob.

But he didn't stop there.

He grabbed two drinking glasses, wrapped them in a dish towel, then set them on the floor. He stomped on them, startling Carol as the glass shattered beneath his shoe.

"Sorry," he said. "I should have warned you."

"No problem," she murmured as she watched him take the towel that was now full of broken glass to the door.

He dumped the contents on the floor and used his shoe to spread it around. He double-checked the locks and made sure the security bar was in place on the door. Then he made a full circuit of the room, even checking into the cabinets in the tiny kitchen.

Carol shook her head in bewilderment as he stood on a chair and checked the air-conditioning vents.

"You don't honestly think someone could wiggle themselves into the room through those tiny vents, do you?"

"No. But they could get a camera in there."

The last of her happy mood died a quick death.

He passed her and headed into the bedroom.

She followed, curious to see what else he thought was necessary to ensure her safety and privacy. One thing was certain: none of the Stellar Security guards had ever gone to this kind of trouble for her. Luke's thoroughness made the danger she was in feel more real than ever, but it also made her feel surprisingly safe and protected. No ill-timed picture was going to leak to the press under Luke's watch, giving away their location to the killer.

After checking beneath the bed and inside the closets, as well as the vents, Luke headed into the bathroom. Carol stood in the open doorway and watched him rap on the mirror over the sink, and then cup his hands against the mirror and press his face up against his hands.

"Why are you doing that?" she asked.

He straightened. "The mirror is on the wall that's shared with the next room, so I'm making sure it's not two-way glass."

"You've got to be kidding. No one even knows I'm here. It's not like the paparazzi are in the next room trying to catch a picture of me taking a shower."

"You'd be amazed at some of the lengths they go to for a picture that can earn them thousands of dollars. If a paparazzo bribed the desk clerk downstairs to send us to this room if we came into the hotel, and the clerk recognized us, we could be on camera right now."

She glanced at the mirror and shivered. "But we're not. Right?"

He shook his head. "No, we're not. This suite is as secure as I can make it." He patted the gun in the holster concealed beneath his leather jacket. "And if the worst happens, I can still protect you. Don't worry."

"I'm not worried, surprisingly. I think I may even be

able to sleep tonight without nightmares. I'm exhausted."
She glanced around, noting there was only one bed.

Luke's mouth crooked up in a half smile. "I didn't want
to blow our married-couple cover or I'd have asked for
two beds. I can sleep on the couch."

"Don't be silly. You're far too tall for the couch. And,
honestly, I'm way too tired to want to sleep on an uncomfortable couch myself. The bed is plenty big enough
for both of us."

His brows rose. "Are you sure?"

"Of course. We're both adults. I'm sure we can be-
have ourselves. Now, if you'll excuse me, I'm going to
take a shower."

SLEEPING TOGETHER WAS a terrible idea.

Luke lay awake long after Carol's breathing had turned
deep and even. He was tired and badly needed to get some
sleep so he would be alert tomorrow. Or at least, he *was*
tired until he'd turned on his side facing her and had noticed how the sliver of moonlight coming in through the
curtain traced the soft, delicate curve of her cheek. Or
how she made a sexy little moaning sound in her sleep
when she shifted her legs, making her long, white nightgown ride up high on her silky thighs, on skin that was
flawless.

Except for the bruises.

Even in the dark he could see the outlines of the fading
marks her husband had left on her upper arms, her thighs.
His hands clenched into fists and he rolled onto his back
to stare up at the ceiling. The minutes dragged by.

"Luke?"

He turned his head on the pillow. Carol was facing him
and staring at him. He had to force himself not to look

down where her neckline gaped, revealing far more of her generous curves than she probably realized.

"Sorry," he whispered. His voice came out a harsh croak. He cleared his throat. "Didn't mean to wake you."

Her delicate brows arched. "It's okay. Is something wrong?"

Yes. "No, of course not. Go back to sleep. I'll try to stop moving around so much."

He closed his eyes and tried to think of anything but the beautiful woman lying beside him, or how she smelled like flowers, or that some of her hair was lying across his right shoulder. His fingers curled into his palms against the urge to thread his fingers through the glorious, curly mass.

The bed shifted and he could have sworn she'd moved closer. He could feel her heat curling around him, making him want to pull her closer.

"Luke."

His eyes flew open. He cautiously turned his head and almost groaned out loud. She *was* closer, almost touching. Her face was just inches from his. All he had to do was roll over and their lips would meet.

He stared at the ceiling again. "Yes?" he rasped.

Her hand slid tentatively across his chest.

He sucked in a sharp breath and looked at her. "Carol, what are you doing?"

She snatched her hand back. "I'm sorry. I thought maybe… I shouldn't have done that."

He grabbed her hand, immediately softening his hold when her eyes widened with alarm. He slowly, ever so gently, pulled her hand toward him and placed it back on his chest. If she was any other woman, he'd know exactly what to do right now. He'd interpret that hand as meaning she wanted him, and he knew exactly what to do about *that.* But this was Carol. She was far too good for someone like him, and innocent in every way that mattered.

Her husband had hurt her so much. She probably didn't even realize how her touch frustrated him and made him want her. And even if that wasn't a consideration, he was her bodyguard. He needed to stay focused. Sleeping with a client was a huge no-no on so many levels.

So instead of pulling her to him and covering her lips with his, instead of sliding his hand down her back, across her hips, and cupping her round bottom against his growing erection, he kept an iron-tight control on his desires.

"You said you thought…something. What did you think, exactly?" he asked, unable to speak above a rough whisper in spite of his good intentions.

Her hand fluttered beneath his. He reluctantly let it go and she pulled it back. She propped her head on her palm, her gaze falling to his lips.

"I met…*him*…when I was innocent," she whispered. "I've never…been with anyone…else. But with him, it wasn't… I mean, in the beginning it was very, but then…" She closed her eyes, her voice sighing out on a shaky breath before she opened her eyes again. "I don't want to be hurt again."

He waited for her to say more, but she seemed to be struggling for words, and if her face got any redder it might burst into flames. He rolled onto his side and cupped his face in his palm, mirroring her posture. He put his other hand on the bed between them, palm up.

She slowly slid her hand across the sheet and looped her fingers with his.

"Carol?"

"Yes?"

"I would never hurt you."

A single tear slid down her cheek. "I know," she whispered.

"If I was going to make love to you," he whispered, "I'd take it slow. I'd be gentle and incredibly...thorough. I'd make sure you enjoyed every touch, every stroke, every kiss. But I'm not going to make love to you tonight."

Her eyes had widened during his little speech, and now she ran her tongue over her lips.

His groin tightened painfully.

"Why not?" she whispered.

The disappointment in her voice had him reaching for her before he realized what he was doing. He stopped himself and dropped his hand.

"Because it's unethical, wrong. You're my client. I'm your bodyguard. A relationship between us is impossible while I'm guarding you."

A smile hovered on her tempting mouth. "Okay. Then consider yourself fired. I'll rehire you in the morning."

He laughed, delighted that she still had a sense of humor after everything she'd been through. Then he sobered. "I'm serious. It would be wrong. I'd be taking advantage of you. Being in danger together forces a kind of false intimacy. It can be an aphrodisiac, but it's not real."

Her smile turned bitter. "I was in danger the whole time I was married. Trust me, it wasn't an aphrodisiac." She reached for his hand. "I want you, Luke. And I haven't wanted anyone in a very long time. If you don't want me, tell me. But if you do, then don't throw logic and reason between us."

He disengaged his hand from hers and lightly traced his finger down the curve of her cheek. "I want you, too, very much. But I don't want you to hate me later."

She shook her head. "I won't." She dropped her gaze

and bit her bottom lip. "But I'm still scared, even though I want you."

He fought a war with his conscience, but the battle didn't last long. He wanted her too much to keep denying the attraction between them. But he didn't want her frightened. He couldn't bear that.

"There's no reason to be scared," he whispered. "You're the one who's in control."

"I am?"

"Yes." He lowered his hand back to the bed. "I won't move unless you want me to. You can touch me, or not. Kiss me, or don't. It's your decision." He rolled onto his back and put his hands behind his head, striking a relaxed pose he was far from feeling. He wanted nothing more than to cover her body with his, to explore every fascinating dip and curve. But he knew that wasn't what she needed, and he sensed she wouldn't respond to that. Not yet, not with her fledgling desire warring with her instinctive fear because of her past.

She flexed her fingers on the sheet, as if debating whether to touch him. "Will you take off your shirt?" she asked.

In answer, he pulled his shirt off and dropped it to the floor, then put his hands behind his head again.

She glanced uncertainly at him, then slowly, so slowly it made him ache, she feathered her fingers up his side, leaving a burning trail in their wake. Growing bolder, she ran her hands across his ribs, testing the muscles there, exploring like an innocent who'd never been allowed the freedom he was giving her.

And maybe she hadn't. Not for the first time, Luke wished he could have met Richard Ashton in another century, when a man could defend a woman's honor on a dueling field. He would have loved to challenge the monster to a duel for the brutal way he'd used and abused this kind, beautiful, caring woman.

Her hand stilled on his abdomen and she looked at him uncertainly. He realized his thoughts of vengeance against her former husband had made him tense. He forced himself to relax and give her an encouraging smile.

Her tentative smile answered his, and soon she was killing him again with the warm slide of her hand across his heated skin. She seemed particularly fascinated with the vee formed by his abdominal muscles and how the dark line of hair disappeared beneath the sheet.

He'd worn his jeans to bed, to preserve her modesty. If he hadn't, there'd be no question on her part about how much he wanted her right now.

She slid up in the bed until her lips were close to his again. "Luke, may I…kiss you?"

"Carol, you can do whatever you want."

She let out a puff of laughter. "Okay, then I'd really like you to take off your jeans, and maybe take a *little* bit of control—because I feel silly now and I don't know what to do next."

He brought his hands down from behind his head and gently cupped her face. Then he slowly, carefully, pulled her down to him, with her on top, in control, and pressed her lips to his.

He kept the kiss gentle, soft, or at least he tried to. But he'd wanted her for so long that the feel of her softness against his had him shaking with need. He deepened the kiss, and when her lips parted, he swept his tongue inside, teasing, tasting, teaching her to kiss him back.

She moaned deep in her throat and dug her nails into his shoulder as she half covered him with her body, her breasts pressed against his chest, burning him through her thin nightgown. Suddenly she pulled back and stared at him, her blue eyes nearly black in the dark room, but wide as if she was stunned.

He reached up and traced his thumb over her full bottom lip. "Are you okay? Do you want to stop?"

She shook her head, her hair bouncing across her shoulders. "I don't want to stop." She reached down between them and tugged at his waistband. "But we aren't going to be able to do much more with you still wearing these."

He arched a brow. "I'll take mine off if you take yours off."

She arched a brow in response. "I'll see your bet and raise you, sir." She rolled off him and stood on her side of the bed. Suddenly her white nightgown fluttered down on top of him, covering his face.

He pulled it off his face just in time to see her fully nude body diving beneath the sheet. She lay back on her pillow beside him with the sheet pulled all the way up to her neck.

Her shyness was his reminder that he was going to have to take it slow.

This was going to be an agonizingly long night. But he was going to enjoy every minute of it. And he was going to make sure *she* enjoyed every minute of it.

He slid out from under the covers and was about to shuck off his jeans and underwear when he realized he didn't have any condoms. He stood in indecision.

"Is something wrong?" she asked, sounding worried that maybe he'd changed his mind about wanting her.

He briefly closed his eyes, his body in agony at the thought of what he was going to have to *not* do. "We can't do this," he said, even as he pulled out his wallet, hoping against hope that there was a condom in there. But since he wasn't in the habit of one-night stands and his last long-term relationship had ended over a year ago, he didn't hold out much hope.

"Oh. I see. Well, I'm sorry. I shouldn't have assumed you wanted— That is, I…" She let out a deep breath. "Just forget it."

His head jerked up.

She rolled over and faced the other wall.

He cursed himself for being an idiot. He rushed to the other side of the bed and squatted down at eye level. "It's not that I don't want you. Never, ever think that." And just to be sure she believed him, he kissed her. And this time, he didn't hold back. He pressed her against the pillow, half reclining on the bed, his mouth covering hers as he poured all his desire for her into that one hot, wet kiss. He stroked her tongue with his and she moaned deep in her throat again, shoving her hands into his hair and pulling him harder against her.

When they broke apart, they were both gasping for air. He felt her heart slamming in her chest against his, which was racing just as hard.

"I don't…understand," she said between deep, rasping breaths. "Why can't we, you know…?"

"Because I don't have any protection," he whispered, bending down and lightly sucking the side of her neck.

She arched off the bed and panted his name. "Protection? You showed me your gun earlier."

He laughed against the side of her neck. "Not that kind of protection, love. I don't have a condom."

Her eyes widened and then she laughed. He thought it was the most beautiful sound in the world.

She pulled him to her and this time *she* kissed *him*. It was even hotter and wilder than the last kiss. By the time they broke apart, his jeans were so tight he thought he would die.

"You're wicked to tease me so mercilessly when we can't go any further," he complained.

"Oh, we're definitely going further. You're going to get some condoms."

He shook his head. "No, can't risk leaving the suite. It's late now. The odds are much higher someone would notice us and might recognize you. Earlier, there were other people in the lobby and we were able to blend in."

"Us? *You* can go downstairs and get what we need. I assume they have them in the men's bathroom? I'll just wait here."

"No. I'm not leaving you. End of discussion."

She arched a brow and shoved him back. Then she slowly and deliberately pulled the sheet down to rest beneath her breasts. Her perfect, mouthwatering, beautiful breasts with little pink buds just begging for his kisses.

"You're not being fair," he groaned, unable to even pretend to lift his gaze from her bountiful display.

She chucked him under the chin, forcing him to meet her gaze. "Condoms. Find a way."

He wrenched his gaze from her body and looked around the room. He practically dived at the phone beside the bed. He pressed every button he could find in the dark until someone answered.

"Room service. What can I help you with, Mr. Johnson?"

He winced at the unfortunate last name he'd used as their alias. "Condoms. I need a box of condoms. Right away."

Silence met his request.

Carol started giggling.

He frowned at her. "There's a hundred-dollar tip if you get them up here in the next two minutes."

"Yes, sir," the clerk said, suddenly sounding eager. "Right away, sir."

Luke hung up the phone. "Johnson. I had to name myself Johnson, then call room service for condoms."

Carol howled with laughter and fell back against the pillows. Luke followed her down, punishing her by tickling her ribs. He followed his hands with his mouth, nibbling and sucking his way across her skin until he settled right where he wanted to be.

She stilled beneath him, her body tensing. "Luke? What are you—"

He fastened his mouth on her.

She gasped and bucked beneath him.

He raised his head. "Do you want me to stop?"

"Don't you dare," she ordered rather forcefully.

He laughed and focused on the delicious task at hand, delighting in the way she moaned and writhed beneath his careful attentions. He was forced to stop when room service knocked on the door. He cursed and grabbed his gun and shoved his shoes on to protect his feet from the broken glass at the door.

"Hurry," Carol panted.

It nearly killed him to leave her for the few seconds it took to throw the money out the door and grab the box from the startled-looking attendant. Luke shoved the door closed, locked it and propped the chair under the knob. Then he ran to the bedroom, shucking his shoes, jeans and underwear as he went.

He dived onto the bed, making Carol laugh at his eagerness. But her laughter quickly turned to sexy mewls of pleasure when he used everything in his arsenal to make her feel beautiful, sexy, cherished. He couldn't make up for five years of hell, but he could take her to heaven for one night.

And that was exactly what he did.

When they were both sleepy and sated and wrapped in each other's arms, she pressed a soft kiss against the side of his neck and settled against him.

"You're an incredible man, Luke," she mumbled, sounding half-asleep. "And not just because you're an amazing lover. You're incredible because I can trust you. You're honest and keep your promises, and I know I can count on you never to hurt me in any way." She kissed him again and was softly snoring a few seconds later.

The warm glow that had filled him after their thoroughly satisfying lovemaking began to fade as her words filtered through his mind. Moments ago he was picturing the two of them after the case was over—going to movies together, taking trips to the mountains, doing everything happy couples did. But now he wasn't sure a happy future was possible. As her bodyguard, he'd made a decision back at the mansion, a decision he'd felt he had to make to try to figure out the identity of the person who was trying to hurt her. It was his primary duty to protect her, so by giving the video card to Alex, that was what he was doing—protecting her.

But as her lover, he knew she wouldn't see his decision as his duty. She would see it as him lying to her, as a betrayal. He'd told her he never broke his promises, and that had always been his policy. But this one time, he'd broken the one promise because she'd be safer if he did.

Now he wondered if he had made a horrible mistake and whether she could ever forgive him for breaking her trust.

Chapter Thirteen

Carol shook her head as she peered out the living-room window of the hotel suite at the horde of vans and reporters eight floors below in the parking lot.

"I don't understand how they always find me."

"Secrets always end up getting out one way or another, especially where money is to be gained." Luke plopped their bags on the table by the door and double-checked that he'd gotten most of the glass from in front of the door. He couldn't get all the little shards without a vacuum cleaner, but he'd done the best he could. "I think that's everything. Ready to go?"

She dropped the curtain and grabbed the baseball cap Luke had bribed off a passing guest in the hallway. She twisted her thick blond ponytail on top of her head and shoved the cap over it. "I look good, right?" She turned around for his appraisal.

In those tight jeans and that curve-hugging T-shirt she looked so good it hurt, especially since she was smiling and acting so happy this morning, when he knew her happiness would come crashing to a halt as soon as she found out what he'd done.

Maybe he should call Alex and tell him to forget the whole thing. But knowing Alex, he'd probably already started sorting through the video. He wasn't one to put important things aside, especially if it meant possibly catching a killer. Luke should have waited, should have just destroyed the video card in the first place.

"Luke?" Her smile dimmed.

He crossed to her and, unable to resist, swooped in for a quick kiss. She clung to him and was grinning when he pulled back.

"I guess that was a yes," she teased.

His head was still spinning from the kiss. "Yes what?"

She lightly punched him on the arm. "Yes that I look good, of course."

He crossed his arms. "You look way too good, actually. And since we sneaked into the hotel with you in jeans, whoever told the press you were here is probably on the lookout for you in jeans again." He glanced around the suite, then hurried to their bags. He dug in his and pulled out the lightweight jacket he'd packed in case it rained. "This might help disguise those curves a bit. Hopefully that and the cap will be enough to let us make it outside."

She shrugged into the jacket. "Are we going out front again?"

"We're going out a side entrance, either through a delivery area or the kitchens, depending on which one has fewer people around. We'll have to hoof it from there for a few blocks."

"Then what do we do? Walk around Savannah all day?"

"No. I called Trudy while you were getting dressed. She's going to meet us in another rental car."

"Trudy?"

He cleared his throat, not relishing the idea of telling her a former prostitute was running his business while he was gone. "She's my, um, office manager. She's filling in because of…Mitch."

Her smile faded. "I'm sorry."

"I know." He put the luggage straps over his shoulders, as usual keeping his hands free. Then he peered out the peephole to make sure it was clear.

His cell phone vibrated in his pocket. "Just a second." He grabbed the phone. When he saw who was calling, he said, "I'll just be a minute."

She gave him a quizzical look as he headed into the bedroom and closed the door. "Luke here," he said into the phone.

Alex tossed a few choice curse words at him.

"Nice," Luke said. "I didn't even know you knew those kinds of words."

"I want to claw my eyes out to unsee everything I saw on that video you gave me. There were months of surveillance on that card because it only recorded when someone came into the room. You do realize what was on that card, don't you?"

"Yes, unfortunately, I do. I saw a little of it."

"Well, I saw it *all*. It was horrible. Richard Ashton deserved to die."

"You won't get any arguments from me on that. Please tell me you found something that might help with the investigation."

"All right. Your hunch was correct. I found something."

GETTING OUT OF the hotel undetected was easier than Luke had expected. They'd gone through the kitchen and no one had tried to stop them. Just a few startled looks from the cooks, and he and Carol were racing out the side door.

Trudy had been their biggest problem. Luke had given

her the keys to the Camaro in the parking garage so she could drive it back to the office, while he'd taken the keys from her to the Mustang GT she'd rented for them. If Trudy had been Mitch, she would have made the trade and hurried on her way, letting Luke take his client and get her out of danger.

But Trudy wasn't Mitch, and Carol wasn't a typical client. She'd refused to get into the car until she sat on the curb and let Trudy talk to her about how much she missed Mitch and a host of other complaints. It had nearly killed Luke not to grab Carol's arm and haul her to the car. But regardless of his good intentions to keep her safe, he couldn't stomach trying to boss her around or force her to do something she didn't want to do.

Finally, Trudy headed back to the hotel and Carol got into the Mustang. Luke drove through the historic district, keeping an eye on his mirrors, doubling back several times until he was convinced no one was following them. Then he drove into another parking garage. When he turned off the engine and twisted in his seat to face her, Carol was watching him with wary eyes.

"Why are we here?" she asked.

"We need to talk."

"That sounds ominous." She offered him an uncertain smile.

He held his hand out, palm up. As had become her habit, she didn't hesitate. She entwined her fingers with his and they held hands on top of the console between their seats.

"Carol, I need you to keep an open mind. I need you to listen to everything I say before you make any judgments or decisions. Can you do that for me?"

"Okay, now you're scaring me. Just tell me whatever it is that you need to say."

"I need your promise first, to listen until I'm finished explaining everything. You're going to be mad, hurt, but I need you to keep a clear head. Don't jump out of the car or do anything that would put you in more danger."

She bit her lip, her eyes widening. "If this is the 'let's be friends' speech, spare me. It was just one night. It's not like we made a commitment or anything."

In spite of her flippant words, he heard the pain in her voice. He cursed. "I can see I'm making a mess of this and I haven't even started. What I need to tell you has nothing to do with last night, which was completely amazing and wonderful, by the way."

Her hand tightened on his. "Okay. If it's not about… us…then I don't see how it can be that bad. Go ahead."

The way she'd said "us" had him silently cursing in his mind. Carol was special. Whatever fledgling relationship they'd begun to build was too new, too delicate to survive what he was about to tell her. But he couldn't keep her waiting any longer. Waiting, wondering what he was going to tell her, was even more cruel than what he was about to say.

"I gave the video card to Alex Buchanan."

She froze, as still as a deer staring at the rifle that was about to end its life, unable to move or do anything to protect itself. And damn it if Luke wasn't the hunter pulling the trigger.

"I'm sorry, Carol. I know you wanted me to destroy it, but it was evidence. I was worried we might ruin our one chance of finding out who had been in the house, who'd broken into the safe. If they were on the video then we'd have a suspect. Cornell doesn't seem to have any decent leads. Alex's investigator hasn't found anything useful. Every hour that passes makes it less likely we'll catch the killer and more likely your life is in even greater danger. I gave it to Alex so he could—"

"You promised," she whispered. She jerked her hand from his and scooted across the seat until her back was against the passenger door. "You promised me. You said you never, ever break your promises."

He dug his fingers into the console to keep from reaching for her. "And I never do, except this once. Listen to me. I asked Alex to look for evidence, something that would give us a lead so we could tell Cornell—"

Her gaze whipped back to his. "Cornell? You gave him the video card, too?"

"What? No. No, no, no. Alex still has it. I'm not giving it to Cornell unless you give me permission. That's what I need to talk to you about. Alex saw—"

"Everything," she finished for him. "He saw my shame, my humiliation. Did he tell you all the sickening details, Luke?" Tears streamed down her face. "Did he?"

He shook his head. "Carol, listen to me. I need to explain."

"Did he tell you how Richard taught me lessons whenever I displeased him? And how he beat me and raped me over and over? Did he tell you Richard made me apologize to him for the imagined wrongs I'd done, and how he made me tell him over and over again that I loved him, when all I wanted to do was scream at him and tell him how much I loathed and despised him? Did Alex tell you that? Did he?"

His arms ached with the need to pull her to him, to hold her and protect her from the memories and the hurts she'd suffered. He wanted to wipe the tears away and erase the hurt, accusing look on her face, but he knew she wouldn't welcome his touch right now.

Maybe not ever.

"Alex is an extremely private person. He didn't know what was on that card when I gave it to him. I promise you he would never show it to anyone else or even tell them what's on it without your permission."

She laughed harshly. "You promise? Really?" She shook her head. "How do I keep doing this to myself? First Richard, then you. How do I keep attracting the same kind of men?"

Luke stiffened. His chest tightened and for the space of a few heartbeats he could barely breathe. "You're comparing me to the man who beat and raped you? The man who ruptured your spleen and almost killed you?" he rasped.

She opened her mouth several times as if to say something, but then she turned and looked out the passenger window.

Luke stared through the windshield, wondering how he'd become her enemy when all he'd ever wanted to do was to protect her. They were both silent for several minutes, then he started up the car.

"You have a choice to make," he said.

"And what's that?" she asked without turning to look at him.

"Alex saw someone on that video card. They went into the master bedroom and opened the wall safe. They took out a stack of papers. From what he could see on the video, Alex believes you may be right, that the papers were a will. That person knew or at least suspected your husband had another will. And when they found it, they took it so no one else would ever see it. There's a good chance they might be the killer."

She slowly turned and looked at him. "What's this choice that I have to make?"

"Whether or not to give the video to Detective Cornell as evidence."

She shook her head. "No. Absolutely not."

"Without the video, we have no way of pointing Cornell to the person Alex saw, no way of pointing him toward another suspect."

"We have to find another way." She swiped at the wet tracks on her cheeks. "Who's in the video?"

"Leslie Harrison."

She gasped. "No, it can't be. It doesn't even make sense. She was his lawyer. She would have a copy of any will he had, so why care about the one in his safe?"

"Because she didn't want anyone else to see that copy. Because it was a will she had no intention of ever filing. If she filed a fake will, then she had to destroy any copies of the true will before someone found them. And there's something else to consider, something Alex mentioned on the phone. Someone had to tell Richard about the cottage you rented. Leslie is the only person besides you who knew about the cottage."

Carol pressed her hand to her throat. "Oh my God."

"We need to give the video to Cornell."

She shook her head. "No. We need to go see Leslie. I want to give her a chance to explain. If she hadn't helped me, if she hadn't given me the strength and encouragement that I needed to escape, I'd have died from that last beating. She was a good friend. My only friend. She deserves a chance to tell her side of whatever is going on here. Let's go talk to her. She should be at her office."

"That's not a good idea. If she's guilty of wrongdoing, even if she's not the actual person who pulled the trigger, she's got everything to lose. When people are cornered with no way out, it makes them dangerous. We need to call Cornell and let him handle it while I take you someplace away from all this once and for all and we wait there until the investigation is over."

"She's a friend, or at least she was until I turned away from her. I want to talk to her."

Her anger at him was clouding her judgment. Somehow he had to get through to her. He was about to try again when his cell phone buzzed in the holster at his hip. He frowned when he saw the number on the screen but quickly answered.

"Detective Cornell, what can I do for you?"

His hand tightened around the phone as he listened. "Okay. Yes, I'll tell her. Thank you."

He ended the call and put the phone away.

"Tell me what?" Carol asked.

He scrubbed his face with his hands before answering. "I'm so sorry. There's no easy way to say this. Leslie Harrison is dead."

Chapter Fourteen

"You don't have to do this." Luke paused in front of the Mustang and put his hand on Carol's arm to stop her from going inside the law offices of Wiley & Harrison. "We can wait until Cornell gets all the papers cataloged and back at the station to look at them."

She glanced down at his hand on her arm and arched her brow.

He sighed and dropped his hand.

Without a word, she went with Cornell into the law office.

Luke didn't bother to follow. The place was buzzing with cops, so she was safe, and Carol didn't want him with her anyway. He leaned back against the Mustang and stretched his legs out in front of him to wait.

"Aren't you supposed to be guarding someone?" Alex stepped around the end of the car and leaned back against it beside him.

"I'm not her favorite person right now. She hasn't fired me yet, but it's probably only a matter of time."

"The video card?"

"Congratulations. You're a genius."

Alex laughed and handed an envelope to him, the same one Luke had left for him hidden in the car yesterday.

Luke shoved it in his shirt pocket.

"You do realize that video card ate up the last of any favors I'd be inclined to do for you, right?" Alex said.

"Yeah, I figured. Guess I should have warned you. But I was afraid you wouldn't do it if I told you."

"You tricked me."

"Yeah. I did. But only because I trust you. I knew if you were the one to review the video, nothing would leak to the press or the internet. That would destroy Carol."

Alex was silent for a moment, then he gave him a crisp nod. Apparently Luke was forgiven.

"Speaking of your client, why is she inside? Isn't that where they found Leslie Harrison?"

"The coroner already removed the body. There are papers all over her office that have to do with Ashton Enterprises, so Cornell asked Carol to take a look and see if she saw anything unusual. My turn to ask you a question. What are you doing here? And how did you even know about Leslie's murder? It only happened a couple of hours ago."

Alex smiled in greeting to a couple of police officers he knew as the cops walked around the Mustang and headed inside the building. "Cornell called me. He gave me a briefing of what happened and asked me to meet him here so we could discuss my client."

"Carol?"

"No. Grant."

Luke waited, but Alex didn't seem inclined to say anything else. "Come on. What gives?"

Alex sighed. "Grant posted bail this morning."

Luke's gaze flicked to the law office. "What *time* did he post bail?"

"Three hours ago."

"That's what Cornell wants to talk to you about. He thinks Grant killed Leslie."

"I'm sure that's how Cornell sees it. Grant did go on and on complaining about his brother's will, accusing the lawyer of filing the wrong one. That's public record, by the way, not a client confidence. Grant screamed about the will back at the police station to anyone who would listen."

Luke swore. "He's obviously the killer."

"Innocent until proven guilty."

"You really believe Grant's innocent?"

Alex's lips compressed into a hard line but he didn't answer.

"Screw this." Luke shoved away from the car.

"What are you doing?"

"Getting *our* client out of here before *your* client figures out where she is and tries to kill her, too."

LUKE GLARED AT the police officer blocking his way into the lobby of Wiley & Harrison. "I'm telling you, I'm a bodyguard and my client is inside. I need to see her."

"And I'm telling you, sir, that this is a crime scene and no one goes inside without a badge."

Luke's fingers twitched at his side. He had to remind himself that getting arrested wouldn't help Carol. He resisted the urge to shove the scrawny cop out of his way, just barely.

"You need to leave, sir. You're blocking the doorway."

Luke ignored him and looked over the top of the cop's head. Cornell stood with a group of officers around a young, distraught-looking woman who was dabbing at her eyes with a tissue.

"Cornell," Luke called out. "Call off your Chihuahua and let me inside."

The detective glanced over and rolled his eyes. "Let him in." He waved Luke forward.

The officer grudgingly stepped out of Luke's way.

Luke made a straight line toward Cornell, glancing around the room as he did so, but there was no sign of Carol.

"What's so important you had to bust in here?" Cornell demanded when Luke stopped beside him.

"You didn't tell me Grant Ashton was out of jail when you called this morning."

"I didn't *know* he was out of jail when I called. I found that out on the way here. You might as well wait outside until Mrs. Ashton is finished inventorying the office. There's nothing you can do in here."

"Where is she?"

Cornell jerked his hand over his shoulder. "The middle door on that back wall, Leslie Harrison's office. If you have to go inside, go, but don't touch anything. You know the drill."

Luke frowned. "Why is the door shut?"

Cornell turned around. His brows drew down. "It wasn't shut earlier. Maybe we were too noisy out here for her."

They both headed toward the door.

Luke grabbed the knob, but it didn't turn. "Why is the door locked?" He banged on the wood. "Carol, open the door. It's Luke."

Cornell motioned at the group of police officers he'd just left. "Get the admin to give me the key to the—"

Luke rammed his body against the door. The doorjamb splintered and the door crashed open against the far wall.

Cornell cursed and followed Luke into the room.

Papers were scattered all over the desk and the floor.

But there was no sign of Carol. Luke ran to the only exit, the window behind the desk. He tried to open it, but it was sealed shut. Layers of paint around the frame acted like glue.

"She must have come back out and I didn't notice," Cornell said. He headed into the lobby.

Luke saw an open door on one side of the office. He ran in there. A bathroom, empty, no window, just a skylight, at least twelve feet up.

He ran back into the office just as Cornell rushed inside.

"No one saw her come out of this room," he said. "And the officer at the door to the lobby said she didn't come out that way, either."

Luke continued his search of the room. He felt along the exterior wall, beside the window.

"I'll lock down the parking lot," Cornell said. "I'll get every officer to search the building and all the cars."

Luke stood back and kicked one of the panels in the wall. It flew open, a hidden door, swinging back on hinges to bounce against the exterior wall of the building. Sunshine flooded into the room.

A sick feeling settled in the pit of Luke's stomach. "Too late. She's already gone."

CAROL TWISTED AGAINST her restraints in the backseat of the patrol car, straining her neck to look behind her as the car swung out onto the highway.

She caught a glimpse of the back of the building. Luke's tall, muscular form filled the doorway where she'd been taken just minutes earlier. Carol would have cried out, but her mouth was covered with duct tape. Instead, she renewed her struggles, bouncing on the backseat, trying to get Luke to notice her. But without her hands free to wave, she couldn't do much.

I'm right here, Luke. Look at me. I'm right here.

But he didn't glance her way, and the building disappeared as the car careened around a curve.

She strained against the tape around her wrists, thankful they were at least in front of her and not behind her.

Her brother-in-law glanced in the rearview mirror. "You might as well settle down and stop trying to get the tape off. You're just going to hurt yourself."

She put every ounce of contempt and loathing she could into her expression as she looked at him through the wire partition that separated them.

He sighed heavily. "I'm sorry, Caroline. I didn't want to do this."

He wiped a bead of sweat from his forehead and made another turn. They were heading out of town on a two-lane rural road. Where were they? She should have been paying more attention to his driving instead of wasting her efforts glaring at him.

The trees seemed to fly by as they headed deeper and deeper into the woods. They hadn't passed any houses in the past few minutes. He was taking her somewhere isolated. She'd never come down this road before. She was certain of it. A sense of panic started gathering inside her.

Her nose twitched. The smell of…manure…seeped into the car. Were they near a farm? Another smell, thick and heavy, made her gag. The unfamiliar, rancid odor was cloying and sickeningly sweet. What *was* that?

The trees fell away and they emerged from the forest. A line of concrete buildings squatted in the middle of a field a few hundred yards in front of them. There weren't any other cars. No signs of any people around, probably because it was late and anyone who worked here would

have already gone home for the day. Up ahead, hanging
on the side of the first building, a wooden sign announced
the building's purpose. Carol's insides went cold as she
read the words: Matheson's Beef Packing Plant.

Chapter Fifteen

Every detective in the Chatham County P.D. had been called in to brainstorm where Grant may have taken Carol. They were assuming Grant was the culprit, but it wasn't much of a stretch. Beat cops canvassed the area near the Wiley & Harrison law office, but still there were no concrete clues about what had happened.

The conference room was practically busting at the seams, with every seat around the center table taken and officers lining the walls. Luke didn't care that he blocked the view of the shorter men around him. He crowded up to the table so he could hear what Cornell said and see the video playing on the laptop.

"Okay, people, everybody be quiet so we can hear the audio," Cornell ordered. "The part we're most interested in should be coming up soon."

The view was from a security camera in the alley behind the law office. It was black-and-white, grainy, poor quality. Apparently, the law firm had the camera for an insurance discount, but they'd gotten the cheapest equipment money could buy, just enough to satisfy the requirements of their policy. And it showed. The picture wasn't even in focus, but it was better than nothing. Or, at least, Luke sure hoped so. If they could at least get a picture of the car, and if all the stars aligned, a license plate, the police could put out a BOLO to tell every law-enforcement agency in a hundred-mile radius to be on the lookout for the car that had taken Carol away.

They already theorized a car had approached from the woods behind the building, as evidenced by crushed grass, broken branches and tire tracks the techs were examining. But other than seeing that the road led to the highway, they had nothing. And gaining any useful data from the crude tire tracks would take time—time they didn't have.

The seconds ticked by in the lower-right-hand corner of the screen. Something metallic flashed in the trees behind the building. A car drove out of the trees, the metal rack on its front grille mowing down small saplings and making a road where there hadn't been one before.

"I'll be damned," Cornell said. "It's a police car. One of ours." He snapped his fingers. "Quick, someone look up the numbers on the side. Tell me whose car that is."

The car parked behind the building.

"It belongs to Officer Jennings," one of the detectives called out.

"Where is he?" Cornell demanded.

"Vacation. He's been out of town for over a week. He took his personal car. The perp must have stolen his patrol car out of his driveway."

The car door opened on the video and a tall figure stepped out, wearing a ski mask—a very familiar ski mask.

"He's tall, over six foot," Cornell said. "And he's got some muscle to him. That's Grant Ashton."

"We can't be sure without seeing his face." Luke leaned in close to the screen. He shook his head. "It could be Grant or his brother, Daniel. They both have the same build." He straightened in disgust. "It could be anyone."

Cornell flashed him an irritated glance. "How many men do you know that size?"

"Including me?"

Cornell rolled his eyes and studied the screen again.

"He has a key," Luke said. "That's why there weren't any scratches on the lock. He's someone who knew Leslie Harrison, or at least someone at the law office."

The rest of the video went by quickly. It only took Grant, or perhaps Daniel, less than a minute to rush inside and come out with Carol. Her mouth was covered with duct tape and her hands were bound in more of the shiny silver tape. Her abductor shoved her into the backseat of the patrol car, then took off into the same woods from where he'd just emerged.

Moments later, the car appeared off in the corner of the camera's view, coming out of the trees a hundred yards away and turning onto the blacktop highway. In the center of the camera, the door to the building flew open again, and Luke stood in the entrance, looking around.

He cursed as every eye looked at him. He'd been standing there like a fool, looking at the trees and the back of the building. But he hadn't noticed the patrol car driving away with Carol bouncing in the backseat, obviously trying to get his attention.

Cornell stopped the video. "We've got a car and a direction, and a rough description of the doer." He pointed at one of the detectives. "Put a BOLO out and send some uniforms to Officer Jennings's place. See if he's got a security system that might have caught this guy on camera when he stole the car. If not, let's hope he has some nosy neighbors who saw something. And get Jennings on the phone. See if he saw anyone hanging around his place before he went on vacation."

The detective hurried out of the room.

Cornell glanced around the table. "Now, quickly, let's go down the list and see if something pops. What do we have on the Richard Ashton murder?" He pointed at the detective directly across from him. "You, run it down for us."

The detective flipped through the electronic tablet on the table in front of him. "Two gunshots, fired close-range, about five feet away. Bullet was .45-caliber. The only fingerprints at the scene were from the vic, the landlord, the vic's wife and Luke Dawson. The vic's wife and Dawson's prints were limited to the front door. Their alibis checked out."

Luke crossed his arms. "Get on with it," he urged.

"Grant Ashton owns a .45, but it was allegedly stolen last month. He filled out a police report."

"Convenient," Cornell grumbled.

"Gas receipt at a nearby station traced to Grant Ashton," the detective continued. "Surveillance footage showed him gassing up his SUV right around the estimated time of death. He's our prime suspect."

"Put the footage up on the laptop," Luke ordered.

The detective next to Cornell looked to him for permission.

"Do it."

Soon the video was playing and everyone was trying to crowd around the table to see it. The quality was much better than the earlier video. The license plate was clearly visible. No question that it was Grant's car. But the SUV was parked on the far side of the pump and the driver was only a vague image on the camera.

Cornell squinted at the screen. "Could be Grant Ashton. The size fits."

"It could also be his brother," Luke offered. "Or me.

All you know from that video is that someone drove Grant Ashton's SUV to that station and filled the tank. Period."

"All right, what's your theory, then? We're just reviewing the evidence here. If you've got something to add, by all means, jump in." Cornell leaned back in his chair and crossed his arms.

"I don't know why Ashton was killed, or Mitch, or the lawyer. And I don't know why Carol was abducted. All I know for sure is that I can link all those people together with only two other people—Grant and Daniel Ashton. They were Richard's brothers. They both attended the funeral where Mitch was killed. They both knew Leslie Harrison through their brother. And we all know the link with Carol—they're her brothers-in-law. It just makes sense one of them is behind all this. What I want to know is what you're doing to find *both* of them."

One of the detectives across from Cornell spoke up. "Every available beat cop is out looking for Grant Ashton, canvassing everywhere he would go. No one has seen him anywhere."

"What about his house, his family?"

"They're not home. Left yesterday to get away from the reporters that have been hounding them since Grant's arrest."

"What about the other brother, Daniel?" Luke asked.

Cornell looked to his left. "You were in charge of that this morning. What have you got?"

The detective shook his head. "He's not our guy. He's been at work since seven this morning. He's still there, with plenty of witnesses. He's the CEO of his own company. He's been in meetings this whole time. He couldn't have abducted Mrs. Ashton."

"Then we focus on Grant," Luke said. "He's a wealthy guy, just like the rest of his family. What properties does he own? Is there anything like a warehouse or abandoned building somewhere he might take her?"

Cornell frowned. "We're not exactly amateurs here. We've been checking that out since the abduction. No dice so far."

Luke raked his hand through his hair. Carol had been gone for over two hours. What was happening to her? He couldn't even let himself think the worst—that it was already too late. No, she was strong. She'd proved how strong she was by surviving living with her abusive husband for so long. She couldn't have survived that hell only to die now.

He'd promised to protect her. He'd already broken one promise. He wasn't about to break another. He *had* to find her.

"What about Stellar Security?" Luke asked.

Cornell's brows rose. "What about them?"

"They're a common thread. They're linked with everything the Ashtons do. I had an investigator look into them, but he didn't find anything."

"What did you expect him to find? You think one of the security guards is behind the murders and Mrs. Ashton's abduction?"

"No, I think Grant abducted her. But he may have had help. As amazing as Stellar Security is supposed to be, Grant was able to break into the mansion and attack Mrs. Ashton a few nights ago even though they were supposedly guarding the place. And in all the time Mrs. Ashton lived in the mansion, and Stellar Security was there, it seems rather odd they never realized the abuse that was going on. They turned a blind eye to it."

"You think they turned a blind eye to murder, too?"

Luke clenched his fists. "I don't know. I don't have

anything to go on except a gut feeling. Carol didn't trust them. That's why she hired me."

"Looks like she bet on the wrong pony in that race."

Luke didn't bother to glare in the direction of the detective who'd issued that statement in a loud stage whisper. How could he be mad when the detective was telling the truth? Maybe his distrust of Stellar Security was influenced too much by Carol's own fears instead of facts. Maybe if he'd told her to stick with the much larger security firm, she'd be okay instead of out there suffering at the hands of another Ashton man.

He shoved his way through the crowd and opened the door.

"What are you going to do, Dawson?" Cornell called out.

Luke shook his head. For the first time in his career, he had no clue what to do.

LUKE SPENT THE next few hours driving his car every place he knew of that the Ashton family owned—from Carol's mansion in town, to Grant's and Daniel's houses, and even out to the country house where he and Carol had been a few days ago. So far, no luck spotting anything that even hinted that Carol might have been there recently.

He made dozens of calls to everyone he knew in law enforcement. He called the private investigator that Alex had hired and spoke to him about what had happened. He asked the investigator to focus again on Stellar Security, because the more he thought about it, the more their bumbling incompetence seemed glaring, as if it had been on purpose.

When he was at the police station earlier, he couldn't very well have told Cornell that Stellar Security hadn't noticed Leslie Harrison going upstairs and getting into Richard Ashton's safe. He couldn't do that without mentioning the video card, and he certainly wasn't going to do that again.

He winced.

Please, God, don't let me breaking a promise and betraying Carol be the last memory she has of me.

A call to a friend at the courthouse landed him an email with a list of every piece of property the Ashtons owned. The list was extensive, over ten pages, and half of the places were within driving distance of Savannah. He forwarded the list to Cornell.

Somehow, there had to be a better way to narrow down where to look for Carol.

He called Cornell and checked in with him frequently, but even though the detective was doing everything Luke would have done in his place, the results were still that the sun was about to set and Carol was nowhere to be found.

A visit to Grant Ashton's house yielded nothing but an aggravated butler who had already been grilled by Cornell's detectives. He emphatically told Luke he didn't know where any of the Ashtons were and the next time someone asked him he was going to fill out a harassment complaint.

Luke drove around with no particular destination in mind anymore. He wasn't surprised when he again ended up outside the office building that Daniel Ashton owned and where he was working today. There weren't that many cars still in the lot since it was so late. Finding Ashton's car wasn't difficult. But even if the lot had been full, he'd know which car was Daniel's. Luke had cashed in just about every favor anyone owed him today trying to get as much information about the Ashtons as he could find. As a result, he knew exactly which car in the parking lot was Daniel's—the forest-green BMW sedan.

Surprisingly, he didn't park in a reserved spot with his name on it as Luke had expected. Instead, he parked way out at the end, near the street. Why? So he could get away quickly if he needed to?

Luke scrubbed his face and rested his head against his seat. He would search every place on the list of Ashton holdings if he had to, but without a starting point, something to help him narrow the list down, it was like looking for the proverbial needle in a haystack. It would take days, maybe weeks, to thoroughly search all those possible hiding places.

Carol didn't have days. She sure as hell didn't have weeks.

He checked his gun at his hip and his backup in an ankle holster. If he thought going into Ashton's building right now and holding a gun to his head would yield any useful information, he wouldn't hesitate. But Cornell's men had already questioned him earlier, and Daniel had been coldly polite, insisting he knew nothing. Luke's hope was that if he followed the man he'd lead Luke to Carol.

Two men emerged from the exit at the back of the building. Luke straightened in his seat. Daniel Ashton was easy to pick out. He towered over the much shorter man walking beside him. The other man talked with his hands as he apparently said something funny. Daniel laughed and shook his head, then waved as the man headed to his car on the opposite side of the lot.

Daniel continued to his car and got in without glancing toward Luke, who was parked in the shadow of some oak trees on the street. Luke waited until Daniel turned the corner. Then he floored the gas and headed after him.

CAROL STUMBLED AND fell onto the hard concrete floor. The door slammed shut behind her before she could make it to her feet.

"Grant," she called out. "Please, don't do this! Let me out of here."

The sound of his footsteps rapidly walking away was his only response.

She ran to the door and tried the knob, unsurprised to find it locked. The upper part of the door was glass, but on top of the glass were iron bars. No way out, unless she could figure out how to pick the lock. That was one "lesson" Richard had never taught her.

She made a quick circuit of the room. A row of tiny windows near the top of the ceiling were too high for her to reach. A fluorescent light illuminated the small room, which wasn't much bigger than her master-bedroom closet at the mansion. The walls were concrete. And there was nothing inside the room, not even a chair to sit in. She moved back to the door. If she was going to get out of here, it would have to be through the door. Somehow she had to figure out a way to get it open.

Would Grant really hurt her? She'd thought so, at first. He'd certainly been rough as he yanked her out of the car and shoved her in front of him, forcing her to go into the processing plant. But he'd turned solicitous, taking her to the restroom and waiting outside for her. Then he'd taken her to an office where he had sandwiches and drinks waiting in a cooler. They'd both eaten in tense silence. She tried to glance around, looking for a way to escape without seeming obvious. He checked the time on his cell phone every few minutes.

They sat in the little office for hours. Every one of her attempts at conversation had been met with stony silence. He'd become more and more agitated the later it got, and when the last of the sunlight disappeared from the windows and he was forced to turn on some lights, he swore and grabbed her arm. He tugged her after him and gave her another chance to use the restroom. She took advantage of every minute he gave her, testing the windows, looking for something she could use as a weapon. He must have grown suspicious at how long it was taking her, because he came in as she was trying to pull a paper-towel dispenser off the wall.

His eyes had narrowed dangerously and, without a word, he'd brought her to this room and threw her inside.

Footsteps sounded again down the hall. She peered into the gloom. A moment later, Grant appeared, carrying what looked like little pieces of paper in one hand and a roll of duct tape in the other.

She moved back from the door, rubbing her wrists at the memory of the tape he'd wrapped around them earlier. But he didn't open the door. Instead, he ripped a piece of tape off the roll and used it to hold the pieces of paper in place on the glass part of the door.

When he was done, he tossed the roll down and motioned her forward.

She hesitated, then moved to the door. She glanced at the papers and realized they were computer printouts of pictures. She gasped and pressed her hand to her mouth when she realized who was in the pictures—Grant's wife and daughter. They were both tied up, blindfolded, gagged. Carol couldn't even tell if they were alive or dead.

Her gaze flew to Grant's.

"I didn't kill Richard, or that photographer." His voice sounded muted through the thick glass. "But I did kill Leslie, and I'll kill you, too, if I have to." He tapped the glass above the pictures. "Daniel took them, Caroline.

And if I don't do what he wants, he'll kill them." He tapped the glass again. "I would do anything for them, Caroline. Anything. Even if that means slaughtering you like one of the cows they butcher in this place."

He turned on his heel and disappeared down the hallway.

Carol sank to the floor and covered her face with her hands.

Chapter Sixteen

Daniel Ashton didn't seem to be in a hurry to get home. Then again, he didn't have anyone waiting for him. He was single, never married, no girlfriends or even close friends that Alex's investigator had been able to find. The P.I. had called while Luke tailed Daniel through the city. The only real news he'd been able to tell Luke was that he'd traced Stellar Security through dozens of holding companies to its real owner.

Daniel Ashton.

Luke had immediately called Cornell and told him the news. He also reminded Cornell that Mitch had once worked for Stellar Security and had quit to work for Luke. While Mitch had never shared the details of why he'd quit, Luke knew something ugly had happened while he'd worked there.

Luke would lay odds that the "something ugly" had to do with Daniel Ashton, either directly or indirectly. And now Mitch was dead. Luke had had a crash course today during all those phone calls about the Ashton brothers, and it wasn't a pretty picture his contacts had painted.

The brothers had always been rivals, but with Richard and Daniel in particular, that rivalry went to extremes. Carol was the one who'd told Luke that Daniel didn't visit the mansion much anymore. And while Luke didn't have proof yet, he'd heard speculation that the reason for that was because Richard and Daniel had gone after the same acquisition, a business takeover, and Richard had come out the winner.

Daniel had never forgiven him.

The business Richard bought had taken him from millionaire to billionaire in less than a year. But Daniel was still a mere millionaire and appeared to blame his brother. The only question was, did he blame his brother enough to kill him over it? Or had the other brother held a grudge no one knew about and *he* was the one who'd decided to shoot Richard?

At this point, Luke didn't care which one had killed Richard. They were both dangerous, a pit of vipers. But they were still family, and Luke was betting Carol's life that there was a bond between the two brothers, a bond that meant that Daniel knew where Grant was.

DANIEL SMILED AT the waitress and stood to leave the restaurant Luke had tailed him to half an hour earlier.

Luke held a menu up in front of him. As soon as Daniel went outside, Luke would scramble after him again and see where else the man went.

"Mr. Dawson, fancy seeing you here."

Luke slowly lowered his menu.

Daniel Ashton stood beside the table, staring down at him as if he were the worst kind of vermin, his mouth curling in contempt. "Why are you following me?"

Luke tossed the menu on the table and slid out of the booth. He rose to his full height, which was only an inch taller than Ashton, but it was enough to make Daniel's smug look fade. He seemed to assess the breadth of Luke's shoulders as they stood toe to toe.

"Where is she?" Luke asked.

Daniel arched a brow. "'She'? I'm sure I don't know who you're talking about."

Luke grabbed Ashton's lapels and slammed him against the nearest wall.

Diners at the next table gasped in shock. Excited voices rose from the nearby waiters.

Luke ignored all of them and pressed his hand against Daniel's throat. "Tell me where she is, you filthy piece of—"

"Now, now," Daniel clucked. "No reason to act so uncivilized, Mr. Dawson."

"Sir, you need to let him go before we call the police."

Luke glanced over his shoulder. A group of five men stood behind him. Three appeared to be waiters. The others, judging by their clothing, were the bartender and the restaurant manager.

"You heard the man, Dawson. Let me go. Now."

The laughter in Ashton's voice had Luke gritting his teeth. He forced his hands to relax their death grip on the other man's lapels and he took a step back.

Daniel straightened his collar, frowning at the wrinkles Luke had made. He flicked the fabric and gave Luke a smile that didn't come close to reaching his cold, dead eyes.

"You should try the filet mignon in this restaurant, Mr. Dawson," he said. "I hear the meat's never frozen. It's freshly butchered." He laughed as if at a private joke and headed out the front door.

Luke moved to follow, but the restaurant manager stepped in front of him. "Hold it, sir. I think you should sit and calm down. Whatever happened between you two—"

Luke shoved the man out of his way and ran through the double doors to the street.

The sound of squealing tires had him turning to see

Ashton's green BMW speeding away. Daniel lifted a hand out the window, waving, before the car turned down a side street and disappeared.

Luke cursed viciously and ran to his car. But ten minutes later he pulled to the curb and slammed his fist against the dash. No sign of Daniel Ashton. His last link to the man who'd taken Carol was gone.

Or was it?

He stilled, thinking about the list of holdings on his phone and the last words Daniel had thrown at him.

You really should try the filet mignon. It's freshly butchered.

He fumbled for his phone and opened the email. He quickly scrolled through the list. Yes, there, on the fifth page—*Matheson's Beef Packing Plant.* Sweat broke out on his brow.

Oh, God. Please. Don't let her die like that.

He slammed his foot on the accelerator and rocketed away from the curb, praying harder than he'd ever prayed in his life that he wouldn't be too late.

CAROL SHIVERED IN the concrete room. It might have been hot outside, but the air-conditioning in the plant kept it chilly, and the longer she was there the colder she became. As minutes ticked away and Grant didn't return, she began to wonder if it wouldn't be better to just try to go to sleep and hope she was cold enough to succumb to hypothermia. It had to be a better way to die than whatever her brother-in-law had planned for her.

She closed her eyes and leaned her head on her arms, resting on top of her drawn-up knees. Footsteps sounded outside the room, but not just one set. This time, there were two. She jerked her head up. Grant rounded the corner, and beside him was Daniel.

The chill that went through her had nothing to do with the temperature in the room.

The men stopped at the door.

"Open it," Daniel ordered.

"Not until you tell me where you're holding Susan and Patty. That was the deal."

Daniel calmly raised his hand and shot Grant in the forehead. He dropped to the floor like a rock.

Carol screamed.

Daniel pointed the gun at her through the glass. "Shut up."

She clamped her shaking hands over her mouth.

He took out a handkerchief and wiped the specks of his brother's blood off his face. He put the handkerchief in his suit pocket then unlocked and opened the door. "Hello, there, dear sister-in-law. It's been a while, if we don't count that little visit at the hospital, or the exchange of pleasantries at the funeral. Before that, I hadn't seen you in a year or more, I suppose."

He clucked his tongue and shook his head as he stepped into the room. "Not my choice, I assure you. Entirely your late husband's. Tell me—" he crouched down in front of her and used his gun to tilt her chin up "—did you miss me? No? I missed you very much. You see, I've always wanted you." He slid the cold barrel of the gun down the side of her neck, then across her lower lip. "Grant wasn't the only person who argued with Richard. He and I argued, too, about business and money mostly. But that wasn't *all* we argued about."

He slid the gun lower, until it pressed against the valley between her breasts.

Carol flinched and flattened herself against the wall behind her.

He smiled, as if delighted by her reaction. "Richard

caught me sneaking into your room when you'd gone to bed early one night. I'd told him I wasn't feeling well and wanted to lie down in the guest room for a bit before driving back home. I guess he didn't trust me, so he checked on me at a most inopportune moment." He laughed. "I wanted you. And he wouldn't let me have you. And that's the *real* reason he died." He grimaced. "Unfortunately, dear old Grant over there suspected I was up to no good. It's a long story, really, and I don't have the time. Suffice it to say, I have contacts in security, and I knew exactly where you went every time you left the house. I knew Leslie was helping you." He shook his head. "She paid for that, of course, after doing me a favor or two. Like switching wills."

"I…don't understand." She tried to keep calm, to keep him talking, stalling for time. "Why would you switch wills? You didn't get much money in the will Leslie filed."

He shook his head. "Still haven't figured it out, have you? I didn't want all that money going to Grant. I wanted it for myself. I knew the courts would suspect something if I got the bulk of the estate, so I played it the other way. I would have gotten all the money eventually, of course. When I married you."

She shivered with revulsion.

His smile faded. "Richard would have knocked you flat for that." His eyes flashed with anger. "I'd planned on killing him at that little cottage of yours and framing Grant. You know, two birds, one stone. But 'Grant the pest' followed me, walked right in after I shot Richard. From then on, it was all about damage control. I'd hoped to make Grant look like a lunatic, a three-way lovers' triangle. I was having fun framing him for everything I was doing, but things got so screwed up."

Nausea coiled in her stomach. She pointed at the pictures on the glass door. "What about Grant's family? They never did anything to you."

"True. Their fate is regrettable, I agree. They were nice enough to me. But they're collateral damage. Nothing anyone can do for them now."

Carol looked past him to the open doorway.

His brows rose. "Thinking you can get by me, eh?" He stood and pulled her to her feet. He reached a hand toward her face.

She flinched and ducked away.

His nostrils flared like a stallion scenting a mare. "Skittish, huh? Well, I can understand that, after living with my brother for so long. I never was one to hit a woman. Not that I have anything against the practice. It just wasn't my thing." His gaze raked down her body. "As for the rest, well, like I said, if I only had the time." He clucked his tongue again and shook his head. "What a waste."

He stepped back and motioned with the gun toward the door. "Come along, Caroline. The only way I'm coming out of this without going to prison now is to make sure no one can connect me to anything. That's why I had Grant kill Leslie and abduct you. I needed him to leave evidence that showed he was a psychopath and a murderer. When you both disappear, the police will assume he killed you and ran off. And I can go back to my life as if nothing ever happened." He waved the gun again. "Let's go. The plant opens in a few hours. I have to get rid of both of your bodies and hose the place down before anyone sees me. Time to disappear."

Carol lunged past him and ran out the door into the hall.

The sound of laughter followed her mad dash through

the plant. There weren't that many lights on, only an occasional overhead round fluorescent light hanging from a pole that didn't illuminate much of the area around it.

"I'll just get rid of Grant first, okay, Caroline?" he called out. "Don't worry, it won't take long."

A whimper bubbled up in Carol's throat. Why wasn't he worried she'd escape? She soon found the answer. When she reached the door she and Grant had come through earlier, it was bolted shut with a chain and a padlock across it. She shoved on the door anyway, rattling the chain and rocking the door against its frame.

Daniel's laughter echoed through the room. "That's the only door, sweetheart," he yelled from somewhere in the darkness. "The only other way into the plant is through the cattle shoots. And they're all closed up nice and tight for the night."

Carol whirled around, her gaze sweeping back and forth across the low, rectangular building. The room was full of all kinds of equipment she didn't recognize, scary-looking machines with sharp blades and what looked like giant nail guns hanging from pulleys on the ceiling with rubber hoses attached to them. She turned in a circle, but it looked as if Daniel was telling the truth. The only other doors were the massive overhead rolling kind, like garage doors, only they were closed and she didn't have a clue how to open them.

The sound of footsteps against the concrete floor had her crouching down behind the nearest machine. Another sound followed in concert with the footsteps, a swishing sound, like fabric brushing against something. She leaned around the machine, peering across the dimly lit area where the sound was coming from.

Daniel passed beneath one of the lights, calmly walking through the warehouse, holding Grant's hand, dragging his body behind him.

Carol clasped her hands over her mouth again, desperately trying not to wretch.

Laughter sounded from the other side of the room again. Daniel must have heard her, and he was enjoying her terror.

An image of Luke's handsome, smiling face floated in Carol's mind's eye. If he were here, he'd protect her. He'd make everything safe for her. For a moment, she remained frozen wishing Luke could save her. But she thought about the pictures on the glass door in the room where she'd been held. Grant's wife and daughter didn't deserve to die any more than Carol did, assuming they were still alive. If she gave up now, she wasn't just letting herself down. She was letting those innocents down, as well. She couldn't cower and do nothing. She had to at least try to escape and get help for them.

She forced her shaking legs to carry her forward, into the dark, to try to find another way out or a weapon of some sort. She stumbled over a hose and fell against a smooth concrete wall in the middle of the room. She leaned over it, peering down into the darkness, following the wall as it snaked back and forth on itself through the room.

It was a cattle shoot, one of the serpentine enclosures the cows walked through from the stockyard to where they were slaughtered. She glanced at the heavy doors behind her. They didn't sink into the floor. They rested flat against the concrete. But the cattle shoots were below floor level, like a subway. Maybe Daniel was wrong. Maybe there *was* another way out. Maybe there were side rooms off the shoot or a control panel that would raise the doors.

    She glanced around but didn't see him anywhere. She braced her hands on the smooth top of the wall, lifted her legs over the side, then dropped down into the darkness below.

Chapter Seventeen

There was no sign of movement near the main building of the meatpacking plant. Luke sprinted from the wooded area where he'd parked and quickly crossed the short distance to the parking lot. He crouched beside the patrol car Grant had stolen and felt the hood. Cold. He hurried to Daniel's BMW and knelt down behind the rear bumper, watching the building.

"Their cars are both here," he whispered into his cell phone. "And there are lights on inside the main building, the one with the stockyards out front. Don't come in hot. You'll have to come in without sirens or lights. I don't want you to spook them. Have you contacted the plant manager to bring the keys?"

"He'll meet us a quarter mile outside the entrance. Just keep the line open and let us know if you see anyone outside," Cornell said. "ETA about fifteen minutes. Do not engage the suspects."

"To hell with that, Cornell. If Carol's inside, there's no telling what could be going on. I'm not waiting."

"Just a minute, Dawson. You can't just—"

Luke punched the button to end the call, then turned the ringer off. He shoved the phone into the holder on his belt and pulled out his pistol. As a force of habit, he popped the clip and double-checked the loading, then popped it back in. He waited a few more seconds, closely watching the high-up windows for movement and observing the shadows around the building.

A distant whining noise filtered from inside the building. Luke's stomach dropped. He knew that sound. *An electric saw.* He took off running toward the entrance.

CAROL DUCKED DOWN at the loud noise. It was coming from another part of the building—close…too close. She swallowed against the thickness in her throat, shying away from admitting to herself that she was pretty sure what that sound was. And since it seemed to be coming from the direction where Daniel had dragged Grant's body, she had a good idea what was going on.

She closed her eyes and pressed her hand to her mouth, trying not to gag. The sound stopped. Her eyes flew open. She had to get moving, had to find a way out. Now.

She took off running down the constantly winding shoot again. It was dark, but since the top was open, the dim light in the factory filtered down enough for her to see where she was going. The walls smelled of disinfectant with an occasional waft of manure. She tried breathing through her mouth and forced herself to keep going even though the shoot never seemed to end.

The tunnel came to an abrupt stop at a solid metal door. She slid to a halt, feeling the door, but there was no knob. She pushed against it, but it didn't budge. A bitter curse word flew through her mind. She was trapped. And all Daniel had to do was peer over the top of the concrete walls and follow them to the end. Then he could aim his gun and shoot her as if she was nothing more than a helpless cow waiting to be slaughtered.

"Oh, Caroline," Daniel's singsong voice called out. "Where are you, dear?"

He was so close! Had he heard her pressing on the gate? Was he about to peer over the wall at her? She bit her bottom lip and started forward, trying not to make any sound that would give away her location while she headed back the way she'd come.

"What are you doing down there, Caroline?"

She gasped and looked up. Daniel was casually leaning over the sloped top of the wall directly above her, shaking his head. "Do you know why the shoot curves back on itself so much instead of going in a straight line? Cows, when they get scared or confused, like to turn around and go back where they came from. So, even though we build the tunnel too narrow to allow them to turn around, we curve the tunnel back on itself. It fools the animals into thinking they're going back where they came from, when really they're getting closer and closer to the end, where death awaits. The animals stay calm the entire time." He grinned. "Makes the kill easier. Brilliant, don't you think?"

Carol whimpered and started running.

"There you go. That's a good girl. Run all the way to the end. You're just making this easy."

She stumbled to a halt and glanced uncertainly behind her.

"Now, now. We can't have you turning around." He leaned over the wall above her and aimed his gun. She screamed and took off running. The gunshot echoed through the tunnel behind her.

THE SOUND OF a gunshot froze Luke on the platform outside the window. He hadn't been able to get inside through the main door because it was chained. The only other possibility seemed to be one of the windows set high up in the wall. He'd used the access stairs for the roof to get to one of the windows. He used the butt of his gun like a hammer and busted the glass. He yanked off his leather jacket and flipped it over the jagged edges in the frame and climbed through the hole, then dropped to the floor.

He landed in a rolling crouch to break the long fall, then leaped to his feet waving his gun in front of him. He hurried out the door, pausing when he saw a trail of blood across the concrete. As if a body had been dragged through the hall.

Please don't let it be Carol.

He rushed out the door into the darkness beyond.

CAROL STOPPED AND flattened herself against the wall. What was that sound? Breaking glass? She looked up. Daniel must have heard it, too, because he'd paused and looked back toward the front of the building. He looked down at her and smiled, then pressed his fingers to his lips as if to tell her to be quiet, before disappearing over the edge of the wall.

Were the police here? Or Luke? She waited, hoping to hear sirens or voices, but all she heard was silence.

"Hello?" she called out. "Is someone there? It's Carol Ashton. Is anyone out there?" She waited. Nothing. Could anyone even hear her down in this pit?

She debated running back toward the gate, but that was a dead end, a trap. The only way out was up ahead, where the cattle were slaughtered. Bile rose in her throat but she fought it down and took off running again.

A MUFFLED SOUND echoed from somewhere up ahead. Luke peered into the gloom and listened intently. Another sound, like someone…running? He spotted curving concrete walls in the middle of the room. They ended at the beginning of the assembly line, where heavy drill-looking machines hung from the ceiling—probably the pneumatic guns used to kill the cattle before they were processed.

The sound echoed again. It was definitely coming from that concrete opening. He glanced around, then sprinted to the nearest curve in the wall. He looked over the side and caught a glimpse of someone running.

Relief swept through him.

"Carol," he called out in a low whisper.

She stopped and jerked her head up, her eyes wide. "Luke, watch out!"

He whirled around and kicked in one movement, catching Daniel Ashton in the chest. Ashton grunted and fell against the concrete wall. The gun he'd been holding went skidding across the floor and wedged up beneath a machine.

Luke brought his own gun up, but Daniel lunged at him before he could get off a shot. His arms wrapped around Luke, forcing his gun hand up. They both tumbled to the concrete floor.

Daniel landed on top of Luke and bit down on Luke's wrist. Luke shouted and tried to shake him, but his hand went numb and the gun dropped from his fingers. Daniel grinned triumphantly and dived for the gun. Luke flung himself on top of Daniel's leg and yanked back, pulling him across the floor before he reached the gun.

Daniel cursed and twisted beneath him, sending a punch flying at Luke's jaw. Luke ducked just in time, but his movement allowed Daniel to scurry out from beneath him and lunge to his feet. The gun was a few feet behind Luke now, but he couldn't grab it without taking his eyes off Daniel.

His foe seemed to weigh the choices in front of him,

glancing from the gun to Luke and back again. His mouth twisted in a bitter smile. He lunged toward the gun, but when Luke moved to intercept him, Daniel whirled around and sprinted into the darkness, disappearing behind a row of machines.

Luke grabbed the gun and ran to the concrete wall. He peered down but didn't see Carol anywhere. He looked back up, keeping an eye out for Daniel, then raced along the curve of the wall, glancing down every few feet, looking for Carol.

He ran all the way to the end of the tunnel before he found her, standing in the slaughter box, her eyes wide, her body shaking as she stared at the bloodstains on the floor beneath her.

"Carol," he whispered. "It's Luke."

She didn't respond. She kept staring at the blood, her face alarmingly pale.

Luke glanced around. "Sweetheart, listen to me. It's Luke. Can you tell me where Grant is?"

She finally looked up at him. "Grant?" She shook her head. "Grant is…Grant is…" She closed her eyes and swallowed.

He knew the end of that sentence. Grant was dead. Luke couldn't say that bothered him a bit. It meant one less lunatic to deal with before Carol was safe.

He peered into the gloom. There was a light directly over the slaughter box, which made it difficult to see anything else, like someone shining a flashlight in his eyes.

"I have to go find Daniel. Wait here."

She shook her head back and forth. "No, no, don't leave me! Don't leave me here!"

His heart broke at the terror on her face, in her voice. "Okay, okay. First, take my gun. Just in case. Here, take it." He tossed it down to her.

She caught it and looked at it as if she didn't have a clue what to do with it.

Luke gritted his teeth. He glanced around one more time, the hairs standing up on the back of his neck.

"Luke, please, help me." Carol reached her arms up toward him.

He flattened himself on the floor at the edge of the box and hung down over the opening, his arms outstretched. "Take my hands. I'll pull you up."

She shoved the gun into her waistband and raised her hands.

A swishing noise was Luke's only warning. He dived to the side just as Daniel lunged at him with one of the pneumatic drills hanging over the slaughter box. It fired, the steel bolt slamming against the concrete before retracting, ready for another shot.

Carol screamed from below.

Daniel bellowed his rage and whirled around, knocking Luke flat on his back. Daniel slammed the drill down toward Luke. Luke clasped his hands on the sides of the drill, grappling for control.

Noises sounded from the front part of the building, voices yelling, feet shuffling. A loud pop echoed through the room. One of the rolling doors began rising.

Daniel cursed and renewed his struggles. The drill lowered closer, closer. He smiled, smelling victory. Luke bucked and twisted beneath him. Daniel lost his grasp on the drill and fell to the side. He must have seen the gun holstered on Luke's ankle because he cried out in triumph and yanked the gun out. Luke grabbed the drill and twisted around just as Daniel came up with the gun.

Luke shoved the drill against Daniel's head and squeezed the trigger.

A sickening crack echoed through the room. Daniel's eyes rolled up in his head and he fell to the floor. He didn't get back up.

"That was for Carol and Mitch, you piece of filth," Luke rasped.

"Police! Freeze!" someone yelled behind him.

Ignoring the order, he tossed the drill aside and crawled the last few feet to the slaughter box. The sound of running feet echoed behind him. He reached down and pulled Carol up and out of the box. Her eyes widened as she looked past him at Daniel's body lying on the floor. Her fingers dug into his shirt. He twisted to block her view, cradled her in his lap and pressed her face against his chest.

She sobbed and a flood of tears soaked his shirt.

"It's okay," he whispered against her hair. "It's okay. It's over. You're safe. You're finally safe."

Chapter Eighteen

Three months later

Luke leaned his forearms on his new desk and looked through the glass wall of his office into the main room of Dawson's Personal Security Services. Fifteen other shiny new desks sat in the enlarged space. He'd rented the office next to his and had knocked down the wall in between to expand. He'd hired eight more bodyguards and an admin assistant to help Trudy since her workload as office manager had gotten so heavy.

The notoriety from the Ashton case had gained him more paying clients—*well*-paying clients—than he could handle. And it didn't hurt that Stellar Security had suffered a severe blow after the investigation proved Daniel Ashton had been fed information from GPS locators on his family's vehicles and that some of the guards had even spied for him. They'd looked the other way when asked—like the night Grant Ashton allegedly "broke into" the mansion.

Business was good, but it didn't bring the joy or sense of accomplishment he'd hoped for. Nothing these days did. And he knew why.

Carol.

He hadn't seen or heard from her since that harrowing night at the packing plant. They'd both been brought into separate interview rooms at the police station where they'd each given their statements about everything that had happened.

Cornell had sent his men to all the Ashton warehouses in the city to search for Grant Ashton's family, based on the warehouse in the background of the pictures Grant had taped to the door at the plant. His hunch had paid off and Grant's wife and daughter were found safe. It had taken a few hours, and Luke had stayed in Cornell's office receiving minute-by-minute updates, until it was over. Then he'd gone out to update Carol, but she was gone.

Luke pulled his top desk drawer open and unfolded the single sheet of paper she'd asked Cornell to give him that night.

Luke, I'm sorry to leave things this way, but I have to get out of here. I'm leaving Savannah and all the ugliness behind. I don't know if I'll be back. Thank you for being there for me. You kept your promise. You saved me. That's a debt I can never repay. All I can say is thank you, and goodbye.

He refolded the note and dropped it back into the drawer. Blowing out a deep breath, he shoved his chair back and crossed to the window to stare down at the street below.

Behind him, in the outer office, the little bell Trudy had insisted on putting above the door tinkled, announcing they had a visitor. Luke didn't bother to turn around. Trudy had taken her role of replacing Mitch as office manager quite seriously. She was like a little general, bossing the bodyguards around, undaunted by the fact that most of them were well over a foot taller than her. Luke had yet to see anyone Trudy couldn't handle.

"Well, hello, there," Trudy called out, obviously recognizing whoever had come in. "It's good to see you again. What can we do for you today?"

"I need a bodyguard."

Luke froze at the sound of that soft, achingly familiar voice. *It can't be.* He slowly turned around.

Carol stood fifteen feet away, her startlingly blue eyes meeting his, her pink lips curving into a smile. "Hello, Luke."

Trudy glanced back and forth between them, then— for once—melted quietly away to the far side of the room without saying a word.

Luke stepped out of his office and stopped in front of Carol, his hungry gaze drinking her in. "You colored your hair brown."

She patted her hair as if self-conscious. "It's as close to my natural color as the stylist could make it, for now, until the roots grow out."

"I like it."

"Thank you."

He wanted to reach for her, to pull her against him. Instead, he shoved his hands in his pockets and cleared his throat. "You told Trudy you needed a bodyguard. Someone's bothering you?"

"No. No one's bothering me."

He frowned. "But you need a bodyguard?"

"Well, I suppose to be more accurate, I'd have to say I need *the* bodyguard. The bodyguard who saved my life a few months ago." She stepped forward, until the toes of her heels pressed against the toes of his dress shoes. "I need *you*, Luke."

Afraid to hope, he cleared his throat again. "You might

need to spell this out for me because I have a feeling I'm misunderstanding you. After that night at the plant, you left. You didn't wait to talk to me. You didn't answer my calls or letters. That doesn't sound like you need me."

She glanced around the office, at the handful of body-guards trying to pretend not to listen to them. Trudy didn't even bother pretending. She sat at her desk, her head in her hands, unabashedly staring.

"Is there somewhere…private…where we can talk?"

He stepped back and waved her toward his office. When she stepped inside, he closed the blinds on the glass walls and door, then turned to face her. "All right. No one's watching, or listening. Except me."

She bit her bottom lip and crossed the room to stand in front of him again. She held her hand out. "Hi, my name is Carol Bagwell. I legally changed my last name. I'm an Ashton no more."

He shook her hand and smiled reluctantly. "Believe me, you were never an Ashton. You've always been better than that."

She grinned. "I think so, too." Her grin faded. "Luke, when I left Savannah, it wasn't you I was leaving. It was…everything that had happened. I was confused, scared. I needed to get my head on straight. I went from living with my controlling, critical parents to living with a husband and having my every action, my every thought, controlled by him. When you came into my life, you were too good to be true. But I wasn't ready for you. I didn't even know who I was anymore. I needed time, and space, to figure that out."

"Where did you go when you left?"

"As far away as I could get without leaving the country. I went to the West Coast, to Seattle. But I couldn't escape my past by running away. I had to work with lawyers to settle the Ashton estate. They located Richard's true will at Wiley & Harrison and refiled. Grant's wife and daughter got nearly half the estate. The other half went to Daniel. True to his nature, Richard left me nothing." Her lips curved in a smile. "But Daniel didn't have a will, and no spouse or children. So the court awarded Daniel's portion to me. I hope Richard is turning over in his grave right now."

Luke smiled. "Good for you."

"I gave it away, though," she said.

He coughed. "What?"

"The money. Half a billion dollars in assets. I gave it to a women's charity. They're going to build a halfway house for abused women right here in Savannah. And with all that money, they'll be able to help women all over the country. Isn't that wonderful?"

He ran his finger down her soft cheek. "I think you're the most kind and generous woman I've ever met. Personally, I'd have kept a few million. But I understand why you didn't want to keep your husband's money. You wanted a fresh start. Right?"

"You *do* understand. I knew you would. I'm in therapy, probably will be for a long time. I'm a mess, actually, in a lot of ways. But I'm growing stronger every day. And there's one thing for sure that I know that I want."

"And what's that?"

"You. I want you. That is, if *you* still want *me* now that I'm a pauper."

He spanned her waist with his hands and set her on the desk so they were almost at eye level. "Carol," he said, "I'm in love with you, in case you haven't figured that out."

He covered her lips with his and consumed her in a searing kiss. Her arms wrapped around his neck, pulling him tightly against her as she kissed him back. When they broke apart, they were both out of breath.

He leaned down and kissed the side of her neck.

She shivered. "Luke?"

"Hmm?" He kissed her collarbone.

"When I told you I gave away a half a billion dollars, I may have neglected to mention something."

He moved to her ear and sucked her earlobe between his teeth.

She gasped. "Luke!"

He laughed and pulled back, looping his arms around her waist. "I don't care how poor you are, or what kind of trouble or baggage you bring with you. I'll take you any way I can get you." He leaned in for another kiss, but she pressed her hands against his chest, stopping him.

"I just need to make sure there's complete honesty between us."

He grimaced. "The video card, right? I destroyed it. I got it back from Alex and I cut the thing into pieces. Then I burned it. I'm so sorry I broke my promise."

She blinked. "The video card? No, no. That's ancient history. I understand why you felt you had to do that. I'm the one with a secret this time." She chewed her bottom lip. "I did give away half a billion dollars, but my portion of the estate was a little bit more than that. I may not exactly be a pauper."

"Oh? Exactly how much are you *not* a pauper?"

She grinned. "I might still have a few million dollars left over."

He laughed and swept her into his arms. "At least I'll know you don't like me for my money. I'm not exactly hurting these days, in case you hadn't noticed. Now, if you're through with all this talking, the rest of this… conversation…requires a bit more privacy."

She giggled and looped her arms around his neck again. "Lead the way, bodyguard. Lead the way."

* * * * *

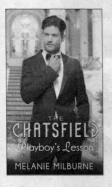

Hot reads!

These 3-in-1s will certainly get you feeling
hot under the collar with their desert
locations, billionaire tycoons and
playboy princes.

**Now available at
www.millsandboon.co.uk/offers**

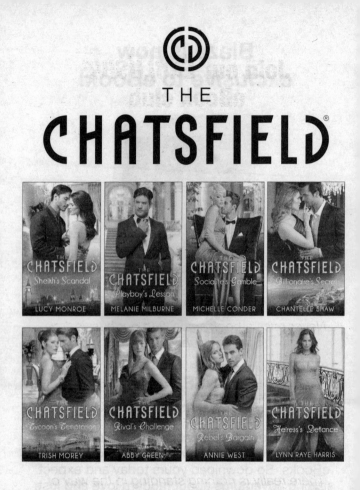

Join our *EXCLUSIVE* eBook club

FROM JUST £1.99 A MONTH!

Never miss a book again with our hassle-free eBook subscription.

★ Pick how many titles you want from each series with our flexible subscription

★ Your titles are delivered to your device on the first of every month

★ Zero risk, zero obligation!

There really is nothing standing in the way of you and your favourite books!

Start your eBook subscription today at www.millsandboon.co.uk/subscribe

The World of Mills & Boon

There's a Mills & Boon® series that's perfect for you. There are ten different series to choose from and new titles every month, so whether you're looking for glamorous seduction, Regency rakes, homespun heroes or sizzling erotica, we'll give you plenty of inspiration for your next read.

By Request

Back by popular demand!
12 stories every month

Cherish™

Experience the ultimate rush of falling in love.
12 new stories every month

INTRIGUE...

A seductive combination of danger and desire...
7 new stories every month

Desire™

Passionate and dramatic love stories
6 new stories every month

nocturne™

An exhilarating underworld of dark desires
3 new stories every month

For exclusive member offers go to
millsandboon.co.uk/subscribe

MILLS & BOON®
Book Club

Join the Mills & Boon Book Club

Subscribe to **Intrigue** today for 3, 6 or 12 months and you could **save over £40!**

We'll also treat you to these fabulous extras:

- 🌹 **FREE L'Occitane gift set worth £10**
- 🌹 **FREE home delivery**
- 🌹 **Rewards scheme, exclusive offers…and much more!**

Subscribe now and save over £40
www.millsandboon.co.uk/subscribeme